Tasting Droplets of the Unforgettable Rain
A Novel By
Adrien L. Montgomery

(... A Presentation Of ...)

(... **Dynamographx**[R] **Paperworks**[TM] ...)
(... The Official Imprint ...)
"... Listen to a Voice Always on the Vanguard"
"... Illustrating the Beauty of Dynamic Motion"

Official Declaration of Authorship (O.D.A.) 2019
Adrien L. Montgomery
(https://www.youtube.com/channel/@adrienlmontgomery)

(Berkeley   San Francisco   Minneapolis   Taos)

Special Note to the Reader:
The author desires to indicate to the reading public the following manuscript-project is the first work of fiction of his composition to receive an official date of publication, thereby, enabling the book to become available for fans of ("['Adult']-Literary")-fiction to review at their convenience.

Official Date of the Project's Original Publication: SAT., Jan. 31, 2026

Information Sheet with the "Opening Titles" (i.e., the Publication's "Title Page")

Tasting Droplets of the Unforgettable Rain
A Novel By
Adrien L. Montgomery

(... A Presentation Of ...)

(... **Dynamographx**[R] **Paperworks**[TM] ...)
(... The Official Imprint ...)
"... Listen to a Voice Always on the Vanguard"
"... Illustrating the Beauty of Dynamic Motion"

Official Declaration of Authorship (O.D.A.) 2019
Adrien L. Montgomery

--()--
I
--()--

Adrien L. Montgomery
Tasting Droplets of the Unforgettable Rain
Original Year of Publication: 2026

(https://www.youtube.com/channel/@adrienlmontgomery)

Berkeley   San Francisco   Minneapolis   Taos

Author's Contact Information:
Telephone: "N/A" (i.e., "non-applicable")
"E"-mailbox: "N/A" (i.e., "non-applicable")
"Cellular"-line: "N/A" (i.e., "non-applicable")
Text-messaging ("Cellular"-line): "N/A" (i.e., "non-applicable")
Text-messaging ("E"-mailbox): "N/A" (i.e., "non-applicable")
Faxline Number: "N/A" (i.e., "non-applicable")

Tasting Droplets of the Unforgettable Rain

(<|Listing of "('Project' ID)"-Notices|>)
01)The "Copywright" in the Author's Name (w/Calendar Year):
   a)"Copywright © 2018 and © 2020 by Adrien L. Montgomery"*

02)"Library of Congress (['Cataloguing-in-Publication'])-Data":
   a)The US "Library of Congress" catalogues the preceding work of
      fictional material under the following fields of literary focus-points:
      --."African-American"
      --."Contemporary"
      --."Fiction"
      --."Minnesota"
      --."Predators"
      --."Sexual Assault"
      --."Urban"

03)The "I.S.B.N." (i.e., "International Standard Book Number"):
   a)13-Digit Number: "978-0-692-13078-0" ("POD"-Edition Copy)
   b)13-Digit Number: "978-1-087-88090-7" ("Digital"-Edition Copy)

04)The US "Library of Congress (['Card Catalogue'])-Number":
   a)"N/A" (i.e., "non-'applicable' ")
      [place "C.C.N." in space here]

05)Official Date of the Project's Original Publication:
   a)SAT., Jan. 31, 2026

"*" Note:
The term "copywright", as it occurs within the preceding chart of "('Project'

--()--
II
--()--

ID)"-notices in its use as seen in the information-window which appears above, also, indicates the terms, heretofore, known on record as "copyright" and "copyrights", etc.)

<u>An Acknowledgement of Pre-Existing Copywright-Statutes</u>

Tasting Droplets of the Unforgettable Rain
A Novel By
Adrien L. Montgomery

(… A Presentation Of …)
(… Dynamographx[R] Paperworks™ …)
(… The Official Imprint …)
"… Listen to a Voice Always on the Vanguard"
"… Illustrating the Beauty of Dynamic Motion"

Copywright © 2018 and © 2020 by Adrien L. Montgomery

Any and all licensing agreements to publish, reprint or adapt the preceding work of fictional material ("Scriptograph[UE] One [The 'Shadowslasher' Volumes (Book I: 'Tasting Droplets of the Unforgettable Rain')]") by parties outside of the work's original author (i.e., Adrien L. Montgomery) are governed by the jurisdictional authority of (and all pertinent regulatory directives found in) both International and Hemispheric (i.e., "['North']"-/"['Central']"-/& "['South']"-American) copywright compacts and conventions as of the date of this publication's official release (i.e., 2025).*

"*" <u>Note</u>:
The term "copywright" as it occurs in the preceding announcement in its use as seen above also indicates the terms, heretofore, known on record as "copyright" and "copyrights", etc.

<u>The Table of Contents</u>
Tasting Droplets of the Unforgettable Rain
A Novel By
Adrien L. Montgomery

<u>Just Unfolding a Map for the Anxious Traveler</u> …
(… <u>Menu of Items in Directory</u> …)
01)Item I:

--()--
III
--()--

Adrien L. Montgomery
Tasting Droplets of the Unforgettable Rain
Original Year of Publication: 2026

<table>
<tr><td>--()--</td></tr>
<tr><td>V</td></tr>
<tr><td>--()--</td></tr>
</table>

--."Author's Announcement Condemning the Mistreatment of Animals"
--.(page#: 'CCXXXI')
48)Item XLVIII:
    --.The "Official Declaration of Authorship"-certificate
    --.(page#: 'CCXXXIII')
49)Item XLIX:
    --.Notes on the "Pinball"-Machine Titles Appearing in the Preceding
       "Narrative"-Project in "Cycle 17"
    --.(page#: 'CCXXXV')
50)Item L:
    --.Our "Made in the USA"-Certification Stamp
    --.(page#: 'CCXXXVI')
51)Item LI:
    --.The Information Page on the Project's "Production Services"-
       Facility (i.e., "Printing"-office)
    --.(page#: 'CCXXXVI')
52)Item LII:
    --.The "Infosheet on the Photographer's ID"
    --.(page#: 'CCXXXVII')
53)Item LIII:
    --.The (["Topside"-]/["Backside"-])-Coversheet Design Credits
    --.(page#: 'CCXXXVII')
54)Item LIV:
    --.The "Endsheet"
    --.(page#: 'CCXXXVIII')
55)Item LV:
    --.The Author's Official Wordcount Report
    --.Notice on the Legal Use of Digital-Images Appearing on Volume's
       "Frontside"-Coversheet and "Backside"-Coversheet
    --.(page#: 'CCXXXVIII', 'CCXXXIX')
56)Item LVI:
    --.The " 'Backside' Coversheet"
    --.(page#: 'N/A')

<u>"The Reader is to Begin Listening Here"</u>
<u>Hello, Dear Reader!</u> ...
    I'm Adrien L. Montgomery, the author of the novel "Scriptograph^{UE} One
[The 'Shadowslasher' Volumes (Book I: 'Tasting Droplets of the
Unforgettable Rain')]". I want to use this opportunity to speak to you about
the particular book-project which I'm, hereby, offering to readers. I do
humbly ask that you now take the time to review this statement prior to
reading the novel itself. (This statement of mine might serve to open the
eyes of any reader anxious to know of the actual intentions which I had in

mind in choosing to create this particular narrative-project for readers.)

This particular book, "Scriptograph[UE] One [The 'Shadowslasher' Volumes (Book I: 'Tasting Droplets of the Unforgettable Rain')]", is, in fact, a *novel*. Permit me to take a moment here to explain to you what I believe a work of writing must be in order to, in fact, qualify as "a novel", that is.

A *novel* is a fictional literary project which consists of a line of incidents (or, events) which presents a "feature" character (i.e., a "protagonist") and the trials (or, struggles) which he undergoes before coming to discover a particular truth about human nature, societal behavior, historical patterns, or his own psychological structuring, etc., etc. What the character realizes upon completion of a personal odyssey could, in fact, relate to any phenomenon which he'd been aware of prior to his journey's start, e.g.'s, his feelings of affection for a specific romantic partner or his devotion to a particular religion, etc., etc. In either such case, the trial which the protagonist undergoes over the course of the novel's dramatic scope merely serves to let him view the particular phenomenon with cleaner eyes and a clearer sight. I.e., he views his particular affection for the specific partner in question with even more gratitude, or he sees devotion to his specific religion as even more of a necessity in the particular world which he just so happens to inhabit.

In the case of "Scriptograph[UE] One [The 'Shadowslasher' Volumes (Book I: 'Tasting Droplets of the Unforgettable Rain')]", this actual *type* of fictional account can be made reference to as being an *adult urban contemporary* novel. The project is an "adult" piece due to the fact that the narrative focuses on an *adult* protagonist who allows the reader to view him and his surroundings from a perspective which he actually uses himself. The book is, in fact, an "urban" story due to the fact that the incidents and circumstances which do appear in the text transpire against the backdrop of *urban* (or, "metropolitan") environments. This fictional work is, also, a "contemporary" novel due to the fact that the character's life occurs in a *contemporary* time period--i.e., one which is almost coincident with the one which exists today (or, rather, one which is almost coincident with the one existing at the particular moment of the book's original publication [i.e., 2025 (... and afterwards, in subsequent editions)], that is).

I must confess that the novel's subject material consists of actions on the part of the protagonist, "Ariq Zarkahn Shoretempel" (which, phonetically, would appear in sound as ... "air-ick zahr-kuhn shor-tem-puhl"), which, of course, would amount to "felony"-level criminal offenses occurring against a particular series of adult females. The character, of course, might, in fact, qualify as a "predator" or, using an archaic term, as a "fiend", regarding his anti-societal sexual habits. The character, "Ariq Zarkahn Shoretempel", without question, permits himself to commit "felony"-level criminal offenses against all objecting females (each of whom ranges in physical maturity from their early- to mid-twenties, that is) throughout the book's text (… pursuing this particular pattern of behavior quite remorselessly), I'm afraid to state here.

The protagonist's first name, "Ariq", is an anagram for the word "Iraq", an arid country found in the southwestern region of the Asian "continent" (i.e., terrestrial landmass, that is) in between the tip of the Arabian peninsula and the Persian Gulf. Ariq was born on May 10, 1977, long prior to either the first "Gulf War" (Jan. to Feb. of 1991) or the "War in Iraq" (Mar., 2003 – Dec., 2011). Ariq's second (or middle) name, "Zarkahn", is the combination of two separate imperial titles which together form one particular word for the protagonist's esteem. First, the first syllable, "Zar", is the phonetical re-spelling of the Russian term "Czar", the designation in use for the sovereign (or, monarch) of the Russian Empire. The old term "Czar" is the Russian-language spelling (albeit in the Roman alphabet) of "Caesar", the term designating the ruler of the Roman Empire (27 B.C. to A.D. 476). The middle name's second syllable, "kahn", is the phonetical re-spelling of the term "Khan", a title designating the ruler of the "Mongol Empire", a land domain that did so flourish throughout the face of Asia, the Middle East and Eastern Europe over a period beginning in A.D. 1206 and continuing until the late 1300's. The most prominent rulers of the "Mongol Empire" (in separate eras) were known as "Genghis Khan" and "Kublai Khan", the secondary name (i.e., "Khan") designating the family name (or "dynastic" name) of those who were sovereign over the landmass of the "Empire of the Mongols". I use a phonetic, English-language variance on the two old terms to form the protagonist's middle (or second) name, "Zarkahn". The fact that two old imperial titles were made use of in order to create the protagonist's middle name denotes the fact that I did foresee in "Ariq" an eagerness to tyrannize an entire subsection of humanity. In Ariq's case, of course, that subsection of humankind would be 1) the particular females which he commits "sexcrime"-assaults against over the course of the narrative, and 2) the totality of the female gender which he constantly maligns as a sector of the human population over the course of the dramatic scenario's text.

The protagonist's last name, "Shoretempel", merely denotes the image of a sanctuary or an official site of prayer which rests upon a shoreline or a coastal stretch of land. The particular structure of an actual religious temple would, to Ariq, denote a zone of inner peace, of course, a psychological state which the protagonist desires to attain in life at some point or another as a reward for satisfactorily completing a successful quest for true human self-enlightenment which he pursues through conducting the variety of antisocial actions which he commits over the course of the dramatic scenario's text against a variety of adult females.

Despite the nature of the protagonist's criminal acts, I do not, through

--()--
X
--()--

this specific production, desire to promote *misogynistic* attitudes towards or promote sexual abuse of <u>any</u> females, i.e., women or girls, to any extent whatsoever. I am <u>not</u> presenting this type of material content to readers in order to encourage *antisocial* individuals to emulate the offenses which the protagonist chooses to commit throughout the text of this "narrative"-project. I am merely offering to the readers an opportunity to witness a certain aspect of human behavior that exists at the extreme end of the spectrum which displays well-known human criminal traits.

I do, hereby, state my actual objection to the pattern of antisocial behavior which the protagonist pursues against females during the course of the particular dramatic text which this narrative will present to you, dear readers. I do understand that the crimes which the character permits himself to commit are deliberate acts which would be particularly objectionable and disturbing to women choosing to read this particular work of ("['Adult']-Literary")-fiction.

Despite the book's material content, I am <u>not</u> attempting to intentionally upset any female who may decide to review this particular fictional presentation. I am in no way demonstrating any support of (or agreement with) the protagonist's decision to pursue sexual offenses against <u>non</u>-consenting females during the course of the novel's narrative material. I must, here, admit that I personally find acts along the lines of those which the character commits to be <u>both</u> *socially* reprehensible and *morally* savage in discussion.

I can admit to you, the readers, that I put in a *very* <u>significant</u> amount of labor in order to complete this particular work of <u>literature</u> for the benefit of readers everywhere. I did commit myself to working in order to produce a <u>final</u> version of the manuscript for this particular book project (quite diligently, that is) over a work schedule totaling an actual term in excess of <u>22</u> years and <u>00</u> months in length (i.e., Dec. 16, 2003 to Dec. 22, 2025)! I can assure you, I did make sure the quality level of the text would be of the highest order known prior to the manuscript's publication, knowing this would be my first "novel"-project actually put into print and my first chance to present a work of mine to the readers deciding to purchase this particular volume of fiction.

I do believe that I did manage to achieve my goals regarding the text's overall level of quality and accessibility to readers "at large". The novel isn't one which the average adult book-buyer would find too cumbersome to work his way through, however. I do trust you, the readers, will see for yourselves, as you review the text on hand, that I did manage to create a "novel" which is completely sound both in its approach and results and, at the same time, coherent and amusing to a degree that guarantees the <u>adult</u> readers will find an adequate amount of delight with the material it offers.

I am, at this point, happy to state that I could not find a higher level of

--()--
XI
--()--

satisfaction with the edition which I have made available to one and all with the specific presentation of the work which I do offer to you, here, my friends. I did desire that the edition's production elements be notably high, as did I so desire the text's level of quality to be solid as well, and I have, in fact, taken the steps that were necessary to ensure that this is, in fact, the very case indeed. The volume itself is excellent in its design and lends credence to the assertion that "Scriptograph[UE] One (The 'Shadowslasher' Volumes [Book I: 'Tasting Droplets of the Unforgettable Rain'])" is a highly exceptional work of ("['Adult']-Literary")-fiction!

I must confess, here, that I've had a lifelong interest in creating fictional works, e.g.'s, short stories, long fiction, poems, etc. I believe my interest in writing *creatively* began at the age of 10! I believe I was twelve years old at the time in which I did decide that I would prefer to eventually become a <u>novelist</u> in life! With the release of this book, "Scriptograph[UE] One (The 'Shadowslasher' Volumes [Book I: 'Tasting Droplets of the Unforgettable Rain'])", I finally did manage to make that particular childhood dream *become* a reality! I believe, through creative writing, I can share with the readers a particularly unique viewpoint on the nature of humanity, the particular truths concerning societal issues in the US (and elsewhere) today, and the psychology of the contemporary individual which the readers of this work can gain both informational awareness <u>and</u> spiritual enrichment from upon reviewing the text of the project.

I do believe an author's purpose in writing a <u>good</u> novel nowadays would be to present the reader with a certain overview on the nature of the Universe which will serve to enlighten the reading audience to a particular degree, permitting him to understand why "Earth" rotates in the particular manner in which she does, in fact, actually rotate. If you do choose to read the following "narrative"-project, I'm certain you will walk away from the experience wanting to review it again, if only to see if you gain even more in the way of enlightenment regarding the various aspects of human individual behavior which I chose to place on exhibit over the course of the narrative text which the book itself includes.

If you, the readers, allow yourselves to review this particular creative writing project of mine, I trust you, just possibly, might never view the Universe or the World (or even yourselves, that is) in the same way again. A novel, such as "Scriptograph[UE] One (The 'Shadowslasher' Volumes [Book I: 'Tasting Droplets of the Unforgettable Rain'])", exists to help its readers see themselves, their world, and, perhaps, even their <u>ultimate</u> purposes in life in a clearer and brighter light.

I'm certain that once you've read "Scriptograph[UE] One (The 'Shadowslasher' Volumes [Book I: 'Tasting Droplets of the Unforgettable Rain'])", you will regard the book to be a volume of literature which you will treasure and choose to return to during the course of a lifetime. The book's material content offers unto its readers a lot in the form of insight, drama, emotion, and individual character, I do trust. You'll probably review the novel's entire text again with the objective of locating particular elements in it which you did happen to accidentally overlook during your first reading of the book.

I, the author, Adrien L. Montgomery, do want, here, to take this moment to thank you for selecting to purchase this particular volume, "Scriptograph[UE] One (The 'Shadowslasher' Volumes [Book I: 'Tasting Droplets of the Unforgettable Rain'])", my first "novel" to actually receive a public release, that is, I should again remind you. (I do, hereby, say the following words in the sincerest of tones to one and all who choose to read the following work: "Thank you very much, dear readers and friends".)

I will acknowledge, at this particular moment in time, that I am currently at work on, yet, another fictional project which will become available to you at some time in the not so distant future, dear friends. If you find you enjoy this novel, I'm certain you'll want to read the work succeeding it, another book which will be just as *spiritually* _and_ *intellectually* rewarding to the adult who chooses to guide himself through its generous allowance of pages.

However, it is my sincerest desire that you do receive satisfaction from the work at hand, "Scriptograph[UE] One (The 'Shadowslasher' Volumes [Book I: 'Tasting Droplets of the Unforgettable Rain'])", dear readers. The novel is a _literary_ project which you will, in one instance, perhaps, find troubling, and will, at another point, find to be a very inspiring perspective on the ultimate purpose of individual human behavior. Hence, I do believe you _will_ enjoy reading this particular work of fiction and I do, hereby, with this statement, present it to you, my dear readers.

Adrien L. Montgomery
Author
--."Scriptograph[UE] One (The 'Shadowslasher' Volumes [Book I: 'Tasting Droplets of the Unforgettable Rain'])"
Minneapolis, Minnesota (U.S.A.)
Date: SUN., Sep. 29, 2019

"Attention! Attention! … Remain Silent While the Author Speaks!"
I do believe and trust the following bytes of guidance I, hereby, present to you might serve to assist the reader in his particular understanding of the actual approach which I'm using in designing both the specific narrative and the particular protagonist which this work of fiction presents to people the world over. To put it simply, the focus, in this particular work, is, of course (and, perhaps, unfortunately), upon the human *individual* (rather than upon the human *community*) and upon the particular system

of values the individual might formulate over the course of a lifetime in order, 1) to survive in, and, 2) to attempt to gain spiritual enrichment from the living community surrounding him. Perhaps you, as well, the individual reader, will gain insights which will benefit you to one extent or another in life if you decide to review the following statements which I've chosen to present on these pages prior to your decision to examine the novel's actual "narrative"-text.

<u>I</u>.

"The most important reward a human can receive in this world is the <u>one</u> particular space in which he's certain to uncover and enjoy an unrelenting peace."
… Adrien's Brief Byte of Knowledge

<u>II</u>.

"The division line existing between 'Heaven' and 'Hell' can have the breadth to it of a human hair's width!"
… Adrien's Brief Byte of Knowledge

<u>III</u>.

"Whatever it might be that you do treasure most sincerely in this particular world, you—'O Human!'—can be certain of one rule: 'Society' <u>will</u> condemn any attempts on your part to earnestly attain it!"
… Adrien's Brief Byte of Knowledge

<u>IV</u>.

"Regardless of the path which 'Fate' has drawn for you to initialize and travel, do not resist for a single minute its particular direction or distance: avoiding the road already set out for you in this world will only guarantee that you find doors, though cleanly open in earlier points, to be completely shut."
… Adrien's Brief Byte of Knowledge

<u>A Note on the Sequences Using "Superscript"-type Appearing Throughout the Project's Text</u>

Throughout the text of the "narrative"-project which I'm presenting to the reading audience with this particular book-publication, I must, here, note there are ("['initials']-combination")-codes which appear in a "superscript"-format of print which occur throughout the text of the following manuscript-project….

E.g., …
(Page Text Appearing in Regular Type)[("['initials']-combination")-code in "superior"-type format]

--()--
XIV
--()--

The ("['initials']-combination")-codes appear throughout the scope of the manuscript-project in order to emulate (or, appear in place of) "official" product-registration markings (e.g.'s, "TM", "SM", "R", "C"), in an attempt to designate the particular "product" in question as having an "official"-level of recognition and legitimate registration, as if the "product" itself of re-cord is <u>real</u>.

The ("['initials']-combination")-codes which appear throughout the text as "facsimile" product-registration markings to denote "products" appearing in an occasional use over the course of the manuscript-project make use of the following alphabetic sequences in order to emulate "official" product-registration markings which appear upon genuine corporate properties in the actual market of "consumer"-goods:

01)"AI":
   --.an ("['initials']-combination")-code representing the term "<u>artificial</u> <u>imprint</u>"
02)"ISS":
   --.an ("['initials']-combination")-code representing the term "<u>illegitimate</u> <u>superscript</u>"
03)"UE"
   --.an ("['initials']-combination")-code representing the term "<u>unidenti-fiable</u> <u>exponent</u>"
04)"ESU"
   --.an ("['initials']-combination")-code representing the term "<u>encoding</u> <u>sequence</u> <u>unknown</u>"
05)"STF"
   --.an ("['initials']-combination")-code representing the term "<u>superior</u> <u>type-facing</u>"
06)"SLTF":
   --.an ("['initials']-combination")-code representing the term "<u>superior-level</u> <u>type-facing</u>"

Again, you will see the ("['initials']-combination")-codes appearing in the preceding list throughout the text of the book-publication project which I'm presenting to you with this particular manuscript-project, which appear in order to, again, *illegitimately* (i.e., falsely) designate the name of the particular "product" in question with "official" product-registration markings in order to denote the particular item in question as a <u>real</u> product with legitimate registration and "official" recognition as a property for sale in the commercial marketplace.

The "products" which do appear with the particular ("['initials']-combination")-codes in "superscript"-type formatting print next to them are <u>not</u> products having any "official"-level of registration or any genuine level of recognition as actual corporate properties appearing in the commercial market for sale to and use by average consumers.

The "products" which do appear with the particular ("['initials']-combination")-codes in "superscript"-type formatting print next to them in the text-data of the following manuscript-project are <u>not</u> genuine corporate properties for sale to and possible use by consumers in the public market of trade, yet, are *fictitious* properties made up for merely theatrical use in the "narrative"-text which this particular publication presents.

I.e., the "products" which do appear with the particular ("['initials']-combination")-codes in "superscript"-type formatting print next to them in the text of the following manuscript-project are <u>not</u> to be seen as "legitimate" corporate properties for sale to and potential use by the public in the commercial market of consumer goods, yet merely appear as *ornamental* fixtures existing merely to illegitimately (i.e., <u>falsely</u>) designate the particular "products" in question as "official" corporate properties having legitimate product-registration status and recognition as <u>real</u> consumer goods.

I'm using this particular precursory note on the ("['initials']-combination")-sequences appearing in the text of the narrative-project which you're about to read in order to explain the actual purpose for their inclusion in this particular publication, in hopes of clarifying for the reading audience what, in fact, the particular alphabetic codes themselves actually stand for, to permit the reader to review the following "narrative"-project without allowing the ("['initials']-combination")-codes themselves to become an obstructive element in any way.

With this particular statement I do hope to clarify for the reading audience the particular purpose I had in mind behind the use of the (" ['initials']-combination")-codes in this particular project (i.e., denoting *illegitimate* "products" as genuine corporate properties having "official" product-registration status in the *actual* "consumer"-goods marketplace), in order to ensure the ("['initials']-combination")-codes themselves which do appear throughout the following text do not become a hindrance or an interference for the reader as he attempts to enjoy the following work of fiction at his leisure.

Adrien L. Montgomery
Author
--."Scriptograph^UE One (The 'Shadowslasher' Volumes [Book I: 'Tasting Droplets of the Unforgettable Rain'])"
Minneapolis, Minnesota (U.S.A.)
Date: MON., Dec. 01, 2025

<u>A Brief Acknowledgement Regarding the Variety of "Typeface"-Designs</u>

--()--
XVI
--()--

Adrien L. Montgomery

Tasting Droplets of the Unforgettable Rain

Official Imprint: "Dynamographx"

<u>Appearing</u> in <u>Print</u> <u>Throughout</u> <u>the</u> <u>Text</u> <u>of</u> <u>the</u> <u>Narrative</u> <u>Project</u> …

Within the scope of the "narrative"-project, I've made use of a variety of differing "Font"-styles (i.e., "Typeface"-designs) with which to present the text-data of the "manuscript"-content itself to those in the reading audience selecting to review the particular work of fiction which I do, hereby, present to all choosing to accept it.

The number of differing "Font"-styles which the "narrative"-project makes use of over the course of its body of text-material is no higher than what you'd most likely find appearing in the "typical" volume of "creative" (or, *fictional*) writing.

I'm selecting, here, to permit the readers to exactly review what particular "Font"-styles I've chosen to make use of in this particular presentation of fiction, that the readers might be aware of the specific "Typeface"-designs which do appear in print over the course of the narrative-project.

I've also chosen to present the name of the "Font"-style (i.e., once again the "Typeface"-design) itself in the list appearing below with text written in print which appears in the particular "Font"-style which the name of the "Typeface"-design itself indicates.

E.g., the name of the particular "Font"-style appearing in the listing of "Typeface"-designs which I've put together below (e.g., "<u>Tahoma</u>") actually appears in print in text (in the list) which uses the "Tahoma" "Font"-style/"Typeface"-design itself.

Again, dear readers, the variety of differing "Font"-styles appearing in print throughout the text of the manuscript-project appear in name in the following listing of "Typeface"-designs in print which utilizes the particular "Font"-style which the name itself indicates.

The following listing of "Font"-styles which appear in print throughout the text of the manuscript-project lists the specific "Typeface"-designs in alphabetical order in accordance with the name of the "Font"-style itself, i.e., the initial letter of the particular "Typeface"-design determines its actual ranking in the list of "Font"-styles which appear in print throughout the following "manuscript"-project.

What follows is a <u>complete</u> listing of the various "Typeface"-designs (i.e., "Font"-styles) which appear throughout the text of the ensuing "narrative"-project which I do, hereby, present to any readers selecting to review the specific volume of fiction on hand:

"**Bodoni MT Black**"
"Lucida Sans"

The <u>total</u> number of differing "Font"-styles (i.e., "Typeface"-designs) which appear in print throughout the text of the specific "narrative"-project

--()--
XVII
--()--

"And the 'Dedication' Goes to …"

I, the author, do, hereby, choose to *dedicate* the following volume of fiction to readers of <u>any</u> location who believe themselves ready to examine a narrative-project which presents to its audience an *unrelentingly* <u>truthful</u> perspective on the human individual's quest--as destructive as it might, perhaps, be--for a *higher* level of "enlightenment" in this world …

Adrien L. Montgomery

"<u>It's</u> <u>Just</u> <u>a</u> <u>Word</u> <u>or</u> <u>Two</u> <u>to</u> <u>Begin</u> <u>with</u>, <u>I</u> <u>Guess</u> …"
(<u>Prologue</u>)

You witness storms which are starting and ending abruptly across the Earth's fresh soils and waters. One spasm rupturing the globe's usual climatic pattern seems identical to the outburst that it's soon to replace. <u>Both</u> the animals *and* the humans fail in recognizing the rare energy of any one particular seizure that occurs in the high tides of air which overrun the world's salty surfaces. But, perhaps, if the motion of a butterfly's wing creates a current which you noisily inhale, on one morning, you'll awake and you'll hear drops of ancient rain falling--in numbers heretofore unseen--to the ground!

Adrien L. Montgomery

<u>A</u> <u>Particular</u> "<u>Dialogue</u>"-<u>Script</u> <u>Excerpt</u> <u>to</u> <u>Only</u> <u>So</u> <u>Noticeably</u> <u>Appear</u> <u>Just</u> <u>Prior</u> <u>to</u> <u>the</u> <u>Opening</u> <u>of</u> <u>the</u> <u>Series</u> <u>of</u> "<u>Sectional-Units</u>"

("<u>Dialogue</u>"-<u>Script</u> <u>Excerpt</u>)

"… I believe no authentic hero could tolerate a ritualistic abuser of females. These men belong in the coldest dungeon known in all human history, eating bread that's no longer good and drinking water that's out of the feeding trough the horses drink from. Such men are horrible threats to the honor and spirit I believe are crucial to guaranteeing the continuance of both human rights and humanity itself…."

Erich-Elisa Reinmaier
a.k.a., "Gustavo De Santa Andrea"
(In the Feature "Motion-Picture")
Running on the Burning Embers of One Belief
(1998)

("<u>Welcome</u>, <u>Ladies</u> <u>and</u> <u>Gentlemen</u>, <u>to</u> <u>the</u> <u>Opening</u> <u>of</u> <u>the</u> <u>Series</u> <u>of</u> <u>Sectional-Units</u> …")
(XOX)

--()--
XVIII
--()--

Adrien L. Montgomery
Tasting Droplets of the Unforgettable Rain
Official Imprint: "Dynamographx"

Tasting Droplets of the
Unforgettable Rain

By
Adrien L. Montgomery

<u>Cycle</u> <u>001</u>:
"If the Jester Wears the Robe and Crown ... If the King Wears the Fool's Motley Suit."

<u>UTA</u> <u>Directive</u> <u>I</u>:
"Attention! Attention! ... All Rail-Transit Guests ... Your 'Railbus[AI]'-System Vehicle's Operator Is Speaking: Welcome ... And, 'All Passengers Aboard'! Repeat, All Rail-Transit Guests ... Your 'Railbus[AI]'-System Vehicle's Operator Is Speaking: Welcome ... And, 'All Passengers Aboard'! ..."
("<u>UTA</u>": <u>U</u>rban <u>T</u>ransit <u>A</u>uthority)

The following statement consists of actual words appearing on an "audioclip"-sample of Ariq Shoretempel's voice in a recording made by an examining therapist during an approximately "up-to-date" psychodiagnostic interviewing session with the subject (i.e., "Ariq"):

<u>Interviewing</u> <u>Specialist</u>:
Dr. Deckster Trillingband, M.D., Ph.D.
(Rehabilitative/Preventative Psychotherapist)

<u>Date</u> <u>of</u> <u>Diagnostic</u> <u>Session</u>: <u>Sunday</u>, <u>August</u> <u>31</u> <u>of</u> <u>2003</u>
"I suspect that I'd find such a house to be almost unsurpassable in comfort. ... One in 'Gamington Farms', a tranquil neighborhood in 'Red Seasons County' (again, the lower section of the twin-county 'Eastern Slopes' region).... One with a view of both the Bay's large pool of saltwater and the high-rise architectural honeycombs on exhibit in northeastern San Francisco."
Interview's Subject: "Ariq Zarkahn Shoretempel"

<u>Notable</u> <u>Traits</u>:
(--26 Years Old--)
(--"African-American"--)
(--Male--)
(--Software-Designer--)
(--Berkeley Resident--)
(--No Known Criminal Conduct--)

(-|<u>Calendar</u> <u>Date</u>: <u>WED</u>., <u>Oct</u>. <u>01</u>, <u>2003</u>|-)
I'm sitting in a "Reign of Fools[ESU]" pizza restaurant found at the east end

--()--
XIX
--()--

of University Avenue in central-eastern Berkeley, California. In the back left corner of the store, there's a TV-set that's up on a displaying shelf, and it's running a Spanish-language program that's part of the Mexican government's "Pirate TV" assault on California, I do here reckon. Y'know, I never knew this store had any *Hispanic* employees. But, at least one of them must be, I s'pose, because of the "Beaner" broadcast I'm now having to unmercifully watch. (... Ha! Ha! Ha!)

There are two African-American teenagers splitting a pizza at a table in the restaurant's dining area. "Hey!" one of the teens says, looking towards the TV-screen. "It's on the Mexican channole!" The boy's friend tells him to quiet himself. ("... Chill!") "I ain't gunna watch this 'Mexi-TV' crap!" the first teen, the teenage TV-critic, says to the employee standing behind the sales counter. "Change the station! ... Hey! Change the station!"

The employee, a "Tahitian"-islands type (a "Son of the Pacific", I s'pose) lifts up a channel-switcher from a shelf under the sales-counter and points it towards the television set. He switches the broadcasting monitor to "RadioNation[AI]" (a cable network which airs music videos on a "24/7"-basis, essentially), which is airing a documentary on a particular "Hip-Hop" artist (a "Rapumentary", it is, I'm assuming). The two African-American teenagers merely return to swapping opinions with each other while enjoying abrupt (and all but feral) mouthfuls of food, that is.

But, the boy who chose to complain about the "Mexi-Vision[STF]" broadcast is himself sporting an "Afro"--circa 1974! (Trust me, if he ever wants a haircut, he'll have to find a handy "sheep-shearing" instrument and a shepherd who's in love with his job. ['... Ha! Ha! Ha!'])

Suddenly, a Chinese employee walks into the store through the venue's rear-entry doors. He wearily drops a pizza-delivery case on the sales-counter and rests his weight against the counter's rail, obviously recoiling from a rather difficult (" 'Pizza-Man' to the Rescue")-runabout. He glares at a table of two African-American females who're sitting near the store's front window sharing a large pizza that's still in its delivery carton. The pair of women curiously pick at toppings before nibbling at the pizza's oven-fresh sourdough bread-sections. I look up at the room's rear wall and see a sign on it that posts the words "30 MINUTE LIMIT AT TABLES". Maybe the Chinaman saw the girls occupying the table when he first left to make the "Fresh Pizza"-deliveries. The Oriental hurriedly rushes over to the guest-seating booth which I'm innocently sitting in at the moment. "Ah, what numbah are you waiting fohr?" the Asiatic "pizzaroom" employee asks me.

I look at the sales-receipt I'm holding and examine the handsize peel of paper for a pick-up number, but cannot readily determine which of the slip's number codes is the actual order number itself. I just hand him the receipt slip for an inspection. "Ah, number '51'. It'll be about ten minutes,"

--()--
XX
--()--

the pizza house's Oriental employee reports.

The Chinaman quickly returns himself to the restaurant's kitchen deck and starts apportioning various toppings to a large plate of dough before the particular order's put into the oven for baking. I'm guessing the Chinaman's dim mood might be due to the fact that the store's dining area is strictly being made use of by an "African-American" clientele at this point in time ... strictly, that is. I'm actually referring to 1), the two black teens at the table feasting on pizza like carnivores, 2), the two African-American women sitting at a table near the restaurant's front window, and, then, there is, of course, 3), i.e., me, the lone diner who's sitting at one of the booths against the store's western wall. ("Yes ... I'll take a table for one, please ...")

If the Chinaman doesn't like what he's witnessing in the pizza parlor right now, he's probably glad he isn't working the "Noontime"-shift. I'm, at this point, recalling the sight of "Cedar Creek High School" students as they walk the main routes to and from their academic campus during their school's "lunchbreak"-period. I can see them carrying paper soda cups with the "Reign of Fools[ESU]"-emblem appearing in ink across them while they make the great trek back to their afternoon classrooms. F.Y.I., "Cedar Creek High School" is an "inner city"-school, which has a student population that is predominantly "African-American". Hence, a likely reason for "Chairman Mao" to sidestep the store's bustling lunch-hour crowd.

Three homeless men enter the restaurant from the sidewalk just outside the foodvending-outlet. One of them, a Caucasian, limps over to my booth with a walking cane and seats himself on the bench opposite to mine. "Yo!" he says to me, in overt mockery of the individual he sees, I must here note. I stare at the vagrant, so as to make him aware of his blatant intrusiveness at the moment in question. He remains at the table with a boyish gleam upon his aging, weather-beaten face. I point my nose towards the open floor of the restaurant, telling him to quickly make himself scarce. He rolls his eyes as if to say I'm as predictable as every other "real" person who has the misfortune of coming into close contact with the specific derelict choosing to park himself in front of me on the exact occasion. He struggles out of the booth and hobbles over to the sales-counter, to beg the employees on hand for a free slice of pizza, I do s'pose.

One of the vagrants, an African-American, starts panhandling in the store, asking different customers for "spare change". He walks over to my booth. "My bruthah! My bruthah! ... Can you spare a dollah?" the inquiring vagabond says.

"No," I say, repeating the response with a hasty nose gesture. "I don't have any cash on me," I state, in all honesty, that would be.

Abruptly, the mood-stricken Chinaman emerges from a storeroom that opens up to the floor running behind the setting's sales-counter. "No!" he

--()--
XXI
--()--

says tersely, glaring at the two men panhandling for coins and, perhaps, free menu items. "No!" the Chinaman repeats, pointing to the store's streetside entrance. He's demanding the two "Nomads" hit the road, preferably Shattuck Avenue, again. Both homeless men exit the restaurant and the "Year of the Dragon" (i.e., the outlet's irate Asian administrator) instantly returns himself to the "on campus"-outlet's rear stockroom.

I watch a young couple enter the store through the twin doors at the dining room's rear wall. The two teenagers (both look like 17-year-olds to me) immediately walk up to the sales-counter and start conversing with the Tahitian-American worker. The girl, then, walks over to a bank of candy dispensers at the restaurant's northern (i.e., back) perimeter. She puts a few coins into one of the candy-vendors and cranks out a handful of nuts with caramel-coating to them. She feeds herself the candy-flavor nuts, popping each into her eager (and quite active) mouth, I do, here, note.

The boy catches up with the girl and the two exit the store through its rear entrance. I don't know if the two even came in to order anything to eat or drink tonight. Perhaps, the teenagers just came in to talk with the store's Pacific-American employee, "Tahiti" O'Neill of the Polynesian Shores.

However, watching the teenage girl hand-feed herself the caramel-rich, candied nuts, I caught, if just for a moment, an example of what a typical, carefree teenager is like in times today. Teenagers, the females in particular, seem to exhibit an apparently unsinkable spirit, which would be a sign of their unfailing energy-level, I do suppose. Yet, my teen years are long over for me these days, I regrettably have no choice but to, here, admit. (((Sigh))). I'm twenty-six years old now, and adulthood's no longer just a next-door neighbor ... it's a full-blown roommate!!! (... Hah! Hah! Hah!)

One of the three vagabonds, who was clever enough to seat himself at a table and then secretively watch his two associates panhandle themselves right out of the store, walks over to my booth. "Say, bruthah, got ten dollahs so's I can get sumthin' tuh eat tonight??"

"No," I say, looking about the venue for the hostile Eastern outlet manager to beneficially present himself once more.

"Then how 'bout five dollahs?" the vagabond inquires.

"No," I repeat. "Hobo Jones" now begins to beg for cash in continually lower US currency denominations, until we come to the trusty, reliable old penny. "Why d'ya want a penny?" I say to the transient.

" 'Cuz, you can spend the pennies too, can'tcha?"

"I don't have any change on me," I tell him. "Sorry."

"Joe Homeless" now starts making his rounds, soliciting short-term funding from the restaurant's other patrons in attendance here tonight. I see a young Asian male walk in through the store's front entrance just prior to exiting the location (just as quickly as entering it), crossing the seating area in walking to the dining room's two back doors. Prior to today, I wasn't even aware that this store actually does, in fact, have a rear entrance. I don't even know what, if anything, is behind this building. I assume it's nothing more than a large (and empty) parking lot.

A "Mexican" family now enters using the parlor's front doors and they seat themselves in the dining booth that just so happens to be right in front of the booth which I'm currently making convenient use of. The father immediately starts amusing the infant son with a routine of ridiculous facial contortions. The mother (or, *"la madre"*, I guess) seems to find delight herself in the "table"-side antics of both father and child. A restaurant employee, Tahiti O'Neill, "Son of the Society Islands", drops two large pizza cartons onto the table which the "Meximerican" family sits around.

"You ordered two cheese pizzas, right?" the youthful "pizza parlor"-staff worker asks. He quickly scans the receipt which the mother hands to him. The employee peeks inside a white paper bag and then rolls up the bag's opening, putting the bag back on top of the pair of pizza boxes.

It's unfortunate *Los Mexicanos* weren't here earlier…. They would have been able to watch the Spanish-language station which the eating venue was showing to its guests at that particular time. What did the teenage TV-reviewer call it … " 'Mexi-TV' crap"?!

The "Son of the South Pacific" walks over to my table and holds up a plastic card right in front of me. "Is this your credit card, man?" the ocean native courteously asks. I look at the plastic bank card and see a "Statue of Liberty"-impression on its front side.

"Nope," I say to the "Son of Oceania". Yet, while watching the employee walk from my table, I can't, here, help but think I should have chosen to answer "Yes". But, once a credit card's lost (or stolen) the genuine cardholder merely needs to make the specific banking institution aware of its absence in order to make the particular financial instrument obsolete. I.e., gaining possession of someone else's plastic isn't really going to amount to any type of monetary windfall for you, my good friends.

I'm at this point remembering my first visit to a "Reign of Fools[ESU]" pizza restaurant. I was an eleven-year-old at the time, I believe. The particular dining room in question was part of a midsize retailing village in "Warring Acres", a community in northeastern Santa Lucia, California. I remember the restaurant interior's air had an almost lethal degree of nicotine content to it due to the ribbons of tobacco smoke polluting the popular eating es-tablishment. (This incident, of course, took place prior to federal legisla-tion banning all cigarette-usage in restaurants and other social gathering places across the US in hopes of safeguarding public health…. Ha! Ha! Ha!)

At home, later that night, due to a particularly adverse reactivity to the tobacco fumes, I *threw up* onto the floor of the upstairs hallway. I remem-ber the spillage of hot vomit itself appearing to be nothing more than bitesize bits of the pizza I'd eaten earlier that evening at the specific "Reign of Fools[ESU]"-location. The remainders of the stomach-wrenching meal did happen to look as though the intestinal acids hadn't ground up the pizza at all. It was strange, however, being able to see something that I had just eaten make a return trip on me…. Yuck!

A white man now walks through the store's streetside entrance with a dog belonging to a lower-scale breed at his feet. He stands beside the sales counter and speaks with Tahiti O'Neill, "The Volcano Dancer". The employee points to a poster on the kitchen deck's side wall which advertises a special pizza order the store's promoting, or, he could just be pointing to the restaurant's rear exit in order to direct the man and his <u>un</u>sizeable animal out of the dining venue. *("No Pets on Store Premises, Please!!")* The customer withdraws a deck of plastic cards from his jacket's outer pocket and looks as though he's about to deal a round of "Blackjack" at a Las Vegas "gaming"-table. He hands a card over to the counter clerk, to pay for an order, I s'pose.

The man seats himself at a table in the eating outlet's dining space, apparently, for the purpose of just lounging comfortably in its chair. The dog (which is in a harness that's at the end of a retractable leash) is on its hind legs and keeps pawing at the man's knees in an ecstatic canine fit. (That little dog must really like Roma tomatoes and Italian dry salami, I would wager.)

I look up at the TV-set's screen, which is still exhibiting the "RadioNation[AI]" feature-documentary program (i.e., the "Rapumentary"), I'd, here, note. I watch the "entertainment industry"-profile report for a minute before examining my watch to estimate the amount of time I've spent in this University-region pizza parlor.

Suddenly, I hear a woman starting to speak bluntly with someone else near the front entryway of the eating outlet. I turn towards the restaurant's southern wall to see what the disturbance appears to be all about. There's a homeless woman standing at one of the tables and she's talking in curt language with another female who's sitting in a chair near the store's south-facing, frontside windows.

"You 'Palestinian' <u>witch</u>!" the homeless female spits out, assuming a combative stance near the other woman's chair. "I wish I could lock myself in a room with you and do to you for ten minutes what you've done to me for <u>ten</u> *years!!* You damn little <u>Arab</u> terrorist! I'm gunnah rot to death in a dirty alley 'cuz uh you, you <u>Afghani</u> brat!"

I unseat myself from the particular booth which I'm occupying and walk over to the large bank of candy-dispensing units standing at the restaurant's rear wall.

The nomadic female continues to verbally harass the patron sitting near the large storefront windows found at the pizza parlor's frontside entrance.

Adrien L. Montgomery
Tasting Droplets of the Unforgettable Rain
Official Imprint: "Dynamographx"

"My life ain't gunna come to some sorta horrible end just 'cuz you keep praying to 'Allah' for it to, got it?" the raving street empress asserts. "You people are all over the place, goddammit. Fucking al-Qaeda's female recruits are everywhere <u>nowadayz</u>! ... Jesus-*goddamm*-Christ!!"

I let the homeless woman's one memorable word repeat itself in my head ... "life" ('life', 'life', 'life', 'life' ...). Standing beside the large bank of candy-dispensing machines at the sitting hall's northern entrance, I, here, have to ask myself ... what—*if* one could ever know—is "life"?! Some would actually assert the purpose of "life" is to complete a voyage of self-discovery, if only for the purpose of self-identification, i.e., once you know who you <u>are</u>, you'll know why you're <u>here</u>. In other words, you'll know what your life could mean in the end—if, by chance, it means <u>any</u>thing at all—to others, to the world, and to the Universe itself. Still others say the purpose of "life" is to find a particular place where you can serve both society ... and yourself (as well) in equal measures. In achieving this, when it is over, you can look back upon your days on this particular planet and see that they were, in fact, not ones which you recklessly chose to toss aside.

I take a closer look at the vagrant female who's ranting near the pizza outlet's front entryway, and realize that I, in fact, do know the woman. Her name is "Elsie Marcher". She believes Islamic conspirators are the source of all of her problems in the world, of course. Y'know, the "linenheads", i.e., the "Qur'an"-quoting madmen of the International Muslim Brotherhood. (She is Jewish, however, i.e., a genuine "heeb", that is.) I don't think she recognizes me at this point, though. But, I usually come upon her after nightfall. I do suppose this particular dining room is too brightly lit in order for her to recognize a face she ordinarily only sets eyes upon as I approach "after hours" under the light of a dimming street-corner lamp.

The Chinaman (i.e., the "Lost Emperor", that is) emerges once again and orders the vagabondette to exit the "Reign of Fools^{ESU}"-outlet. "Elsie" backpedals her way out of the "Campuszone"-diningtime house while rolling her upright cart outside with her. Standing outside on the concrete sidewalk, she continues to curse at the restaurant's Asiatic manager and at the woman who's sitting near the store's street-facing windows (i.e., the " 'Palestinian' Witch").

I, at once, do make note of the entrance, as it, *here*, occurs of a "Caucasian" couple (a woman and a man--most likely "30something"-types), who join the dining floor's assembly of guests and find for themselves a table (in the dining hall's center, one built to seat four guests, actually) to occupy before enjoying the menu of options which the specific "Reign of Fools^{ESU}" restaurant offers to clientele-members choosing to pay visit to the facility during its evening hours of operation, that is.

"<u>Hey</u>! It's been at least <u>ten</u> minutes since we placed that 'order', hasn't it?! It should be ready by about <u>now</u>! 'Cuz **we're** certainly *ready* for <u>it</u>!" the

--()--
XXV
--()--

Adrien L. Montgomery

Tasting Droplets of the Unforgettable Rain

Original Year of Publication: 2026

female partner of the onsite Caucasian-pairing declares unto the presence of staff personnel inside the "Campus"-region's pizza-vending outlet.

The observably moody "Chinaman" immediately carries what appears to be an "All-The-Toppings" Xtra-Large pizza to the table which the Caucasian duo chooses to use in tandem on tonight's particular visit, quickly placing the large serving tray atop the couple's table and retrieving the sales-receipt which reports to store employees the specific order number which the pair of "thirtysomething"-types did receive at the time of their purchase earlier on.

I spot a penny that's on the floor next to my right foot and decide to pick it up. Whenever I see a copper piece on the sidewalk, I remember the following old saying: "… See a penny, pick it up, and all day long you'll have good luck!" I don't necessarily know if there's actual truth in that statement, yet I trust there could possibly be. If you just so happen to put a penny into your pocket and fortune doesn't appear to find you on that particular day, the penny merely might have been a guardian against any misfortune that would have found you had you not had the coin on you at the time. (Huh? …) Which is to say, even if a penny doesn't appear to bring you good luck on a particular day, you still might be benefitting from its presence if in fact you are capable of avoiding any possible misfortune (or, "bad" luck) which the "single cent"-piece manages to safeguard you against by being held well in hand on the specific occasion in question. (See?! …) Therefore, it's not as if you have a real option any time the chance to lift a penny off the sidewalk's cement surface arrives, do you?! The next time you find Old Abe's profile under foot, do not hesitate to pick up the coin someone else carelessly sought to discard.

I do reseat myself at the table which I earlier chose to occupy and notice the Mexican family that is still sitting in the booth that's right in front of mine. I s'pose the family is now claiming "squatter's rights" to it at this point. (… Hah! Hah! Hah!) The Tahitian tribal scout walks over to my booth and places a pizza box on top of the booth's table. "Here you go, 'Bro'! You have a good night, now!"

I do, here, lift the pizza carton's top half to inspect the food, as if I could determine whether the correct flavoring items were on it or not. I can just about taste the widely-chosen ("Reign of Fools[ESU]")-menu item in the aroma freeing itself from the box as its lid is up. I choose a slice of that Italian ingredient (i.e., the pepperoni, that would be) and quickly place it into my mouth (which is, at this point, all but twitching with anticipation due to the single-course meal it's about to thankfully enjoy). I allow my tongue to sample juice from the steaming piece of oven-fresh, deli-style meat. For a moment, I think about eating a small pinch of the Canadian bacon right here in this pizza-vending outlet before leaving the "campus"-region's eating venue in order to head back home … but I don't. (((Sigh))).

--()--
XXVI
--()--

Tasting Droplets of the Unforgettable Rain

By
Adrien L. Montgomery

Cycle 002:
"Yes, You're Saying You've Had Breakfast at Tiffany's … But, I've Had Sunday Brunch at Saks Fifth Avenue."

UTA Directive II:
"Attention! Attention! … Caution! Passengers Must Not Attempt To Open Side Doors While The 'Railbus^{AI}'-System's Carriage Is In Motion! … Repeat, Caution! Passengers Must Not Attempt To Open Side Doors While The 'Railbus^{AI}'-System's Carriage Is In Motion!"
("UTA": Urban Transit Authority)

Scenario:
(-|Calendar Date: MON., Jul. 12, 1982|-)
In the kitchen of a suburban house, three children are sitting around a table cautiously reviewing the particular "breakfast menu"-item that's presently available to each of them that morning …

Boy '1':
"I'm not gunna try it! … You try it!"

Boy '2':
"I'm not gunna try it! … You try it!"

Boy '1':
"I'm **not** gunna try it! … You try it"

Boy '2':
"Hey! I know! … Let's get Ariq!"

Boy '1':
"He won't eat it. He hates *everything*!"

(The two older boys watch while a five-year-old "Ariq Shoretempel" begins lifting spoonfuls of the cereal bowl's mixture of grain nutrients to his mouth.)

Boy '2':
"He *likes* it! … Hey! Ariq!"
(XOX)

--()--
XXVII
--()--

(The two older boys watch in amazement as the five-year-old "Ariq" continues to munch on the cereal's ingredients with a mouth anxiously in motion, as the child's face exhibits a smile and begins to brim with delight.)

<u>Epilogue</u>:
"LIFE" … Don't just pour it into a bowl on your kitchen table every morning and eat it…. Go ahead and add a few ounces of milk. Why don'tcha?!

(-|<u>Calendar Date</u>: <u>SAT</u>., <u>Oct</u>. <u>04</u>, <u>2003</u>|-)
It is, here, merely a moment after sunrise. I'm standing in bare feet on the cold tiles of the bathroom floor, preparing myself to spend a brief session in the shower. I'm adjusting the temperature dials and fingering the water pellets escaping the shower faucet's adjustable, chrome-built release port. I, of course, prefer very warm water when venturing behind the shower curtain and then, once my flesh relaxes under the touch of the bathtime sprinkler, I prefer to let a milder water temperature generously sweep over me. (Even if a *higher* temperature doesn't really lessen the shock of the shower water's assault on the morning skin, because you *think* it's a safer bet than cold water would be, the hot fountain blast must actually be easier for the skin to accept, I'd, here, have to say.)

I first let the lines of water spray moisten me, moisturizing me all over. I, then, let myself drink thirstily from the shower head's hard release. "Chugging" from the shower head while you're naked and under the discharge is a very refreshing sensation, I'll, here, make note of, my friends. Try it, sometime, if you haven't. The colder the water, the more baptizing the H_2O's ounces *actually* are. I guide the bar of deodorant soap over my skin and then grow soap-foam in a wash-cloth I use to free myself of any flesh pollutants which I've let myself acquire over the previous "24-hour"-term. I shampoo with a mineral-rich orange soaping gel. Y'know, I shampoo my genital section's hairs and armpit hairs with the same "tangerine"-like syrup, too. The bottle's label doesn't claim the shampoo's just for the scalp, does it?? … Ha! Ha! Ha!

I live in "The 'Tyrolla' Building" at the top of Allston Way in central-eastern Berkeley, California. The apartment complex is just across the street ("Oxford Street", that is) from U.C. Berkeley's collegiate campus. One thing I can't for my life understand is why any genuinely wealthy person would choose to live inside of an apartment building. (??? … Mind you, I am <u>not</u> a wealthy individual.) I've never had any particular fondness for New York City--**never!**--but, to think of one of New York's <u>wealthier</u> residents forking over fresh green "Federal Reserve"-prints for what is essentially a "matchbox" above the ground is, to say the least, puzzling, and, to tell truth … <u>sickening</u>!! (… Ha! Ha! Ha!)

The fact that the "Manhattanites" all choose to inhabit what amount to

--()--
XXVIII
--()--

nothing more than "full feature" hotel rooms (selecting to essentially occupy what is merely a lavishly built-up shelfspace) makes me cringe at whatever trait constitutes the nucleus of that particular city's psychosocial universe. (<u>Ahem</u>! ... If you can afford to purchase a house outside of the "Big Apple"--in CT, NJ, Long Island or "Upstate"--just do it and stick yourself on a train line to "Gotham" each morning.... <u>Jeez</u>!!) A rich man who chooses a penthouse in "Central Park West" over an ideal out-of-town estate must really, **really** love NYC! I can't wait until I can move into a *real* house of my own one of these days. I want to stand at my front door and open it without the fear of someone exiting through it on me, or the fear of someone standing behind me while I fumble through a briefbag for the key to the door at the building's entryway.

And, additionally, apartment-leasers must put up with a housing complex which is overrun with tenants who can separate you from your specific degree of sanity more quickly than the ear-tweaking screams of a blood-wet, horror-ridden warzone could, in fact, manage to do. A certain number of the residents inhabiting the particular building I'm currently occupying would make life in a barnyard of livestock seem almost noiseless in comparison. In this actual residential property, you hear voices in the hallway that come to haunt you as a *poltergeist* (i.e., a "rambunctious ghost") would come to tyrannize the unwilling listener with its virtual typhoon of infernal sounds. I just can't wait until I have an *actual* house of my very own at <u>some</u> point in the future, hopefully a future not so distant at that, I might, here, choose to add. In truth, the building's "nine to five" manager just quit on us. I suspect that she could no longer tolerate dealing with the daily irritation which the building's more aggravating residents would cause her on an hour-by-hour basis. The main offense against the property's occupancy code would appear to be narcotics distribution (i.e., "dope-dealing", that would be) by various building-residents. (Those damn in-house "ice"-vendors!)

The narcotics-sellers use the "tenant"-registry to unlock the apartment building's set of front doors (i.e., the "inner" door and the "outer" door) to let any crack-addicts enter our private residential spaces at all hours of the overnight term. A dope-pusher from a lower floor will come up to my floor and knock on another dealer's front door, telling him to bring all his "junk" to her place for her "regulars" to take a look at for possible selection. I've tried to get the drug-dealers thrown out of the building, because I can no longer emotionally survive the annoyances which these particular subcreatures serve up to me on an almost daily basis. I remember seeing a write-up in a local newspaper about dope-fiends who had the opportunity to seize a vacant apartment in one of the area's buildings and chose to make camp inside of the unit for the ensuing two weeks until one of the building's <u>actual</u> tenants chose to notify the local police department of the

--()--
XXIX
--()--

intruders.... I.e., if you happen to be in a particular conversation that features the area's dope-dealing constituent, you just so happen to be discussing nothing other than the most primitive form of human life yet known to exist, I'd care to note, here, my old friends.

Yet, I'm going to jump aboard a "BART"-train to San Leandro sometime early this afternoon. I have to visit an outdoorsman's emporium to search for a few items which I'm certain will turn out to be quite useful to me in the near future. Then, I'm keeping a promise to drop by an old friend's house to peek at a new litter of infant dogs which his Cocker Spaniel bitch just saw enter the world by way of her canine womb. Later, I'm going to stop at "The Screening Room" on Shattuck Avenue to rent a DVD-title which I'll probably watch sometime tonight or early tomorrow morning. Today's itinerary will end with a trip to "Campus Mart", the one on Telegraph Avenue, not the one on University Avenue. [!!Emoticon Alert!! (} : > (] I have to purchase a couple of single-liter "eXcellor^{AI}"-brand "Lime-a-Lot" cola bottles. I'm momentarily without so much as a single drop of the particular soda concoction in my at-home refrigeration unit and *that*, my friends, is a violation of the personal code of urban-area survival which I vehemently live by, if I must, here, admit to you all.

Under the fountain's warm water, I press the open face of my right hand, the stronger hand, against the tip of my (sometimes) "sexual" organ (... or, my "joystick", or, my "sin stick", or, how 'bout, my " 'all day'-sucker", huh??). Simply choose the label which you find yourself to be the most at ease with, my good friends. I start squeezing the elastic shaft of the penis with my anxious hand while envisioning the sight of a young girl I once saw several years back. The girl--a princess in a "practice bra" (... ha! ha! ha!)--was standing on a residential street running east from Shattuck Avenue. I was trying to charge home from a screening complex ("PhotoScope^{UE} Union 8", actually), because I hadn't let myself pause to use the exhibition complex's restroom after filling myself with about a hundred ounces of soda during one of the film-screenings.

I told myself aloud, "I'm going to pee like a platoon of drunken soldiers when I get back to the apartment in a minute". And the girl, probably thirteen years in age, began laughing at me, obviously overhearing what I had just said to myself. Anyway, I remember her smile and the pre-womanly radiance on her adolescent face as I ran frantically past her in a mad dash back home. I'm now attempting to excite myself by recollecting her image as I stand in the shower stall gripping my magician's wand with my fuzzy little right-hand palm. (You really *will* grow hair on your palms if you keep toying with the old garden hose, got me?! ... See, a woman's vaginal realm is comparable to a garden, is it not? And a man's got the lawn-care system that's necessary to irrigate the delectable patch of sprouts, right?)

There are other ills, to be sure, that result from the art of "self-arousal",

--()--
XXX
--()--

my old friends. Any hazard you choose to negotiate, my friends, whether we're discussing alcohol, cigarettes, or manhandling your own "power" tool (ha! ha! ha!), is something which will demand a toll from you, eventually. You must recognize this truth from the beginning, or you'll awake one day not knowing what the Hell just came out of the sky and landed upon you! Use caution, once again, whenever treading upon footprints that others left in their tracks prior to meeting up with certain (yet, quite serious) injuries. I believe that I, a veteran of the "Self-Abuse Battles", must be the one who warns the next generation about the perils which might arise if one chooses to solve his "sociosexual" problems with a "hands on" approach, so to speak. (... Ha! Ha! Ha! ... Get it? A "<u>hands on</u>" approach! ... Ha! Ha! Ha!)

What I *must* do now is inform those who are just beginning to explore their own anatomical regions (<u>literally</u>, that is--ha! ha! ha!) that certain techniques musn't be put to use when one is attempting to get a grip on one's love life with all the dexterity found in one's right hand, to put it bluntly. Anyway, all boys within earshot (and men who still require the wisdom which only a "guru" can offer unto them) should listen carefully to the following allotments of advice that I choose now to generously bestow upon each of you. May your nocturnal "self-help" procedures only provide you with peace, my little wolf-pups....

<u>(The Start of Ariq's Fourteen Laws on Self-Arousal and Relief)</u>
<u>Law #001</u>:
You should only attempt "masturbation" while in a private bath or shower stall and **only** use your right (or, <u>stronger</u>) hand to manipulate the genital organs, O my anxious sons! In this case, the cock's pungent cocktail instantly withdraws itself into the drain-pipe's port and, hence, there's no physical evidence of your orgasmic action which anyone else might potentially discover.

<u>Law #002</u>:
You must never attempt to achieve orgasm by engaging in any activities of intercourse involving an inanimate object, e.g.'s, a pile of grass clippings, watermelon slices, or a toy doll (i.e., a "Teddy Bear"). In other words, never substitute a physical object for a human figure.... You might end up trying to impregnate an inflatable plastic woman for cryin' out loud. *(Geezus Christ!!)*

<u>Law #003</u>:
Never--**never!**--ejaculate onto anything other than the floor of a shower stall. If you attempt to gratify yourself in your bedroom and you don't manage to capture all of the ejaculatory matter, your personal nocturnal(X)

quarters will begin to assume a particularly objectionable odor. And visitors to your room will, without exception, notice it. There is **not** an adult in the world (male or female) who can't recognize the scent of human semen.

Law #<u>004</u>:

Do **not** attempt to constrict, interrupt, or accelerate any physiological processes in order to accentuate the sensation you experience during one particular "climax" (i.e., an incident of ejaculation, that is). (I've read stories about people actually strangulating themselves while masturbating because they unwisely let themselves assume oxygen-deprivation would intensify the level of euphoria at the moment of orgasm…. Mmmmm??)

Law #<u>005</u>:

You should **not** attempt to masturbate in any <u>public</u> location. Someone might show up unpredictably and you'd be left without having had the opportunity to "complete" the particular task occurring at the time. (Would <u>you</u> want to shake someone else's hand if you were already aware of what that person had just had in it?? … *Ughh!)*

Law #<u>006</u>:

If gratifying yourself in a bedroom, make sure you're "hidden" from any possible onlookers. I haven't slept in a bedchamber to this day which couldn't be easily seen by someone somewhere nearby. When you attempt to entertain yourself, you don't want to entertain anyone else as well, do you?!

Law #<u>007</u>:

Do not attempt to manipulate the genital organs with a foreign instrument of any type, i.e., such as a tool or any sort of vise. (I once tried to satisfy myself by putting my own "hot rod" in between a couple of bath sponges, in order to squeeze the old pepperoni roll until I did manage to accomplish an adequate level of hormonal arousal.) You might end up damaging the barrel of the penis or a testicle. (Just imagine yourself hopelessly attempting to explain *that* particular injury to a doctor: "I swear, it was a bicycle accident! …")

Law #<u>008</u>:

Do not excite yourself to the point of erection in public, O little lion cubs. I remember amusing myself with a sexual fantasy once in my 12th-grade "Oriental Civilization II" class. The wingless reptile reared up on me while I was quietly lounging at my desk. I had to struggle mightily to withdraw myself from the land of "The 'Faerie Tale' Sex Follies" that I had just begun to eagerly explore. But trust me, the stench of the ejaculatory juice would have made the entire classroom foul with its odor, my friends.... In other words, <u>be</u> *careful* out there!!

Law #<u>009</u>:

You musn't try to masturbate (i.e., "reach for the brass ring", that is) in anyone else's house. I remember visiting an aunt of mine once while at the age of nineteen and I irresponsibly left a spot of semen on one of the futons in the study which I slept in. That's not <u>exactly</u> being the most gracious guest, I know. Yet, I was in a particularly desperate state of sexual neediness that particular summer and due to the high temperatures even the females had no choice other than to wear as little as was possible. Hence, what I saw walking past me each day drove me to recklessly spotting my aunt's new futon with the teaspoon of hormonal soup.

Law #<u>010</u>:

<u>Never</u> masturbate (i.e., "deal from the bottom of the deck", that would be) inside of an automobile, either (whether it's in motion at the time or not). Once again, you'd be unable to purify the vehicle of whatever odor is left by the semen and your routine passengers will be able to detect how you've been passing the time while sitting at intersections. (With that nimble right hand of yours clutching the old familiar gear-knob, again.... *Ha! Ha! Ha! Ha!*)

Law #<u>011</u>:

Do <u>not</u> attempt to masturbate (i.e., "wave the magic wand", that is) before venturing forth into the public world. I remember initiating a session of self-abuse right before I was to venture to a shopping mall and I overheard a pair of women at the mall commenting on me ... y'know what I'm saying, my secret associates? The females could still detect a fragrant hint of the ejaculatory juices which I'd left upon me. In attempting to add a minute of self-manipulation to your day-to-day routine of "jobs to do", you do not desire to see yourself turning into some sort of social pariah, my faithful followers.

Law #<u>012</u>:

Do <u>not</u> even try to masturbate (i.e., "fight with one hand tied behind your back", that is) if you happen to inhabit an apartment along with someone else, i.e., a roommate. No matter how secretive you try to be with your late-night handiwork, that "roomie" of yours will always find out what it is you're up to after hours. And if there's one thing people love to talk about, it's the nocturnal exercises of a "self-help" disciple. (Do <u>not</u> self-arouse if you are sharing a residential space with any life-form that's even remotely

--()--
033
--()--

close to you on the food chain…. Even *Golden Retrievers* are known to gossip on occasion…. Ha! Ha! Ha!)

Law #<u>013</u>:

Do <u>not</u> masturbate (i.e., "burn the candle at both ends", that is) while on the run. I.e., do not try to squeeze in a little self-abuse time while readying yourself for school or for work. Either, you will not do what you have to do to complete the task, or, conversely, you'll end up making yourself late for the previously scheduled appointment. Merely choose to release any tension you have when you have ample opportunity to do so, O little leopard kittens.

Law #<u>014</u>:

Do <u>not</u> attempt to masturbate (i.e., "give yourself a warm round of applause", that would be) while watching television or while listening to the radio. One event will simply distract you from the other. If you're helping yourself to yourself while in front of the TV, you're going to miss the show, or vice versa … what's on TV will keep you from fully enjoying the "hands on" experience you've set up for yourself, my eager, flagrantly anxious sons.

(The <u>End</u> <u>of</u> <u>Ariq's</u> <u>Fourteen</u> <u>Laws</u> on <u>Self-Arousal</u> & <u>Relief</u>)

Hence, you must, my puma cubs, use care if trying to set free your sex drive by seizing the shifting knob with your right (<u>not</u> *wrong*) hand, that is. I.e., acknowledge the wisdom of the preceding words, my pupils, and you'll avoid the heartache that many disciples of the "Do-It-Yourself" dogma have come across in their shadowy search for just a handful of happiness while here on Earth. However, I know you'll use extreme care from this day forward whenever handling the old sprinkler head, y'know what I'm saying? Have a joyful old time embarking on your sinful voyage of self-discovery, my anxious "Self-Help" disciples!!

When I was nine years old, I would see a TV-commercial every morning before the start of school which did happen to feature a group of kids eating fruit-flavor popsicles in a park-size backyard. I remember seeing a young girl among the garden playmates smile and nibble at a "Cherry"-flavor popsicle bar. I'd always focus on her while watching the "Breakfast"-time TV ad and would fantasize about knowing the girl and would imagine the two of us as being a "steady" couple (i.e., "<u>boy</u>friend & <u>girl</u>friend", y'know). I'd envision her smiling at me with the same glowing shyness which she would display in the morning television commercial. (To this day, I'm still capable of remembering the snack-advertisement's sing-along tune.)

But the innocence of such fantasies ended with the earliest of my years,

--()--
034
--()--

my ever-loyal listenership. By the time I was eleven, I was fantasizing about a girl in my "6th"-grade class who had the same quiet beauty as the girl appearing in the old "morningtime" TV popsicle commercial. Though, I wasn't dreaming about us nibbling on "Tangerine"-flavor popsicles together in a park after school, that is. I would, at the time, fantasize about sodomizing the girl and about forcing my pinkie finger up her rear end and about probing her anal cavity with just about any instrument I could place my pre-pubescent hands on. ("... <u>Attention</u>! <u>Attention</u>! ... 'Dr. Shoretempel' to the 'OR'! ... <u>Attention</u>! <u>Attention</u>! ... 'Dr. Shoretempel' to the 'OR'!")

By "6th"-grade, however, my sexual fantasies had already grown to a level of perversity which even "kiddie porn"-productions probably didn't happen to showcase on screen. Of course, beyond elementary school, the daydreams I'd play back again and again were both misogynistic and antisocial to an ever-escalating degree. But, whatever, my *"oh so faithful"*-followers, occurs in the realm of fantasy amounts to what I would refer to as "victimless crime", I do believe. There aren't any elbow-scars, knee-burns, or foot-scrapings due to whatever I choose to imagine in the sexual visions I happen to create for my own personal amusement. Through fantasy, though, I've built a panoramic landscape around myself which I'm, perhaps, incapable of ever fleeing from, my dearest fellows.

These frank confessions of mine may lead you to assume that I'm, perhaps, a "pedophile", i.e., an *adult* who seeks sexual relations with "minors" (i.e., children), whether such relations be consensual or not. Yet, such a guess on your part would be unwise, folks. I'm not necessarily someone who selects "Gradeschool" girls for use as replaceable sexual acquaintances now and again.... For, in truth, I do <u>not</u>. My genuine belief is--as I, here, suggest ... children exist behind a highly-secure portal which adults cannot (and *should* not) ever attempt to open. I do, occasionally, think of opening that grand gateway and stepping in between those walls which isolate the child from the adult. But, I primarily select not to go where I would most prefer to. I'm not the type to toss caution to the world's farthest winds, y'know what I'm saying, O loyal brethren?

I have yet to truly achieve in sexual heroics any feat which would be of genuine historical significance, my friends. But, if I do make history through any hypersexual stuntwork, I'll make you, old mates, the first ones to be aware of the specific case. I can safely admit to this, however--I have, to this date, seen myself commit no <u>illegal</u> acts with respect to my particular sexual practices or preferences. Hence, I've nothing grim or unseemly to report to you at this actual point, my *oh-so-secret* associates.

I remember instances of sexual activity in the summer of 1990 (when I was only thirteen years in age) with a particular girl who had the keen sense to reside at a street address just one block away from mine inside of a working-class "condominium"-district (i.e., the "Condos", as all of us would affectionately term the actual neighborhood), which we were sharing in the southwestern corner of "Warring Acres", a suburban *housing* community in Santa Lucia, California. The beehive of single-family houses was known, fittingly, as the "Eucalyptus Patch", because, that is, in fact, what the area, at one point, only had to present to the public and nothing else besides. The particular region of land was, at that time, nothing more than a planting ground for tract after tract of "eucalyptus"-tree groves. The actual female was, in fact, a twelve-year-old that summer, who hadn't yet become a student at the junior high school that I'd begun attending during the most recent schoolyear (i.e., "Belheller Junior High School"). She'd just come out of the "6th"-grade, "graduating", so to speak, from the local elementary school, "Red Earth Elementary". I can, at the moment, remember enjoying sexual intercourse with this particular girl on the family room's sofa on one certain Saturday afternoon while the house was otherwise empty. *('Family' room?? ...* Huh?? Note: In the state of California, the "family room" is [of the two downstairs "meeting rooms"] the one with the TV and "entertainment"-center in it, people. The empty sitting room that's near the front entrance of the house is known as the "living room" in that particular state.... Got it, old friends and loyal associates on hand??)

On weekdays, she would usually drop by in the late morning, probably around 11:00 a.m., P.D.T., and we'd execute various sexual acts in the car garage ... correct, on the cold, concrete, dust-ridden floor of the car garage. (What the Hell did I care?! It was up to the girl to lie upon the concrete's unwelcoming cement surface, y'know. I, on the other hand, would merely position myself neatly right on top of her. She had the cold concrete floor to lie upon, whereas I had **her** to lie upon.... Hah! Hah! Hah!)

I remember attempting sexual "experiments" with the girl on the carpet-soft floor of my bedroom in the afternoons throughout that particular "Summertime"-season (of 1990, that would be). She would just show up at the front door, as if she were simply looking for another kid to talk with. I'd have the child out of her clothes and on the floor of my bedroom within just a few moments of her most fortunate arrival, I can assure you, my old friends. I do, at this particular moment, also recall enjoying sexual acts with this one same girl in a car-parking space which was apparently built to overlook the condominium complex's ("['Upper']-pool")-area. (There were two recreational pools belonging to that particular "neighborhood"-housing development, an "Upper"-pool and a "Lower"-pool.) Once, under a starless nighttime sky, I actually did manage to convince the actual girl in question we would have the necessary privacy right in front of the unlit headlights of a pickup-truck which was sitting in a space in the otherwise empty lot of asphalt parking-sites.

Years later, a friend of mine in the "Patch" (a term put commonly to use by area inhabitants in noting the region they held residential status within)

Adrien L. Montgomery
Tasting Droplets of the Unforgettable Rain
Official Imprint: "Dynamographx"

would admit to me that he and a girlfriend of his had regularly had sexual intercourse inside the whirlpool bath's iron enclosure after nightfall drove all the other swimmers indoors. Yet, when these nocturnal escapades actually took place both he and his sexual playmate were merely sixteen-year-olds. Of course, there wasn't a chance under the distant, winking stars overhead that I would have tried to sneak the twelve-year-old into the whirlpool bath's rusting perimeter posts. (… "<u>Deanna</u>"! … Yes, that was the twelve-year-old girl's name, if I am, at this moment, correctly remembering it.) The whirlpool bath's spacious concrete deck was open to anyone's eyesight through the gaping iron bars which stood as a barrier around the sitting pool's roomy deck area. In any one of the condos along the ("['Upper']-pool")-area's open side, someone could have easily begun conducting surveillance upon whichever couple was at play in the bath's basin of hot, chlorine-rich water. Or, someone walking atop the dirt walking trail that ran in between the condos and the ("['Upper']-pool")-area's own see-through, black iron fence could have caught the two of us increasing the hot bath's water temperature with the steam rising from our busy adolescent bodies.

I can, at this particular instance, also recall committing acts upon "Deanna" inside the confines of a crawlspace which ran under a stretch of eight condominium-units that were just up the street from the address which my own family kept as a residential-unit at the time. Deanna's family did inhabit one of the eight condos which the large, unlit cavern ran underneath. The tunnel space had a floor of cold, pale dirt … dirt which had, perhaps, never felt the weighty heat of sunlight in its term beneath the lineup of family housing-units. The cave's interior had an openness that would permit any kid in the neighborhood the ability to walk through it without having to watch for any of the overhead beams which were built to provide foundational support for the housing structures which sat right above the chilly, hollow "underfloor" tunnel-space. Also, at any particular time another neighborhood kid could have ridden or taken a bicycle right through that sunless, dirt-ridden corridor. But, whenever I was in that cold, musty hall fiendishly exploring Deanna's most personal components, no one ever chose to enter the sun-absent chamber only to discover the two of us in the midst of frenetic sexual actions.

I remember once in college a floormate of mine saying to me, if he were to ever become sexually "anxious" enough he'd choose easy prey for him-self, such as an eleven-year-old, he'd s'pose. (He did fail, I must, here, note, to specify the juvenile's exact gender, male or female, however.) Others on the "residence hall" floor quickly said in agreement that this particular individual was, perhaps, emotionally defective for entertaining such antisocial sexual objectives. (Or, maybe the guy's admission was really just a hoarse scream for help … y'think? I would not know, nor could I, at this moment in time, even pretend to care about such an issue as this one.) But, on campus, you frequently hear dispatches on random sex from housemates who are all too eager to inundate your ear canals with entries from their personal *semi*-criminal up-to-date "sexlife"-portfolios.

One night, a floormate of mine told me he knew a guy who <u>strictly</u> sought "blond" women! (Let's see, I s'pose that would strictly refer to a woman having <u>blond</u> scalp hairs, <u>blond</u> under-arm coils, and <u>blond</u> vaginal sprouts.) "... Just **blond** women", this particular friend made an effort to explain to me at the actual time. This schoolmate of mine, a "Persian" by birth (i.e., an Iranian-born arrival), told me that he, as well, would secure companionship *exclusively* from "blond" females, *if* only he could achieve such a romantic feat for himself, that is. He said he chose to regard the frail, attractive "blonde" as the most desirable of all female physical types. I remember a particular floormate of ours ridiculing him for preferring "skinny" women. (In adding to the widescale scorn, "Ha! Ha! Ha!" I readily stated to him.) And his reply to the on-campus critic in question? ... "The pretty ones are always <u>skinny</u>". He'd point to what he saw as an acceptable specimen if he just so had the chance to catch sight of one on TV while the two of us were sitting in the dormitory's "TV"-lounge, watching whatever program we would regularly view along with any other students happening to enter and assume seats for themselves in our midst on the occasion.

But, I can now remember sitting atop my dorm-room bed on one night in particular and hearing someone in the room next to mine bumping himself against the wall which ran in between the two "residence hall"-units. The puzzling sound of human limbs banging up against the wall which was separating our side-by-side rooms kept occurring over a lengthy span of time. I ran into the guy the next day, the floormate who slept in the bed which was on the other side of the separating wall. ("Kant", if I'm remembering correctly, was the specific guy's name ... "Kant Ramsey", that would be.)

"Man! What was going on in your room last night?!" I said to him (... to "Kant", that would be). "What I heard sounded like 'Ring Riot: Part IX' on *WrestleFest: Arena & Ring!"*

"Yeah? ... Well, I definitely did have someone 'pinned to the mat'," he said, showing me a proud smile. "Yeah, she was definitely 'down for the count'," Kant said, at that point releasing a virtual leakage of laughter ("... ha! ha! ha! ha!").

I remember I'd watch a couple of campus girls, i.e., co-ed's, march into Kant's room on the occasional Friday night.... <u>Two</u> at a time?!! *Whoa-hoh!* The college's own "Casanova", I'd venture here to say.

Every year is different. I remember an older dormmate of mine explaining to me that the residence hall's level of sexual energy occurring over the preceding academic year (A.D. 1994 to A.D. 1995, that is) was(X) probably nine or ten degrees higher than the level of in-house activity I was seeing occur around me during my own particular "Freshman Year" on campus (A.D. 1995 to A.D. 1996). In the earlier year, as the particular floormate chose to inform me, you could hear females uncontrollably inhaling in an overtly boisterous state of sexual ecstasy from residence hall rooms found up on the 5th-floor. (The one floor which was, specifically, the housing-site's "all female"-floor [or, the "_female_ only"-floor], that is. The girls in residence on the 5th-floor would routinely permit their male acquaintances overnight bedspace, I do s'pose.) This particular friend of mine ("Kimi", a Japanese student … a "Japan-American", or, a "Japamerican", you could say) said you could hear the mattresses squealing beneath the weight of each hip-thrust which they had to sustain during the overnight sexual exercises occurring inside of the dorm-rooms found on the campus hall's 5th-floor.

"Every year is different," Kimi said to me. "This year's … not like _that_." … Indeed. During my two particular semesters in the "Dorms" (as the particular rooming-hall was known by those of us residing in its virtual beehive of units) there wasn't a great deal to comment on regarding events occurring in the field of sexual exercise, or "sexercise", I, regretfully, must, here, admit. Uhmmmm … particularly _not_ in my room, I, unfortunately, must (yet, again), here, confess to one and all within adequate hearing range.

On the "all male"-floor (or, the "_male_ only"-floor), i.e., the 3rd-floor, that is, physical face-offs could erupt rather easily, if only for the reason that incompatible floormates had to cohabitate with each other on what would be a "night and day"-basis. Yet, I came to notice one repeating rule, however, concerning the result of any specific dustup, which I'd state as follows--the dude who chose to initiate a standoff would _always_ be the one who, in the end, had no other choice than to regret having begun such a smackdown. _(… Ah hah!!)_

I'm, at this point, remembering a pair of friends I had, actually, who didn't appear to care for each other at all, engaging in a lively round of "intramural" mayhem on one particular evening. The three of us were idling in the floor's "TV"-lounge, watching whatever programs were airing at the time, and "Nuywan" (which you'd pronounce as "nee-whan"), a _Korean_ friend of mine, threw a card (or _some_thing) at another friend of mine, "Puarov" (which you'd pronounce as "pahr-off"), an _Indian_ (of the "Subcontinent" in Asia, that is, not of the "teepee-dwellers" in the US). And "Puarov" just starts swinging at "Nuywan", perhaps upon finally coming to wit's end over Nuywan's ceaselessly annoying persona…. Mmmmm?? Yet, Puarov at once becomes aware of one particular inconvenience, that would be, in the midst of the "Rooming Hall"-brawl … Nuywan (ah, yes) knew a style of the _martial_ arts, "tae kwon do", I do note, which is, of course, the

Korean variation on the ancient Oriental man-to-man sparring technique. Alas, Puarov quickly finds himself holding an "All Day" admission ticket to an event amounting to nothing less than "Martial Arts Expo 1996", a panorama of Oriental hand-to-hand dueling skills, I must, here, confess to all members of the audience in attendance here today.

Anyway, "Nuywan" began knocking "Puarov" against the walls of the floor's "TV"-lounge and I, at once, chose to alert the dorm-monitor on duty (the one in charge of the building's lower section of stories [1st through 4th]), who had a room just one stairwell up from us, on the fourth floor, that is. The monitor, an in-house "Inspector General" for the residence hall's current roll-call of onsite inhabitants, was a profusely robust African-American dude, a third-year student, I believe him to have been at the time (i.e., *"Fat Albert: The College Years"*, I assume). As I ran into the stairwell leading up to the residence hall's fourth floor, someone did try to warn me against notifying the "Floor Watch", yet, I knew if one of the amateur "ringmasters" were to damage the TV-set inside the lounge the entire floor (each one of us, that is) would come under fire for an incident of "University"-property damage. "Round Albert" reluctantly agrees to follow me back to the dormitory's third floor (out of sheer obligation, I guess, with him being the in-house monitor, of course) and puts an immediate stop to the "twin bill"-episode of *"Casino City Boxing Presents!"* And, on the <u>very</u> *next* day, in the <u>very</u> *same* lounge, Puarov asks me if I was the particular "floormate" who chose to summon the dormitory's "Peace Officer" to the "Fight Night" spectacle which, regrettably, took place on the previous afternoon.

"<u>You</u> were the one who ran and got 'Kendall', right, Ariq?" Puarov doesn't hesitate to inquire at this particular moment.

"Yeah," I had no other choice, here, than to admit to him. "Nuywan knocked you right into one of the doors leading out to the 'Sundeck'.... That thing rattled like a brass gong inside of China's 'Imperial Palace', or sumthin', didn't it? I didn't want to see anyone thrown headfirst through it, <u>OK</u>? The shards of glass alone would've taken <u>all</u> of us an entire day to clean up, I betcha."

"I *knew* it was <u>you</u>," Puarov says, rolling his eyes as if to show adamant disapproval. Yet, if I hadn't had the dorm-monitor ("Kendall", remember) interrupt the virtual funeral service which "Nuywan" was preparing him for, Puarov would have quickly become yet another entry into the local PD's "crime file"-reports recording current "campuswide"-assault statistics, I do, of course, not doubt, at this point, due to actions by those participating.

Nuywan walks into the floor's "TV"-lounge and selects for himself a seat that's just next to mine on one of the room's sofas. The two recently-retiring ring professionals, Nuywan and Puarov, choose, here, not to speak to each other, yet Nuywan still doesn't fail to seize the opportunity on hand to characterize Puarov's abilities in the game of self-defense as those, perhaps, belonging to the star of an all-male dance-troupe.

"Oh! … It's another <u>lame</u>-ass show," Nuywan says of the broadcast material which the TV-screen is displaying at the moment. "<u>But</u>, it's not as lame as *'Puarov'* is!"

Puarov, the snooty "Son of India", merely chooses to dismiss Nuywan's attempt to initialize an era of cordial post-combat relations with an obvious and impatient exhalation. (Ah, Nuywan's attempt to end any uneasiness existing between himself and Puarov quickly fails!) … The ex-amateur fist-fighting foes simply continue to ignore each other and focus themselves on the programming material airing at the time on the floor lounge's television set.

The tenancy building I'm residing in, "The 'Tyrolla' Building", chose to open its entry doors to any eligible lease-holders on Friday, July 20th of 2001, that is. As it happens, I was able to sign a "leasing"-agreement on an apartment-unit in this particular housing complex on Monday, September 30th of 2002. However, it just so occurs, I found myself in a different room at the start of my specific era of tenancy in this actual residential operation. The apartment in question was, in fact, a "studio" on the building's top level. Yet, after the punishing remains of a "supertyphoon" out of the Northwestern Pacific (originating within the range of a clustering of islets just southeast of Japan) struck the San Francisco Bay Area in early December of 2002, a leak did quickly appear in one spot of the granular surface of the studio-apartment's ceiling. The ceiling's outer lining began dripping after the arrival of a build-up of rainwater upon the building's roof on a Saturday morning, around ten o'clock, and the housing complex's "maintenance" man, a Mexican dude ("Philip", or *"Felipe"*, that is) took a look at the exhibition of interior precipitation and told me I could immediately relocate myself and any personal possessions into a "temporary" unit available among the residential establishment's inventory of inhabitable rooms. (He did suspect, wisely, the ceiling could crumble and collapse over the weekend if the rainwater had already had the chance to begin rotting the room's insulating "overhead" material to an extreme degree.)

I quickly began to transfer all the household-items which I kept on hand in the first room I held as a building occupant into an apartment sitting at the opposite end of the hallway which lead, at first, to the room which I unfortunately chose for myself in September of 2002, the day I did sign onto a "tenancy"-agreement. Yet, the 2nd option which the building's "maintenance"-supervisor let me occupy on an "emergency"-basis (due to the crisis occurring inside the unit I had to inhabit at the particular time) did prove to be a most *beneficial* change for me, to say the very least, dear friends. The first unit I chose to "rent out" for myself had a "south facing"-

exposure to it, i.e., its offering of windows did look southwards, that is, hence, on days of higher temperature in the "East Bay"-region, inhabiting that particular apartment did prove to be an excruciating test for my usual degree of emotional stability. But, I've had the particular "studio"-unit which I'm occupying <u>now</u> for just over nine-and-a-half months--from Saturday, December 14 of 2002 until today, Saturday, October 04 of 2003.

There is actually a "soda"-dispensing appliance on the floor that is just below the one I occupy, offering to us tenants 12-oz. cans of "eXpree[STF]"-brand beverages, unfortunately. (I am certain I've made mention before to you of the fact that I actually happen to prefer whatever particular chemical formulation exists in "eXcellor[ISS]"-brand "Lemon Lime"-cola to the recipe existing in any type of rivaling soda-concoction.) It is, O faithful fellowship at hand, the ingenious coupling of the artificial sugaring agents alongside of the imitative coloring ingredients which, I s'pose, both combine to produce a particularly "addictive" solution (in my case, at any rate), which I trust the manufacturers deliberately assemble in the "bottling"-process to ensure consumers such as I (i.e., those of us at the mercy of the specific soda formulation) continue to purchase the specific brand-name in question (i.e., "eXcellor[ISS]") upon each visit to a supermarket in the area.

Anyway, one night I did choose to purchase a 12-oz. can out of the cola-dispensing system standing on the floor just below the building's top-level story and I didn't want to bother with putting on an outfit of "outdoor" (i.e., "street"-ready) apparel. I'd often seen female tenants walking up and down the hallways of "The 'Tyrolla' Building" in their "Teddies" (... Mmmmm??) and did come to realize if women are O.K. with traveling the residential property's open traffic-routes in only nighttime undergarments, I should be, as well. Anyway, I was just wearing a pair of cotton boxer-shorts at the time I took to hiking down the two flights of steps to the "vend-a-cola" dispensing-machine. *"Felipe"* (or "Philip"), the property's Hispanic custodian (i.e., "maintenance"-man), caught sight of me in the hallway and instantly fell into jitters of "hyperqueer" delight. I could watch his lips close and I could see his eyes dilate and glisten in what must have been an involuntary hormonal response to the particular sight he was able (at that specific moment) to conveniently behold. (Oh, an "assmeister", huh? ... Ah! Hah! Hah!) And <u>that</u> (O ever-attentive attendees) was, in fact, the <u>last</u> time I sought to travel beyond the safety of my own apartment's front door while wearing nothing more than a pair of cotton "boxer"-shorts I can safely, at this point, confess to you all. This, <u>people</u>, **is** the "San Francisco Bay Area", you got that, guys and girls?! ... The region attracts "queers" and "dykes" like a gravitational field in space attracts planetary debris still afloat after a suicidal asteroid's apocalyptic surface-collision with the celestial sphere.

My primary short-term goal would actually be to obtain a leasing-agreement on an apartment found on the soil of San Francisco, California.

Adrien L. Montgomery
Tasting Droplets of the Unforgettable Rain
Official Imprint: "Dynamographx"

We are, at this particular point, in the beginning of October of 2003. I will probably make the "Great Leap" across the "San Francisco Bay" and will hit dirt in the "City" (i.e., "Frisco", that would be) at some point in March of 2004, I do trust. I do not particularly enjoy "residing", here, in the city of Berkeley, California. (I use that particular term ["residing"], because I wouldn't precisely identify what it is I <u>actually</u> do here in Berkeley as genuinely "living".) This is what we'd call a college town, the location of the state university campus "U.C. Berkeley", etc., etc. There are just **too** many university students in these particular parts. Trust me, folks, they'll make your blood's undetectable heat-level escalate to a virtual boiling point.

I remember visiting a "Galaxyland[UE]" fastfood-vending outlet once, the actual venue being the one at the northern end of Telegraph Avenue. And--*I swear*--an entire floor of "residence hall"-inhabitants just came into the restaurant right in front of my unbelieving eyes! I was, at the particular time, just sitting at a table looking over the items appearing on the menu board right above the sales-counter and these "fraternity house"-rejects barge in and just walk right up to the service-clerks without even acknowledging the fact I, already standing on the outlet's premises, did actually arrive on site before they all quite merrily came marching in. It took the kitchen-staff twenty minutes to serve the "residence hall"-tenants, for cryin' out loud. And at the time I was faltering under the death throes of an almost crippling hunger, for Heaven's sake.... <u>Goddammit</u>!!

And, yet, an additional point, the town of Berkeley's got a few too many police officers on hand, if y'know what I'm saying, old friends.... You've got the U.C. Police Department, the BART Police, the Berkeley PD, the Alameda County Sheriff's Office, and the Albany Police. (Albany's a city just northwest of Berkeley, but its squad cars, nonetheless, still patrol Berkeley's busiest streets after the skies overhead turn dark *each* and <u>every</u> evening.) On Saturday night, Telegraph Avenue looks like a sales lot in use for the liquidation of surplus "police patrol"-vehicles, for the love of Saint Pete and all the Apostles. I don't happen to know why the copper "badges" monitor Telegraph so overtly, when Shattuck Avenue's the city's unofficial "strip" (i.e., its "Main Street"), so to speak. The city's "collegians" primarily park themselves on Telegraph Avenue or on Durant Avenue come each Saturday evening in the campus's neighboring acres. Hence, those two runways (or, "drag strips") are, apparently, where all the problems begin each Saturday night, at least as far as local "police squad"-patrolmen would evaluate the picture on public-safety within the vicinity of the college, I assume.

Despite the scenario being that the campus itself attracts people from all parts of the planet (and, it, sometimes, appears, from places even outside any known terrestrial boundaries—ha! ha! ha!), you still feel as though you're "doing time" in a "small town"-environment (i.e., inside of a "micropolis", that is). You simply cannot *breathe* in this particular community the way you would, perhaps, feel at liberty to do in a larger city (i.e., in a "megapolis", that is) ... like a Phoenix, or a Dallas, or a Los Angeles, or a Miami, I would s'pose. In the city of Berkeley, California, you <u>never</u> do feel as though you're just another "face in the crowd". You <u>do</u>, however, feel as though you are an individual whom people in the community-at-large become increasingly familiar with over the continuing course of time. And you, as well, become familiar with local inhabitants who run across you on a daily basis, with the phenomenon of others, in due course, determining you to be a known area-resident occurring just after the amount of time necessary for someone to come to perceive a regular passer-by as a frequent acquaintance has had the chance to predictably expire. Yet, I choose not to seek any particular level of familiarity with such casual "strangers". I would also merely prefer to think that these "outsiders", who also inhabit the municipality of Berkeley, assume that they know nothing of me in particular ... at all.

The primary complaint I must, here, make against Berkeley (old friends and collective comrades on hand), arises due to, once again, the town's police department ("public safety" officers, as the cops call themselves ... ah ha[?!]). Patrolmen come upon you at night, you receive citations for various "infractions" (which are not akin to genuine "breakages" of the official city-, county-, and state-level legal codes which regulate the local citizenry's behavior), and these same cops recognize you in "daylight"- hours, as well, from time to time. Worse yet, the patrolmen notify their departmental "colleagues" about you and (once that particular transaction occurs) you've got other officers maintaining surveillance on you on a day- to-day basis, as well, old folks and friends alike.

I remember leisurely hiking up to the campus on one Saturday morning and regrettably running into a U.C.P.D. foot policeman. Apparently, there'd been an act of thievery in one of the academic buildings, "Palantine Hall", actually. At any rate, this "campus"-badge told me that he'd been seeing me around on occasion.... Mmmmm?? Odd, because, at the moment, I had no genuine recollection of ever having seen him before on campus. Yet, this was, I suppose, a scenario in which an earlier U.C. police officer had spotted me around the academic park from time to time and, then, chose to alert this particular squadmember of his to the apparently unwelcome presence I was able to embody whenever choosing to set a single foot upon "University"-property, that is. (Like I said, I'm twenty-six years old and no longer a paying guest, or "student", of the state-run university in question, that is. I.e., I have no "legitimate" reason to travel to the school's central campus grounds at any particular hour of the day [or night], according to the amateur "on campus"-lecturing I often hear from these "collegiate level"-hall monitors.)

--()--
044
--()--

Adrien L. Montgomery

Tasting Droplets of the Unforgettable Rain

Official Imprint: "Dynamographx"

"Hi, can I talk to you for a minute?" the Keystone Cop says to me. At this particular moment, I merely choose to freeze myself in my tracks. "There was a 'break-in' on campus earlier this morning."

"Yeah? ... Which building?"

"The burglary? ... It was 'Palantine'. Did you see *any*thing?" the pig dares to ask me at this moment.

"No, I didn't see *anyone*," I cautiously answer, wondering, briefly, if the cop, in fact, has chosen to approach me with the aim of happily making an onsite mid-morning arrest.

The cop pauses, conspicuously guiding a stare all over the figure of the innocent (i.e., unoffending, that is) individual standing squarely in his midst, i.e., me, that is. "Usually, the thieves don't stay on campus after hitting an office," the campus security agent explains. "They're usually long gone by the time we arrive," the school's "peace officer" says to me. "I've seen you around. Are you a U.C. student? ... If you're not a 'U.C. associate', that doesn't permit any cop on campus the right to openly hassle you for anything. I don't have the right to hassle you if it's 'cuz you might not be an actual UC 'student-body'-member," the lawman continues, here. " 'Cause I <u>know</u> what it's like dealing with cops who are nuthin' but <u>S</u>.<u>O</u>.<u>B</u>.'s! I've gotta deal with 'A-hole' cops whenever I'm in Oakland.... 'Bottom Line', my friend, you're <u>not</u> an *asshole*. I'm <u>not</u> an *asshole*...."

"Agreed!" I say.

"You didn't see *any*thing today?" the persistent "campus patrol"-agent inquires, again.

"No, I did **not**," I repeat to the state-run school's all-too-talkative "Daytime" copman-in-arms.

"O.K., thanks for your time anyway. You have a good day now, sir," the man (a "College District"-badge who's soon, perhaps, to be occupying shelfspace in the county morgue's refrigeration chamber) says to me. The officer of the law's soon to occupy a human-size storage locker at the area's primary hospitalization-facility, I would not doubt at this moment.

Yet these "Protect & Serve" apostles always do manage to ruffle my feathers, y'know that, companions of the "**oh** *so* close"-variety, that is.... Uhmmmm, perhaps not this particular "badge", I s'pose. Still, I've run into **too** many cops who are simply <u>not</u> capable of dealing with the local citizenry (or, perhaps, with just me, in particular) with the courteous and polite approach each taxpaying resident should come to expect out of the area's lineup of local "law enforcement"-agents. There are moments in which I feel I want to submerge the tip of a switchblade into a cop's naked eyeball as its pupil dilates and quivers in a seizure of mortal panic!

I just so happen to know a certain gentleman who rents a room in a "residential hotel" that's merely a "stone's throw" to the southwest of Market Street's Civic Center "BART"-station's entrance. The man's name is

Adrien L. Montgomery

Tasting Droplets of the Unforgettable Rain

Original Year of Publication: 2026

"Armin Krushinski". But he prefers to refer to himself as "Armin K. from Arkhangelsk". (He's originally from the city of "Arkhangelsk", which would be in the country of … Russia, of course, i.e., the Russian Federation, that is.) However, there is one particularly notable aspect to "Armin K." (… from Arkhangelsk, that is)--he's a *homo*sexual. Or, putting it in other terms, he's a "Rear Admiral" (ha! ha! ha!), or, a "proctology apprentice" (ha! ha! ha!), or, a "sword-swallower" (ha! ha! ha!), or, a "mouth to feed" (ha! ha! ha!), or, a "snake-charmer" (ha! ha! ha!), et cetera, et cetera. Just select the term of affection which you find you're the most at ease with, O dear (… and near) old comrades whom I keep around me.

I first came across "Armin K." while upon an aimless walk along Market Street's southwestern stretch. I chose to stop and stare into a retail outlet's "storefront"-exhibit and take a peek at a "Photocamera" on display and "Armin K.", who--at the particular time--stood just next to me, occupying himself with a cigarette break, instantly came over to me and took a moment to ask me as to whether or not I had a particular pastime which he also found amusing, the shooting of casual photographs, with it, apparently, being a hobby of his. (… Mmmmm??) He told me, at the time, he'd already bought a camera model similar to the one in the storefront "window"-display and that I *could* actually take a set of pictures with it if I would only be so bold as to merely follow him up to his crashpad, which was, conveniently for the both of us that would be, not far from the retailing outlet's "streetside"-window. (<u>Right</u>? … No problem at <u>all</u>, sir!)

Inside of the hobbyist's residential hotel room, "Armin" shows me a new "Photocamera" and comments on a few of its distinguishing features. Also, Armin (… of "Arkhangelsk", of course) then admits to me that the roll of film inside the particular photography-instrument already has "explicit" photos on it in what would amount to nothing less than a very abundant number, that is. I'm inspecting the <u>state</u>-<u>of</u>-<u>the</u>-<u>art</u> "Japcam" and Armin K. informs me that <u>all</u> of the images on the camera's cartridge of full-spectrum iron-rich "35-millimeter" film-stock feature men in specific posings while completely <u>nude</u>?! ("Say, '<u>What</u>'?!") I choose to delicately place the marvel of modern engineering on top of the nearby "cedarwood" dresser. Abruptly, Armin confesses to me that he's actually a "<u>queer</u>" (i.e., he just so happens to possess membership in one of our society's counter-sexual subcultures, that would be) and that he is originally from "Arkhangelsk", a port appearing on the northwestern coastline of the Russian Federation, at a harbor found at the mouth of a southward-running river.

"My name's one that's <u>real</u> easy to remember," he says to me. "Just think 'Armin K. from Arkhangelsk', *right?*" A moment later, Armin tells me he would regularly *sodomize* his little brothers at night while in his "teens" back in his old Eastern European homeland. He, old "Armin K." claims, was

Adrien L. Montgomery
Tasting Droplets of the Unforgettable Rain
Official Imprint: "Dynamographx"

one particular teenager fully aware and quite fond of possessing authentic "man's man" status, that is. (… Hah! Hah! Hah!)

In Armin's childhood home, all of the boys apparently slept in one large bed. *(Ah Hah! … Convenient for Armin, to genuinely understate the obvious.)* As a member of the "Krushinski"-household, L'il Armin made the most of each opportunity on hand to form a "bedtime"-bond with each of his three "kid" brothers, I do, here, assume. Yet, Armin's naughtiness while atop the bed's large "body board" did, in fact, permit the other boys to see exactly how <u>big</u> "Big Brother" Armin actually was, I s'pose. (… Ha! Ha! Ha!)

"I used to fuck them all 'up the rear' <u>each</u> *night* … uh, Ariq," Armin tells me, without so much as a hint of remorsefulness in the voice he proudly speaks with at this actual moment. Armin explains to me that he, "Gay Armin K.", that is, grew up in a large "Old World"-family, of course. In other words, Armin's childhood house was, in itself, a virtual Eastern Slavic beehive, I'd venture, here, to state.

"Your little 'broes' let you do all that crap to 'em?!" I ask of Armin as I sit beside him upon the residential room's "twin" bed. (Inside the "rent-by-the-week" accommodations-venue unit, Armin's <u>only</u> got the bed and a separate piece of "sofa"-furniture [i.e., a large chair] available for himself or a guest on site to sit upon. And the sofa-seat's already overrun with the old-timer's underwear items as it is, my ever-present companions and always-faithful cohorts. Hence, the only spot offering a visitor any sort of acceptable "guest seating"-space at this point would be upon the aging queer's bed, all right, good people?)

"And why *wouldn't* they?" Armin offers me in response. "In any *traditional* 'Russian' household, the motto that's embroidered and framed up on the dining room's wall is *'Love Thy Family and Thou Shalt Ne'er Be Lonely Nor Lost'*. All you try to do in a Russian family is love all them others that's inside the house. You simply try to love your 'sister', your 'mother', your 'father'…. And I, of course, tried to share *any* <u>love</u> I could with my three little 'bros'. A-hah! Hah! Hah! Hah!" (On hearing this, I am just about ready to *orally* expel my most recent meal … one "egg-salad" sandwich, if I do remember.) Armin, at this juncture, offers me a twenty-dollar bill (i.e., $20.00) if I would *only* allow him to do a "rag shine" job on my cock with his elderly man's "weather-beaten" tongue. (… Huh?!!!) I, *of course*, hereby, do most vehemently <u>refuse</u> to submit to the specific act of physical inter-course which Old "Armin K." insists on enjoying at this exact moment in time inside the "bargain"-price residential hotel-unit.

"Armin", here, explains to me that he currently works as an "industrial" painter. (… Mmmmm??) That is, he coats the walls of business outlets, office complexes, housing establishments, hotel lobbies, etc., etc., … with gallons, half-gallons, and quarts, etc., of *non*-toxic interior enamel coloring agents. He, as well (here), shares with me that he puts in "bids" for various "brush 'jobs' " around the city of "Frisco" in order to receive contracts permitting him to perform painting assignments for the developers initializing the specific construction-projects originating in the urban back-drop's newly-built "theater"-scenery. Old "Armin K." says the stack of requests for construction permits he's recently seen tells him old 'St. Fritz' is just about set to *erupt* with new "job"-assignments for those practicing the ancient trade of indoor, decorative re-coating. (… Remember, at all, the "Cave"-paintings found inside primitive habitats archeologists discovered several years ago inside the locales in mountainous regions in France's southeastern sector of vacant "topographical" terrain??) Old "Armin", here, admits to me, without so much as the briefest *hinting* of caution, that is, that he's been a resident here in the city of "Frisco" for about <u>seven</u> years by this particular location inside the overall grand schematic of time. He adds, here, that he's been the sole occupant of the specific room which he's been leasing as "Tenant" at the current moment for about *six* of those (yet, again) <u>seven</u> years "… in the 'Bay' ", that would be.

He does *appear* at ease, although, while sitting right next to me on the room's "Twin"-size bed, viewing me, all the while, through a large set of "sight"-correcting lenses. "This building's actually run by a couple of 'queerz', y'know that?" good old Gay "Armin K." tells me. "The manager and his assistant (or substitute) are '<u>fairies</u>'. Most people livin' in this hotel are 'homoes'." I figure, at the moment, *every* person currently residing in this low-rent "Tenancy"-operation at this particular point in time <u>is</u>--without question--a <u>homo</u>sexual, or, at least <u>all</u> the *male* tenants are, I s'pose. I do trust the hotel's security guard, janitor, <u>and</u> "maintenance"-man are a traveling trio of "Happy Assbandits", as well, I am afraid, here, to state. Armin, at this moment, selects to inform me that most of the "residential"-hotels found within the town's "Central Commercial District" are … "Homosexual"-housing <u>establishments</u> or, perhaps, "Lesbian"-lodging <u>facilities</u>. (The famous "Retailing-and-Tourism" District which the area of San Francisco presents to its variety of "Out-of-Towner" guests is inside the northeastern sector of the Bay's central hub, i.e., the heart of the region's coastal counties, that is. Hence, all "Downtown"-properties which the town offers to its locals and tourists alike are actually in an "Upland" or <u>non</u>-central zone of the widely-known "Pacific Rim"-settlement.) … Meaning, *if* <u>you</u> were to ever rent a housing-unit in any of these particular "Hotel Industry"-buildings, you wouldn't want to, *ever*, pay the Innkeeper any "back rent" (ha! ha!), or to, *ever*, fall "behind in rent" (ha! ha!), or to, *ever*, pay "up front" (ha! ha!), or to, *ever*, make a "security deposit" (ha! ha!), or to, *ever*, subject yourself to a "forcible eviction" (ha! ha!), I'd venture to state at this specific moment in time. I <u>am</u> correct on this am I <u>not</u>, dearest folks and friends alike?

Old "Armin K." tells me here that, as a child, he would prefer to think of himself as a "<u>Bi</u>sexual", though after a certain term of "maturation" (set to occur due to a standard transpiring of events bound to happen in the due course of time), he quickly began restricting himself to a "Cock Heavy"-menu, of course, i.e., a diet with a lot of "dick" in it, that is…. I.e., he made a choice to *exclusively* practice "man-to-man" mating habits at one particular point during his period of "psychosocial" human development. I find this type of evolutionary course to be true of <u>most</u> homosexuals (i.e., "man-fags")…. That is, early in the term of "adolescence", the "queerflies" assume they desire females as well as males, i.e., they're under the false illusion that they can, hence, *legitimately* refer to themselves as "Bisexual", that is. Yet, they--*ultimately*, that is--learn (albeit, through the most unfortunate scenario of circumstances, in certain cases, I'd have no other choice than to assume) that they--and other individuals of similar "neurohormonal" configuration, no doubt--are merely deceiving themselves (and, all the while, deceiving others as well). They, at one point, see that they're "Assmasters" (i.e., "Faggit-butts") *through* and *through*, possessing <u>no</u> desire whatsoever for sexual contact with the <u>other</u> gender (i.e., women, that would be)…. <u>Surprise</u>! <u>Surprise</u>! <u>Surprise</u>!

Armin (… from "Arkhangelsk", that is) says to me (at this actual moment …) that, at the age of just <u>fifteen</u>, his new stepfather made the decision to evict him from the premises after learning that little Armin was a *"queerer than thou"*-type of youth…. Ahem! Armin then tells me he found himself "on the streets" for an entire year after that particular incident of adolescent misfortune. And during that time, he would "suck 'cock' " to earn the necessary amount of cash capable of serving as "eating" money, that is, *each* and <u>every</u> day. Meaning … he would *eat* 'dick' in order to *eat* <u>meat</u>. I.e., in order to put a mouthful of meat into his gut, he <u>first</u> had to put a handful of meat into his mouth. (… Hah! Hah! Hah! … *Sick!)*

The Russian Federation's ex-Soviet citizenry (i.e., the country's national community, that is) obviously makes a sincere agenda of promoting their "hemisphere"-size homeland as the "Land of True Brothers" (i.e., "Comrades-in-Arms", I do s'pose [… Hah! Hah! Hah!]). This particular self-promotional slogan could, in Armin's case, refer either to the "brethren" or "brotherhood" found among the Queer community's official membership in the Federation of Russia … or to the "Slumberland"-orgies little "Armin" would unload upon his brothers during the "teenhood"-era which he underwent back in the oceansize "Motherland" of Russia. (Be sure to re-member the subsequent excerpt of "Christian" Scripture, old friends: *"… And do love thy brother as thou wouldst love thyself….")*

Armin's family name, "Krushinski", is, of course, <u>unmistakably</u> *Russian* in extraction. He continues to assert that the overnight sexual scrimmages against his male siblings were activities that were merely indicative of lengthily-held "Old Russian" family values. But, Armin declares, to this day, his brothers refuse to come to any type of reconciliation (or, "common ground") with him over the issue concerning Armin's *homo*maniacal behavior during his term of adolescence. Gay "Armin K." claims that his siblings are "homophobes", i.e., that they would prefer that he would keep himself at a "reasonable" distance from all of them. (... You know, I can't imagine why that would be??!!)

"I said to my brothers, 'When we were younger, I used to use the reliable whammy-hammer to screw you boys up the rear end **all** night, **every** night!'" Armin explains at this point regarding his current level of communication with all siblings still at large. "And then they said: 'That's a separate matter! Y'see, back then we didn't know that you were a fuckin' **queer**! *Now* that we know you're a goddamn faggit, we don't want nothin' to do with you anymore'." Armin's smile grows at this specific moment and his overtly mature face begins to gleam with a bashful, perverse radiance. (The Russian immigrant appears to be a member of the age grouping that would specifically label individuals who are experiencing the mid-"fifties", an "age range"-subset appearing in the chronological dating chart tracking each person's private timeline [i.e., 54, 55, 56].) "How big is your dick?" the old-timer asks me with a grin uncontainably brimming in all directions of the apartment's interior-airspace.

"I really wouldn't know," I answer. "I've never put a yardstick to it." (A lie, of course, my listenership and ever-loyal legion of faithful followers. I've chosen to gauge the length of the old adjustable antenna--that "telescopic" ejaculator--dozens of times in my life, just like *every* other male who might undergo fits of high anxiety over any possible inadequacies he could very well have in that particular area of physical anatomy.) "Besides, it might not be that large by your--shall we say, 'queer'--standards. How big must a cock be to be big to **you**?!"

Armin puts his palms together in the amount of air that's right in front of him and then separates them, essentially indicating that the inches of empty airspace existing in between the left hand and the right hand would quite easily equal the length of an appetizing male sexual organ, I s'pose. (The distance that separates Armin's pair of upheld hands is roughly equal to a healthy foot-and-a-half of available breathing room.) ... Surprising? ... No. Like I said just a moment ago, the old queer's name must be "Ol' Captain Assjacker". (... Ha! Ha! Ha! Ha!)

Like I said earlier, I grew up in Santa Lucia, California (... United States, that is). Through the course of my upbringing (if you would care to refer to the particular period of childhood I had to unfortunately undergo as a recognizable era of "upbringing", actually), I had to change street addresses on many an occasion in that particular "urbanzone" and in its surrounding outlands. I'd made bed, so to speak, in eight different houses by the moment I left the "High School" which I did successfully manage to graduate from at the age of eighteen back in June of 1995. I, at least, had the opportunity to attend just one particular high school ("Green Treeleaves High School", that is) over the term of years which ran through that specific span of academic seasons (the "ninth"-grade through the "twelfth"-grade, with such terms being the "Freshman"- through "Senior"-eras in the series of grade-levels concerning one's "secondary" [or, "senior"-level] education).

I remember at one point receiving the opportunity to interview the city's chief executive (i.e., the mayor, that would be) for a piece in the junior high school's newspaper, *The Belheller J.H.S. Citizen Dispatcher*, of course. (Regrettably, amateur political reporting did not genuinely seize the attention of the seventh-grader fulfilling the assignment of speaking with the city's top administrative officer, I can assure you, folks and old friends that you are.)

I can, at this particular time, recall aiming at leisurely motorists with almost lethal water balloons (or, "liquid-grenades", as we would call them), as the unknowing street-pilots would innocently roll by a hedgerow that kept my best friend's driveway well-hidden from any passing driver's peripheral eyesight. I can also remember ripping up a neighbor's mail, only to later see both husband *and* wife, victims of the postal-abuse incident, complain to my parents about my act of throwing out a credit account card which *Continental Crossroads*, a finance company offering deserving consumers "exclusive" lines of available credit, sent to the couple. ("It wasn't my fault, though," I told the man and wife. "I'm not the one to blame for this.") An older boy I knew would thieve material from mailboxes, tear it all up into stringy ribbons of confetti, and, then, feed the paper meal to the mouth of an open drain in the neighborhood's sewer-system. He alone chose to shred the neighborhood's mail to spaghetti noodles. (Uh huh ... that's exactly how it was all right, to my knowledge.)

What I can also recall at this point are the times I slept overnight at the house belonging to a particular neighborhood playmate of mine. This friend of mine's family home was just uphill from the house I was living in at that specific period of time. On one night, his dad caught the four of us--i.e., me, my friend, my friend's sister, and the sister's overnight guest--without a single stitch of clothing to be seen upon any of the panic-stricken members of the fun-loving foursome found "off-guard" inside of my friend's bedroom. (There are people who **should** simply remember to "knock" before entering a room, aren't there, huh?? ... Geez!!) Remembering correctly (I s'pose), I believe my friend, his sister, his sister's "sleepover" guest and I were all "gradeschoolers" at that particular time, however. (When you play "Spin the Bottle" with those belonging to the other gender, you really should quit by a certain point, y'know what I'm saying, my *oh-so-close* associates? ... Perhaps that would be before the entire room resembles a campsite crawling with slap-happy "nudists", huh?)

Adrien L. Montgomery

Tasting Droplets of the Unforgettable Rain

Original Year of Publication: 2026

I clearly do remember a classmate I had, "Robbie", attracting the attention of a girl whom I saw as the tastiest treat since chocolate icing straight from the wooden mixing-spoon, that would be.... I can, at this point, remember myself captaining a "go-cart" down an asphalt slope too steep to walk up without the use of Himalayan climbing equipment. I can, as well, at this time, also remember losing a contest for "Student-Body" President in the "Sixth"-grade by no more than a handful of ballots. Funny thing, though, on the day after actual votes were cast, everyone kept coming up to me and telling me that I'd lost by just a narrow margin and, at the school day's finish, when the results were <u>officially</u> put on record, I found out I'd lost the election by merely a minor gap in the overall tally. (I guess the candidate <u>is</u> always the last one to know.... Mmmmm??)

I can now also recollect seeing a couple of my neighbors "shoplifting" (i.e., *stealing*, that would be, in stores at a "stripmall" we'd stop at on our way home from the local gradeschool, "Red Earth Elementary School".)

"Are you shocked at what I did, Ariq?" one of the delinquents asks me after leaving the supermarket with about half of its sales-merchandise on him underneath his conveniently loose articles of clothing.

"<u>No</u>," I say, answering the wayward child rather indifferently. (By that point, I'd been ransacking candy shelves for two or three years myself.... I've known since the earliest of ages that I'm a *habitual* offender, my loyal listeners and ever-present public.... Ha! Ha! Ha!)

"I cried the first time I did it," the boy told me, as if pangs of guilt could successfully separate a naïve, innocent thief from the true social parasites who remain "at large" among the rest of us upstanding citizens.

Oh, my agreeable and ever-present guests, I work at a "software"-sciences "Research and Prototyping"-operation which is found inside San Francisco's "Central Commercial District". I'm responsible for re-directing all of the "E-mail" cyber-traffic which enters our "Sybernet[STF]" system through the corporation's online consumer-service "Superpage". I'm the one who carries out the specific task of directing all consumer "E-mail" inquiries on our series of special "software"-instruments to the appropriate product-support technicians in the company's "Research/Design"-division, which constitutes a department that occupies the entire ninth floor of the office building which the firm currently leases for its programming projects. I'm in a "partition"-pen that's on the north side of the highrise construction's tenth floor. The north-facing windows overlook the brightly ornamental pathways that actually appear to map out the pedestrian-friendly acreage of San Francisco's well-known "Chinatown"-District, hosting the folks from the "East Orient". I'm also responsible for forwarding all "Voicemail"-messages from affiliate or subsidiary groups regarding the "Research/Design"-division laboratory's system-software, specifically concerning the actual capabilities of the particular "Flexiware[AI]"-product in question, to the appropriate tech-development experts on staff. Sometimes, I inform the particular E-mailer that the specific inquiry has to be put on a momentary "priority list" in order to permit me the time I require in order to locate the actual team-members responsible for explaining the E-mailer's particular concern regarding a certain product's performance issue. I sometimes inform the individual inquiring on the software-product item itself to contact a particular group leader which the design center charges with supervising "multi-integrative/dual-system" network projects (i.e., our "Netware[AI]"-products, that is).

I have the ability to pre-scan "E-mail"-notices sent to various technical-services personnel and to read the diagnostic summaries which the devout programmers float to each other via the corporation's "Supernet[UE]"-directory regarding one of the particular operational capabilities which the software-product in question offers to our consumers. Occasionally, I'll monitor "E-mail"-notices coming in through the company's network and see an "E-mail" containing language which is overtly <u>uncivil</u> in character (e.g., one software-research leader threatening to *kill* a rival group manager's secretary for stating in conference that the first research group is already over-budget and over-schedule in developing its latest programming assignment). Such cyber-mailings would, in fact, amount to unprofessional (and, I guess, indictable) behavior on the part of the specific individual producing the "E-mail"-notice on record. I basically inspect and deliver messages which people submit to our company's "('Software')-Research"-groups through the firm's online "Xpressmessage[UE]"-system. (I'm in charge of sorting through the technical inquiries on "soft-system" product performance in what you might possibly refer to as a "basement"-level mailroom-office under the echo-ridden corridors of *oh-so-isolating* "Corporate 'E'-space". [... Ha! Ha! Ha!])

I am, at this point, sitting on a sofa in front of the TV-set, eating from a carton of doughnuts ... *Old-Fashioned Buttermilk*, that is (... Yumm!!). I probably feed myself too many items that are on the World Health Organization's current "Watch List" of plutonium-rich available eating op-tions which the nation's food-industry corporations produce on an annual schedule. One woman that I know, with whom I had had a "midnight affair" on at least a couple of occasions, told me about "Juergen-Meiz[AI]", insisting that I try the "Mocha & Peanut Crunch" European frozen-yogurt desserts. At that particular time, this woman was working at a nearby supermarket and said the frozen-yogurt popsicles she brought to me came straight out of the market's extra-large refrigeration-units. <u>Ahh!</u> ... The woman stole from her own place of employment, I've no choice, here, but to assume. (I doubt that she actually <u>paid</u> for the pricey, freezer-kept, after-dinner dairy-products.) Anyway, every time I'm in a supermarket's dessert section, I al-ways make note to pick up a couple of cartons of "Juergen-Meiz[AI]" dessert bars (e.g.'s, "Milk Chocolate & Cream Chocolate", "Vanilla Caramel & Crème De Leche", "Fudge & Crispy Peanut Butter", etc., etc.). The woman in question doesn't happen to work at the neighborhood foodmart which she, in the earlier era, had had employment in, but, I s'pose, she, *at least*, did what any good employee *should* do. She made me, potentially an avid consumer at the market, aware of a particular sales item which the specific retailing venue kept in its merchandise aisles. It's funny, though, after din-ner, I'd bite right into a large hand-held treat ... and she would, <u>too</u>!! (Ha! Ha! Ha! Ha! ... Get it? ... The large, hard popsicle in my pants, that would be, folks and constant companions of mine.)

Well, my "apostles", I suppose I should, at this actual point, present to you the <u>genuine</u> system of beliefs on "Self-Enlightenment" which I certainly do plan on abiding in and adhering to from this particular moment forwards. (If I am not able, <u>today</u>, to tell you people all that it is which I truly do think, I fear that I might never have what is necessary in order to offer to you similar statements concerning my personal viewpoints regarding matters of self-promotion and personal gain in the world which we all currently happen to inhabit.) The words which you're about to review, my ever-obedient disciples, amount to nothing less than the opinion I do, at present, possess with respect to the tremendously difficult process which a human individual <u>must</u> undergo in order to achieve an unquestionably high level of "enlightenment" in his time in this particular realm which human beings just so happen to inhabit....

<u>(The</u> <u>Start</u> <u>of</u> <u>Ariq's</u> "<u>Philosophical</u> <u>Perspective</u> <u>on</u> <u>the</u>
<u>Process</u> <u>of</u> '<u>Self-Enlightenment</u>' ")

<u>Section "A"</u>
<u>001</u>.
I'm certain **each** act of *seriously* <u>antisocial</u> conduct (i.e., any genuinely "evil" deed) which I do commit is just an additional step towards becoming an individual who can *truly* refer to himself as a "Being of Enlightenment".

<u>002</u>.
With *every* act of <u>true</u> "evil" which you choose to *openly* commit against any one particular human or against the most *ancient* of human laws, you will certainly gain a degree of enlightenment (i.e., *"spiritual* knowledge") which no other human will be in possession of.

<u>003</u>.
In the "Ancient Scriptures", "Adam" (i.e., the world's first "human") chose to eat fruit of the "Tree of Knowledge of Good and Evil" in the hope of *ultimately* obtaining granules of the <u>wisdom</u> which *only* its produce could

--()--
054
--()--

Adrien L. Montgomery
Tasting Droplets of the Unforgettable Rain
Official Imprint: "Dynamographx"

offer unto him!

004.

Yet, in committing such an act, "Adam" stood in violation of the *very* laws which the Creator (i.e., "God", that is) told him--on an earlier occasion-- amount to rules which he is <u>never</u> to ignore or violate.

005.

Just as "Adam" had to commit an action against the Creator's laws to gain a particular degree of wisdom for himself, I, "Ariq Zarkahn Shoretempel", **must**, likewise, <u>violate</u> the earliest of *ancient* human laws in order to gain the specific level of "Enlightenment" which I desire to see myself *ultimately* obtain as an individual inhabiting the Earth.

<u>Section "B"</u>
<u>001</u>.

I believe *if* a man were to obtain <u>each</u> measure of Enlightenment (again, "spiritual knowledge", that is) which he, for himself, had a craving, he *would*, <u>ultimately,</u> grow to be a " 'God'-like" individual in his lifetime.

002.

In other words, the particular human being in question (after receiving a total level of "Enlightenment", that is) would be <u>un</u>like any other human individual on Earth.

003.

My <u>one</u> particular goal would be to *violate* the most <u>ancient</u> of human laws in order to obtain the level of Enlightenment which I desire myself to *ultimately* be in possession of, just as "Adam" had to violate the laws of the Creator in order to gain whatever wisdom he, at one point, sought for himself.

004.

Once I have, in fact, become an individual in possession of a <u>total</u> level of Enlightenment, I ("Ariq Zarkahn Shoretempel") will be, in all, a human that is " 'God'-like" in the easily observable stature which I will, then, possess.

005.

In other words, I <u>will</u> be an individual who is <u>un</u>like any *other* human being existing *any*where on "Earth".

006.

Yet, *each* separate act in the commission of <u>genuine</u> "evil" is merely a *single*

--()--
055
--()--

step towards my final goal of attaining a <u>complete</u> level of human Enlightenment.

007.

With *each* single act in the commission of <u>true</u> "evil" (once again, against
any one particular human being, or against any of the most *ancient* of human laws), I am bound to gain a specific degree of wisdom which <u>no</u> other
creature on "Earth" will be in possession of at such a time.

008.

And, once I commit what I--in particular--view as the <u>ultimate</u> action of <u>anti</u>-
social conduct (i.e., inarguably recognizable "evil", that is), I am certain to
receive the <u>largest</u> measure of *"spiritual* knowledge" (as a result of such an
action) available to me or to any other human being on Earth.

009.

I, <u>then</u>, will be <u>un</u>like any other "earthbound" creature, and will be <u>only</u> such
as the "Almighty One" Himself, i.e., "God".

010.

In other words, after achieving the <u>final</u> step towards the *total* level of
human Enlightenment (i.e., *"spiritual* knowledge"), which would be found
in committing the <u>ultimate</u> act of human "evil" (i.e., an *unquestionably* <u>anti</u>-
social act), I will become an individual possessing *every* degree of mortal
wisdom available to a human being in the world today.

011.

Once a "human being" gains <u>every</u> measure of Enlightenment from *each*
separate action which he commits against the earliest (i.e., most *ancient*)
of human behavioral codes, and once he commits what would amount to
the <u>ultimate</u> act of "evil" in deeds (an action which would be the equivalent
of nothing other than an act of "self-violation", that is), the individual in
question will, <u>then</u>, receive a <u>cumulative</u> level of *"spiritual* knowledge"
which he alone will benefit from, and he (the particular human in question)
will, <u>then</u>, be unique in all the mortal world!

<u>(The</u> <u>End</u> <u>of</u> <u>Ariq's</u> <u>"Philosophical</u> <u>Perspective</u> <u>on</u> <u>the</u>
<u>Process</u> <u>of</u> <u>'Self-Enlightenment'</u> ")

   These particular views, my anxious apostles, are the basic set of beliefs
which I do plan to strictly abide in and adhere to from this moment forward.
Because I have just told you what it is that I plan on seeking and securing
for myself in this world, i.e., attaining a level of <u>total</u> human enlightenment

Adrien L. Montgomery
Tasting Droplets of the Unforgettable Rain
Official Imprint: "Dynamographx"

(i.e., "spiritual knowledge"), I will not keep any additional viewpoints appearing to be of a highly personal nature from you after this particular moment in time…. I do, hereby, promise you this, my all-too-agreeable guests.

I eat up the final bitesize remains of the breakfast which I found in the "Bakery Goods"-carton in the kitchen's bread-storage chest and I walk back into the kitchen's limiting floorspace. I carefully place the empty "cake products"-carton into the kitchen's large trash-holding container. I start filling up a large barroom mug with water from the kitchen sink's faucet head. The handy example of glassworking-skill came to me, actually, as a gift which one of the "next door"-neighbors which I had back in Santa Lucia brought to me after a "Winter Break" with his family. He, his wife, and their three kids travel *each* and <u>every</u> year to Salt Lake City, Utah, to visit skiing venues in that particular "resort"-going region found in the US states known for featuring land frequent with "high altitude"-levels of recreational terrain. After one of their winter trips, my neighbor came back with a drinking mug which had the words **"Salt Lake City"** and a black outline of alpine peaks set into ink onto its exterior-side. I drink the water that's still inside the "Mormontown"-mug and put the souvenir with its open-side down on top of a large, maple-wood cutting board. *(What* [… Oh! <u>What</u>?!] would a true member of the local "Mormon Church"-fellowship fill up the mug with?! … Mmmmm?? … Hot milk, I suppose, huh?)

I quickly look inside the refrigerator to see if I've got any "Gruenelheim[AI]" cans left. (I <u>only</u> buy the "Gruenelheim[AI]" <u>signature</u> 14-oz. "Barrel Cans[UE]".) I see that there are only two cans of that particular brand sitting on the refrigerator's top rack, the specific rack which I've deliberately set apart for the various can-held fluid refreshments which I consume on a perdiem-basis (beers, "eXcellor[ESU]"-brand sodas, fruit juices, "energy" drinks, etc., etc.). I pick up a pencil and start to scratch out a reminder to myself on the top page of notepad sheets to visit a local supermarket to purchase additional ounces of the Dutch-made alcohol-rich refreshment formula, which has, I, here, have to admit, become a primary weekending priority of mine in recent months.

I would have to, at this point, remind myself, and, thereby, inform you, as well, that perhaps my favorite morning meal (eatingtime in the "A.M.", that is) would, doubtlessly, be that which anybody could order at a local "Charlie's Ark[TM]" franchise, i.e., that old "Animal Sanctuary" which nourishes its captive group of customers quite adequately, I'd have to, here, state, being one who frequently pays visit to the famous "fastfood"-venue. Y'know of the place, I reckon … the "Floating Zoo", the "Barnyard on the High Seas", etc., etc. When I choose to visit the "Charlie's Ark[TM]"-outlet found in my particular area, I usually order the "Wilder-than-Life[ESU] Platter": a waffle, sausage patty, biscuit, fried potato strings, with an "Egg Nest[AI] Sandwich" and two cups of "Wildfruit[UE] Juice".... Mmmmm!! (... Yummy!!) If I must, upon review, confess, here, to you good and friendly folks (... oh outgoing group of eager guests that you are).

Tasting Droplets of the Unforgettable Rain

By
Adrien L. Montgomery
Cycle <u>003</u>:
"Alongside of Other 'Railsystem'-Guests, I Just So Happen to be Sitting in the Boxcar of a Freight Engine Currently en Route to the San Francisco Bay Area ..."

<u>UTA</u> <u>Directive</u> III:
"Attention! Attention! ... Upon Arriving At The System-Route's Final Terminus, All Rail-Transit Passengers **Must** Immediately Offboard Themselves! <u>Repeat</u>, Upon Arriving At The System-Route's Final Terminus, All Rail-Transit Passengers **Must** Immediately Offboard Themselves!"
("<u>UTA</u>": <u>Urban</u> <u>Transit</u> <u>Authority</u>)

<u>Television</u> <u>Network</u> <u>Announcer</u>:
(<u>At</u> <u>the</u> <u>Start</u> <u>of</u> <u>the</u> <u>Episode's</u> <u>Broadcast</u> ...)
"Welcome to the Inter-Satellite Television Supercasting Service's 'Evening World Newswatch'. On Thursday, the Ninth of October, Two-Thousand and Three. **Now** ... the anchor of ISTSS's 'Evening World Newswatch', Ariq Shoretempel ..."

<u>Ariq</u> <u>Shoretempel</u>:
"Good evening, ladies and gentlemen! ... Today, on board a 'commuter'-transit system in the San Francisco Bay Area, a conference on the 'Crisis in the Middle East' was almost jeopardized due to a man found to be ... *masturbating* in one of the train cars?! ... Say, 'What'?! Oh, God!! This *can't* be a true news item!! ... But it appears as though, it *is* <u>true</u>?! (<u>Whoah</u>!!) I'm sure you'll all want to take a look at the video-footage we've got on file for this report, folks!! (... <u>Whoah</u>!!) ... Just when you think it's safe to anchor a nationwide network's evening newscast, something stranger than anything happening before it seems to occur! ... And you heard about it <u>here</u> first, folks!!"

(-|<u>Calendar</u> <u>Date</u>: <u>THU</u>., <u>Oct</u>. <u>09</u>, <u>2003</u>|-)
Hello, again, O ever-present pupils and always-loyal public! I'm standing on the boarding platform of Shattuck Avenue's "Center Street" "BART"-station, waiting for a train to the "Civic Center"-station in downtown San(X)

Francisco's southwestern end. I can still hear the street musician performing on the concourse that's just up the flight of exiting stairs from the rail-accessing floor. The man (a male Caucasian, being approximately 23 years in age) is singing a "Blues"-Rock ballad and accompanying himself with an acoustical guitar. I know not if the rail transit musician's performing an original piece, however. *("... Remember, all guests. From far or near, when traveling through the Bay Area's shoreline landscape, climb aboard BART--the commuter's mobile music club!")* To me, it seems as though a crowd of the local hoboes inhabiting this particular section of the state are musicians or song-composers of one variety or another. (The transit system's underground stations are venues offering its visitors a virtual festival of free music for each rail passenger to conveniently encounter on his way to the workplace, or on his way back home from it.)

At this particular moment, one immediately familiar face approaches me, however. "Hello, my bruthah! I got a dollah-fifteen. If you gots a 'korduh'--(he's saying: 'quarter')--I can get sump'n tuh eat. If yuh do got sump'n to spare today ... family." The host of the urban transit-site's daytime telethon continues to push a "SuperSipper^{STF}" cup towards the rail-friendly faces which are quickly moving past him. I've seen this particular individual before (... frequently, that would be), just one particular cast member appearing in Berkeley's comic street theater. (... NOW PLAYING in Berkeley's "Open Air" Drama, "Scenes of the Underclass [Part II: 'Urine Nation']".) This one panhandler's typically found campaigning for coins outside of the "Farmgate Foods" market which stands at the northern end of Shattuck Avenue. Harassing the populace for "spare" change on a "BART"-station's boarding platform is, of course, against the transit system's code of commuter conduct, a book of rules which this particular panhandler is apparently unfamiliar with. Hastily twitching my nose, I inform the hungering avenue cat that I'm temporarily out of US currency units (whether such units themselves be of paper or metal construction).

I innocently stroll towards the boarding zone's southern end and discover (in a moment that inflames in me the instinct existing in all mortals which compels us to flee from any instantly recognizable threat) a huge amount of <u>fresh</u> excrement on the platform floor, just next to a large supporting column. There is also an extensive puddle of hobo pee on the platform floor, attempting to gradually overrun the open platform space existing around the puddle's particular point of origin. For a moment, I pause to guess at whatever it could be that you might select to blame for such an urban fright.... Perhaps, one particularly large dog could be the culprit in question? I, sometimes, see "guide dogs" with blind passengers on board the "BART"-trains. But, there's simply too much   material on exhibit in this actual case. (There's just a little too much "shittage" for one "K9 Sight^{ISS}" dog to have left in its path upon the station platform.) I guess one of the local street-corner "Kings" found himself in serious need of some instant toilet time and came to realize, due to his ass's especially eruptive condition, he didn't have the agility left to rush to a restroom inside of one of the several "quick service"-outlets found just up the staircase on Shattuck Avenue's crowd-heavy street-level.

I see people disembarking from a transit vehicle at rest while en route to the "Richmond"-station up in "Contra Costa County". I realize I should step away from the exhibit of shit and the puddle of pee (a startling example of inappropriate public behavior, I would venture, here, to state) before a "BART"-user strolls by and figures I'm afraid to abandon the crap pile due to reasons of emotional attachment on my part. Uh huh … the person will assume I just want to stand by it and gaze upon the results of my one great effort on Earth with a sense of tearful pride and achievement. (… "Oh, <u>Hell</u>, No!")

The overhead "digital notification"-screen announces the immediate arrival to the commuter deck of the "SFO/Millbrae"-train. I can hear the train carriage's rail wheels rolling towards the transit station as it advances through the subterranean tunnel prior to entering the open space of the underground "commuter rail"-depot's boarding zone.

The "SFO/Millbrae"-train speeds into the "Central Berkeley"-station from the North Berkeley stop merely on the energy remaining from its seismic, machine-era momentum. I am, at this point, wondering what it would actually feel like to cast myself onto the rails lying just in front of one of the "BART"-system's oncoming passenger vehicles. (I.e., I'm guessing as to what in fact would be the specific degree of psychosis necessary to compel me to do such a thing to myself on the fleeting birth of a moment, etc., etc.) And, alternately, I'm attempting to determine what it is I would feel if I were to force somebody *else* onto the track right in front of an onrushing commuter engine that's just entering the train station's boarding stage. (Truth is, I've heard that in New York City, people standing upon subway boarding platforms maintain their distance from the edge of the station's loading deck. *Everybody* there knows someone will knock you onto the rails right in front of an incoming rail-liner if the opportunity to do so just so happens to conveniently present itself to hobbyists idly passing time at the mass-transit stop. That would certainly bring rush-hour commutes to a "dead" halt, wouldn't you think?! … Hah! Hah! Hah!) The public transporter comes to a complete rest aboard its rails and I step into one of its open passenger cabins. I find an empty seat for myself at the car's northern end, just next to the "see-through" (i.e., "transparent", that is) exiting panels which permit one's entry into the train compartment which is adjoining to the one which I'm selecting to assume seating space in.

I'm occupying a spot that's right up against this particular "BART"-compartment's rear-boundary doors. Instantly, a Mexican-American (or, a

--()--
060
--()--

"Meximerican", that is) man puts himself in the "sectional" of four seats that's just in front of the particular spot which I'm currently sitting in inside of the commuter's train carriage. He isn't facing me, however. Like me, the Hispanic man is in a seat which places its occupant in a position to <u>only</u> face the commuter car's southern end. Two "African-American" men enter the "BART"-cabin through the transparent sliding screens that open and close to permit foot traffic to visit and exit the compartment adjacent to the one which I'm in. One of the men snatches a seat that's across the aisle from the spot which I am occupying, however. The second one places himself in a spot that's in front of (and opposite to) the spot which the first one is currently occupying at this particular point. Hence, the two black commuters visiting us from the next compartment over are, here, directly facing each other aboard the traveling mass-transit car, and each is sitting across the aisle from me at the specific moment aboard the commuter rail-system.

I survey my exact area inside the "mass transit"-cabin and quickly see that I'm sitting in the seating section known commonly to area "rail transit"-travelers as the public vehicle's "Harlem"-district, once again, I fear. At the "northern" end of any compartment in a "BART"-system carriage, there's a particular seating zone which is basically a sitting area that's set apart from the compartment's central section of available seats. (Why, then, do blacks assemble themselves at the *northern* end of a rail train's compartment, you might possibly ask me at this moment?? … How in the abysmal canyons of "Hell" would I know the answer to that, my good friends?! But, y'know, to escape enslavement in the southern US states [prior to the "Civil War"-era, that is] "runaway" slaves always knew to head *north! … Ah-Ha! Ha! Ha! Ha!* That's the reason, isn't it, my comrades?!) On occasion, you'll find African-Americans, regardless of age, sitting in a rail compartment's *north*ern section of seats during a "BART"-transporter's cross-Bay commute. I suppose the "MetroTransit[UE]"-system's black passengers choose to seat themselves in this particular section, at the rail container's *north*ern end, due to the fact that the seats are right next to the pair of transparent (i.e., "see-through") sliding panels, which open to permit any passenger to exit into the next rail cabin adjacent to the one you already happen to be in. I.e., if you see you *must*, for any ordinary reason, maneuver to avoid a person just coming aboard the train at one of its official route-stops or just stepping into the car through the pair of entry panels at the train carriage's opposing end, you can quickly step through the two transparent screens and escape into the adjoining commuting car, easily avoiding detection and any possible endangerment which the intruding presence apparently presents to you, my old friend. Perhaps the black passengers choosing to seat themselves at a "BART"-compartment's *north*ern end assume sitting right next to the carriage's pair of exit screens will permit them to crawl away from a threatening street rival or from a "BART"-security officer just entering the train car to inspect it for travelers being in obvious violation of the official "public rail"-code outlining acceptable commuter conduct. Yet, for whatever reason, black rail-passengers (not the <u>whites</u> or other <u>non</u>-blacks [i.e., Asians, Latinos, "Native" Americans, Arabs, etc., etc.] aboard the "MetroTransit^{UE}"-system) refer to the sitting section found at the *north*ern end of a "rail system"-compartment as "Harlem"--a designation which (in itself) serves as a reference to the predictable, and constant, use of the notable guest-seating section in a commuter cabin by the public transporter's "African-American" clientele-members.

I <u>do</u> know that in the "Segregation"-era South (i.e., commencing with the Civil War's end and continuing to the start of the "Civil Rights"-movement in the mid-1950's), blacks on board public-usage buses would normally sit in the seating floor's rear section. This practice on board public commuter buses was "customary", i.e., <u>not</u> an actual requirement by any sort of civic penal code in existence at the time, yet a pattern which all traveling by public bus would readily acknowledge and *voluntarily* abide by. And today, the habitual behavior which black passengers respect in assuming seats for themselves at a "BART"-compartment's *north*ern end, near the pair of "see-through" exiting screens, is "elective" (i.e., voluntary or by one's own choosing), not *mandatory* under the public-transit authority's code of appropriate commuter conduct.

The black rider sitting across the aisle from me begins talking to the co-passenger, i.e., the friend who came aboard the rail-carriage with him, who's occupying the seat directly in front of the space which the first black compartment guest is sitting in. "Just turned **forty-seven** on Saturday. I just did number '47', dig?" the man says to the co-traveler sitting right in front of him. "I was born on October Fourth, Nineteen Fifty-Six."

"It smells like <u>damn</u> *burrito* in this place," the other black passenger replies, showing no interest at all in the Birthday Boy's attempt to explain the chronological chart which he's attempting to maintain on himself on an "up-to-date" basis at this particular point in his lifetime.

The "Birthday Boy", sitting across the cabin aisle from me, unfastens his watch's metallic wristband for whatever reason, as if to rid himself of any timepiece which could still serve to remind him of the clock that ticks off whatever minutes in his life there are which might just remain, considering the recent event transpiring, most alarmingly (it would appear), in the bio-graphical timeline which he so adamantly maintains. He begins to stare at the "Latino" man who still happens to be sitting right in front of me, in a seat that's facing (as mine is) forwards (i.e., towards the rail container's *south*ern end), requiring he sees what I, as well, am, at this point, looking towards. "This <u>Mexican</u> is in the *wrong* spot and he ought to <u>know</u> it," the

"Birthday Boy" says to me, referring, yet again, to the unspoken, yet widely known rule which (informally, albeit) guarantees the section of seats near a "BART"-cabin's *north*ern exiting screens are to be <u>exclusively</u> set aside for the "African-American" passengers who choose to travel by use of the public-transit system. "Yoo! ... Yoo! ... Yoo in the wrong place, *buddy!*" the "Birthday Boy" says to the "Mexican-American" rail-commuter, i.e., the "Meximerican" passenger, I s'pose. "<u>Jose</u>! ... <u>Miguel</u>! ... Whatever yo' name is, <u>amigo</u>!" the black public-transit patron continues, here. The "Birthday Boy" turns to make eye-contact specifically with me at this particular point aboard the southward-running metropolitan rail-vehicle. "He's sittin' right <u>here</u> and he knows it ain't cool," the "B-Boy" says, again, in reference to the unwelcome presence of the Latin-American man in the commuter car's *north*ern section of passenger seats, the specific seating section being, once again, held on "reserve" for the benefit of the transit compartment's black passengers, even if such a railway agreement is kept intact by ticket-holding travelers on a silent (i.e., <u>un</u>official) basis, which might be troubling to an extent to many of us who travel aboard the "BART"--the Bayside commuter rail-system, I assume.

The Hispanic man turns towards the black traveler, to the loud anti-integration advocate aboard the rail-traveling train-compartment. The Latino simply nods at the protester and quickly turns away to face forwards once again, ignoring the black man and his plate of highly audible opinions which would appear to be promoting the instant adoption of public "Apartheid" aboard the Bay's "mass transit"-rail network.

"<u>Yo</u>, *man!* ... Where you at?" the commuter-system's traveling segregationist says to me, directly.

"Huh?"

"I mean, how *old* are you?" the "Birthday Boy" inquires of me at this moment.

"What?" I answer, being--at the moment--in complete bewilderment due to the awkward obligation of needing to respond to such a personal level of questioning which one rail-passenger opportunistically decides to present to another.

"I said '... how *old* are you?' " the stranger repeats for my benefit alone.

"I'm twenty-six," I admit to the train cabin's self-chosen public inquisitor.

"I'm **forty-seven**!!" the "Birthday Boy" announces, without even needing to make that particular declaration again for those of us sitting inside the public rail-system's passenger-cabin.

It's upsetting, to an extent, to watch myself undergo an inquiry at the hands of the aging rail-traveler. For there is an attractive Hispanic woman in the "BART"-compartment's central section of passenger seats and she appears to be smiling rather unreluctantly at me at this particular moment.

(... **Whoa**!! **Boy**!! Hee! Hee! Hee!) Hence, the old man (i.e., the transit system's unofficial public orator) has become an unwelcome nuisance, a genuinely distracting figure. For me and, I s'pose, for the female passenger aboard the rail-carriage, as well. Her attention's drifting to the train car's "en route" inquisitor, the elderly "African-American" rail-commuter, rather than remaining where it should truly remain--*strictly* upon me. (... Am I wrong on this, *oh-always-loyal* associates?!) I need the "community rail"-client, currently suffering through the throes of a "midlife" crisis in full public view, to "**cease** and **desist**", so the Latina can concern herself *strictly* with me once again.... **Geez**!!

"Birthday Boy", the elder practitioner in the art of "public address", here, asks the Hispanic male sitting in front of me for an impromptu word on the USA's on-going occupation of <u>Iraq</u>, one of the "Persian Gulf"-region's Arab states. The host of the transit car's international affairs panel lifts a wrinkling paper bag to his gaping mouth, sipping, no doubt, from the bottle that's inside of it. ("Tumbleweed[ESU]"-brand Rye Whiskey, I bet.) The "winos" (i.e., drunken tramps) litter the streets of San Francisco's "Central Commerce District" with empty bottles of that commercial liquor manufacturer's best-known label of easily available alcohol. The whiskey-wielding traveler hands the brown bag of "rye" to the other black man aboard, who's sitting on the seat directly opposite his own. An unfortunate development for me, I suppose, for I can see, once again, the Hispanic maiden's focus is resting upon the bottle-happy interplay of the two black passengers who are sitting just across the aisle from me at the moment. (**Drat**!!) I'm afraid the appealing flower of "Latina" maidenhood I'm able, here, to observe has the attention span of a "preschool"-age child suffering with overt hyperactivity issues.

At "MacArthur Station", a group of fat hippie concertgoers steps aboard the open "BART"-system's carriage. The acidheads, a jolly band of beerbongers, walk into the compartment and seat themselves in the passenger container's central commuter section. The group of antiwar activists is most likely heading to the "Futile Conflict" show, one of the well-known "Alt-Rock" act's stops along its "World Tour 2003", apparently, set to happen tonight at one of the auditoriums appearing up and down the southwestern end of San Francisco's urban thoroughfare, "Market Street", I see. The group (two boys and two girls) instantly erupts with loud, pointless chatter aboard the public-transit carriage.... I.e., engaging themselves with what's commonly known as "commuter rail"-commentary and such, I do s'pose. Y'see, these "hippies" (or <u>hippos</u>, I should say, in view of each one's sheer measurements) are in items of attire that would earmark each one of them as a "Poster Child" for the "American Legal 'Weed' Society" in its nationwide campaign to acquire privately-run seed-planting grounds set aside for the exclusive purpose of fostering cannabis-production. (Well, what else could you expect from such "hippies"? ... Yet, another element of the Bay Area's citizenry which anyone intent on safeguarding his own emotional stability could do without, I'd venture, here, to state, O colleagues and *ever-so-close* confidants.)

After the "12th Street" rail-system depot (i.e., the "Central Oakland"-station), two Caucasian teenagers enter the mass-transit car by opening the pair of "see-through" exiting screens at the "BART"-compartment's southern end. The adolescent males allow themselves to select a "twin" seat near the commuter cabin's main "Entry/Exit"-doors. The two teenage boys converse with each other briefly until one of them begins to continually peek in my direction and, in addition, starts to whisper odds and ends about one thing or another into the second boy's ear (... *continually*, that is [... Mmmmm??]), using an open hand to protect his voice from releasing a potentially audible broadcast relaying his private opinions throughout the airspace inside the traveling "public transit"-vehicle. The second teenage boy now starts to glance slyly in my direction, as well (... uh huh?? ... okay??).

"That's <u>not</u> *him!"* the second teenage passenger states to the boy sitting beside him, the rail carriage's curious companion, I'd venture to note at this point.

"Yes it <u>is</u>!" the first teen, the one conducting covert commuter-cabin surveillance, insists. "I got five uh the episodes on a 'DVD' at home. I'll show 'em to you, *okay?* ... It's *him*, all right!"

To summarize the proceedings, folks, apparently, the duo of adolescent males are arguing over whether or not I, Ariq Zarkahn Shoretempel (humble "Berkeley" resident, that is), am a member of a certain "Primetime"-schedule network sitcom's cast or not. (Of course, I can at this point reassure everyone in attendance in noting, here, that I, of course, *currently* am <u>not</u> [nor have I *been*--at any point in the recent past] a member of a "Primetime" TV-network sitcom's cast.) The uncertain twosome of teenagers continues to steal glances at me (by both boys), alternately peeking across the floor of the rail-running "BART"-compartment. The two teenagers near the passenger cabin's main "ENTRY/EXIT"-doors are busy deciding one way or another as to whether or not I am a well-known "Primetime" network television entertainer. Why, certainly, of course!! *(" 'BART' ... A ticket buys you more than just a ride home. It pays for the type of recognition only celebrity impersonators could encounter in public." ... Ha! Ha! Ha!)*

"I've got it on 'DVD' at my fuckin' house!" the first teenager says, again, to his partner in public transit, a comrade aboard the commuter train, I s'pose. "I'll betcha **five** bucks, *bitch!"*

"Fine," the co-passenger eagerly replies. He turns to look at me again ... smiling, as if to assure himself, yet again, that I, Ariq Shoretempel, certainly <u>couldn't</u> be the actor which the other observer (the commuting companion) claims that I undoubtedly am.

"Fine, you owe me **five** bucks, *bitch!*" the first teenage rail-traveler announces to his onboard underage associate.

At the "West Oakland" system-stop, a fat Caucasian man in an Oakland "Raiders" team jersey enters the rail container through the two transparent panels at the vehicle compartment's southern end. He rests his scandalous weight upon a seat that requires he faces the pair of seats which the Latino man (i.e., *"Jose!"* or *"Miguel!"* [… remember]) already sits in--the "Raiders" fan's seat itself being right in front of the one which the Latino passenger is already occupying. The cabin seat which the fat man sits on is actually right next to a bench that's against the rail-carriage's side wall and just a few feet from the passenger container's main foot-traffic doors. The proud citizen of the "Raider Nation" puts himself upon a seat that permits him to conveniently gaze upon *both* the "Meximerican"-commuter and **me**, the "BART"-customer sitting directly behind the Spanish-speaking passenger.

The Caucasian "Silver & Black"-addict smiles merrily at the "Mex-American" man *("Jose!" … "Miguel!")* and, then, at me, the public-transit guest who, unfortunately, finds himself in a space directly behind the "Hispanic" commuter at this particular moment along the "East Bay" public-transit system's southwards route. The hefty "NFL" fan has a little gray and black shoulder-strap pouch with him, a carrying kit for the "game day"-ticket holder, which he opens up and starts rooting through. He, at once, produces a large bottle of whiskey and exhibits the manufacturer's label to the pair of African-American mass-transit "pals" occupying seats just across the aisle from my specific spot aboard the train-carriage while upon the trans-Bay rail-voyage ("Old Charlie Swinrow's[ISS] Carolina Corn[SLTF] Whiskey 'Red Label[ESU]' "). The bottle's stick-on product detailer seems to genuinely incite the two black transit-patrons still sitting across the aisle from me.

"Oh! Let me ho'd it! Let me ho'd it! Righ'tcheer--in **this** hand!!" the area transit-authority's former "commuter affairs"-investigator says, while in an almost ecstatic state. "I'll give you uh dollah … uh, a 'kohrduh' (the public rail patron is, here, saying 'quarter'). Just let me ho'd it **here** in this hand, my **fine** whiskey-drinkin' *friend!*" the black commuter begs, expressing an enthusiasm for the famous grain-alcohol formula which the weighty Caucasian passenger appears to merely revel in at the moment.

"I ain't even broken its cap off, yet," the porky "NFL"-season enthusiast reports. The "pigskin"-fan must be planning to consume the liquor while sitting at the 50-yardline after the First Half's kickoff. "I ain't even gunnah share 'dis here bottle with a 'niggah' I got I'll be meeting at the game," the white game attendant admits to the pair of African-American males on board the southbound public transporter, apparently referring to a "Gametime"-playmate which the fat "Raiders" fan plans to sit with in the stadium's extensive "guest seating"-zones.

The chain of rail-transit cars enters the Transbay Tunnel, initializing the four-and-a-half minute trip through the commuter-traffic channel which runs underneath the large bowl of saltwater existing in between the Peninsula and the coast-side region's eastern counties. While aboard the Transbay track, the radiowaves pulsing through the expanse of air, all but instantly, undergo deletion by the enclosing concrete barriers of the public-transit tunnel, ensuring the "cellular service"-subscribers are unable to receive or transmit sound-data signals using their hand-held "mobile"-communication devices. Many passengers aboard the "BART"-system's carriage which I'm sitting in quickly fold up and slide their "wireless line"-units into coat pockets or purses until the rail container exits the underwater commuter traffic channel at the opposite end of the Bay's large body of scenic, coastal water.

An adult male (curly hair, with a beginning beard) enters the "BART"-cabin from its eastern (i.e., "Alameda County") end, while, simultaneously, a "BART"-system technician enters the passenger compartment from its western (i.e., "Peninsula") end. On meeting in the open floor-space near the train container's eastern "Entry/Exit"-doors, the passenger, probably a Jew (i.e., a "kyke", there is no cause, here, to attempt to determine the identity of the man's actual ethnological legacy at all, O familiar and ever-faithful associates and co-conspirators), complains to the system-technician about a mass transit incident occurring the previous night, aboard the "East Bay" train at the "Pittsburgh/Bay Point"-station …

<u>Passenger</u>:
Where were **you** *last* night when I was trapped on the train?? *(Here, the Jew turns and glares at me, as if I'm someone he's able to blame, as well, for whatever public-transit problem he had to undergo aboard the "BART"-system occurring on the previous evening.)*

<u>Transit Technician</u>:
What??

<u>Passenger</u>:
I got stuck on the train. I told this other guy with me, "Hey! Man! We're stuck on the train!! We can't get off!!" *(The "BART"-passenger seems to genuinely re-channel the panic he apparently felt on the previous night upon instantly surveying his unfortunate circumstances while at the "Bay Point" rail-system depot. Here, once again, the Jew turns to me, as if attempting to explain himself to a bystander while, at the same time, rudely engaging the tolerant public-transit employee. Ah!!! … Perhaps he believes I was the <u>other</u> passenger aboard the train during last night's episode of momentary captivity at the "East Bay"-station and the panic-ridden transit-*

user is merely attempting to solicit my voice to lend credibility to the complaint which he's attempting to make against the commuter system's busy mechanic…. Just like a "kyke", to blame employees of a "municipal"-level bureaucracy for a moment of misery which he obviously took steps to bring upon himself.)

Technician:

See this red bar?? (*The "BART"-system's "maintenance"-agent [perhaps growing impatient, mildly, with the complaining mass-transit client] points to a large metallic red pipe found on a swivel-joint attaching it to the carriage's cabin wall near the pair of eastern "Entry/Exit"-doors.*) It says "EMERGENCY DOOR RELEASE"!! If you're ever stuck on the train, just lift this handle and these two doors will automatically separate for you! … <u>All right</u>?!

Passenger:

Oh, yeah?! (*The Jew comments, in a challenging tone, as if not believing the "BART"-employee's explanation on "commuter safety"-procedures.*) … Well, I didn't see that <u>last</u> night! (*The Jew comments as though the passenger-protection advisory and the door-release handle, which the rapid-transit technician chooses to make note of here, are precautionary issues which just magically--and conveniently--came into existence today. Here, the Jew turns to me, yet again, with a clueless expression, as if to inquire of me as to why the two of us hadn't been able to notice the door-release handle under its "EMERGENCY"-notice near the train-compartment's pair of "Entry/Exit"-doors on the previous evening, during the Jew's moment of temporary entrapment. ["Say, '<u>What</u>'?!"] Both men aboard--i.e., the "BART"-system's "rail repair"-technician and the commuter cabin's panic-stricken "Judaic"-transit guest--go their separate ways and each man exits the commuter vehicle's rail compartment at the end opposite to the particular set of "see-through" exiting screens which he, specifically, had to make use of in order to first enter the railway-system's passenger carriage.*)

At the " 'Embarcadero' Station"-platform, a black girl (about nine years in age, I s'pose) enters the commuter cabin and contacts the railsystem-vehicle's "onboard"-conductor by use of a two-way "speakerphone" in order to alert the mass-transit employee about a particularly odd set of circumstances transpiring at the current moment inside the adjoining train container:

--.Conductor: Yes??
--.Girl: Umm, they'z a man playin' wid hiz self!!
--.Conductor: <u>Where</u> <u>is</u> <u>he</u>?!

--()--
068
--()--

Adrien L. Montgomery
Tasting Droplets of the Unforgettable Rain
Official Imprint: "Dynamographx"

--.Girl: In the next car, "Car 3815D".
--.Conductor: <u>All</u> <u>right</u>!

The black girl and another one, a friend of the first girl, start giggling, almost gleefully, over the surprising scenario which the two of them, in this particular instance, find themselves in and walk the aisle towards the compartment's *western* end--the end opposite the one which the two had to use to enter the system's passenger cabin--in order to exit the carriage through its pair of transparent sliding screens.

At the "Ritterman Street"-rail depot, an Oriental woman (... probably Chinese) enters the container and asks me what she has to do in order to maneuver herself from her current spot aboard the "rapid transit"-system to the "Fremont"-station's boarding platform. I tell her, because the "BART"-train we're on is, apparently, already in motion, the woman cannot disembark and step aboard the "eastbound" train preparing to exit the commuter transportation hub over on Station Platform "B". I tell the female (unmistakably a daughter of the Asian nations) to disembark from the train she's currently standing aboard at the station that's further down the rail line, i.e., the "Powell Street"-system station, and, then, to walk across the boarding platform to Platform "B", in order to await the next eastbound rail-vehicle, which she can board to travel to the "Fremont"-transit depot. I tell the "Asiawoman" (i.e., the "Chinamerican"-type, that is) that she, then, will have to stand aboard the loading deck and await a "Fremont"-bound train, rather than a "Bay Point"- or "Richmond"-bound transporter. Once the "public rail"-engine arrives, she'll need, then, to step aboard one of its carriages and, subsequently, remain on it until the commuter-transit car reaches the "end of the line", i.e., the "City of Fremont", which would serve as the public carrier's ultimate point of termination.

I, however, continue to sit aboard the cabin until it reaches the "Civic Center"-station deck, the stop at which I am to disboard the regional rail-network on this occasion. At the "Civic Center"-stop, I offboard the transit compartment and direct myself towards the boarding platform's escalating traffic ramp. The public conveyor's shuttling commuters from the boarding platform's "rail level"-deck to the "BART"-station's "Concourse"-level. I begin to walk with caution towards the commuter-traffic compound's automatic exiting ramp.

Two "BART"-system "policemen" (i.e., "transit officers") enter the train compartment which I just left, presumably to search the adjoining container for the "Ejaculator-on-Board", i.e., the self-abusing system-guest which the black girl told the transit vehicle's conductor about earlier using the two-way "speakerphone". I merely stand by and watch as the two railsystem cops tackle the black narcotics-user as he exits one of the vehicle's cabins, using the open "Entry/Exit"-doors leading travelers to the floor of the urban transit-exchange, wrestling him abruptly (and quite physically) to the boarding platform's dust-ridden loading deck. The dope-doer is too unaware (considering the particular level of alertness, he, at this moment, possesses in view of the current degree of chemical-driven numbness which he's suffering under here) to realize what's actually happening to him at this specific moment in time. The individual himself appears to be a visitor native to the African continent of "developing" nations. He's actually wearing the official jersey of Nigeria's 2002 men's national team, the country's "F.I.F.A. World Cup"-squad ... the light turquoise, large-collar soccer shirt with the Nigerian Football Federation's official emblem appearing just below the tournament jersey's neckline.

The onboarding mass-transit passengers are, at this moment, witnesses to the on-the-floor struggle of "Cops vs. Commuter" on Platform "A" of the station's rail-accessing floor. The visiting sub-Saharan soccer fan continues to wriggle about (not unlike a pet goldfish caught momentarily outside of its aquarium, in air which the marine creature cannot breathe) as the pair of " 'BART' System"-security agents struggle to handcuff the man's wrists to each other behind the African football fan's back. I turn away from the scene of the transit-station arrest and merely step aboard the escalating ramp which elevates me towards the railsystem-depot's "Concourse"-level deck.

Yet, because of the amount of "Kitchenshelf[ESU]"-brand coffee (i.e., " 'Oldtime' Roast[STF]"-recipe) which I drank earlier in the day (a liter of it, at least), I am, at this point, suffering through what, to me, at least, seems to be an almost "narcotic" condition regarding the level of at-the-moment consciousness which I'm maintaining. I've never chosen to consume any illegal substances (e.g.'s, cocaine, heroin, methamphetamines, PCP, hashish, etc.), but my central nervous system instantly appears to overheat from what is itself an electrochemical injection that the coffee's detectably active ingredients (i.e., "caffeine", etc.) are currently inciting inside of me. I am, at once, aggressive--I want to accelerate my fist through the nearest hallow wall, or anything else as easily destructible (due to its inferior grade of constructional materials)--nervous, edgy, and ill-at-ease. (I feel as though I could exit the "rail network"-depot and punch a total stranger in the face if for no reason other than knowing such an instance of exertion would offer me the opportunity to free my system of the excess energy which it's recklessly bursting with at this actual moment of time.) I feel as if I am invulnerable to bodily injury to any degree, as well, at the specific moment. (It's as though I could now hurl myself from a building's third-story window and watch myself undergo a straight drop [i.e., a "freefall"] to the unmerci-fully solid asphalt ground below without incurring any damage whatsoever or feeling any level of pain at all as a result of the inescapable body-to-earth impact.)

--()--
070
--()--

Adrien L. Montgomery
Tasting Droplets of the Unforgettable Rain
Official Imprint: "Dynamographx"

I suppose these sensations are what someone under a resolutely intoxicating dosage of "PCP" (i.e., the elephant-tranquilizing agent) must undergo as well … aggression, nervousness, agitation, invulnerability, and the delusion that one possesses a "hyperhuman"-level of physical strength. I assume those who regularly utilize synthetic adrenaline boosters enjoy the *super*diesel charge that puts the individual's nervous system into a moment of *over*drive, permitting one to detect a virtual burst of unnecessary energy which only serves to instantaneously consume the particular individual himself. But, I'm **not** at all, here, comfortable with the degree of odd voltage which my morning caffeine milligrams have me suffering with at this specific point in time, my associates and *oh-so-close* confidants.

Upon reaching the "Concourse"-level of the "Civic Center" "BART"-system station, I immediately begin walking towards the rail depot's northwestern exit, the one with the parallel escalators, one of which ferries people up to the west end of "United Nations Plaza", an open square on the northside of the world-famous thoroughfare known as "Market Street". An elderly man appearing in San Francisco "Giants" team apparel, i.e., the paraphernalia of the average gamegoing fan, having an overgrown, unkept graying beard, as well, stops me and asks for assistance. "How d'ya get out to 'Ocean Beach'?" the aging "baseball"-enthusiast asks me.

I point to a sign inside the perimeter of the "Metrorail[UE]" service's public-entry deck that appears above the conveyor-system that's lowering people to the boarding platform of the "Metrorail[UE]"-system's urban-transport train.

"That's how I get out to 'Ocean Beach'?" the older National League fan asks, again. "Aboard the 'TOWNTRACK[AI]'?"

"Yeah," I answer. "It's just one floor below us." I start, yet again, towards the rail station's exit and see an African-American man panhandling near the foot of the twin escalating ramps, sitting on a low stool and holding up a hand-drawn sign in front of him. The section of cardboard which the man presents to the public-rail commuters indifferently walking past him displays the following set of words appearing loudly on it in red marker-ink: "HOMELESS, my ass! I just wanna get HIGH!" I step aboard the escalator and ride the automatic mass-transporter patiently up to the southwest corner of "United Nations Plaza". (Why hurry yourself while aboard an escalator belt by actually attempting to *walk* up it? … Unnecessary, to say the least, wouldn't it be??)

At the escalating rampway's end, I turn to my right and immediately see an SFPD cop getting off of a "Police Squad"-cycle, a "motocross" patrol ve-hicle which cops in San Francisco use in order to drive themselves up the steep asphalt streets which the region's road plan commonly offers to its community of route-sharing motorists. The policeman begins to bark at a group of "Filipino" teenage males who are just beginning to disperse from another boy who's standing next to the guard-rail near the entry-walk to the "Civic Center"-rail transit depot. "Get the <u>hell</u> back *here!*" the "Motorcop" shouts to the assembly of teens, i.e., the "Sons of the Pacific", who are attempting to quietly draw themselves away from a particular teenager who appears to be standing next to an open duffel bag of "black market"-merchandise. (Probably CD's or videogame-cartridges, I'm here assuming.) The children of "Oceanica" stop themselves at once on the police officer's directive and I turn towards the eastern end of the footpath, walking anonymously across the plaza's ornamental flooring, which would be the large rectangular plates--an imitation of pale red brickwork, that would be--in order to escape the crowd of urbanites currently appearing in the cosmopolis's expansive public square.

Tasting Droplets of the Unforgettable Rain

By
Adrien L. Montgomery
<u>Cycle</u> <u>004</u>:
"Uhmmm ... Table for One" (... Or, "Evening Feast in the Lair of the Slumlord")

<u>UTA</u> <u>Directive</u> <u>IV</u>:
"Attention! Attention! ... We'll Be Delayed At This 'Railbus^{ESU}' Station Momentarily. We Do Make Apologies For The Inconvenience.... Repeat, We'll Be Delayed At This 'Railbus^{ESU}' Station Momentarily. Again, We Do Make Apologies For The Inconvenience."
("<u>UTA</u>": <u>U</u>rban <u>T</u>ransit <u>A</u>uthority)

<u>Cable</u> "<u>TV</u>"-<u>Station</u> <u>Announcer</u>:
(... Interrupting the Station's Ongoing Programming Material)

!!CRISIS RESPONSE ALERT!!
!!CRISIS RESPONSE ALERT!!
!!CRISIS RESPONSE ALERT!!
!!CRISIS RESPONSE ALERT!!

We are conducting a test of the Local Crisis Broadcasting Response. What you are about to listen to is only a <u>test</u> alarm. If this were a genuine crisis scenario, you would receive additional information on public-safety precautions from your Local Crisis Broadcasting Bureau. We repeat, this is only a test alarm. If this were a ... *(the announcer, here, begins hearing the high whine of a siren initialize)*.... What the <u>Hell</u> is *that?!!*

| --()-- |
| 072 |
| --()-- |

Adrien L. Montgomery

Tasting Droplets of the Unforgettable Rain

Official Imprint: "Dynamographx"

(((!!!Ehmmmmmmmmmmmmmmmm!!!)))

Goddammit! <u>Who</u> is cueing up that alert signal?!! Not yet!! I'm still trying to announce our mission statement.

(((!!!Ehmmmmmmmmmmmmmmmm!!!)))

Stop it!! I'm *still* reading the "audioscript"!! <u>Whichever</u> one of you boys back there's responsible for this--just quit pushing that "effects" key, *all right!!*

(((!!!Ehmmmmmmmmmmmmmmmm!!!)))

Just stop it, <u>dammit</u>!! It's driving **me** up the <u>Goddamn</u> wall!! That's it!! ... This concludes our test of the Local Crisis Broadcasting Response today. Keep tuning in to "KMIN-TV" for subsequent information on public-safety precautions necessary in the event of an actual "crisis"-level broadcast. We will now resume the airing of this station's regularly-scheduled programming.... Jesus!! I'm not makin' a live announcement at the start of any "L.C.B.R." tests after this, O.K.?!! My God!! Somebody tell the station manager to keep an eye on that "f/x" key during "crisis alert" notifications!... <u>JEEZUS</u> *Christ*!!!

(-|<u>Calendar</u> <u>Date</u>: <u>TUE</u>., <u>Nov</u>. <u>18</u>, <u>2003</u>|-)
I'm sitting in the lobby of the "Focuspoint[STF]" store on "Rocolo Arcade", the retailing thoroughfare, in the central-northern sector of Minneapolis ... in the state of ... Minnesota, that would be. I'm sitting on a twin-cushion seat which rests against the panel of windows found at the front of the outlet's street-level entryhall which opens up to the traffic-ridden sidewalk outside, or, "Rocolo Avenue", the pedestrian channel running through the well-known retailing venue of widely chosen shops, bars, and restaurants, etc. I've got a pair of large paper shopping bags with me which I have a multitude of household merchandise-items in ... cleaning brushes, bottles of anti-bacterial disinfectant, dust pans, scrub sponges, rubber gloves, re-sealable plastic sandwich bags, canisters of air-freshener, etc., etc., for the new "studio"-style apartment I'm in which is in the "Laurel Park"-neighborhood, a section of the urban region which lies just south of Minneapolis's "Central Commercial District", or its "Downtown" area, that is. It's 7:35 p.m., C.S.T. (mid-November, state of Minnesota, the "Northern Plains"-region, under skies exhibiting a somewhat scenic gray coloring to them, with a "metallic"-tint appearing in the layering of stationary clouds hovering overhead) and I'm readying myself for the atmosphere of cold Autumnal air which I'll encounter during the lengthy foot voyage home ... back to "The 'Falconeer' Building" on the corner of Reddington Avenue and

Courier Street.

At the moment, I'm watching a tall, lean teenage girl standing in the middle of the entry hall's beige foot carpets as the pairing of companions with her, also teen females, collects around her just before the entire threesome of highschoolers decides to exit through the rotating doors found at the outlet's front in order to march into late Autumn's cold climate, here, in the "Northern Plains"-sector of the United States. There's a Caucasian woman who walks past me across the floor of the retailing venue's "street"-level and smiles eagerly at me. (For a second, I think of asking the woman for a car ride home, just to avoid the walk in the frigid, Midwestern air's inconveniently low temperature made note of in the forecast preparing citizens, if so choosing, to venture outdoors tonight.) Though, I do see that she's bridging the racial gap at the moment by communicating with an "African-American" individual (i.e., me, that is), in order to extend to another human being an open hand in the name of interracial co-existence. (… Ha! Ha! Ha!)

I watch a boy with red hair, i.e., a "carrot top" (probably a ten-year-old), ride habitually up and down the store's pair of paralleling escalators which conveniently lead customers up to or down from the retailing station's "Airwalk"-level, a maze of indoor catwalks forming a labyrinth of climate-friendly footpaths sheltering pedestrians from the harsh winter elements collecting upon the urban streets beneath its unending infrastructural network of "warm air"-corridors. He's obviously playfully passing the time while his mother, perhaps, browses the merchandise outlet's floor plan of multiple aisles. (The kid obviously thinks this particular "Focuspoint[STF]" store is, perhaps, yet another Starr Shield Companies[SLTF] "Mystic Fortress" theme park location, I s'pose. [… Ha! Ha! Ha!])

There's a second Caucasian boy (about nine years of age, one with brown hair) who walks right up to me and peeks inside the pair of large "Focuspoint[STF]" paper shopping bags which I've set up right beside me and starts smiling inexplicably at me. (A group of four people soon gathers around the small, intrusive child.) I do <u>not</u> (repeat: "do <u>not</u>") enjoy children staring at me whenever I'm visiting any public venues, y'know that. You're always afraid the child in question will utter words amounting to one sort of insult or another and, of course, you, being the innocent adult, would have no rights whatsoever in safeguarding your own dignity in any way at all by responding in similar tone to the child's openly offending remarks. After all … a *child* <u>is</u> just a *child*. They're free to say, think, and do *whatever* it is they desire to without having to offer any apologies if the underage individual in question succeeds in presenting himself as one beset with an obvious absence of social manners. (Am I correct on this count or not, my old friends?)

The child at hand (the boy with brown hair) begins to complain to both of his parents about *"that old lady"* who apparently had the unusual daring to accuse him of attempting to shoplift an item of merchandise inside of the "Focuspoint[STF]"-venue, I'm assuming at this point. The talkative group of people appears to constitute a family of 5 persons: 1) the "Mom", 2) the "Dad", 3) the first "Son", 4) the "Daughter", and 5) the second "Son". (The annoying boy [the nine-year-old child with the brown hair], who took an inappropriate look inside of my paper shopping bags, is the older of the family's pairing of "Sons".)

There's a cafeteria just next to the retailing outlet's entryhall area and, in the dining room's interior airspace, I can detect the flavor of "hot dogs" which the eating space's guests purchase and consume, i.e., the "all beef"-brats, pickle-relish, mayonnaise, mustard, ketchup, onions, and bell peppers, etc., etc., that people enjoy while sitting at those tables found not far from where I currently sit. The alluring aroma rising off the cafeteria's menu of ready-to-eat items makes me, at present, all too aware of the distance which I have to cover until I can prepare an acceptable dinnertime-option for myself once I'm back in the apartment which I'm occupying at this particular point in time. (... Dammitt!!)

I do, here, desire to make known to you, old friends of mine that you are, that the state of Minnesota is a taste which I assume any new arrival must gradually acquire a steady appetite for over a period of time ... much like the craving for measures of peanuts and butter instead of just "peanut butter", or the love for measures of mud and pie instead of just "mud pie", or the hunger for measures of ice and cream instead of just "ice cream", or the yearning for measures of tomatoes and paste instead of just "tomato paste", y'know what I'm saying, O *ever-so-close* companions and convenient cohorts?? I do, here, desire to make known to you, dear friends, that I might have just accidently overshot my pre-existing--and significantly more preferable--landing site, the USA's "Cereal Belt" (i.e., Nebraska, Iowa, Illinois, and Indiana), which is, in fact, the particular environment which I actually would have chosen to quite happily inhabit, I trust, if I had genuinely had that specific opportunity on hand at the time at which I left the "Bay Area". (The "Land of 10,000 Lakes" is the state of Minnesota's popular motto which actually appears on the state's "motor vehicle"-plates, if you ever care to look at one of them, folks and friends alike.) ... Uhmmmm, F.Y.I., the state of Wisconsin's got 15,000 lakes and the state of Michigan's got 11,000 of the "freshwater"-pools! ... Hah! Hah! Hah! Take that, you " 'Gopher'-Staters"!! (That's the particular mammal which the population of this actual state has, apparently, chosen as the animal to *officially* represent their specific geographical sector as a public mascot ... the <u>gopher</u>.[??!!]) Y'know, residing in the state of Minnesota is not that unsimilar to entering the "Great Hereafter", i.e., the "Otherworld", or, the "Underrealm", or, "Coffins 'R' Us", etc., etc., or, that region in which a local can rent a feature motion-picture's "Blu-ray™ Disc"-copy without fearing he'll incur any actual penalty for returning the title after the rental deadline expires, etc., … i.e., a real "Casketville", that is. This metropolis's "urban atmosphere" serves, I think, to undermine whatever it might have been that had once, perhaps, made the city of Minneapolis authentically *rural*, i.e., agrarian both in its soul and in its scenic arrangement.

I gather my pair of large "Focuspoint^{STF}" paper shopping bags and summon, I s'pose, what I'd deem to be a reliable amount of *instant* courage which I'll, here, make use of in order to exit the retailing venue's street-level entryhall (conveniently under current climate-guidance by a state-of-the-art "ComfortLevel^{AI}"-brand air-regulation system) and travel through the rotating screens which turn inside of the tall cylindrical enclosure amounting to the lobby-level's port of entry for guests intent on browsing the outlet's aisles for sought-after merchandise-items. I make, here, a mental note of the cold air coming into the lobby's space of pedestrian traffic *each* and <u>every</u> time someone opens one of the side doors which permits people to enter and exit the retailing location's "streetside"-level and set foot onto the sidewalk outside the outlet.

I notice that there's an "African-American" female panhandling and randomly approaching customers walking through the consumer venue's busy entryway, apparently requesting casual "donations" for children in need. The black female vagrant approaches me, however, after appearing to momentarily consider a venture into the cafeteria's dining room, and asks me for a donation in order to help feed "her" children. *("Wanna help me feed some kids?"* the beggar-woman asks of me.) Yeah…. Uh huh…. Those damn kids she's got at home, always eating, they seem to be. Poor woman. (((Sigh))). Why didn't the Good Lord see the wisdom in providing this particular woman with children who have no need for edible dietary substances?! She's just one of those persons having had the misfortune of entering our world (at birth) under an unfavorable (and poverty-stricken) configuration of celestial bodies which did simply happen to appear over her crib, I s'pose, to instantly condemn the black woman to bearing offspring who surprisingly possess an appetite for vitamin-rich nutrient materials on what is, unluckily, a <u>perdiem</u> basis!! (… Ha! Ha! Ha!)

I exit the shopping outlet's interior atmosphere as made suitable by the "touchscreen"-system controlling it and venture into the frosty outside air still at large on this late Autumn evening. People are hurrying themselves home up and down "Rocolo Arcade", the thoroughfare of "retailing industry"-outlets that stretches through the northern-central sector of Minneapolis's official "city"-acreage. The bustling crowds of pedestrians still hurry into the front hall of the large "Focuspoint^{STF}"-outlet with hopes of making quick purchases inside the huge merchandise depot (the site being but one of dozens of similar venues existing across the US which all belong to the well-known chain of upmarket retailing houses) before the retailer formally closes its front doors to the public tonight, that is.

There's a Caucasian man cursing at a white panhandler on Rocolo Avenue, presumably to put the beggar on notice, warning the vagrant against any future pleas for meager rations which are meant to maintain the outspoken loiterer's day-to-day personal upkeep. I see a second pan-handler on the corner of 10th Street and Rocolo Avenue sitting on the concrete walking path outside of a "Real Fiesta Mexicana Grill" restaurant. The panhandler's holding up a cardboard sign in front of him for the benefit of any onlookers who happen to take note of it while passing by. ("I JUST PEED IN MY PANTS--I NEED $3.50 TO DO MY LAUNDRY TODAY--PLEASE HELP!!") Mmmmm?? ... What's the vagabond going to wear while he's laundering the pee-ridden pants he's got on, huh?? (Answer me that, O *ever-so-convenient* companions.) These panhandlers don't thoroughly think through their petitions for cash prior to sketching out specific requests for personal assistance with the "felt tip"-end of a "Funny Dropper[ISS]" ink-pen, y'know that?

I see people entering the "Iron Horseshoe Saloon and Grill", a barbequing house on the eastern side of the well-known pedestrian corridor ... "Rocolo Arcade". I walk by the "All For Fitness[UE]" exercise club and see its patrons striding atop the rotating belts running inside the workout room's treadmilling-systems and pedaling the stationary cycles in the "gymnasium"-venue's roadside "personal training"-facility. I can, at this moment, see a small group of vocal protestors standing on the southwestern corner of Rocolo Avenue and 11th Street. (I'm wondering what the circle of urban social activists meeting on the crowd-ridden thoroughfare is attempting to make a noble stance against on this particular occasion?? ... The "War in Iraq"?? ... Or, crimes against the environment??) I see a group of black men (i.e., "transients"--without question--that would be) who've set a "drumfire" for themselves inside of an old tin oil barrel in the employee lunch park of the "North Hawk Bank[AI]" Mall.

"You fellows try to stay warm tonight, OK?" I say to the assembling of vagrant males as I quickly walk Rocolo's broad concrete pedestrian path towards the apartment in the "Laurel Park"-residential district that's awaiting the imminent arrival of its current occupant.

"Wat'choo think we doin'?!!" a man standing among the band of black vagabonds quickly replies. "Spare any change *tonight*, my <u>brother</u>??"

Upon leaving the party of derelict males, attempting to safeguard themselves against the Autumnal air-temperatures on a mid-November evening with the "fire-in-a-pan" approach which they've chosen for themselves to utilize on the occasion (i.e., using the empty oil barrel as a makeshift, "oldstyle"-iron stove ... the kind permitting homeowners to burn up logwood in an old-fashion "kitchen"-unit which channels smoke through a stack which runs up to the room's ceiling in a cabin-style, "Frontier"-era log-built house), I continue to trek southwards, to the apartment in "Laurel Park", which yet awaits its lease-holding tenant's oncoming return.

I do, here, encounter, yet another group of persons, who appear to all but immediately engage my attention in what would still be nothing more than an additional moment of street-level chatter. In this particular instance, the pairing of Caucasian males on hand offers to me a tale detailing the difficulties of locating the particular hotel which a friend of theirs (the third member of the traveling trio, that would be) sought to reserve a suite in prior to the threesome's arrival in the metropark found by foot-travelers in the north-central sector of Minneapolis. The two males (… short, each with a blond "ponytail" hairstyle, appearing to, most likely, hail from a spot, also, in the "Midwestern"-region [e.g., perhaps, Indiana]) are standing outside the entry drive to the "Oakmont Classic Inn", apparently just waiting in between 13ᵗʰ Street (which is just to the north of them) and "Grandgate Avenue" (which is just to the south of them).

There's one in particular, who speaks on behalf of the trio (the third, and, hereby, absent member of the traveling Caucasian troika, is, apparently, across the street, inside the "Orbital Hotel", attempting to determine as to whether it's the place in which he tried to put a suite on reserve for the band of travelers just prior to their landing in Minneapolis). The male who, apparently, assumes the role of "official" party spokesman, asks me if there's a "Shopmart1000ᴱˢᵁ" (the title of a widely-known chain of "convenience"-outlets existing across the Midwestern region of the US) anywhere in the particular area which he currently finds himself inside.

"Is there a 'Shopmart1000ᴱˢᵁ' somewhere nearby?" the vocal member (i.e., impromptu orator) belonging to the wandering group of out-of-town Caucasian males plainly asks me.

"There's a 'Shopmart1000ᴱˢᵁ' at 2001 Rocolo Avenue South, at the corner of Rocolo Avenue and Skylight Street, and there's another one at 1100 Hennenburgh Avenue, at Hennenburgh and 11ᵗʰ Street," I answer in order to inform the recent "out-of-state" arrival.

"Yeah, it looks like we'll be headin' to a 'Shopmart1000ᴱˢᵁ' after just a bit, as soon as our 'friend' can find us the right hotel," the young out-of-towner explains to me. "At first, we thought it was this one," the traveler says, gesturing to the entryway of the "Oakmont Classic Inn", which stands just a number of yards behind him. "Now, he's across the street, in that one, tryin' to see if that's where our 'reservation' is," the arrival, here, makes note of, pointing to the entrance of the "Orbital Hotel", which stands just across Rocolo Avenue from where the twosome waits on the occasion. "Problem is, after he made the reservation, he forgot to write down the name of the hotel. Which means, when we got here, we didn't know where to go. <u>Only</u> thing he seemed to remember about the hotel was that its name started with an 'O'!?? … Good hands we're in, *huh?!*"

As the group's self-chosen spokesperson continues to share the peculiar plight which the trio of unhappy travelers find themselves, at least at the moment, unluckily needing to endure, the 2nd member of the "streetside"-pair of out-of-town guests merely shifts his focusing between me and the entryway of the "Orbital Hotel", inside of which the "friend" of the pairing, i.e., the trio's third, and, hereby, absent groupmate, is, apparently, attempting to re-secure a room reservation for the hapless band of recent arrivals, watching (as the silent member is), intermittently, the entrance of the "Orbital Hotel" site, which stands on the eastern side of Rocolo Avenue, for, perhaps, any signal indicating the pair waiting upon the street opposite the "accommodations"-venue can safely enter as authentic guests on that particular evening.

"It's been a long day," the vacationer, obviously a true <u>amateur</u> concerning the art of "weekending"-travel, I can safely, here, assume, offers to me at this point, while the three of us merely stand upon Rocolo Avenue, just outside the "Oakmont Classic Inn" visitation compound, as it is about 08:00 p.m., C.S.T., according to the wristclock which I'm currently wearing. "What I wanna do is just go to a 'Shopmart1000^{ESU}' and pick up a 'sixpack' of beer just to chill out for a while."

"Uhmm, I believe there happens to be a bar in that hotel, across the street … 'The Orbital'," I say to the pairing of hapless out-of-town travelers, while pointing to the streetside window appearing alongside the tourism site's front drive built for use by the motor traffic of actual guests selecting to stay at the extensive complex of lodging suites offering to its occupants the usual "rent-a-room" conveniences which such places make available to their newly arriving visitors. Behind the large panes of transparent glass, one can apparently see the typical interior and necessary assets which would belong to any hotel bar found on said facility's "lobby"-level, i.e., the clerk's counter, the lengthy customer countertop, the large rack of wine glasses, the bank of wine and liquor bottles, the barstools, the set of beer-dispensing taps, an extra number of napkin-dispensing pails for particularly messy customers to request be put on the counter in front of them for reliable use when clearly most necessary to them, etc., etc.

"Well, that's probably <u>exactly</u> where we'll be headin', as soon as this 'friend' of ours can work out the reservation in there and we know we got a room for ourselves tonight," the luckless trio's self-chosen chief communicator in public-relations wearily responds.

Almost at once, the traveling threesome's third, and, heretofore, absent member, i.e., the one who didn't remember to make note of the name of the "hoteling"-industry venue (i.e., the lodging facility, that would be) at the moment in which he apparently chose to make a reservation for the trio of weekending travelers, emerges from the cylindrical enclosure surrounding the rotating doors for use at the hotel's spacious guest-entrance.

Standing inside the cylindrical enclosure itself, without so much as taking a single step outside of the venue's circular entryway, the male out-of-state arrival (about 21 years in age) raises a single arm and begins to burdensomely motion to the pair of companions standing upon the opposite side of Rocolo Avenue, i.e., the "western" side, to signal to them he, apparently, the group leader, has, <u>in fact</u>, been able to make a reservation for the three visiting tourists at the front desk of the "Orbital Hotel"-lobby. Hence, it appears, at this point, it is appropriate for the pair of traveling partners standing impatiently on the street outside to enter the actual venue, there being no need any longer for the duo of unhappy loiterers to linger upon the sidewalk across from the "accommodations"-facility for word of success on the part of the group's third (and, apparently, leading) member.

"<u>There</u> he is! ... Right <u>there</u>!" the first traveler says, the group's apparent "Chief-of-Communications" or self-chosen "streetside"-correspondent. "That's our friend! ... Thanks for all your help." The first member of the trio of out-of-towners offers me gratitude once again for assisting him in locating the whereabouts of a "Shopmart1000^{ESU}" outlet in the area and begins to walk across Rocolo Avenue with his silent sidekick (the other Caucasian companion) towards the cylindrical glass enclosure of the accommodations establishment which the three assistance-seeking arrivals will apparently check themselves into tonight ... with the twosome of incoming adventurers, at the moment, following the third member of the vacation-going party of three through the circular gateway surrounding the rotating doors which turn on demand inside the facility's visitor's entrance. After watching the trio of helpless travelers disappear into the lobby of the "Orbital Hotel" venue, wherein (you'd want to think) a suite awaits the band of out-of-town tourists (at least for the night), I re-initiate my southwards trek towards the residential building in "Laurel Park", inside of which a particular apartment will soon receive the occupant currently holding a 12-month leasing-contract guaranteeing "tenancy"-status in the rooming space of the specific rental-unit in question, i.e., yours truly, "Ariq", of course.

Tasting Droplets of the
Unforgettable Rain

By
Adrien L. Montgomery
<u>Cycle 005</u>:
"Ah-Ha! ... If One Just So Happens to Be Caught Using the Native Tongue in Public, Again, One Must Remember, Henceforth, to Abide by the Ensuing

--()--
080
--()--

Advisory to Avoid a Re-play of the Maneuver: 'Keep the Mouth Closed!' "(X)

UTA Directive V:

"Attention! Attention! … 'MetroTransit' Passengers Must Not Park Bicycles Near The Rail Compartment's Side-Entry Doors! Repeat, 'MetroTransit' Passengers Must Not Park Bicycles Near The Rail Compartment's Side-Entry Doors!"

("UTA": Urban Transit Authority)

Radio-Station Promotional Byte:

"Each morning, after you awake, make sure to roll the radio's tuning pin to 98.3 KKOF 'The Coffee' FM…. New Scandia, White Bear Lake, Little Canada, Eden Prairie, Brooklyn Park, Maple Grove…. Make us your weekday warm-up before the workday starts. Be sure to enjoy a large cup of caffeine-free 'Adult-Rock' before the office opens…. Make all of your co-workers take notice. Let yourself begin an 'office affair' with 'The Coffee' FM. How do you spell true love? … 'K-K-O-F'. Take your cereal and toast with a little KKOF! Compliments of the True Choice[AI] Radio State Companies and all affiliate stations…. Dawn just got a bit more delicious!"

Radio-Station Promotional Byte:

"KMHK 'The Mike' 95.5 FM invites one and all to tune in each weekday morning for fresh slices of 'Soft Jazz' in HD 'High Definition' Digital FM Stereo…. Minneapolis, St. Paul, Coon Rapids, Bloomington, New Brighton, Golden Valley…. Help yourself to a home-cooked menu of 'Soft Jazz' selections from our ever-expanding library of contemporary favorites. Breakfast at 'The Mike' is always a satisfying morning meal…. 'K-M-H-K'! We're in the Crossnational Communications[UE] System of Home Radio[ISS] Channels. Serving samples of 'Soft Jazz' with a smile and extra cream. At breakfast, we toast sets of music 'til they're good 'n' crisp … and then we add the butter!"

(-|Calendar Date: SAT., Nov. 22, 2003|-)
Partition 001:

Trekking around the region's old expanse of urban terrain isn't as simple as it might, at first, sound, O fraternity of *ever-faithful* friends. One night, you might end up stuck on a street corner in the Midwestern metrocenter's section of southern districts, with a marathon of shadow-ridden hostile blocks to hurdle before you make it back to the familiar "playpen" later on. If you're ever standing alone on "Arquette Avenue" after hours without cash on hand for a taxi-cab, just hitch up with the motoring queer, who's cruising the streets to search for what could possibly be a "one night" affair. But, remember, old friends that you, of course, are, that

--()--
081
--()--

car ride home ain't gunna actually be "free of charge", y'know what I'm saying? You won't be using that old right hand you have use of to reach into your front pocket later on in the evening in order to extract the wallet out of its regular place of easy access. Yet, you will be (can I say …) "whipping"(?!) out the one particular worldwide passport that permits a person frequent tours into this northern metrozone's "Lion's Den" mansion of excitable men. (Hah! Hah! Hah!) After hours, on "Arquette Avenue", there's no need to signal a taxi if, in fact, you require any temporary vehicular privileges to ship yourself back to the old "cribhouse". Just go a-head and be sure to "cat call" the closest queer motorist. That old familiar organ which you've got inside your pair of underpants (*if* made easy for other men to obtain and quickly awaken) will pay for any public-transit fees which the male traveler might incur on any road trip back home after the clock's midnight chimes have eventfully rung…. Trust me. [!!Issuing 'Emoticon' Alert!! (} ; > o]

<u>Partition 002</u>:

Aaaaggghhh!!! Minneapolis is the Queen of the " 'Queer Sister' Cities", that's for certain, my fine, quite familiar, old friends. This place has gotta be the Lesbian "Mecca" of the USA's "Middle States"-region…. "Lesbo Central", and that's without a doubt! ("… Hello, this is 'Directory Assistance'. Operator 'Leslie' speaking…. I'm searching, sir, but there is no local listing available for a 'Scarlett Cockburn', not in the Greater Minneapolis Metropolitan Area. I'm afraid you'll have to dial an out-of-state number carrying a long-distance charge. I regret that I can't retrieve any information on a 'Scarlett Cockburn' under any area-code appearing in our statewide-subscriber's database. I'm sorry, but it seems as though there is no 'Scarlett Cockburn' to be found in the state's listing of network service-line subscribers, sir.") It's the refugee camp for all "faggettes" (that's female faggots, to one and all) fleeing the farmlands of the continent's interior acreage of crop-ridden earth. Y'know, you see "Dykes on Parade" along the municipal epicenter's prime traffic routes on Friday afternoons. ("Warning!! … Dyke Alert!!") You see " 'Dyke Pride' Day" T-shirts cluttering up the streetside windows of memorabilia shops in the area's "Central Commerce District". ("Warning!! … Dyke Alert!!") You see "lesbo" clubgoing clusters gathering outside of "after hours"-bars and music venues in the "Brick Wall"-District on Saturday nights. ("Warning!! … Dyke Alert!!") There's the annual "Kiss a Dyke--Earn an 'A' " contest at U of M's "Westside Campus"-location. ("Warning!! … Dyke Alert!!") I must, here, note this specific urban-center's a virtual "Dyke-a-Rama"!! This particular "Northern Plains" town appears to be nothing less than an actual legion of lesbos who just so might happen to be marathoning up and down that epic continental waterway, i.e., the southwards running river known as the "Seismic Mississippi"! (Oh, Good Lord Almighty!!) On my first instance of overnight "adventuring" in the state of Minnesota, a diesel dyke (i.e., "Captain Cunt Job") tried to solicit my assistance in persuading a prostitute to let the lesbo orally explore the whore's vaginal region. I, of course, could offer no argument on the "boot" cunt's behalf in order to assist her in achieving the particular objective which she sought to attain on that specific occasion, unfortunately, my *oh-so-loyal* association of overnight enthusiasts and urban foot scouts.... (((Sigh))).

<u>Partition 003</u>:

Aboard the "Cititraxx^{STF}" system, on a trip from the Minneapolis/St. Paul International Airport, the "rail transit"-vehicle stops outside of the "Metrodome", a spacious indoor "field" venue built to host athletic contests in various events of public competition, i.e., the local spectator site, inside of which the "Minnesota Twins" of the "American League"-rules baseball association <u>and</u> the "Minnesota Vikings" of the "National Football League" organization of "Pro"-level athletic clubs compete in "home"-games during each team's annual schedule of " 'regular' season"-events. One man, being twenty-one years in age, perhaps, steps aboard the "mass transit"-carriage with a group of females, all appear to be campus ("University of Minnesota", that is) citizens in current standing. The man initializes an orator's account of a recent incident which the assembly of "public transportation"-guests all just had to regrettably undergo. The females-- **three**, that is--start laughing (merely giggling, yet in an almost <u>frantic</u> manner) due to their apparent recollection of the recent episode which the male commuter (the foursome's readily available "communicator-in-chief") speaks of to no one other than the trio of female "mass transit"-users. After recovering from a virtual seizure of gleeful laughter, the male transit client appears to sneak but a brief peek at me, the only <u>other</u> rail traveler occupy-ing the vehicular compartment alongside of the fun-loving foursome of collegiate "public rail"-companions. The male transit passenger smiles quickly at me and attempts to abruptly appraise the presence of the only <u>other</u> male aboard the "commuter rail"-system's passenger-container. On, once again, realizing he's in the midst of a trio of talkative, hysterical female "MetroTransit"-goers, the man's carefree character, all at once, appears to become quieter by, I'd suggest, several detectable degrees in scale and, at the moment, begins to rapidly disappear. He seems, in one brief instant, ill at ease, standing among the threesome of chatting, laughing campus-age women, as if he's aware that the females would appear (to an outside observer, i.e., me, for example) as though they're selecting to associate *exclusively* with him by a common, and all too intentional, choice, that is. A particular social arrangement which, apparently, he'd choose to undo at this specific moment in time, if such an example of "Will versus Reality" with respect to the desire on one's part to instantly alter that which **is** into that which *should* be were at all possible

Adrien L. Montgomery
Tasting Droplets of the Unforgettable Rain
Official Imprint: "Dynamographx"

at this point in the evening's itinerary of events. The male "public rail"-guest attempts, again, to smile (albeit, nervously) at me, as if saying, due to the female "rail mobility"-customers surrounding him at the moment, communication with me can only occur on but a *visual*, secretive (and, basically, <u>non</u>verbal) level at this point in time, my friends. He seems, here, to signal to the females, as if to tell each one of the eager collegians to lower the volume-level on the particular individual's own voice, due to the fact that the foursome of University-level "academic enrollees" are not *exactly* alone aboard the "public rail"-carriage at this specific moment. One of the three women turns around in order to get a quick glimpse at me, the only <u>other</u> male aboard the "MetroTransit"-system, and frowns, as if noting that my very presence is prohibiting the formerly happy foursome from fully setting free the camaraderie that any group of midnight "transit vehicle"-users would be likely to exhibit aboard a rolling "public transportation"-compartment, I'd venture, here, to say. The females obligingly lower their voices while speaking aboard the "commuter traffic"-container, as if suddenly conscious of the fact that they're in the presence of a stranger, i.e., a man outside of their private, pre-graduate "rail cabin"-party. In quick, fleeting turns, my collegiate male counterpart, again, attempts to take a shy peek at me, smiling cautiously and brightening a bit about the eyes with each specific incident which allows him to contact, though stealthily, the *other* traveling male "rail transit"-goer (i.e., me, that is) aboard the urban "railroute"-compartment. At this point, O favorite, ever-faithful followers, I've no other choice than to assume that this particular "on campus"-comrade (found standing amidst the assembly of collegiate females) is--nothing less than--a **bi**sexual, due to the attention which he often strives to offer to me, though he himself is in the very *rare* company (<u>indeed</u>!!) of three attractive (... and just as noticeably distressing) campus-age co-ed's. (((Sigh))). Well, I guess this is just one example which serves to validate that old well-known rule regarding the peculiar degree of "quirkiness" which drastically tints adult behavior after dark, which to, once again, re-state the old (and undeniably famous) principle, would be: "... The freaks only **come out** at night". In this actual moment, all I would have in offering to the audience a statement that legitimizes this old, well-known opinion concerning the personal habits which appear to publicly transpire after the event of sunset conveniently concludes itself would be: "Seeing <u>is</u> Believing". [!!!Issuing 'Emoticon' Alert!!! (} ; >)] ... Hah! Hah! Hah! Hah! Hah!

Partition <u>004</u>:

("... *If not for the winter, what would you call yourself, my friend?*") ... "<u>Ladies</u>" *and* "<u>Gentlemen</u>", welcome to the city of Minneapolis, Minnesota, or, as the surviving locals like to call it, "Mother Nature's Clinic on Human Refrigeration Research". (Hah! Hah! Hah! Hah!) ... Ever wonder why anyone

--()--
084
--()--

possessing an average blood-level reading of 98.6-degrees Fahrenheit would volunteer to live in a state featuring <u>every</u>thing the state of Alaska has *except* the "Eskimos" and the "Igloos"?! At least those choosing to reside in the "Land of the Midnight Sun" receive the opportunity each Winter to keep themselves reasonably secure from the outdoor elements by *iglooing* themselves inside of "family"-size fortresses of fresh, overnight snowfall. Personally, I've only been residing in the "Land of 10,000 Lakes" for seven-and-a-half weeks at this particular moment in time, yet *(already)* realize that the reason people choose to remain in this particular sector of the "Northern Plains"-region of the Midwestern US is, perhaps, because choosing to relocate to a "mild temperature"-climate would require the individual necessarily abandon the costly "Wintertime"-wardrobe assets which the person unquestionably spent several years and a high count-up of dollar-bills acquiring for himself as obvious "Wintertime" survival gear in this particularly frigid span of the USA's "Mining Belt"-region.

I remember visiting a specific "minimart"-outlet, here, on one "Summertime"-afternoon several years back during a visit to the state to see a particular aunt of mine residing locally who, unfortunately, has since left this world for the next one after, and hearing (upon that occasion at the actual "minimart"-outlet) the counter clerk state to me the uncomfortable prospect she faces in having to work indoors on such an ideal "Summertime"-afternoon considering the atmospheric conditions presently transpiring in the local geographic region. She told me, at the time, she deals with the uncomfortable scenario of being caught inside on a climatically preferable day by 1) refusing to look out the window, and by 2) *pretending* it's a cold, Winter's day outside.... Mmmmm?? Living in the state of Minnesota and *pretending* it's a cold "Wintertime"-afternoon is like being a dolphin and *pretending* to go for a quick dip in the Pacific Ocean. In other words, this particular convenience-outlet clerk chose to deliberately ruin what was an environmentally suitable "Summertime" day by convincing herself the morning weather report had had in its forecast a drastically different scenario for area residents to endure on that particular date with respect to the level of precipitation which we all could expect to pay witness to on the occasion at hand. We do have to necessarily endure a number of frigid, Wintertime afternoons in this particular state without needing to purposely deceive ourselves into assuming Winter's frost-bearing embrace has come to us at some moment in between the nighttime fireworks of the "Fourth of July" and the daylong backyard barbequing of "Labor Day".

But, she, at the convenience outlet on that particular instance, sought to indicate what it is, unfortunately, most Minnesota natives appear to suffer from, the *plague* which some (originally, born in the state) receive from their parents, and which others (originally, from out of state) acquire

only after residing in Minnesota over a lengthy term. Which is to say, even if there <u>isn't</u> a snow-ridden, "subzero"-level landscape to behold outside, with the ground-level layer of low-temperature air chilling each of us outdoors from "head to toe", the "typical" Minnesotan still sees to it to *pretend* Wintertime's ice-ridden wrath waits just outside the front door which he seeks to exit each morning (either, if leaving the house for work, or, as with the case of the young female "convenience"-outlet clerk, if arriving at the jobsite for the day's shift).

I suppose for those of us selecting to inhabit this particular state in the "Upper-Central" zone of the USA's Midwestern section, those frigid, Wintertime temperatures which come with the chilling, ice-heavy "Wintertime" days amount to a particular micro-environment which any True Minnesotan cannot seem to do without, or even forget about, if even *momentarily*, though the "Sun"-borne season of the Summer might quite well be very abundant around us all. For the typical Minnesotan, the Winter is to us like the "Paparazzi" is to the celebrity (e.g.'s, the film star, "TV"-star or "Pop"-music star) … in other words, it's something you will claim to despise, but it's also something you could not honestly *survive* without.

A "celebrity" who has no "Paparazzi" around him (… photographing him, harassing him, and pestering him) is, *obviously*, no longer a <u>genuine</u> celebrity. And, *likewise*, a Minnesotan, who isn't witnessing the presence of a frigid, "low temperature"-air oppressing the local environment which he unluckily just so happens to inhabit at the time (… chilling him, biting him, and freezing him) is, of course, no longer a <u>genuine</u> "Minnesotan".

A "celebrity" (i.e., the film star, "TV"-star or "Pop"-music star) is an individual who comes to believe he was born to enjoy the lights of the "Paparazzi", just like a true "Minnesotan" is an individual who comes to trust he was born for the sweeping winds of the frigid, ice-ridden "Wintertime"-season, here, in the "Northern Plains"-region of the USA's Midwestern section of states. Just as the "celebrity" would find himself to be quite unhappy without the "Paparazzi" around to bother him on a perdiem basis, the true "Minnesotan" would find himself to be just as unhappy without a frigid Wintertime season to, once again, ruthlessly submerge him in a layering of snowy "subzero"-level air. Case in point, once again, the apparent decision on the part of the "minimart"-outlet employee to deny herself the benefits of witnessing an atmospherically ideal Summertime afternoon, and to (instead) *pretend* Winter's snow-ridden arrival had already come and the frost-bearing season was in abundance around her.

Meaning, each time you venture outside the front door which you seek to exit each morning (if either venturing to the job or elsewhere in the area) on one of the cold, frost-ridden Wintertime afternoons soon to pay visit to the "Northern-Central"-sector of the Middle-States region, and the air automatically chills you, once again, from "head to toe", reminding you of where, *precisely*, on the USA's territorial grid of coordinates, you just so happen to reside on that particular occasion, start to smile … and prepare yourself for the "close-up" shot which "Mother Nature" 's private satellite camera is taking of you, and realize without days like these to bring a ground-level layer of "low temperature"-air to the particular zone which you reside in, you would no longer be able to call yourself a true "Minnesotan", would you?! … For the *Minnesota MetroReport Page*, I'm Ariq "Odious Arrival" Shoretempel, speaking to one and all from domestic confines found easily in the "Laurel Park"-sector of Minneapolis (Minnesota). And I certainly do hope to talk to you good folks again (next week, that would be, of course) in, yet, another "Weekending Edition" of the *Minnesota MetroReport Page*.… Goodbye to one and all, i.e., the *oh-so-near* and ever-loyal listenership at large!!

Tasting Droplets of the Unforgettable Rain

By
Adrien L. Montgomery
Cycle <u>006</u>:
"Even in its Mask, with its Ears, Eyes, Nose and Fangs Safely Unseen … the Wolf Can't Help But Drool!"

<u>UTA</u> <u>Directive</u> <u>VI</u>:
"Attention! Attention! 'Cititraxx^{STF}'-System Users Musn't Leave Their Trash Inside Of The Rail Compartment. Be Sure To Exit The Rail Compartment With Any Trash You Wish To Discard! Repeat, 'Cititraxx^{STF}'-System Users Musn't Leave Their Trash Inside Of The Rail Compartment. Be Sure To Exit The Rail Compartment With Any Trash You Wish To Discard!"
("<u>UTA</u>": <u>U</u>rban <u>T</u>ransit <u>A</u>uthority)

(-|<u>Calendar</u> <u>Date</u>: <u>MON</u>., <u>Aug</u>. <u>15, 1988</u>|-)
(Scenario: Two eleven-year-old boys are standing under a tree in the middle of a clearing which appears at the top of a low-standing hill next to a street which ends with opposing ["cul-de-sac"]-boundaries in the southern section of a ["('condominium')-tract"]-style residential estate in Santa Lucia, California.)

Boy "01": "Your mother's like a 'Cadillac™' limousine: big, black, and from Detroit."

Boy "02": "Your mother's like a 'high-speed' roller-coaster: everyone who hops aboard her has to hang on for dear life."
(XOX)

--()--
087
--()--

Adrien L. Montgomery
Tasting Droplets of the Unforgettable Rain
Official Imprint: "Dynamographx"

Boy "01": "Your mother's like the U.S. Army: she'll take any man right after the guy's left high school (with a 'failure to graduate') behind him."

Boy "02": "Your mother's like a subway station's turnstile: she wants men to absorb her impact just below the beltline."

Boy "01": "Your mother's like a hurricane: after she gets herself going, the state of Louisiana's all wet."

Boy "02": "Your mother's like a coffin: the man who's inside of her ain't ever gettin' up again."

Boy "01": "Your mother's like a boomerang: the man who tries to toss her away soon sees both of her legs rushing towards his head … at full-speed, I might add."

Boy "02": "Your mother's like an elevator: just push the right button and she starts to go down on you."

(Epilogue: The point of it all? … One child can always insult another child by implying the other child's mother is … "of questionable moral character", might we suggest [i.e., a "harlot" of sorts], and through such an assertion, due to early discoveries in the science of biogenetics, one can, hence, conclusively state that the child which the first child is insulting is, under scrutiny of easily obtainable physical evidence, the "**son** of a bitch".)

(-|Calendar Date: TUE., Nov. 25, 2003|-)

I'm standing up on the rooftop of the "Gottenburgh Building", one of several "storefront" business constructions which anyone can easily find up on Reddington Avenue, in the "Laurel Park" section of Minneapolis, which is a neighborhood just due south of the city's "Central Commerce District" (or its "Downtown"-section of acreage, that is). The "Gottenburgh Building" is, also, just two-and-a-half blocks to the south of the housing complex which I'm now residing in (i.e., "The 'Falconeer' Building", found on the southeast corner of Reddington Avenue and Courier Street), which is inside the "Laurel Park" community, as well. The first level, or "floor", of the "Gottenburgh Building" is a beautician's salon, I believe, a beauty "make over" shop serving many of the local female residents as regular patrons, known by regional inhabitants as "Queen Chloe's Parlor". The remaining properties lining the eastern side of Reddington Avenue are streetside outlets of one sort or another (e.g.'s, an "Oriental"-foods market, a store operating as a package-shipping and mail-receiving depot, a "Punk"-retailer

Adrien L. Montgomery
Tasting Droplets of the Unforgettable Rain
Original Year of Publication: 2026

selling music albums, T-shirts, posters, skateboards, etc., a hole-in-the-wall bar with its glossy, electrically-lit "neon" bottle-label designs in the frontside-window displaying the specific beer brands which the bar sells on tap, a little grocery store run by an Indian family ["subcontinent", that is], and an "East African" gaming room [card tables, I assume] which serves "Hot Chai" to its strictly male clientele, primarily Ethiopian and Somali immigrants, etc., etc.).

Yet, upon this one *particular* rooftop, there is, I've had the opportunity to note, a *vagrant* female, i.e., a homeless woman ("Theresa Heams", being the street urchin's name, if I am remembering reliably here), who makes a noble attempt each night at erecting a makeshift shelter for herself at the building's Reddington Avenue location. To my knowledge, the woman's just an area scavenger who's making camp on the roof of the "Gottenburgh Building" in order to avoid any overnight contact with local patrol officers who are known to pester residents choosing to nest themselves in the easily-seen, ground-level spaces around the urban-grade neighborhood.

"Hey! … Do you want a can of beer?" Theresa asks me, as she reclines against the roof area's perimeter wall at this one particular moment of the "graveyard"-shift which we're choosing to spend with each other atop the commercial structure's roof, i.e., its "open air"-level. She's already made herself "at home" tonight, I see, resting in a full-length sleeping bag, to stay, I assume, as comfortable (and as warm) as she possibly can atop the residential complex's frigid rooftop-level space until the morning arrives.

"No.… Thanks, anyway, 'Theresa'," I answer. "I don't need one at this *exact* moment. I'll take one later on, maybe.… If you still got any of 'em."

"Theresa" is a Caucasian female, who's twenty-four years in age, with "butterscotch"-blond hair (i.e., a "beach sand"-color of blond with light brown streaks through it, as highlights, I s'pose) which she keeps "swept up" in a neat "purse" above the back of her neck. She's always wearing knee-high leather horseback-riding boots, as if she's preparing to compete in some sort of equestrian contest *each* and <u>every</u> afternoon. [!!Issuing 'Emoticon' Alert!! (} ; >o] I've also come to be quite familiar with encountering this particular transient female while, in fact, the woman appears to be wearing a full palette of beautification treatments upon the tic-ridden face which this walking illustration of social refuse exhibits to the local population of area-inhabitants *each* and <u>every</u> day of the week.

I can see theatergoing couples crowding up the northern crosswalk at 16th Street and Reddington Avenue in order to make it to a performance hall that's on Rocolo Avenue, which is just one block to the east of the "Gottenburgh" 's rooftop, with the intent to attend a comedic "musical" production ("… Crying on the Inside", being its title, I believe) in the well-known "Laurel Park"-area auditorium, "The Old Showroom". I, "Ariq Zarkahn Shoretempel", note, for one, have (I do, here, gather) never—to date—been capable of discovering any delight whatsoever in what would be commonly known as the "THEATER" (i.e., stage dramas, musicals, the ballet, ensemble comedic productions, operas, "acrobatics"-exhibitions, demonstrations of magic, juggling acts, clowns in full costume, etc., etc., etc.), at any point in the current era, nor at any point in an earlier period of life. I, also, have no particular level of fondness whatsoever for that actual subset of citizens (male and female, *or*, young and old, alike) who have become, collectively, known to the world-at-large as the "Theatergoers", i.e., the local playhouse's regular round-up of reliable attendees, that would be.

Indeed.... *These* ... the insipid, pompous, elitist, and bourgeois "patrons of the stage", i.e., the "fans of the incandescent footlights", etc., etc.

This particular rooftop (at the top of the "The 'Gottenburgh' Building"), however, does serve an assortment of different purposes for those residing in (or for those merely choosing to casually pay visit to) the one corner of the "Laurel Park" residential development zone which Theresa and I conveniently inhabit. One ... it seems to serve our specific "biogeographic"-quadrant quite readily as a "dope den" for area "crack"-addicts, i.e., those belonging to that overtly unsavory urban "sociochemical" plague. [!!Issuing 'Emoticon' Alert!! (} : > (] Two ... the exact area's addicts-in-residence, apparently, see this particular housing structure's roof as a site that's acceptable for illegal pharmaceutical injections and as a crib which keeps this specifically criminal habit out of sight if considering the local "on duty" patrol personnel. Three ... local disciples of vagrancy, on occasion, return to the Gottenburgh's "rooftop"-level if for no other reason than to set an overnight "campfire" inside of an old tin oil-storage container in order to keep themselves safe from the infamously low nighttime air-temperature levels. Four ... frequently, young adults trek towards the tenancy house's roof-site for no other purpose than to consume "spirits" high in alcohol content (e.g.'s, Scotch "whisky", Irish whiskey, rye whiskey, Bourbon, or vodka) and to pass around the old "Peacepipe", i.e., the marijuana roll. *(And, without further ado, that is* ...) Five ... a variety of unsavory individuals choose to relocate themselves to the roof, if only for the moment, to use the Gottenburgh's open arena of floor space, seemingly, to escape the watch of the vigilant "Public Safety"-office employees who might, in fact, have good reason to meet up with possibly more than just a few of those belonging to this guilt-ridden variety of citywide-fugitives.

Perhaps, at one particular point in the past, Theresa may have become victim to one or more of the crack-addicts appearing atop the roof (a sort of makeshift opium parlor for local narcotics-users) in an unfortunate "crime case"-entry to the file-sheets which record updates on statistics concerning "Metro"-region incidents of "sexual assault"-crime. I.e., it's highly unsafe for a vagrant woman to select to lie asleep in a spot which any street addict ("... that's too **po'** for a **ho'** ", as the old expression states, i.e., "... that's too **poor** for a **whore**", that is) could easily gain access to during an overnight shift of hours.

Standing next to 'Theresa' on the housing location's roof, I, suddenly, catch sight (*and*, more alarmingly, <u>sound</u>) of an African-American male (being in age just 21 years), who is appearing to head south on Reddington Avenue's western sidewalk, right in between 16th Street (the asphalt road which's in back of him) and 17th Street (the asphalt road which's in front of him). The man appears to be performing a particular "Popmusic" anthem while merrily marching Reddington Avenue's western pedestrian path in the closing moments of Tuesday, November 25, 2003. (The wristwatch I'm currently wearing announces the time at this particular instant to be at just a handful of seconds after 11:30 p.m., C.S.T.) The adult "African-American" male offers up to all standing within the territorial limits of the soloist's range of voice-projection the very first verse of a familiar "Popmusic" tune (*"Last Friday Night's Affair"*, being the specific music track's actual title). The amateur vocalist's first outdoor recital fails, I do fear, to exhibit any true artistic abilities upon the performer's part, however, i.e., the street singer eats it, that is, and quite <u>sloppily</u>, too, I must, here, add!! [!!Issuing 'Emoticon' Alert!! (} : > (] The bold outdoor recitalist delivers to all caught inside the auditorial range of the proud songmeister's coarse oral output the subsequent series of lines originally appearing in the original recording's lead vocal track:

I've gotta far march out to the town's "Bar Park" tonight ...
*I'll search 'til I find a room brimming with **both** a high song and spirit.*
I'm gunna march 'til the doors of the "Bar Park" cross into view!
*Tonight, I'll **know** the spot that's got the right heart—indeed, I'll hear it.*
The past workweek's just a faint, ghostly, mist-hidden dream ...
*In just this one elapsing minute, I am, **at last**, alive again!*
The road I'm on tonight will lead me right to "Heaven's Stairs"!
I'll find the "The Brickstreet Cellar" and enter it through its door—
*Hear me sing in praise just **once**! In closing, what must I say? ... <u>"Amen"</u>!*

Theresa appears to be strongly at odds with respect to the man's decision to pollute the avenue's urban airspace with such an unacceptably crude tribute to the familiar " 'Pop' Radio" music anthem. The black pedestrian's song, the "a cappella" (i.e., "for-the-voice-only" composition) tune is, if I'm retrieving information on it correctly, an "Adult Rock"-favorite famous from a particular point in the late 1990's. The record's title, I do trust, is, once again, *"Last Friday Night's Affair"*, a track by an acoustical Rock act out of Orlando, Florida, who refer to the ensemble they, together, amount to as "Ghettoblaster Farm". The CD (... uhmmm, which I think I, at one point, had in my music "library" until lending it, regrettably, of course,

Adrien L. Montgomery

Tasting Droplets of the Unforgettable Rain

Official Imprint: "Dynamographx"

to an acquaintance residing in the particular "Lawn and Garden"-district which I held tenancy in, as well, through that one specific span of time) is, by title, "Seeing the Immortal Church Burning". The single itself (i.e., *Last Friday Night's Affair"*), if I'm able, once again, to correctly recall at this point, became a widely popular selection request which "Rock" and "Pop" radio channels along the dial would continually re-cue for constant airplay throughout 1998's "Summertime"-era calendar months (June, July, August and [last ... yet not least] September).

I am, at this specific moment, remembering an encounter with a local "Hippie" male (... indeed, in <u>these</u> parts, no less, i.e., the "Northern Plains"-sector of the USA's Midwestern table of states, that is) which came about on the floor area of the "roofspace" which "The 'Gottenburgh' Building" provides to its occasional guests—yet, on one particular moment at around "Midnight" not that long ago. The young specimen of countersocial anti-authoritarian activism (he did appear to look around 24 years in age at the time), on that particular overnight-shift of the "after hours"-era, makes a confession to me concerning an occasion occurring earlier that evening. Due to its specific notableness on the police squad's crime-patrolling scope, he appears to be sure he's got himself caught up in a criminal incident and, also, in, quite possibly, a specific "felony"-level charge, I s'pose. ("Trafficking With The Intent To Sell", I'd venture here to sate.) The "Hippie" talks of attending a bustling house party in the initial hour of nightfall and of crashing its gates with a "kilo" of cocaine in a "quartsize"-storage bag which he brought with him to the "addiction pit". He next tells me the cops (i.e., the "M.P.D.") hit that particular residential address after hearing "call girls" were in attendance and crimes of "solicitation" were transpiring upon the premises of that specific "suburban"-zone residence.

The "Hippie" (i.e., the relic of 1960's-era countercultural adolescent isolationism) says to me that he ran from the gathering site upon hearing police squadcars rolling up to the house, but, he, carelessly, left the scene of peace and good cheer without recovering the kilosize bag of "coke" which he took with him to the "not-so-inside-the-law" party of "NextGeneration" derelicts, outsiders, and outcasts occurring at the residential property. The "Hippie Kid" ("The Lost Orphan of the Age of Aquarius") is afraid people at the party did **not** hesitate to designate him, the anti-societal saboteur, as the sole proprietor and solitary consumer of the illegal, yet, widely-known, agent of instant anesthetization. *"I ... I ... I ... knew the probable consequences of my behavior and I ... I ... failed to factor into the equation any damaging possibilities that such actions upon my part could most likely produce tonight,"* the Hippie says to me in a frantic moment of on-the-spot openness. *"Y'know what, man? ... I'm afraid I'm gunna go to jail tonight."* The Hippie nervously consumes a few mouthfuls of faucet water from a red floor-rinsing hose that's running from an iron release-pipe near the roofspace perimeter's safeguarding wall.

The Hippie, I'm guessing, made use of the building's rusty "fire escape" ladder to ascend the Gottenburgh's outside brickwork and crawl to its "terrace"-style overnight public recreating venue. (Yet, one never knows with these "hippies"—**damn** weed-eating radicals! ... Rather, he simply may have chosen to powder himself with a pocketful of "Pixie" dust, i.e., the opiate of the flying "sprites", thereby, enabling himself to float up to the building's upper deck without use of the iron ladder altogether!) He expunges any need for extra water (which the existing flight from local law enforcement personnel apparently produces inside of him at this point) and shuts off the roof area's running "utility" hose. He stares at me blankly, as if I were just standing there to offer what might be just a marginal degree of assistance which could help to remedy the circumstances which the member of the anti-establishmentarianist microsociety (i.e., the "Hippie Nation") currently finds himself having to deal with. Unfortunately for the particular addict-at-large, he appears to have no time on his hands as of late to campaign for the passage of liberal, penalty-free "marijuana"-legislation, which could adequately <u>de</u>criminalize public use of the infamous, haze-producing cannabis leaves.

"Well ...," the Hippie says, sighing in order to disrupt an otherwise empty and lengthy pause in interpersonal communication which is still transpiring between the two of us aboard the "after dark" roof-level refuge. *"... I gotta get back to the street-level, y'know. I can't—I can't—stay up here all night. I know the cops'll be searching this place later on.... But, thanks for listening to me, man,"* the Hippie says to me, just prior to crossing the empty floorspace of the building's highest surface to get to the iron siderail that descends the side of the "Gottenburgh" building's 90-degree face to permit anyone fleeing endangerment found atop the building to safely set foot upon the alleyway running parallel to "16th Street", the (['moto-traffic'])-route set alongside the large "Laurel Park"-construction project.

I see the "hippie" excuse himself from the building's roof-level "open air" club and initialize the steep, yet, steady drop to the ground-level asphalt by using the rusting iron "fire escape"-ladder which extends from the roof to the pedestrian-grade streets on the urban acreage running alongside the building which I, regrettably, find myself standing upon at this moment in the era transpiring after the advent of nightfall.... "Hippies"?? ... "Poster Boys" of a heart-felt nostalgia for the "1960's"-era of modern history *or* the lingering debris of an ever-fading period of antisocietal post-adolescent activism? ... You decide, O legion of loyal, *ever-so-close* associates. (... Ha! Ha! Ha!)

But, <u>here</u>, back atop the private, rent-free roofspace of the "Gottenburgh"-complex, Theresa stands beside me on the floor of the building's outdoor rooftop arena and begins to mumble incoherently while an expression of uneasiness begins to appear across the face which the community the female vagrant resides in apparently selects to routinely ignore on a perdiem basis, I've no other choice than to assume. The transient female starts conversing on one particular subject of high concern to both of us—the biographical profile on a recently-arriving female tenant residing, at present, in a housing establishment at the southern end of Reddington Avenue. "D'ya know her?" the vagabond lady asks me. "I see her around a lot. She told me that her parents were immigrants from 'Belarus' ... and that they were <u>Jewish</u>. I think she's the daughter of Belarusian **Jews.**"

"Yeah, I've seen her around lots of times," I answer, standing next to Theresa atop the Gottenburgh's outdoor "after hours" amphitheater. "Y'know ... I gotta tell ya, I'd like to put a burning torch to the synagogue that that one's got on her.... *Oh*, boy! You can <u>believe</u> me on that one!!"

"What??" the homeless woman asks, beside me in the unlit urban auditorium. The moon itself appears as the only audience member in attendance at the tenement-district's after-dark, nightside showroom, the "Amphitheatre-in-the-Lunarlight". "You'd like her to *'<u>Burn</u> <u>in</u> <u>Sin</u> <u>for</u> <u>God</u>'?!* ... What's all of that mean?! Are you a '**Christian**' or something? ... Is that why you don't like her?!"

"No ... I'm not a <u>Christian</u>," I answer the woman, while the two of us stand beside each other atop the Gottenburgh's almost vacant upper-level "open air" stage. "I'm just saying what you said—that the girl's **Jewish**! A 'synagogue' is a temple of Jewish rites, a spiritual sanctuary, of sorts. I'm just saying she's a sizzlin' <u>hot</u> 'Heebwoman'.... That's all!"

"All I know is that, **one**, she gives me $5.00 *every* time I run into her. ("That's pretty cool, huh?" Theresa says, as we wait patiently inside the hobo female's "Back-to-Basics" private roof-level estate.) "And, **two**, I ain't gotta do <u>nuthin</u>' for it! It's just $5.00 for **free**! That's *really* cool, huh? She's really bitchin', ain't she?"

Theresa roots out a handful of "condoms" (i.e., "prophylactics", "rubbers", "Christmas stockings", "['Snacksize']-fridge bags", "['Quarter']-rolls", etc., etc.) from a traveler's pack found among the assortment of items which she keeps in an upright push-cart earmarking its owner as a "drifter" afloat in the world which she, *not-so-happily*, inhabits and holds the almost appetizing abundance of bright, foil-kept, easy-to-open candy-wrappers up for me, tonight's client on hand, to examine. "Which one d'ya like?" she asks as an uneasy stare seems to almost commit itself to remaining upon her pale, yet, arguably appealing and unjoyful face. I choose just one of the several "safe sex" accessories which the derelict female offers to me while the both of us occupy the rooftop retreat atop "The 'Gottenburgh' Building", eagerly expecting me to outfit myself with a particular pocketsize protection tool. She places the unchosen, little "foil"-

paper packets back into the carry-all bag which she keeps with the rest of the "Roofsite Survivalist" gear she's got in her upright cart of worldly possessions.

The particular "roofspace" arrangement which I've been keeping with "Theresa Heams" occurs according to a pre-chosen regularity equal to one episode of "After Hours"-interaction *every* month of the calendar year. With the specific episode of intercourse in question transpiring at one point during the monthlong timespan's final workweek. (I.e., the specific occasion of rooftop "sexercise" [i.e., "sex" + "exercise" (ha! ha! ha!)] with the vagrant woman which I choose to gleefully participate in occurs as an end-of-the-month ritual.) I do, I will admit, always offer the building's roof-happy maiden a total of $25.00 in compensatory benefits for enlisting herself in the voluntary, permonth, outdoor "Peace-on-Earth" practice that occurs, in earnest, in the name of Human Goodwill *and* community spirit.... Trust me, here, O *ever-faithful* assembly of amiable admirers.

I split open the corner of the "protective aid"-packet and open up its reflective, foil-paper wrapping. I, then, withdraw the coinsize roll of elastic plastic material that's neatly kept inside of it. I.e., that little "slip on"-suit of lightweight nocturnal combat armor. Well, "ladies and gentlemen" ... here we **go**!! [!!Issuing 'Emoticon' Alert!! (} : >)]

Tasting Droplets of the Unforgettable Rain

By
Adrien L. Montgomery
<u>Cycle 007</u>:
Fresh "Cutting Room" Footage: Tyrannosaurus Sex (... Or, a Day in the Life of the "Daemonio")

<u>UTA Directive VII</u>:
"Attention! Attention! ... The 'Railbus^{AI}' Will Remain At This Station Until Transit Central O.K.'s Our 'Go-Ahead'! Repeat, The 'Railbus^{AI}' Will Remain At This Station Until Transit Central O.K.'s Our 'Go-Ahead'!"
("<u>UTA</u>": <u>U</u>rban <u>T</u>ransit <u>A</u>uthority)

<u>Television Network Announcer</u>:
(<u>At the Start of the Episode's Broadcast</u> ...)
"Ladies <u>and</u> gentlemen, from the Inter-Satellite Television Supercasting Service's 'All-World ArenaVision^{STF} Park' in Glendale, California ... in 'Stage Number Ten' on the First Floor of the International Broadcasting Center's Superplex ... in the heart of the Nation's Television Capital ... it's 'America After Dark'! ... And <u>here</u> ... once again, it's your host *and* mine ... Ariq Shoretempel!!"

--()--
095
--()--

Adrien L. Montgomery

Tasting Droplets of the Unforgettable Rain

Official Imprint: "Dynamographx"

<u>Ariq Zarkahn Shoretempel</u>:

"Thank you!! Thank you!! Welcome, one and all, to Glendale, California, or, as we at 'AAD' like to call it … the Southland's answer to 'Shangri-La'. ((audience laughs)) … 'But, seriously, folks …' ((host pauses)) … Today, the Pentagon announced more American casualties in the 'War in Iraq'. Unfortunately, ISTSS's new Thursday night lineup was actually counted as one of them. ((audience begins to jeer in response)) … All right, all right, just settle down a bit, OK? The CIA now claims they're almost 100% certain of where Osama bin Laden is secluding himself! Several local residents will report they've witnessed the suspect working behind the counter of a 'RedBannerUSA^{STF}' outlet in the city of Las Vegas, Nevada. ((audience laughs approvingly)) … Hey! Did you hear the news about 'Beverly Hills' today?? Apparently, local residents have now agreed to spy upon wealthy Arabs who currently reside in that particular city. People in Beverly Hills are, un- fortunately, now living in fear of their Arab neighbors, thinking the Middle-Easterners might be a part of some new 'al-Qaeda' cell. Can you imagine <u>that</u>? You and your family just move to Beverly Hills from the United Arab Emirates and you've got the cast of 'The Widowmaker' hiding in your backyard with a 'zoom lens' camera and a cellphone. ((audience laughs with delight)) … Apparently, even in San Francisco, local residents are wary over any new possible terrorist attacks that could soon potentially occur. A new city ordinance requires <u>every</u> gay dance club in San Francisco to stop playing the song 'Magic Carpet Ride'. ((audience responds with laughter and mild jeering)) … Hey! Did You hear the Prime Minister of Greece is visiting the White House this week? It seems that Bush told the Greek PM that their meeting would occur in the office at 1600 Pennsylvania Avenue. After the Greek premier heard that the 'Primetime' dramatic series 'Office at 1600' had been moved from its original broadcasting spot by the HomeVision^{UE} Corporation, he got back on his plane (assuming the meeting with Bush had been cancelled) and flew back home to Athens in disappointment. ((audience responds with large laughter and scant jeering)) … All right, all right, everyone. Just calm down, OK? …"

(-|<u>Calendar</u> <u>Date</u>: <u>SUN</u>., <u>Nov</u>. <u>30</u>, <u>2003</u>|-)

I'm standing in the open courtyard of the "True Minneapolite Church of Christ's Cross", a Protestant "house of prayer" which stands on the south side of Eleventh Street and appears directly in between Hennenburgh Boulevard, the thoroughfare to its west, and Blainboro Avenue, the commuter-track to its east. The Christian communal site sits (squarely) in the middle of what tonight, at any rate, appears to be a dark, noiseless, urban-built block. This particular setting of "New Testament" faith and fellowship stands at the southwestern edge of the Urbanzone's recently re-built "Central Commerce District", or its "Downtown" acreage, the particular

--()--
096
--()--

backdrop being a virtual beehive of daytime activity occurring in Minneapolis throughout the workweek.

On the southeastern corner of Tenth Street and Hennenburgh Boulevard, there's a Digital Clockboard[ISS] that rests against the northern face of an exterior wall belonging to the "Millennium III Farmhouse Insurance[ESU]" building. I just chose to walk past the giant time-readout screen roughly 10 minutes ago and could see the Digital Clockboard[ISS] announce the regional time at that instant as being at 12:05 a.m., C.S.T., i.e., it is—at this particular moment—still within the early minutes just after 'midnight', O *ever-so-close* associates and outdoor enthusiasts.

Due to the almost "polar" temperatures the eastern-central sector of the state is experiencing on this specific night, the "avenues" and "streets" are absent with respect to the usual foot traffic which the area's prime commercial "real estate"-zones would typically host during the overnight hours. (… The bar patrons, the clubgoers, the "out-of-state" arrivals offboarding "Frontiersman[AI]" Diesel-coaches [i.e., Interstate roadliners], the dope-vendors, the vagrants, and all constituting the consuming end of the local narcotics market, who are, at this hour, just regaining awareness after the once-a-week, opiate-heavy, marathon spell of unconsciousness, etc., etc.)

About 30 minutes ago, on KDHG "The Dog House" 93.9 FM, the DJ (i.e., the one and <u>only</u> "Bizzie Dixx") read off tonight's temperature forecast at 0-degrees F, with a mild, constant snow shower and a potential of -12-degrees F (with a "windchill factor" of -27-degrees F as the "arctic" extreme that's set to become the overnight session's absolute temperature floor). Due to the public's apparent decision to abandon the asphalt gridwork of the city's northern-central section (its prime urban district for nightspots), I do believe I will not, tonight, need to concern myself regarding any interference from unwelcome onlookers or pedestrians who just might so happen to come by. [!!Issuing 'Emoticon' Alert!! (} ; >)] In the cold urban coordinates I am, at present, occupying, the air itself is too still to authentically originate anything but the lifeless simulation of dead silence at the particular moment, old friends and faithful followers on hand.

I gaze up at the sky passing me overhead and I notice a gray, fading cloak … appearing quite similar to the top layer of ocean water in a moment just prior to the arrival of a seismic, rupturing sea storm. To be truthful, I'm incapable of ever recalling a single moment, prior to this one in particular, that is, in which I could detect in the atmosphere around me a level of easiness matching the degree of peacefulness which apparently permeates the environment I'm in at this specific moment in time. The stillness which exists at present inside of me appears almost as a pool of inner emotional quiet which, I must admit, I (1) have, until this point, never before known, and, I (2) have, until this day, perhaps, taught myself to perceive as impossible to ever humanly encounter. (((Sigh)))…. Mmmmm??

I, again, do believe the actions which I desire to see myself initialize at this specific location (inside the due course of time) will certainly be secure from the watch of any possible onlookers which the area in question would usually include at this particular hour after the arrival of nightfall. With the prospect of an interruption no longer a concern, I am certain I need not possess any lingering fears due to a choice on my part to pursue the particular course of behavior I, at present, do predict I am about to embark upon, O *but-so-close* associates and companion-like cohorts.

I'll note, here, I must be decisive in the path of action which I adopt to-night, seeing myself, at once, as possessing the necessary mindset which the specific exercise will require, and, also, as being, basically, invulnerable to any harm which the activities I'll attempt to complete at some point soon would ordinarily cause me.

There exists in the soundless urban airspace, a stillness that starts to assume an almost intolerable stench, with the odor itself expanding outwards through the surrounding environment, like a weighty panic which the streets are beginning to detect as a highly intrusive burden.

At once, a seizure of adrenaline, as if an ignition charge due to a sudden injection of Diesel fuel, enthralls me … inciting me with enthusiasm over the incidents which might soon occur inside the dark floorspace of the Protestant church's open courtyard. A tinge, albeit in the faintest of nocturnal winds, of doubt (or, a moment of merely being nerve-ridden to a degree or two), at once, washes over me, prompting me to pause but for a brief point … in order to question the exact purpose of my visit to this specific churchyard tonight.

I'll not set aside this particular period in time as a moment in which to report on the actual intentions which I have regarding this early morning outing, for any such admission of an agenda at this minute would amount to words which would needlessly expend both my time and yours as well, my old friends. The personal "stakeout" which I'm attempting to conduct at this precise location amounts to what is basically a demonstration in the art of nocturnal surveillance, a discipline which I've taught myself to excel in over the past several months, I have to admit, here, folks.

Sexual assault, i.e., criminal sex, is a particularly *human* pursuit which I trust I am actually capable of (at some point) achieving and I believe myself to be adept in this specific matter, actually thinking this for what would appear to be a substantial amount of time pre-dating and leading into the specific Autumnal morning I witness before me at the moment in the churchyard I, here, do stand in. Due to the lengthy term of self-instruction which I chose to diligently put myself through, today's rendezvous with the mandate existing in a pre-spoken and prophetic tablet comes after a period of discomforting inactivity … and <u>impatience</u>!

I see the peculiar acoustics existing inside the audible impatience of the outdoor airspace I'm standing in at this moment are uniquely solid, as if the night sky itself is anxious to see what is set to soon unfortunately transpire inside the forward "patio" area—here at this house of Christian instruction and guidance in the Urbanzone's "Downtown"-District.

I am, here, at this specific set of urban coordinates, my "wolfpups", to determine if the occurrence of "criminal sex" is capable, in one's life, of imparting to the individual predator in question a particular degree of true enlightenment (i.e., "cosmic knowledge" or "spiritual wisdom", that is), if you, my class of trusting listeners, do, at this point, remember the "Philosophical Perspective on the Process of 'Self-Enlightenment' " which I did present to you on an earlier occasion.

I'm ready, I trust, to launch the one particular exercise in barbarism (or, primalistic ritual) which I'm imagining (in this specific instance of time) upon, alarmingly, encountering the arrival of an appropriate human target. (One that would amount to that famous and, yet, most tragic type—the unwitting, and, regrettably, unwilling female.) [!!Issuing 'Emoticon' Alert!! (} ; >)]

Due to the "Thermoscale^{ISS}"-measuring instrument presently reading the levels on the latent energies which I, at this point, trust I do possess, I believe I'm safe in assuming I will not object to completing the specific path of actions I've set up for myself to perform inside this hidden space tonight. I'm like a leopard, hungrily, yet, noiselessly lurking … expecting the antelope to begin grazing in the long shoots of fragrant savannah grass (on the sun-swept, open plain found atop the interior acreage of the habitat-rich continent officially known as "Africa"). Yet, it is only the stalks of the soil-borne roots themselves in which I keep myself hidden while monitoring the feeding animal, the clueless object of the merciless appetite emerging within me at the specific moment with an unrelenting rise.

Yet, I must admit to all, I do possess, at this point, not so much as even the mildest tone of that mortal, self-sustaining fear which surfaces inside of anyone about to enter a risky combat scenario, to express myself with such terms, if I can at this point, my comrades and ever-so-constant companions. The fear in each veteran hunter … that instinct that ignites in the rear boundaries of the brain, causing the potential predator to pause before placing himself in what might be a predicament endangering him to an unsafe extent, possibly. I must confess, to one and all, that I am, at this precise instance, inside the solid grip of a specific grade of happiness that I cannot remember knowing at any particular point over the past several weeks (… if such a level of inner satisfaction has, in fact, been able to occur within me at any moment at all over the course of the life I've had no other choice than to live in this world).…. Mmmmm??

Peeking towards the sky, I watch a muscular cloud float towards the southeast, like a large cargo boat carrying millions of liters of liquid in its "moisture"-storage spaces, to a drier region of terrain anxious for the merciful inundation of skywater. Bursting winds accelerate through the branches of surrounding trees, allowing the leaves to tremble in silken whispers, a noise not unsimilar to the lapping sound which wavelets make in the shallow waters at the shoreline, permitting the tree-leafs to shift like soft chimes in the street's cold, urban air currents. I do, here, catch the flight-track of a beige sparrow as it silently shoots through the blank airspace just above Eleventh Street's vacant asphalt lanes.

A taxicab (the "vanwagon", with the words " 'Star of the North[AI]' Cabservice" across the large passenger door on its driver's side) cautiously crosses Eleventh Street at its intersection with Blainboro Avenue and heads south, perhaps traveling to the Minneapolis/St. Paul International Airport.

Today, Saturday, ({ : >), I woke up, if I'm remembering correctly, at 7:24 a.m., C.S.T., and I ate a couple of Daughter Jeanette[SLTF] "Breakfast Rolls" (the item being a microwavable breakfast sandwich having a sausage patty, a "scrambled" egg, and a cheese slice between two halves of a large croissant roll). I also had about 24 fluid-ounces (or, just over 700 milliliters) of Gulfshore Groves[ISS] "Old Floridian" orange juice, which I put into a large beermug right before gradually sipping my way through the flavorful, "punch"-tasting refreshment.

I, then, had to walk to the nearest "RedbannerUSA[STF]" outlet (that's a "minimart"-system that's prominent, here, in the state of Minnesota and in other states found in the upper-central sector of the Midwestern region of the US, i.e., North & South Dakota, Nebraska, and Iowa), in order to purchase one 1-liter bottle of "Crystalwater[ISS]" Diet Lemon soda and one 32-oz. carton of "Pinball Land[STF]" fruit candies.

For lunch, later in the day, I had a "chopped" tuna salad on potato bread sandwich, Vernon's[ESU]-brand "Ripple Ranch" potato chips with a container of Vernon's[ESU]-brand "Borderland Onion" dipping sauce. At dinnertime, which I had right before 7:00 p.m., I ate about four slices (which would amount to _half_) of an "Endzone Village[SLTF]" pizza (a large "Italian Deluxe", an option featuring "steamed vegetables" as its plate of "topping"-items). Tonight, I chose to avoid eating the usual "dessert" after enjoying Dinnertime's menu, however. That is, I choose to reserve the hunger I have for sweet eating options until a particular point in time that's soon to occur, old acquaintances, in these, the late, noiseless hours after nightfall's reliable arrival. [!!Issuing 'Emoticon' Alert!! ({ : >)]

Oh, yet thank each star in the Heavens, I, at once, do!! But, in an instant, though, I do see a potential human target entering the unlit belt of parking spaces which runs alongside the Christian prayer house's eastern property limit.... *"And, lo, the footman came and, thus, he chose to place the _first_ sacrificial female on the altar as a gift to 'Wisdom', a tribute from the warlord emergent in him, a soul irrevocably sworn to abide by an oath of loyalty to Enlightenment itself!"*

The female I see, a "Latina" woman, walks with intent to the car awaiting its driver's return, the lone automotive machine in the southeastern corner of the religious service venue's block-size sector of asphalt terrain. The female marches herself through the "guest parking"-zone, the one human in transit upon the surface which her personal "moto-vehicle" rests patiently upon, the small black "ragtop" (a 2004 "X-Lyne^{UE} 'Team VIII' Q-Series 'Equator^{STF}' ") that sits in the shadows made by the skeleton-like figures of the leafless, "out of season" Birch trees. (It is, yet again, "Autumn-time", here, in the USA's "Northern Plains"-region, folks.)

I can assume, safely, I s'pose, that there would, apparently, be—at this point—no one else inside of adequate viewing range concerning anyone just happening to, momentarily, set eyes upon the courtesy parking corridor outside the house which the Good Shepherd's flock returns to *each* and every Sunday morning to receive reliable guidance against the potential hazards which the world, at times, offers to us all. I do, however, acknowledge, friends, the opportunity is at hand, if I choose to assign myself to it, to pursue criminal sexual conduct on the particular occasion which presents itself this morning in the church's guest vehicle lot at this specific interval. [!!Issuing 'Emoticon' Alert!! ({ : >)] I must, at this time, I realize, maintain control over the psychomechanical reaction that's accelerating through the neurochemical network of nerve-channels which quickly ignite themselves instantaneously inside of me. But, I'm already starting to twitch with fits and tics of a psychopathic hypersexual force ... in anticipation of the highly *anti*social activities which are soon to occur on this acre of sacred Christian soil, in the northeastern section of our vibrant urban center's primary footage of retailing and dining.

The Latina female, a pleasant Hispanic specimen, I'd suggest, if I must, here, report to the audience at hand on such immaterial matters at this moment, arrives at the new ragtop (the 2004 "X-Lyne^{UE} 'Team VIII' Q-Series 'Equator^{STF}' ") that's alone atop the parking surface's newly-built and odor-rich black asphalt-built flooring.

There is, if I'm remembering accurately, a well-known slogan *("Always Come Prepared ...")*, or words vaguely similar to these, which, perhaps, the company known solely by the name of "Boy Scouts of America" uses as a corporate motto that is, also, I trust, taken as a personal oath of good citizenship among the youngsters in its loyal ranks found quite frequently across the USA's "coast to coast" (and further afield) terrain. I, Ariq, never having worn a "Scouting" uniform in childhood, nonetheless, do solemnly swear by the famous fraternal organization's long-beheld rule of responsible conduct. I am, I do believe, quite "ready" to guide myself through the particular series of physical "stress tests" which I must perform inside this lot of "Protestant" Metro-central land tonight in order to initialize the program of spiritual "self-enrichment" which I'm attempting to ultimately achieve graduate-level stature in…. Remember the "Philosophical Perspective on the Process of 'Self-Enlightenment' ", my eager-to-learn litter of leopard-kittens?!

I've got, hidden safely, inside my jacket's inner chest pockets the following assortment of urban "Sexcrime"-survivalist tools: 1) a "FineCrafters^AI" boxcutting knife with a 25-millimeter blade, 2) an aluminum canister that contains 100 grams of pepperspray, and 3) a set of large stainless steel interrogation cell, inmate-immobilizing heavy-duty wristcuffs. [!!Issuing 'Emoticon' Alert!! (} ; >)]

With an outdoor temperature dropping to -12-degrees Fahrenheit, and with a negligible, almost unnoticeable snowfall the ceiling of precipitating clouds overhead anxiously rids itself of, while moist flakes of winter's arriving weather softly collect themselves upon the flat, stone-built floor of the church's shadow-ridden courtyard patio, I let myself respire noisily—inhaling and, emotively, exhaling … to prepare myself for the ordeal of maturation which I must at once undergo upon the specific site of Christ's Sunday assemblies wherein I do presently stand. I reach into my jacket's inner left chest pocket and conveniently withdraw the FineCrafters^AI boxcutting blade. The well-built utility knife (ordinarily put to use in cutting construction tape, opening cardboard packages, shredding paper shopping bags, cutting boxboard-cartons, e.g., one for a 12-pk. of 12-oz. cola cans, etc., etc.) is in its light green aluminum grip-case and features a switch along its top edge that lets you produce and retract the 25-millimeter stainless steel cutting blade which the hardware instrument permits its user to conveniently access on demand. I grip the knife's light green aluminum casing and use my thumb to slide the switch upwards along the handle's top edge in order to expose the razor-like boxcutting blade that's inside the lightweight, protective aluminum shoe.

I begin to walk (inaudibly, that is) towards the potential human target, the Latina woman, appearing to be about "23" (in years of age), as she stands in quiet isolation beside the black ragtop sitting at the southeastern corner of the all but noiseless parking surface, the 2004 "X-Lyne^UE 'Team VIII' Q-Series 'Equator^STF' ".

I step with extreme caution towards the attractive Latina female, using genuine restraint so as to ensure I do not make any detectable sounds that would forewarn (or alarm) an unsuspecting woman as to the fact that an assailant is approaching—one who just so happens to arrive with a particularly lethal knifing instrument in hand. I'm walking unnoticeably up to the victim herself, still certain she, at this point, is clueless as to the predicament about to pay visit to her particular path in the world, i.e., the circumstances indicating an assailant is selecting her as a potential "statistic" to instantly appear in "police file"-records compiling "up to date"-

data on incidents of urban "sexual assault"-crime occurring in the Minneapolis "Metroregion". I (at last) come upon the female Latina (an action transpiring with no detectable warning whatsoever), seizing her slightly-built left shoulder with one hand, while (with the other) pushing the safe edge of the box-knife's blade against the space of exposed "Latina" flesh that's open to view and to the cold moonlit air as well, i.e., the spot appearing on the right side of her delicate neck, a neck still pulsating at the prominent arterial vessel which carries blood to the woman's unworrisome brain at this particular moment in time.

But, in half the time necessary to complete the flexing of a heart already accelerating due to a sudden, alarming danger, the victim gasps loudly in response to the troubling demands which I've, at once, here, made upon her time, attempting, in a state of alertness, to turn to me to face the nuisance daring to harass her on what had been merely a typical (and, most likely, safe) road-trip back home. Just to be on the cautious side, I pressure the woman's left shoulder with a more anxious assertion of strength, attempting to make the female aware as to the exact degree of misfortune which she, at this specific moment, seems to have finally caught up with in the world we're all here to quite happily inhabit together. ("… Oh, why?!")

"**Don't** turn around, *hermanita!*" I say to the onsite exhibition of what the Hispanic man (i.e., the "Meximerican"-type) receives as a partner, companion, and helpmate in life. (… Ha! Ha! Ha!) "**Don't** even *think* about screaming—got it?!" I am, with a particularly high level of forcefulness, seizing the handsome woman, who will soon, with my help, encounter the nightmare which the stars illuminating the Earth from the skies overhead chose to tragically place upon her "lifepath" on the day which the Hispanic female was *necessarily* born—if I can, here, but offer a modest opinion on the particular matter itself…. Ha! Ha! Ha!

"We're walking back to the church's front deck, okay?" I glare at the Latina female, who, I've come to note, seems, actually, to have a gentle smile on her face—a face that seems to genuinely brighten with a little help from the after-midnight air which we both (under a moon brimming with lunarborn light above) are breathing. "Let's **go**! Start *walk*ing! I re-secure the tense hand-grip I've got on the lady's left shoulder and continue to keep the blade's "safe" (i.e., <u>non</u>-cutting) edge against the ribbons of straining muscle tissue which run along the right side of the woman's neck.

"**Remember**, keep your trap shut, *muchacha!*" With the care-free Hispanic female coming along (so far, held well in hand), I return to the secure space found in the Protestant sermon hall's shadow-dark forward entry court.

"**Don't** even *think* of running, *mujera!* … This boxblade's still anxious to draw forth fresh <u>female</u> blood!" I find, for the two of us, a safe spot on the floor of the open reception yard next to the assembly house beheld en masse by the "Flock of the Lord" crowd *each* and <u>every</u> Sunday morning, a particular space well hidden by trees standing in round plots of fresh "nursery"-depot soil which appear in a deliberate pattern that runs along the large concrete "churchyard"-deck region.

The apparently compliant "Mexicana"-woman is standing atop the spacious cement floor of the pastor house's eastern entry area in a well-cut women's business-suit (wearing a blouse, a jacket, a knee-length skirt, hosiery, and heels).

"Hispanicamerican <u>Female</u>":

Why are you doing **this** to me?! Do you want a <u>date</u>?! We can drive back to my house?? My car's just over there … in the parking lot, y'know?? It's the black "soft top".

"<u>Sexcrime Assailant</u>":

Are you **crazee**?? You want **me** to get into a car and drive with **you** back to your goddamn <u>house</u>?! Do you think I'm <u>stoopid</u>?? Just **shut** <u>up</u>, remember, *senorita?!*

"Hispanicamerican <u>Female</u>":

Why do you want to do **this**?? I've never done anything to <u>you</u>?? Maybe you are angry because of *some*thing, huh? But it's not <u>me</u> you are angry at! I have done <u>nothing</u> to you, <u>sir</u>!

"<u>Sexcrime Assailant</u>":

Just keep it good and closed, *"chiquita".* I've got pepperspray and wrist-cuffs inside my jacket's inner pocket … just in **case** I need them. You'll <u>do</u> what I want you to <u>do</u>, *got it?!*

"Hispanicamerican <u>Female</u>":

If we have to do this, sir, <u>not</u> at a church, OK, sir? We can just go back to **my** house. I just live over in the " 'MetroWest' District"-area. It'll just take a quick "ten minute"-drive and we are there, yes?? Just wait another "ten minutes", yes? Is that good, <u>sir</u>?!

"<u>Sexcrime Assailant</u>":

Better still, I'll give you my name and address and you can stop by my house sometime next week when you're available to do so. That sounds even more convenient than the car ride, doesn't it? In *fact*, you can bring the cops with you and I'll just put myself in these handcuffs when the "pigs" arrive. Saves 'em the trouble of bringin' and extra pair of cuffs themselves, I say … all right??

"Hispanicamerican <u>Female</u>":

Y'know, what you are doing to me is a **criminal** act! Also, it is a <u>sin</u> in the eyes of "**God**". Of course, we're at a <u>church</u>, if I can remind you, <u>sir</u>? It's not too late to stop this and just turn around, y'know?! I'll pray for you, <u>sir</u>! Let's pray together, that the "Good Lord" gives you the wisdom to stop this **horrible** sin against "God's Embassy" in the world.

--()--
104
--()--

<u>"Sexcrime Assailant"</u>:

I'll decide what's a "**sin**" against *"God's Embassy"*, you motherfucking <u>Mexican</u> "whorelady". Keep talkin' and I'll use this boxcutting blade to cut out the tongue you got in that *enchilada*-loving mouth, all right, you <u>Mexican</u> "slut-and-a-half"?!! You're going to swallow lots of cock, tonight, dear. 'Cuz I gotta **BIG** dick, *mamasita!!*

<u>"Hispanicamerican Female"</u>:

If you want to curse yourself to "Hell"—then—do <u>it</u>! But, **don't** take <u>me</u> with you! I don't want my soul to be condemned tonight! <u>Raping</u> me on a church property—on "**Holy** soil"—will send me to "Hell", too, don't you see??!! Let's do <u>this</u> at my house, O.K., <u>sir</u>?! Look, if you don't want to drive all that way, we can just go some place quiet, not that far away, and do this … <u>OK</u>?!

<u>"Sexcrime Assailant"</u>:

Now, don't you worry one bit, little mama. Ain't nobody goin' to "Hell" tonight. But, one of us **is** goin' to "**Heaven**"!! (Ha! Ha! Ha!) Get ready to give it up for the Lord on the "Lord's Day". Tomorrow morning, the Good Shepherd's flock of faithful sheep will gather upon these premises for the "Sunday Service". (Ha! Ha! Ha! Ha! Ha!) Let us <u>praise</u> God! (… Oh, in<u>deed</u>!)

<u>"Hispanicamerican Female"</u>:

I will <u>not</u> comply!! Not **here**!! You'll just have to **kill** *me.* At least I will <u>die</u> a *Christian* on "Christian" soil! My soul, then, will still be pure and eligible for citizenship in "Heaven's Nation".

<u>"Sexcrime Assailant"</u>:

Well, I've got a boxcutting knife with a 1-inch stainless steel blade, a canister that contains 100 grams of "pepperspray", and a set of large wristcuffing instruments, which all say YOU will <u>comply</u>. And, if you <u>don't</u> cooperate, I'll make you strip off all those clothes in tonight's subzero layers of midnight air. It's 12-degrees <u>below</u> "Zero" out here, mi *hermanita!!*

I tell the attractive Latina female to kneel upon the square, solid sections of concrete building material which comprise the congregation hall's spacious entry deck and to ready herself to orally arouse me … i.e., to expect she'll soon permit the tasting sensors in her tongue to savor a proud foot of anxious, predatory (i.e., penile) flesh. [!!Issuing 'Emoticon' Alert!! (} ; >)]

"The 'boxknife' I'm handling says you'll <u>eat</u> what I tell you to <u>eat</u>, *woman*, with the 'boxblade' itself coming courtesy of 'FineCrafters[AI]'." And … (almost instantly), our panic-ridden Latina assault-victim quickly begins to orally arouse the erect organ that is both, 1) here, "on hand", and, 2) still, "at large", on this, just one of several "sinful" evenings appearing in Ariq's personal chronicle of antisocial "sexcrime"-file incidents.

The odd, warm touch of the Latina's suddenly hungering mouth seems to offer to me a strange coupling ... a "flesh on flesh" contact that is, at once, both pleasing and, frankly, puzzling.... Is the female in question *(La Republica Mexicana's* famous "Mouth-to-Feed", that is), at all, "liking" the savage human encounter which she and I (here) do equally partake of in this overtly unfortunate (yet, undeniably satisfying) moment of time? ... Mmmmm??

"Keep eating, *senorita!* That yogurt I'm discharging has nutrients in it that will fortify any growing girl's daily assortment of well-balanced menu items." The woman continues to concentrate (wholly, that is [??!!]) upon the muscular instrument I've got that's open to such oral excitation, whether such a unique gesture on the part of a consenting (or—as is the case with the current participant—<u>non</u>consenting) female happens to occur just *after* sunrise <u>or</u> just *before* sunset. "This boxcutting tool's on watch for any lapse in attention you might, at some point, suffer from, *'mi mujera'*. In other words, I want you to add a <u>higher</u> level of heat to that old nightstick of mine with a little more of the 'head-to-head' action, *mi hermana.* Put a little more of that tongue into it, you 'South-of-the-Border' bitch!" I raise the boxopening blade over the female's head, easily forwarding the blade's access switch with my right thumb in order to ensure the tool's lethal edge is readily available for use and is, in each one of its millimeters, eligible for a meeting with any square-inch of viewable female flesh which I find to be undeniably defiant to any degree whatsoever.

I, at once, absorb a cold, semi-polar current that races through me without so much as a wink in the way of any warning, chilling me *"from head to toe"* (even altering the air exiting my respiratory channels into a visible frost, with its sub-"Zero" level of atmospheric temperature).

While the "Hispanic Whore" maintains our romantic moment together by generating an adequate level of hormonal arousal in me, I can see, overhead, the layering of precipitation cloudlets, i.e., stormbeds floating across the skies found above us, which (apparently ripe with a threatening release of torrential fluid) begin to besiege the both of us (the Mexicanamerican "cunt" and I, that is) with a fragile showering of moist (but <u>only</u> temporary) crystal flakes which all happen to land, noiselessly, atop the square, cement-built sections constituting the church patio's front entry floor, which encompasses several of the large block-shape concrete spaces for any sermon-going Sunday guests. A strong surge of "Arctic"-level air abruptly aims itself into both the Latina lady and me, as she and I loiter (criminally, of course) within the spacious boundaries of the empty (other than us, that is) lot of urban property ... catching me with its wintry grip, just for an instant, before I exhale, and, in addition, suspending, but only <u>briefly</u>, the attractive female's surprising "after hours" appetite for the footlong section of human flesh which I do, hereby, offer unto the "Mexicanamerican"-woman, who is, without question here, ready to appear among the Metrowide police agency's set of "criminal assault"-case statistics in an up-to-date record of felony-level offenses on current report.

I look up and can see (dripping from the patchwork of Autumnal cloud-layers ready to inundate the earth beneath with heavier precipitation still) flakes of ice, i.e., frigid winter leaflets—samples, that is, of the air-temperature occurring in the regional sector (i.e., the "Mining Belt") in the latter stage of the Fall—rush towards the solid land which I stand upon, touching me squarely in each eye and melting into the exterior membrane of each lens which is open and alert to the lavish climatic exercise that appears to begin in the night sky on this particular occasion. I must, I think, look like I'm tearing up (crying, that is), due to the build-up of water left by the crystals of ice that melt into the outer surface of my eyes after the confetti-like flakes outgrow the bedding which the overhead pool of cloud-matter permits them to crop up in before the ribbons of cooling liquid fall towards the particular urbanside backdrop which the local " 'Born Again' Society"-members use in order to celebrate their sacred, lengthily-held beliefs *each* and <u>every</u> Sunday appearing in the yearlong calendar.

I, at once, determine the erotic routine which the *"Mexicana"* victim continues to perform on my behalf to be, by this point, adequately at its end and, hence, no longer necessary to maintain beyond the moment at hand. I.e., in my estimation, the enjoyment which I sought to acquire with the aid of the Hispanic Woman's oral sexual action is, in view of all available evidence, *undeniably* <u>in</u> hand at this specific moment of time!

"That's good enough, *mi hermana*. The 'cockjob' is <u>complete</u>! I want you to, **now**, do something else for me tonight, 'Angelina', **all right**??" I hold the "safe" (or, the *razorless)* edge of the "FineCrafters^AI" boxcutting instrument up against the bare flesh appearing on the right side of the female's chilling neck, ensuring I'm still capable of easily coercing the Latina towards one of the several "Quaking Aspen" trees which stand "at attention" atop the congregation house's eastern patio area in the round soil vessels offering to each statuesque plant its necessary bed of nutrient-rich earth. (The FineCrafters^AI boxopening blade is the one weapon which I conveniently refer to as the "Hellrazor", due to the view on my part the tool itself is, in fact, a genuine "Hell"-raiser, i.e., a device which is certainly capable of *raising* a sufficient measure of "Hell" which I'm able to summon forth into this world from time to time after the actual moment of Midnight arrives on occasions such as the one transpiring on the "Protestant"-church property at this particular point in time…. Ha! Ha! Ha!) "**Now**, you're going to 'Hug-a-Tree', just like you were taught to do back in gradeschool, got it, *Chicana?*" I say to the faltering Hispanic female. "I want you to embrace Nature tonight like a 'Save-the-Planet' psycho-type would do, little sister…. Now, just walk right over **here** and put yourself up against the trunk of this 'Quaking Aspen' tree, *senorita!*"

I do, here, select to apply but gentle pressure to the visible webbing of nerve-endings which route themselves through the tense bands of muscle tissue appearing in the back of the Latina's lean, feminine neck. I carefully direct the woman's compliant figure towards one of the several strong, high-standing "Quaking Aspen" infants that nest themselves inside of soil beds held in the spherical barrels at rest upon the floor of level pavement which greets weekly guests to the Protestant "safe house" which Christ's disciples residing in the nation's " 'Upper-Central' Midwest"-region come to in order to share common ground each Sunday morning, I can safely assume. I position the victim's right shoulder up against the pale, barkless trunk of the childsize (… for a tree) "Quaking Aspen" plant, which appears to adequately (at least, at this particular point) support the full weight of the "Meximerican" female's upright (and emotionless) figure.

I, conveniently, return the FineCrafters[AI] boxopening knife to its previous place of safekeeping inside the inner left chest pocket I have inside the lightweight, nylon jacket which I chose to wear earlier tonight with the empty hope of safeguarding myself against the sub-"Polar" air-temperature levels which are, without question, officially registering on local climate-reading gauges at this specific instance of the morning on which "Sunday Service" will be held at a time not far from this actual minute. I, at this moment, reach into the nylon jacket's inner right chest-pocket and withdraw the large set of high-caliber metal wrist-shackles, i.e., the good 'n' useful "Interrogation Rings", which, I can trust, will secure our victim's arms in a binding hold which will, then, permit me to bring to conclusion the epic endeavor of seeking "Self-Enlightenment" which I find myself attempting to execute, here, upon the acreage of the God-seeking community group's Sunday gathering-site.

"Just keep yourself right up against the pillar of that sturdy old 'Quaking Aspen' tree, *mi hermanita*, all right? This will all be over with before you know it, little Christ-loving lady. Until it ends, just enjoy the ambience which this quaint Christian church locale presents to us, got it, *mamasita??!!*"

<u>"Meximerican Woman"</u>:
Do not do this to me, *sir* … I mean, "<u>my</u> brother". We can stop *right* <u>now</u>, no?? We've already enjoyed a wonderful *sexual* encounter, **yes**?? I do not wish to become pregnant. I do not believe in "abortion". It's against my religious views. You must know, **now**, sir, that I have many venereal diseases!! "Latina" women are known for that! … We carry various infections with us starting in our mid-teens. I'm just warning you, <u>sir</u>!

<u>"Ariq Zarkahn Shoretempel"</u>:
Oh, yeah? Which venereal diseases do you have, little mama?? Gonorrhea??

--()--
108
--()--

Syphilis? Chlamydia? Herpes? "HIV"?? Watchoo got, woman? You ain't gotta worry about gettin' pregnant, sista. "<u>Homeboy</u>", here, is gunna take care of *every*thing <u>tonight</u>! Now, you just keep that Spanish-speakin' face of yours looking straight ahead and I do **not** want to hear any screamin' outta y'all, senorita! Just my luck—I guess—to end up with a scum-ass Mexican **bitch** with all the "VD" in the world in her! Yep! … Just my luck, I guess.

"<u>Meximerican Woman</u>":

We musn't, **sir**, continue to commit such a criminal act against the High Lord upon the grounds of His own "house". I want you to come home with me tonight, my "brother". Let me cook for you an old-fashion offering of <u>expert</u> cuisine. I'm known by friends for making good, home-cooked … *and* nutritious meals. I can make for you a wonderful dinner—with *"tostadas"*, *"tortillitas con aroz"*, <u>and</u> *"tamales carnes"*?? I can offer you a large glass of cold pineapple juice to drink while you enjoy the meal of classic (… and good-tasting) "Mexican"-style cooking. Sounds good, sir, huh?? After you eat the meal of traditional "Mexican"-cuisine I'll prepare for you, I will speak with you on the blessings of knowing "Jesus". I will awaken you to the <u>true</u> joys only those who know the Good Lord can savor *each* and <u>every</u> day. You and I will celebrate the path "Jesus" left for all of us while we're back at my house, away from all the falling snow and the cold, harsh winds. Sounds <u>good</u>, huh, my **brother**??

"<u>Ariq Zarkahn Shoretempel</u>":

Look, *mi chicanita*, I've already told you that this encounter of ours will be over with before you can say *"Cinco De Mayo"!* And I'm not *exactly* open to suggestions from the audience at this point, all right? I'm not ready to alter tonight's pre-arranged itinerary of activities, little sister. Things will go a <u>lot</u> quicker if you'd stop running your mouth like you're a <u>damn</u> "air traffic"-control operator. Just take a look around you! Isn't the "Autumntime" environment just exquisite!! Let's just enjoy the arrival of the snowflakes and the crispness of the cold climate, here, in the country's frosty "Northern Plains"-region. (… Hah! Hah! Hah! Hah!)

"<u>Meximerican Woman</u>":

I will pray that the Good Lord will give you the strength to stop this high atrocity against the "House of God". I ask only that you, sir, begin to pray *with* me. If you continue to conduct yourself in such a <u>sinful</u> manner, I do not doubt the Lord will condemn your very soul to the pungent fumes and ghastly flames of "Hell". But, if you stop **NOW** and surrender yourself to Jesus—**then**—your soul will soon find redemption in the eyes of the "Father Almighty". Accept the Lord Jesus **NOW**, <u>sir</u>!! Tonight, you have the wonderful opportunity at hand to turn yourself away from the habits of sin you're pursuing and surrender your soul to God Himself!!

"<u>Ariq</u> <u>Zarkahn</u> <u>Shoretempel</u>":

Shut up about the "Good Lord" and the "*… flames of 'Hell'* ", all right, *mu-jera?!* Just close those pretty eyes you have and get ready to receive the "greatest gift of all"—the standing flagpole comin' right outta my pants. (Ha! Ha! Ha!) I'm gunna run this boxopening knife right through the flesh of your throat if you keep working that loud mouth you got, <u>got it</u>?! You'll be back home before you know it, little *chicanita*. But you might not make it there in <u>one</u> piece if you keep *irritating* <u>me</u>—**got it**?!

The "beaner" woman is still steady, with her delicate right shoulder in solid, static contact with the lean, pale beige pillar of the northern forest's "Quaking Aspen" nestling, i.e., the childlike tree nursing at the barrel-size crib of re-enriching soil through its mushrooming array of thirsting roots. I, here, rather easily, press the Latina victim's two arms together in a pinch behind the woman's back in order to prepare the female to accept the large set of high-grade metallic "Interrogation Room"-wristcuffs I'm carrying with me with the aim of securing the lady's arms in a hold guaranteeing *mutual* safety (i.e., hers … <u>and</u> mine) over the course of a strenuous session of <u>criminal</u> "rear cavity"-penetration which is to transpire rather soon, I trust. (Ha! Ha! Ha!) [!!Issuing 'Emoticon' Alert!! (} ; >)] I carefully attach the heavy set of wrist-locking rings to the Latina woman's lean, frosty lower forearms, the frigid touch of the victim's flesh serving, here, as an indication as to the amount of time which she and I have spent outside within the midst of the state's Autumnal front of almost "Arctic"-like ground-level air tonight.

With my right hand, I jerk up the knee-length skirt that completes the "executive" ensemble which the "Mexicanamerican"-woman is wearing on this particular moment occurring inside the early hours of Sunday—the week's <u>7</u>th (or, final) 24-hour term, upon which ancient "Christian"-school rituals are to be held on site—hereby, exposing the flesh of the female's lower limbs to the ongoing flurries of sub-"Zero" air which start to beach themselves against the large, ornamentally decorative windows comprising the eastern face of the sleekly-built temple of Jesus Christ's local community of "Salvation"-seeking converts.

I reach into the lightweight, nylon jacket's inner left chest pocket in order to retrieve the "FineCrafters[AI]" boxopening blade (i.e., the old, reliable, and "always-at-the-ready" "<u>Hellrazor</u>", that is—Ha! Ha! Ha! Ha!) for easy and urgent usage, finding it all, at once, necessary to slice away the "Mexicanamerican" woman's tissue-like lingerie garment, i.e., the pair of silk panties appearing to protect the female's most personal (and presumably private) areas of interest. [!!Issuing 'Emoticon' Alert!! (} ; >)] I cut through the Latina lady's costly silk-made section of attire, all the while

--()--
110
--()--

separating the fragile garment into a loose, unusable article of underwear, using extreme caution the whole while, so as to avoid actually wounding the woman's outermost layer of skin (having, here, no desire myself to watch fresh droplets of the female's blood dot me in any particular spot with any milligrams of the exiting, intravenous fluid).... Yuck!!

I carefully return the "FineCrafters[AI]" boxcutting razorblade to the nylon jacket's inner left chest pocket—its specific place for safekeeping—and, at this point, I, gradually, pick at the *Chicana* female's silken piece of delicate insulative material, until the fine item of "womenswear" dangles at my curious fingertips, the creamy pair of panties being, by this particular moment, completely free of the Hispanic female's highly arousing lower region. (Hah! Hah! Hah! Hah!)

I (using caution so as to avoid seeing the female's enticing private item fall to the open floor of the prayer hall's eastern concrete yardage) place the woman's pale, "cream"-looking clothing necessity atop one of the lean, skeletal limbs of the recently re-grounded "Quaking Aspen"-plant, the decorative landscape addition that's ornamenting the lineup of window panels which stand at the eastern limit of the sermon house's area of interior floorspace built for seating the sanctuary's eager legion of "Seventh Day"-attendees. The apparatus which I'm soon to make use of at the time in which I begin engaging the victim (i.e., the "Meximerican" maiden, that is) in direct "ass canal"-intercourse (ha! ha! ha! ha! ha!), i.e., the old pistoning penis, is, as of this particular minute, "at the ready", and is, also, under scrutiny of every available visible indicator, unarguably anxious for the additional excitation which *genuine* flesh-to-flesh contact will certainly (here, on these acres) incite. I.e., the indecent organ (nothing else than my crime-happy cock, of course) is, "for the record", ready to intimately explore the alluring Latina female's anal orifice.... [!!Issuing 'Emoticon' Alert!! (} ; >)]

I am (I do s'pose), at this particular point, to adopt the offensive posture that would, in fact, put me in a position that is, assessing the circumstances at hand, the one that is most appropriate, considering the type of criminal occurrence I'm certain to occupy myself with soon ... seeing (as I, here, do) myself loitering, anxiously, just inches to the rear of the Latina female's visibly nude hindquarters (i.e., her <u>posterior</u> region), while the "Meximerican" woman waits, with disbelief, in the immobile stance which I've just had the opportunity to position her in. I do, at this time, place my hands around the female's midsection, in the soft spot (i.e., the "beltline" that's just below the ribcage and above the hipbone), in an attempt to re-secure my footing prior to the exercise in highly "criminal" physical intercourse that's about to ensue aboard the rectangular plates of recently re-built concrete, in the eastern public assembly deck of the Pro-Christian Party's weekly sermon hall ... which one would locate just southeast of the

Metrocenter's primary "Dining and Retail"-district, i.e., "Rocolo Arcade".

I do, hereby, begin to penetrate (choosing, here, to use both caution *and* control) the Latina female's rectal canal (i.e., the cavity of the "Meximerican" female's "rear"-orifice) by introducing, of course, the erect male (reproductive) organ that's enlarging due to an overt level of excitation, as I trust I'm seeing that which, at this point, appears to be an opportunity (here, at hand) to occupy myself with a certain interpersonal pursuit (ha! ha! ha!) which might become, within moments, an instance which the anxious erection will feel is as rewarding as any "consensual" encounter which the specific cock in question has ever had the ability to entertain itself with during the after-midnight hours. I do notice, almost instantly, a somewhat alarming wavelet of rapid air rushing at the "Sunday Service" site's recently re-built "standing room"-only floor with a particular rate of travel which abruptly interferes with the comfort I've come to let myself accept through the efforts I'm, here, making in ecstatically committing myself to the criminal penetration of the Hispanic-American woman, who, almost lifelessly, keeps herself upright by shouldering the "Quaking Aspen" tree specimen standing in its hand-built spot of dark, underground earth.

I decide, on the needle-like point of a half-moment, marveling, really, at my particular level of cleverness, that I'd, in fact, be able to increase the specific degree of human-born heat that's emanating outwards, directly from the one specific figure in motion, i.e., me, that is ... <u>here</u>, in the "Metro-Christian" choir's private urban compound (in this hour after sunlight's sought other tracts of earth to flood on the planet's opposing hemisphere) ... <u>now</u>, in the midst of these, the ending stages of Autumntime inside the USA's tranquil "Northern Plains"-sector of Midwestern states. The Latina victim, the lady which I appear to be (at this particular juncture of the morning's early minutes) quite handily violating, that is, seems all but asleep, ready—apparently—to offer almost nothing at all along the lines of any recognizable signs of awareness other than the abruptly tense clenching of the chords of muscle tissue found at the rear of the woman's elegantly-drawn neck, as if receiving, from time to time, a pulsation of alertness that momentarily revitalizes the apparently spiritless frame which I'm currently distressing by forcing against it the full weight of an adult male figure.... *A-ha! Ha! Ha!*

Yet, on the murmuring last remains of a moment, I catch a sudden glimpse of a dashing squirrel, a pale brown urban inhabitant (i.e., a tail-bearing "urbanite", that would be, or a "city critter" [ha! ha! ha!]), that's racing eastwards across the cement floor of the sacred assembly site's outer patio-space, towards the recently re-built black asphalt ground of the "Guest Parking" field, in order, I will, securely, assume, to free itself from a locational setting that presents to it a *criminal* action which I am, here (while not using caution), committing myself to in (1) overwhelming a woman's own individual rights as a citizen in a "civil" society and (2) overturning a temple's own inviolable rules which do preserve it as a sanctuary of self-humbling communication with the Holy Lord.

Upon the occurrence of a predictable (and, quite odor-rich, that is) conclusion to the felonious incident on hand, if I must, myself, admit to, I do, regretfully, decide to close out this specific session of "after hours" criminal intimacy, seeing that this particular episode of overnight anti-feminist aggression has come, over its due course, to a notably unfortunate ending. (((Sigh))). [!!Issuing 'Emoticon' Alert!! ({ : > (] And, in light of these circumstances, the enlivening action of illegal intercourse that I, in all honesty, found to be quite necessary and, perhaps, truly reviving to engage myself with, must, in this moment, sadly expire, if I can, at this specific moment of the nocturnal sector transpiring inside of the perdiem time-cycle, make final comment on the surprisingly convenient one-on-one criminal encounter which the house of salvation-seeking "Born Again" Sunday-morning Bible-browsers (helplessly) had to play unwilling host to on the aforesaid occasion. (... Hah! Hah! Hah!)

The unlawful act which this "early morning" physical affair has proven itself to (in fact) be, has, I fear, come to a foreseeable (and quite—do I say—'heartbreaking'[?]) end, leaving the both of us (i.e., the *Mexicana* maiden and me, that is) with nothing other than the late Autumn climate's tide of inbound airwaves, chilling the stream of exhaust I exhale with each recurring round of respiration into a pale, evaporating head of moonlit, silent mist. I quickly re-close the open section of clothing (i.e., the "zipper"-fly) that's at the top of the pair of black denim jeans (i.e., the "Backbay[UE]"-brand "Crescent Series[STF]" Black Denim, 5-pocket, "Slim"-fit Jeans) which, I confess, do appear as the primary piece in the exhibition of "urbanwear" which I chose to outfit myself with earlier on—in the evening—seeing that the occasion of anti-societal, person-to-person interaction is (as of this particular moment in the beginning hours of the "Day of Service") only a faint, inaudible echo of its former seismic self, of course, with the incident of "criminal" intercourse occurring at this site (which is soon to host ritualistic Sunday exercises in promoting the re-affirmation of Christian faith) being, here, at its end.

The incident of intentional *sexual* misconduct, which (I'm noting at this particular point) came to its comforting (and quiet) close atop the outdoor patio's floor of concrete squares which appears just to the side of the Protestant pastor house's eastern entry doors, is, in a word which I assume summarizes the criminal occurrence which I've seen myself adeptly achieve upon a property belonging, specifically, to Christ's purposeful urban apostles ... "**HISTORY**"!!

I swiftly unlock the set of large "prison"-grade, metallic wrist-shackles which did let me bind together the Latina victim's forearms throughout the lengthy incident of <u>non</u>consensual coupling which just came to its unproblematic end--hereby--freeing the female's upper extremities from the <u>compliance</u> hold which the reliable "interrogation room" arm-locking rings kept them safely in during the series of unlawful sexual exercises which I just let myself unrelentingly perform on this specific morning against the young "Mex-American" woman. [!!Issuing 'Emoticon' Alert!! (} ; >)]

I cautiously return the metallic "interrogator's" wristlocking cuffs to the inner right chest pocket of the black nylon jacket I chose to put on at the very start of the overnight shift's urban "flesh run" (i.e., the "hunt for easy cunt", which this action most likely appears to have become), knowing the arm-shackling rings are "antipersonnel"-aids, of course, built, at one point, to appear in the service of certain agents seeking truthful answers from prisoners refusing to promptly respond to various inquiries despite facing a <u>genuine</u> promise of undue torture.... Hence, I'll always see (as I should) the large pair of restraining wristcuffs as invaluable instruments of nocturnal warfare, which one must keep on hand on occasions such as the instance transpiring in the initial hours of the specific morning on which our local pro-Christ contingent chooses to use in communing with "God" in but one of the High Lord's many earthbound houses. Though, here, the festive affair which I just had the privilege of witnessing myself enjoy has, unhappily, seen itself come to its unsuspenseful close, in the midst of the local Protestant public's place of Sunday prayer.

The all but lifeless lady (i.e., the "Meximerican" female, that is), still supporting her trim figure's full weight by pitting her narrow right shoulder up against the "Quaking Aspen" infant, the ornamental landscape addition put on the premises for the Sunday gathering of "Urbanside" disciples to see, offers almost no signs of vitality whatsoever at this moment ... only a faint, almost inaudible burst of groaning that is gradually escaping the Hispanic victim's hoarse oral passage. Although I am, at this recognizable marker in time, still standing nearby, the Latina woman, I realize, fails to even acknowledge me at this point, refusing to acknowledge, I s'pose, the assailant selecting to violate her female form (that sacred secular vehicle) and, alongside such a remorseless criminal incident, selecting (as well) to violate the precious faith which she's chosen to abide by (those God-fearing religious viewpoints one such as her would hold in high regard), while, over the entirety of the "felony"-level action on record, being atop the territorial expanse of the Central Commerce District's urban church-compound.

The Hispanic lady is, at this specific moment, absolutely soundless, as if already asleep, exhibiting nothing at all in the way of any signs usually indicating alertness, awareness, or the ability to revive one's self to any degree whatsoever on the part of a woman having just undergone an episode as highly traumatizing (in its specific purpose) as the actual episode which she just had to undergo upon these solemn grounds at my

--()--
114
--()--

abominable hands…. Hah! Hah! Hah!

I, O ever-faithful and familiar followers on hand, at this specific moment in the "after hours" menu of antifeminist "on street" actions, push the "Latinamerican" maiden onto the cold concrete-built flooring of the Protestant sermon center's eastern entry-deck, i.e., the open patio space greeting churchgoers to the MetroChristian "Worship Service" site *each* and <u>every</u> Sunday morning, that would be. I do, here, withdraw the plastic canister containing the micro-granular "pepperspray"-agent, a 100-gram volume of the nontoxic aerosol-form inhalant kept inside its chamber's black disposable casing, from within the dark nylon jacket's inner left chest pocket. I aggressively "fumigate" the Metrozone's unfortunate "sexcrime"-statistic, striking the "Hispano-American" female directly in the face with the evaporating cloudlet of microscopic solid molecules (as the youthful "Mexicana" mama, at this particular point, lies atop the church lot's assemblage of spacious, cement-made sections), just offering to the "bilingual" Latina "beautie" an excessively generous sampling of the microchemical, antipersonnel "aerosol"-compound, exposing the woman's vulnerable interior respiratory channels to the irritating particulate mixture of hazardous, inhumane matter.

I swiftly return the canister which contains the debilitating formula of anti-respiratory ingredients to the inner left chest-pocket inside the black nylon jacket which I'm wearing at the moment in order to ward off the outdoor air's Autumnal temperature, prior to preparing myself for a final escape from the hallowed Protestant house of "Evangelism Society"-citizens in order to initialize a flight on foot through the expansive maze of urban streets which warily awaits the arrival of tonight's emergent fugitive, member to a solitary strikeforce inside the southwestern spaces of the Metrosite's "Central Commercial District".

"Ariq <u>Z</u>. <u>Shoretempel</u>":

I do, hereby, insist that you <u>must</u>, at once, agree to acknowledge and agree to abide by the following series of advisory comments, my all-too-familiar female friend …

"<u>One</u>":

Do <u>not</u> **contact** any "Sexcrime" detectives currently on staff at the "Minneapolis Police Department"!

"<u>Two</u>":

Do <u>not</u> **contact** a local "Rape Crisis Counseling Center" in order to initiate a program of <u>recuperative</u> therapy!

"<u>Three</u>":

Do <u>not</u> **contact** any well-known non-profit nationwide "feminist" organizations!

"<u>Four</u>":

--()--
115
--()--

Adrien L. Montgomery
Tasting Droplets of the Unforgettable Rain
Official Imprint: "Dynamographx"

Do <u>not</u> come into **contact** with any individuals known to suffer with tropical bacterial contagions!

"<u>Five</u>":

Do <u>not</u> accept an optometrist's recommendation for any sight-correcting "**contact**" lenses!

"<u>Six</u>":

Do <u>not</u> accept any supposition claiming extra-galactic lifeforms are now attempting to **contact** humans inhabiting "Earth"!

"<u>Seven</u>":

And, *finally*, do <u>not</u> make use of ("['Email']-message")-transmission to maintain **contact** with friends or relatives, yet, rather, rely <u>solely</u> upon "telephonic"-communication, for (as we all <u>know</u>) there's nothing quite so inspiring as the sound of the human voice! … Ha! Ha! Ha!

I am, at this point, still having to hear Sunday morning's undeniably tragic *Mexicana* woman (i.e., the "Metro"-District's current "police file"-case soon to be found in a report under the "sexual assault"-crimes category, that is), who is struggling, here, with various respiratory issues due to the soluble antipersonnel irritant, i.e., the police Riot Squad's "faerie" juice, which I sent into the Hispanic lady's open air-conducting channels just a minute earlier. I quickly turn from the Latina subject existing as the investigative centerpiece in the emergent "sexual assault"-case's table of detectable forensic evidence as she lies (being all but immobile) atop the rectangular sections of cement material forming the eastern greeting deck's outer entry floor in order to quickly vacate the church building's plot of prime urban property and maneuver myself through the mazework which amounts to the Central Commerce District's "motor"-traffic planning grid in order to navigate a path leading me to the specific "tenancy"-unit found on the basement-level of "The 'Falconeer' Building", which I do, in accordance with the official "occupancy"-agreement, maintain "leasing"-status on at this point in time, O comrades and *ever-faithful* associates on hand.

I soon find myself on "Hennenburgh Boulevard", traveling southwards towards the "Laurel Park"-District, the acreage that is, in fact, locational host to "The 'Falconeer' Building", the real estate facility that is, again, physical home to the apartment which I am, at this actual juncture, residing in within the borders of this specific "Midwestern"-region state. On coming to the intersection of Hennenburgh Boulevard North and East Greenleaf Street (… halting, safely, at the traffic-signal hub's northeastern corner to acknowledge the "crosswalk" sign for pedestrian travelers), I spot a Latino man (i.e., *another* Spanish-speaking citizen[!]) standing at the "autotraffic" re-routing port's southeastern corner uttering words in the Hispanic man's native language aloud … to no one other than himself, however.

--()--
116
--()--

Adrien L. Montgomery

Tasting Droplets of the Unforgettable Rain

Original Year of Publication: 2026

The "Mejicano" keeps himself at a standstill, ignoring whatever instinct there is in him to physically re-collect himself to any extent ever again, upon the southeastern corner of the empty autotraffic "navigational" concourse, or "route exchange"-juncture. The Spanish-speaker spots me on the corner that's, to him, due north, just a single asphalt driving track (containing a path of three eastbound automobile lanes) away from the section of pedestrian cement which he (with a particular level of *genuine* eeriness), at this time, occupies as one aimlessly traveling on foot ... at the noiseless intercrossing of Hennenburgh Boulevard North and East Greenleaf Street.

The Latino man, i.e., the "Hispanomerican" male, is, apparently, attempting to clarify with finer resolution the graphical aspects appearing in the physical image which my presence would offer to any random onlooker at this point, as I, hereby, assume outdoor space upon the corner opposite the one which the "Espanophile" temporarily stands upon just about 30 feet in measure across from where I do uncomfortably await the signal permitting foot traffic to cross the asphalt roadway. The tortilla-eater ("Spinach"-flavor, most likely, rather than the usual "Flour"-variety of burrito wraps) appears to permit a fearful expression to emerge upon the aging Hispanic face which I see staring across "East Greenleaf Street" at me ... i.e., <u>me</u>, the innocent "after hours" assailant—uh, I mean, "associate", that is (Ha! Ha! Ha! Ha!)—who just so happens to be committing an action amounting to one that is no more offensive than what I'm doing in merely anticipating the fluorescent green "Walk" signal that's soon to appear in the "pedestrian"-traffic sign that's found just over the Spanish-speaker's head to allow me, at that point, to cross "East Greenleaf Street" and, thereby, continue the trek which I'm making to the particular unit which I do, at this time, occupy in "The 'Falconeer' Building", that is.

The "Meximerican" raises an arm towards me, pointing across the white separating lines of the "motor traffic"-track, as if to warn anyone else nearby that I, Ariq, the "Lone Outdoorsman", stand motionlessly on the corner of a pedestrian footpath and, thereby, could potentially locate other obviously defenseless individuals who would be unfortunately caught outside at such an inhospitable hour and in such inhumane climatic circumstances as those which do besiege the urban backdrop which I'm maneuvering myself through on this early Sunday morning.

The proud product of Spain's "New World"-nations decides to announce aloud (due to, apparently, the extreme circumstances occurring on hand) a stream of highly impolite language, while in the midst of staring northwards across East Greenleaf Street, towards me, Ariq Z. Shoretempel, the Metroland's "Overnight Outlaw" ...

<u>Latino</u> <u>Man</u>:

--()--
117
--()--

(While standing on the intersection's southeastern corner …)
"El Demonio! … El Demonio!"
(In English: "The Demon! … The Demon!")
"El Demonio! … El Demonio!"

The loud "South-of-the-Border" mouthpiece, again, appears to be under the influence of *epic* terror, the fear, once more, beginning to appear upon the face which presents itself to me from across the motor-route which the everyday street helmsman steers himself through towards the specific automobile's eventual terminus—all of this occurring inside the moments which I spend upon the corner of Hennenburgh Boulevard and East Greenleaf Street … merely awaiting the signal prompting foot travelers to safely traverse the road originally built for traffic with wheels.

I am, of course, at serious odds with the accusatory comments which the "Hispanicamerican" man is apparently making, at the moment, in hopes of publicly designating me, i.e., Ariq, the "Bladehandling Sex Bandit", as an assailant "at large"—one that remains footloose and, safely, free from the confining restraints of local "law enforcement"-agents. Being made to feel ill at ease (however) by the "Meximerican" man's indicting remarks, made, I'm certain, in an attempt to mischaracterize me as a *predatory* nocturnal presence, I quickly decide to circumvent the vigilant watch of the Hispanic man (tonight's makeshift "street crossing"-guard, I guess) and maneuver myself east, towards the intersection of East Greenleaf Street and Blainboro Avenue. Upon arriving at the autovehicular interchange of East Greenleaf Street and Blainboro Avenue, I do here become anxiously alert for any possible signs or sounds of mototraffic which might problematically be approaching the single square-yard of outdoor urban property which I do, at this moment of time, individually occupy. I, then, quite uncomfortably, that is, march myself across the empty asphalt pathways towards the car re-routing port's southwestern corner, just prior to walking alone along Blainboro Avenue's spacious pedestrian sections of pavement towards the "Laurel Park" neighborhood and (upon seeing myself successfully arrive at the particular locale itself) to the actual "tenancy"-unit which I do, at this point, occupy by right of pre-existing lease-holding agreement in "The 'Falconeer' Building". [!!Issuing 'Emoticon' Alert!! (} ; >)]

I'm swiftly walking the solid concrete blocks which the sidewalk itself comprises, which span the length of Blainboro Avenue, leading me south, that is, on foot, towards the "Laurel Park"-District, a residential neighborhood that rests just outside the pre-existing boundaries of the Metrosphere's "Central Commerce Zone"—the prominent square-footage of public urban property which the regional citizenry visits "en masse" *each* and <u>every</u> weekday, apparently. After I anonymously traverse several empty urban blocks, noticing no other "early hours", outdoor guests idling upon the streets of traffic-worn, vehicle-weary asphalt, I do arrive at the mouth (i.e., the top) of the long alleyway which anyone can just so happen to find running right behind "The 'Falconeer' Building", the constraining rear road-lane which runs in between the two bordering auto-commuting routes— Reddington Avenue (i.e., the street sitting beside the tenancy building to its <u>west</u>) and Rocolo Avenue (i.e., the street sitting beside the tenancy buil-ding to its <u>east</u>). Upon entering the lengthy alleyway which traverses the block behind the private housing operation which I do, currently, maintain "room occupancy"-status within, I do, here, in this specific space appearing upon the urban gridsystem, quickly encounter a teenage girl (a girl whom I'm already quite familiar with), who, at present, appears to be guilty of "loitering" (without any "criminal" intent, I'd agreeably select to offer) near the pairing of large-size entry doors which open up to the alley at the rear of the imposing (yet, noticeably aging) "room leasing"-facility, this particular girl being a 17-year-old "runaway" child known to "crib" (on occasion) with a Lesbian woman who occupies a unit on the residential building's ground-level ... apartment "#109", that would be.

The youth, in this case, an Italian-American girl (dark hair, with a skin tone indicating a particular ancestry originating on the coasts of the salt-heavy waters of the Mediterranean Sea) usually appears about the building premises wearing a black baseball cap—one that seems to only rest atop the girl's head in reverse, i.e., with its head visor appearing in the back and its plastic cap-strap appearing across the girl's forehead. The teen girl, also, seems to usually appear on the site wearing a pair of dark denim jeans, sporting a "crew cut"-hairstyle, with large green tattoos (such decorations being merely ornamental in intent) which are seen up and down both of her arms, and with a set of unmatching earrings adorning her pair of teenage earlobes.

I do trust (almost absolutely) that the teenager of record, i.e., this Italian-American girl, would find herself ... unmistakably <u>vagrant</u> (i.e., "homeless") if, in fact, the "Lesbo"-female residing in the tenancy operation's first floor rooming-unit did not permit the social castaway to assume an amount of indoor space, as found in terms of "cubic-footage", inside that one particularly boisterous housing setup which the two women freely make use of as an "after hours" couple on a ... "free of charge"/"dusk 'til dawn" agreement for penniless (and, it would seem, sexually permissive) guests which the Lesbian woman apparently selects to offer to the street orphan on a night-to-night basis, that is.

<u>Teen "Runaway" Girl</u>:
The "Teen" *spots me entering the rear alleypath which runs behind* "The 'Falconeer' Building", *a passageway that basically comes to form a lengthy roadway which connects* "Reddington Avenue", *the one ... commuter route*

--()--
119
--()--

Adrien L. Montgomery
Tasting Droplets of the Unforgettable Rain
Official Imprint: "Dynamographx"

leading autotraffic past the tenancy building's <u>westside</u> with "Rocolo Avenue", the one commuter route leading autotraffic past the tenancy building's <u>eastside</u>. Upon recognizing the face of the adult male who's approaching her at this point, the "Teen" *instantly initializes conversation with me …*

"Oh! Hi, there, 'Sweetie'!! Hey! … Du'yuh got any 'weed'? Hey! … Du'yuh smoke it?!! Du'yuh got any 'booze'?!! Hey! … Du'yuh got any 'hardstuff'?!! … Uhmm, I'll give you—'I'll give you'—two dollars for a couple of cigarettes, baby?"

Ariq <u>Shoretempel</u>:

I, here, continue to walk the rear alleypath's fading asphalt footage, past the pair of large iron trash-storage tanks, past the large blue plastic recycling bins, past the pieces of pale birch plywood room-furnishings which somebody in the building—i.e., a "tenant"—*chose to set aside as refuse not that long ago…. I head gently towards the pairing of rear-entry doors at the private housing facility's southern perimeter.*

"I ain't got any 'weed' on me tonight, little mamma. I ain't into that stuff, anyway. I ain't got any cigarettes on me, either…. Uhmmm … I'll be going to 'Bourning Hill Grocery & Tobacco' tomorrow for more whiskey and malt liquor. Why don'tcha catch up with me tomorrow night, O.K., 'Hunnie Bean'?"

Teen "Runaway" Girl:

The "Teen" *offers herself a brief peek in between the framing boards of a back bedroom window which is facing the lengthy rear alley-route in the far wall of a rental-unit that's on the large tenancy complex's "first floor"-level of residential spaces. The girl (i.e., "17", being her known age, once again) quickly taps a small fist against the rectangular pane of glass which is sitting inside the surrounding framework's lower "window assembly"-unit.*

"Hey, 'Sweetie'! I'm locked out again! See … the women in there aren't letting me in?! Hey! Can you let me into the building?! I usually have to climb into the apartment through the 'alley'-side window. I don't wanna do that tonight, though."

Ariq <u>Shoretempel</u>:

I'm soon noticing, sitting up against the concrete side of the housing property's rear-boundary wall, a duffel bag and a bedroll, the transient girl's overnight "survivalist"-pack, apparently, proving itself to be the only assortment of personal items (i.e., possessions) which the runaway teen-ager makes legitimate claim to on this particular planet.

"Hey! Wait a minute!? … Where do you sleep when you can't get into the

--()--
120
--()--

building, 'Hunnie Bean'? … Over <u>there</u> in 'Laurel Park'? … It's probably monitored by the cops at night due to the people looking to buy dope."

<u>Teen "Runaway" Girl</u>:
"No! Up at the 'Emergency "Drop-In" '-shelter on Columbia Avenue and Crassleburgh Street. They've got thirty beds inside their 'Overnight Guest-room'. I gotta admit, it's like spending the night on an Army cot inside the 'Greyhound' station's 'pick-up' zone, man. See, 'Sweetie', the women in #109 wouldn't let me in one night and it was bitch'n muthahfukkin' rainin' that night, y'know. I told 'em, *'… Come on, let me in already! It's muthahfukkin' rainin' shit on me out here, you bitch-mothers!!'* The women in #109 wouldn't let me in and *that* night I had to sleep up at the 'Emergency "Drop-In" '-shelter up on Crassleburgh Street. It's those two goddamn muthahfukkin' bitchcunts in '#109', y'know what I mean, man!! Jeezus!!"

<u>Ariq Shoretempel</u>:
"You gotta take care of yourself at those fucking so-called 'shelters'!? Those places ain't safe for ya, at all, 'Hunnie'. I read a news report about one dude who got *raped* up at a local men's shelter by another bum-ass dude!? Up at the 'House of Hope', the temporary shelter run by the 'Sons of Adam', y'know, the gay charity group? It's like, one 'hobo' butt-rumbling with another 'hobo', if you can imagine that?! It's <u>sickening</u>, huh, 'Hunnie Bean'?!!"

<u>Teen "Runaway" Girl</u>:
"Oh, <u>yeah</u>! I know all about how 'dangerous' these muthafukkin' places are that feed and house the 'homeless' crowds. I used to go to one of the local 'Charity Kitchens' up on 8th Street and Santa Fe Avenue, near 'Vandenburgh Park'. It's at the 'Present Day Epistles Church'? … Or, the 'Church of the Sacred Ram', or sumthin' like that??"

<u>Ariq Shoretempel</u>:
"Oh, you mean it's at the 'Present Day Apostles Church of the Scared Lamb'! Oh, yeah!! That's just one block south of the 'Hennepin County General Hospital and Medical Complex' up on 7th Street."

<u>Teen "Runaway" Girl</u>:
"<u>Yeah</u>! I used to go up there to eat breakfast occasionally, but muthahfukkin' riots would break out over the food in there, if you can believe it? Some dude punches another dude for snatchin' a muffin and the whole muthahfukkin' place is rockin' like a sinking boat of Haitian refugees. You just gotta grab what you can get in all the mania and run the

Adrien L. Montgomery
Tasting Droplets of the Unforgettable Rain
Official Imprint: "Dynamographx"

Hell outta there!"

Ariq Shoretempel:

"You should apply to the County 'Social Services' Agency for admission into a first-of-its-kind program that provides 'rehabilitation' for 'runaway' **teenage** addicts. The program offers its enrollees an apartment <u>and</u> a job!? (See, they'll give **you** a place to crib *and* a place to work!) There's also an 'in clinic' 'dependency treatment'-class which includes lectures on recovery from former users and 'in-group' therapy sessions! What d'ya think, huh? Sounds good, huh??!"

Teen "<u>Runaway</u>" <u>Girl</u>:

"Y'know, I still have the option of movin' in with my 'granmummah' down in Omaha, Nebraska. But, the old 'prairie wagon' is fukkin' seventy years old, man! I don't want to deal with livin' with no seventy-year-old 'prairie wagon' at this point in my muthahfukkin' life! ... I'm still just <u>seventeen</u>!! I couldn't even get around town with the car, 'cuz she'd always come back home without it, forgettin' where the Hell she parked it at the local mall, y'know what I mean, man!? That's why she's gotta take the station-to-station busroute back home. Old-timers can't remember if they fukkin' took their medications earlier that day or not!? <u>Geez</u>!! That's why they have their fukkin' 'heart attacks'.... 'Cuz they forget to fukkin' take their goddamn blood-pressure capsules! ... Ha! Ha! Ha!"

Ariq Shoretempel:

"Y'know, our last building manager—'Mackie MacGowan' (or, 'Black Mack' MacGowan [... he had a black beard])—quit just before Halloween. It's odd, but the dude just bailed on us on just a week's notice. Our new building manager, 'Suzie Wolvershire', works out of the landlord's 'leasing'-office up on 'Autumn Leaf Circle'. And I don't think she's ever going to be occupying the manager's residence (... that's apartment '#001' on the building's basement-level floor). I'm sure she's always absent from the property once it starts getting late. She just stops by on occasion after work on weekdays between 6:00 and 7:00 p.m. Which means, you won't need to worry about anyone contacting the building manager about the noise all of you women make in unit '#109' at night anymore! That's bitch'n, huh, 'Hunnie Bean'?"

The carefree "runaway" teen girl is, by her actual name, known as "Candie Brazonelli", and this one, i.e., the secondary (or, the "hereditary") name which the upbeat, spunky youth (selecting, I s'pose, to adopt the particular existence at this point of the garden-variety "adolescent-in-exile", a life ... which she is acclimating herself to all too adeptly, it would appear)

--()--
122
--()--

would, since her birth, automatically come with, is, of course, to appear, in one's pronunciational (i.e., <u>vocal</u>) approach to it, as "brats-oh-nell-ee". The girl's first (i.e., the "familiar") name (that being "Candie", of course) would, obviously, act as a variant of the child's original personal title, which would be "Constanza", this, the youth's "individual" name, together with the waif's paternal name (i.e., "Brazonelli"), of course, genuinely appearing to identify the teenager as, undeniably, "<u>Italian</u>-American" with respect to the runaway girl's original (or, *familial)* background.

I use the large "nickel"-built tenant's key to unlock the rear entry door to "The 'Falconeer' Building", the back entrance to the huge "tenancy"-house which one would easily find once inside the lengthy alleyway which runs from west to east (in between "Reddington" and "Rocolo" Avenues, with each appearing on a separate perimeter of the block of urban property which the private "room leasing"-facility sits upon) in the northeastern sector of the "Laurel Park"-region, of course, one of the Metrosphere's <u>developing</u>, "inner" districts. I permit "Candie", the scrappy underage societal castoff, to enter "The 'Falconeer' Building" right behind me, a gesture upon my part, which is, actually, in violation of the residential complex's statement of pre-existing occupancy codes, i.e., this act amounting to a "rules infraction" in permitting a "<u>non</u>-tenant" to gain admission to the premises without the express permission or knowledge of the specific building resident who's to (at least, temporarily) play "host" to the particular "guest" who's entering beside you, the hospitable "doorkeeper", in the particular instance transpiring.

"Candie" (... once again, being "Brazonelli", as well, that is) the lively "throwaway" youth, walks up the short, yet steep, series of steps that leads one from the entryway's landing to the building's "first floor" lineup of "Easternside" private rooming-units. While I, Ariq, the "Lunarmaniac", start to walk down the lengthier flight of "back door"-steps which leads to the housing operation's basement-level floor, and to the apartment (room "#002", that is) which is awaiting me in the cellar area's southeastern corner.

I swiftly maneuver myself into the large rental-unit that's in the "Falconeer" building's cellar-level floorspace and I, then, easily re-set both the keyhole's locking lever and the half-a-foot safety chain that serves as a "back-up" defense-mechanism if the tenant in question (i.e., me, of course) selects, at any particular time, to partially open the apartment's front door in order to communicate in a "face-to-face" manner with any certain visitor who's come to place a surprising call on the complex's lone, yet, <u>not</u> *lonely*, occupant (i.e., me—"Ariq"—of course, that is).

Inside the apartment hall's basement-level tenancy-unit (room "#002", again), I do trust that I, Ariq (the "Urban Eclipse"), am, at this point, undeniably kept free from any (and all) levels of existing endangerment(X)

--()--
123
--()--

which the emergent consequences of the anti-feminist criminal action transpiring upon my part not long ago (consequences, perhaps, including both injury and doom—specifically to me, it might appear) could have possibly (earlier, that is … on the apocalyptic occasion occurring tonight) set misfortune for me, the culprit in question, to unluckily encounter later on. [!!Issuing 'Emoticon' Alert!! (} ; >)]

I, at once, decide to go to the "fridge" that's inside the apartment's kitchen and withdraw from the upper shelving rack in the appliance's "fresh foods"-storage compartment a 24-oz. bottle of "eXcellor[UE]"-brand "Diet Sourfruit[ESU]" Sodapop—a recent entry, I'd guess, into the lineup of US "cola market" contestants, which I had the good fortune of encountering on a recent trip to a local "minimarket" just one night ago (i.e., the "RedBannerUSA[STF]" "convenience mart"-outlet) on the corner of Laughsley Ave. So. and Sleighton Street (… on November 29, early Saturday morning, at around 1:30 a.m., C.S.T., that is).

With an anxious hand, I unscrew the large bottle's "twist off" plastic cap and place the red bottling piece on the nearer end of the kitchen's lengthy pale "maple"-wood countertop, and (almost *too* suddenly, considering the undeniable rareness of the objectionable circumstances transpiring earlier in the night) permit myself to consume a detectably flavorful "serving size" of the cold soda fluid…. And (… inside of just a handful of moments), I allow myself even extra measures of the frosty commercial cola beverage in a snap decision to digest an additional serving of the deliciously brisk cold soda recipe just prior to gently resting the long, full bottle of "eXcellor[UE]"-brand "Diet Sourfruit[ESU]" Sodapop upon (yet, again) the nearer end of the kitchen's spacious "maple"-built countertop, putting it just alongside the large "Pop" bottle's red plastic mouth-cap.

But, <u>here</u> I stand … on the dark floor of hard cherrywood boards (the rectangular sections themselves appearing to be "wine"-like in surface coloring), which all seemingly serve to spatially highlight the central interior section inside the housing facility's cellar-level rental-unit, casually inspecting the familiar assortment of household "odds and ends" which the basement's apartment appears to (at this particular point in time) predictably possess…. And I do realize that I am, <u>here</u>, standing atop the building-unit's dark hardwood floor panels, <u>safely</u> *home*, despite the variety of public "penal code"-offenses which the antisocial behavioral pattern of my deliberate making has, apparently, let loose inside the course of the morning's early hours, due to decisions of my design to release nothing less than an inhumane array of indecent outdoor criminal incidents. (Oh, *yeah!* **Baby**!)

Alone, inside the one leasing unit that serves as, sort of, the apartment building's final "boxcar", I permit myself to merely smile (… quite visibly, that would be), upon realizing that I've just proven myself to be capable of officially concluding a specific type of felonious anti-feminist assault … yet, one which I (on a certain level, that would be) have sought to see myself commit and complete for quite some time by this specific moment, in the final phases of Autumn in 2003.

As this moment—indeed—is genuinely a rare one, in fact, for one to encounter while enjoying a particularly tranquil frame of mind (or, while experiencing a phase of spiritual temper which is, at the moment, free of any degree whatsoever of anxieties). A moment such as the one I am, in the minute, beginning to know is, I trust, a transition from the maniacal state of emotion which I just had to see myself undergo in the hour over which I chose to pursue an instance of criminal *sexual* misconduct to (preferably, I must add) the sedate (or, more illustratively, "pacific") state of emotion which I do find myself undergoing in the minute, being here at home, i.e., in a "leasing"-unit of "The 'Falconeer' Building", on the hardwood flooring boards (of "wine"-color in natural grain), consuming the cold cola ounces found in the bottle of "eXcellor^{UE}"-brand "Diet Sourfruit^{ESU}" Sodapop.

Well, I'm <u>here</u> (and, once again, alone), comfortably inside the "metropolistic"-level private housing facility's "single"-occupancy tenancy space … becoming all the more at ease due to a recognition ("head on", I s'pose) of the episode of antisocietal sexual aggression, i.e., the select assignment I chose to bestow upon myself, which I've just had the opportunity to see myself successfully accomplish—unquestionably beset with a particular degree of self-satisfaction which all willful violators of those restricting measures appearing in legal codebooks found at the civic-, state-, or federal-level, perhaps, will have the chance to undergo upon completion of whatever single action against public peace the particular *"bandito"* of record has both had the opportunity and ability to skillfully complete in the particular hour of self-enriching, antisocietal criminal conduct which he sought to see himself commit. (… <u>Whoa</u>, boy!! And that is merely the moment at which almost everything—<u>here</u>—begins, my ever-loyal legion of faithful followers!! … Ha! Ha! Ha! Ha! Ha!)

Tasting Droplets of the Unforgettable Rain

By
Adrien L. Montgomery
<u>Cycle</u> <u>008</u>:
"Anything Wrong with Re-Living a Grand Moment in Life? … In the Playback, the Sonic Qualities of the Recording are Enhanced Over Those Offered in the Original Performance, Anyway."

<u>UTA</u> <u>Directive</u> <u>VIII</u>:
"Attention! Attention! … The 'Railbus^{AI}'-System's Commuter Train Will Now

--()--
125
--()--

Momentarily Reverse Itself To Return To The Previous Station. Repeat, The 'Railbus[AI]'-System's Commuter Train Will Now Momentarily Reverse Itself To Return To The Previous Station."

("UTA": Urban Transit Authority)

The following announcement occurs during an on-the-air broadcast by the program's hosting "DJ" while aboard the station's presentation to the loyal contingent of listeners choosing to tune in to the station's specific frequency as it's found on the local radio market's FM-band of channels to hear what the station's on-air commentator chooses to entertain the broadcast's audience with inside the specific segment the radio host leads for the benefit of the channel's listenership at large ...

"Good morning, loyal fans and all-night 'R&B'-addicts, still up after a nightlong spell of consuming cans of the cheapest malt liquor available at local bottle-shops, I assume. This is Tyrone 'Rambling Man' Turner, at WHRN "The Horn" 93.9-FM ... in Cottage Grove, Minnetonka, Eagan, Shakopee and Maplewood ... the only choice on the local dial for what is the coldest, oldest and latest in 'R&B'. The best in today's 'R&B' superhits are right here on the tuning dial, at 93.9-FM.... I just got off the phone with a listener named 'Ariq' in 'Laurel Park'. He requested this next song to go out to a woman he claims he just broke up with. (Sorry about that, Ariq. Hope you find someone else soon.) It's called 'One Night Together' by the 'Black Suits'. Find yourself a new girl soon, Ariq, and, for fans around the station's signal radius ... enjoy our menu of premium 'R&B' selections!"

(-|Calendar Date: SUN., Dec. 07, 2003|-)

Hello, dear friends and faithful followers, one and all. This, of course, yet, again, is Ariq Shoretempel, as I select to lounge comfortably on a loveseat in the family room, or, at least, the front room, of the crib I continue to maintain residential-status in as a subscribing lease-holder, ensuring I do maintain myself as a tenant currently occupying the rental-unit in question ("#002", of course), on the basement-level of the housing-complex, i.e., the "Falconeer"-building, found in the cellar space's southeastern footage, that would be.

I'd like to indicate to all listeners on hand, those of you in the audience I've managed to amass for myself as a self-chosen tour guide announcing to any in attendance news on incidents transpiring in the surrounding region I often choose to travel through for various reasons from time to time. Unfortunately, what transpires in the following segment of notices I keep on an up-to-date basis for any and all selecting to review such items which I have chosen to present is basically a *summarization* of an incident which did happen during an earlier instance in the "narrative"-drama you're paying witness to, my friends, which I'm choosing to <u>re</u>-examine at this particular moment in order to ensure the members of the audience on hand are aware of the *exact* reason as to why I did choose to violate the particular "victim" in question, that is. Of course, the primary motivation for the decision on my part to select to violate the woman of record (i.e., the "Latina" female, remember … occurring seven days ago, on SUN., Nov. 30, 2003) was, of course, to begin and, then, to complete the 1ˢᵗ-stage <u>necessary</u> in the agenda which I'm attempting to fulfill in order to finalize the steps found in the process of achieving individual "Self-Enlightenment", which would amount to a program of stages I set forth for myself to complete earlier in the dramatic presentation itself in order to secure for myself what I trust, in the end, will amount to a higher degree of wisdom (or, "cosmic knowledge") in the world, which I will, ultimately, be able to bestow upon others who approach me in order to seek a higher level of wisdom (of the "spiritual"-variety) for themselves as well.

01)<u>Note</u>:
   a)<u>Assignment#</u>: 001
   b)<u>Date</u> <u>of</u> <u>Assignment's</u> <u>Occurrence</u>:
     --.SUN., November 30, 2003:
   c)<u>Specific</u> <u>Task</u> <u>to</u> <u>Fulfill</u>:
     --.The single instance of a felony-level "sexcrime"-assault against a female target whom the assailant (i.e., Ariq) determines can serve him as a suitable victim in the particular case in question
   d)<u>Summary</u> <u>of</u> <u>actions</u> <u>transpiring</u> <u>in</u> <u>the</u> <u>attempt</u> <u>to</u> <u>complete</u> <u>the</u> <u>specific</u> <u>assignment</u> <u>on</u> <u>record</u>:

I, of course, as the audience is already aware of, did commit a "felony"-level "sexcrime"-assault against a non-consenting Latina victim on the grounds of a "Protestant Church"-property within the vicinity of the Urbanzone's "Central Commerce District" as of the date of SUN., Nov. 30, 2003 in order to initialize what I view as a campaign which will *ultimately* reward me upon the agenda's successful culmination with a higher level of enlightenment than that which the average human would ever be able to obtain for himself in his particular lifetime on Earth. The act itself occurs in accordance with the steps necessary to fulfill the "Philosophical Perspective on the Process of 'Self-Enlightenment' " which I outlined for the reader's benefit earlier in the "narrative"-drama. I believe if I complete all stages necessary in the process of self-enlightenment I will become, in the end, a fully *enlightened* individual, and, hence, a "God"-like figure who is, then, able to bestow certain measures of wisdom (i.e., "cosmic knowledge") upon other members of humanity seeking wisdom as well. If I am *ultimately* able to achieve such a position for myself in the world, i.e., one

Adrien L. Montgomery
Tasting Droplets of the Unforgettable Rain
Official Imprint: "Dynamographx"

who has a higher degree of wisdom which I'm willing to bestow upon any members of humanity, I can then see myself as a "good" person, i.e., as an asset to the human species, rather than as a "bad" person, i.e., as a parasite who feeds off of the world for the sake of benefitting himself without offering anything of value to humanity in return.

I trust with each instance in which I select to violate any of the most ancient of laws which humans deem to be necessary to guarantee the stability of a humane and decent society, for instance, violating official penal codes established to protect the rights of one citizen from being infringed upon by another who decides to act as assailant in the commission of a crime against another individual's person or property, I will, then, achieve a certain measure of "wisdom" for myself. If I next commit what I believe is the *ultimate* act of violation with respect to the most ancient of laws established to guarantee the stability of a decent and humane society (i.e., self-violation at the hands of another perpetrator, that would be), I will then receive the *highest* measure of wisdom available to mankind as an individual human specimen. I will, in the end, then, *cumulatively*, be in possession of the *highest* level of enlightenment which a human can receive as an individual in his particular lifetime on Earth, and, hence, then be ready to bestow such wisdom on others, fully assuming my role as "benefactor" in the world, i.e., one who is able to <u>help</u>, as opposed to "parasite" in a society, i.e., one who is *only* able to <u>harm</u>.

I chose to violate the Latina woman on the grounds of the "Church"-premises at the "True Minneapolite Church of Christ's Cross" in the early morning hours of Sun., Nov. 30, 2003, on the day of an upcoming service for attendees of the prayer-site in question, with use of the nocturnal assailant's kit which I keep with me on such occasions. I did commit the 1st "sexcrime"-assault incident in attempting to complete the agenda which I'm pursuing in order to fulfill the requirements in the "Process of 'Self-Enlightenment' " which I set forth for myself to eventually finalize.

I, of course, view the act of violating the Latina woman on the particular occasion itself as being *necessary* in my attempt to pursue the agenda I've set forth for myself to finalize in the "Perspective on the Process of 'Self-Enlightenment' ", viewing the incident as the necessary <u>1</u>st-stage in the process which I'm attempting to fulfill, a violation against the ancient laws which humans sought to establish to safeguard the stability of a decent and humane society for the benefit of such a society's citizens with respect to their well-being and peace of mind, those being specific values which the citizenry trusts they're entitled to possess as "civilized" creatures co-habitating with each other in a human community. With the completion of the incident itself, I trust I'll receive what amounts to a particularly high degree of enlightenment (i.e., "cosmic knowledge"), which I'll benefit from after the conclusion of the entire program of stages in the process of self-enlightenment, permitting me to, thereby, impart such wisdom unto others seeking enlightenment, as well, in the world.

At the site of the violation itself, I had with me, of course, the assortment of "nocturnal"–warfare instruments which I keep handy for use once attempting to conduct an assault against a female in the attempt to pursue the agenda on "Self-Enlightenment" which I, again, in Minneapolis, have chosen to fervently adopt for myself. I had with me the boxcutting-blade, the 100-gram canister of "pepperspray", the anti-respiratory inhalant formula able to pollute the recipient's air-channeling passages with microscopic granules of toxic-level powder which the human lungs are incapable of adequately absorbing and expelling, and the stainless steel wrist-locking rings for beneficial use at the time of the incident in question to immobilize a nonconsenting female.

At the site of the violation itself, I did commit an act of forced oral-stimulation of the male sex organ (i.e., penis), and, once again, an incident of sodomy (i.e., "rear-cavity" penetration) against the Latina crime-victim, while, yet again, the woman in question was conveniently bound with both arms behind her back with use of the stainless-steel wristlocking-instruments which I had available to me on the specific occasion.

Prior to initializing the "sexcrime"-assault against the particular female at the time of the incident in question (the assault I chose to commit one week ago, that would be, old friends), I—just prior to approaching the victim on the occasion—did choose to utter, for the benefit of those on hand in the listening audience at the time, the following words, as if to announce a declaration of victory in my quest to locate a suitable victim to serve me as a target in my attempt to complete a <u>necessary</u> stage in the agenda I'm attempting to fulfill in order to finalize the process of self-enlightenment … *"And, lo, the footman came and, thus, he chose to place the <u>first</u> sacrificial female on the altar as a gift to 'Wisdom', a tribute from the warlord emergent in him, a soul irrevocably sworn to abide by an oath of loyalty to Enlightenment itself!"*

I did, of course, on choosing to part ways with the woman on hand, decide to announce to her a final statement (i.e., from "victimizer" to "victim", that would be), those being the last words which I chose to speak to the Latina female on site, at the close of the "sexcrime"-assault incident, just prior to the moment at which I chose to exit the scene of the criminal act itself.

I, hereby, do choose to remind those of you in the audience at hand, in walking from the scene of the felony-level assault, I did inform the victim, as she suffered in a state of respiratory-restriction due to the inhalant-formula I chose to fumigate her with using the "pepperspray"-canister, not to inform local "law enforcement"-authorities (or anyone else, for that matter) about the actual incident of violation just so happening to transpire against her at my unmerciful, crime-happy hands. (… Ha! Ha! Ha!)

Tasting Droplets of the
Unforgettable Rain

By
Adrien L. Montgomery
Cycle <u>009</u>:
"Just Climb Aboard the 'Merry-Go-Round' and Reach for the Brass Ring One More Time."

<u>UTA</u> <u>Directive</u> <u>IX</u>:
"Attention! Attention! … The 'Railbus[AI]'-System Cannot Proceed Until The Commuter-Vehicle On The Tracks Ahead Of Us Travels Down The Line To Distance Itself. Repeat, The 'Railbus[AI]'-System Cannot Proceed Until The Commuter-Vehicle On The Tracks Ahead Of Us Travels Down The Line To Distance Itself."
("<u>UTA</u>": <u>U</u>rban <u>T</u>ransit <u>A</u>uthority)

The following announcement is made "on air" by the hosting "DJ" serving as segment-guide for an afternoon broadcast on an affiliate-station of a nationwide radio-network which operates stations around the US found on the local dial's FM-band, with the majority of affiliate-channels existing in the nationwide chain of FM-stations offering to its listenership a playlist of music consisting of songs belonging to the category which would earmark the outlet as an ("['Adult']-Rock/['Soft']-Rock")-music station which radio-listeners can enjoy upon rolling the receiver's tuning pin to a familiar frequency found on the local market's dial of channels:

"Once again, you're listening to WSNG 'Riversongs' 93.3-FM in the 'Twin Cities'-region, serving both sides of the Mississippi—Minneapolis and Saint Paul—on a Sunday afternoon here inside the climate-friendly confines of our broadcasting studio at the station's central facility on Arquette Avenue in the 'Commerce District'. It's currently 25-degrees, under cloud-heavy skies, seeing a light rainfall at the moment and projecting a light coating of snow for the evening. Ready to wheel out extra helpings of 'Adult'-Rock for our listeners out there, on either side of the river today. Here's an old favorite that's going out by ('E-mail')-request to 'Ariq', who's just sitting at home today in 'Laurel Park'. He's ridin' easy on a Sunday, I s'pose…. It's 'No Longer Alone After Dark' by Diamond Starlight. And I certainly do hope that *you're* no longer alone after dark, Ariq. This is, once again, DJ Robbie Rosterberg, on WSNG 'Riversongs' 93.3-FM, here, in the 'Twin Cities'."

(-|<u>Calendar</u> <u>Date</u>: <u>SUN</u>., <u>Dec</u>. <u>14</u>, <u>2003</u>|-)
(XOX)

--()--
130
--()--

What transpires, old friends, in the subsequent section will amount to what is essentially a necessary *summarization* of a particular incident which did happen earlier, a week ago to be precise, on SUN., Dec. 07, 2003, a recent moment, of course, in the "narrative"-drama unfolding in front of those choosing to observe the actions I volunteer to guide them towards, permitting those on hand to pay witness to any scenes which I determine to be noteworthy examples of behavior on my part which the audience must have the privilege of observing on a direct basis, of course. I did choose on the occasion in question to assault a 2nd-victim in the incident itself, in order to complete the 2nd-stage necessary in the agenda which I'm attempting to fulfill in order to guarantee I finalize the steps in the process of self-enlightenment, which itself comprises a program of stages which I set forth for myself to conduct at an earlier point in the drama to ensure I secure for myself what I trust, in the end, will amount to a higher degree of "cosmic knowledge" in the world. I will, then, be in a position to bestow such wisdom upon others seeking enlightenment for themselves in the world as well.

01)<u>Note</u>:
   a)<u>Assignment#</u>: 002
   b)<u>Date</u> <u>of</u> <u>Assignment's</u> <u>Occurrence</u>:
     --.SUN., December 07, 2003:
   c)<u>Specific</u> <u>Task</u> <u>to</u> <u>Fulfill</u>:
     --.The single instance of a felony-level "sexcrime"-assault against a female target whom the assailant (i.e., Ariq) determines can serve him as a suitable victim in the particular case in question
   d)<u>Summary</u> <u>of</u> <u>actions</u> <u>transpiring</u> <u>in</u> <u>the</u> <u>attempt</u> <u>to</u> <u>complete</u> <u>the</u> <u>specific</u> <u>assignment</u> <u>on</u> <u>record</u>:

I chose to commit a <u>second</u> "sexcrime"-assault at a "church"-property in the "Uptown"-District of the central-eastern "Metropolitan"-Area (i.e., at the "First Metropolitan House of the Ancient Gospel", a "Protestant"-faith site of fellowship, found not far from the spot in the "Laurel Park"-region in which I currently reside). I began the overnight-episode's adventure at a "RedbannerUSA^STF"-outlet and then had to walk towards the church-location itself on foot as I sought to initiate the most recent criminal encounter on record for any companions on hand to review, here. Near the specific "church"-location I was quickly able to encounter the target which I saw as suitable, a young Korean-American female who chose to park her car on a street two blocks from the church's property and then chose to attempt to walk herself home past the church building. The "sexcrime"-assault itself did occur on East Franklin Street, several blocks east of the corner of North Rocolo Ave. and East Franklin Street, a specific intersection upon which a

"RedbannerUSA[STF]"-minimart location is to be easily found for immediate use by any traveling through the area. On the occasion in question, I chose to loiter outside the minimart-outlet for a number of minutes after purchasing a soda and a couple of hot dogs (wieners, with mustard, onions, pickle-relish, and multigrain sausage-buns) at the outlet's grilling station.

I had no choice but to converse with another outside the venue who did approach me in order to request a small onsite donation of "spare change" to assist in maintaining the man's personal upkeep on the date in question. After eating the two hot dogs on the patio outside the front entrance of the "RedbannerUSA[STF]"-outlet, I next chose to proceed to march myself towards the east on East Franklin Street in hopes of positioning myself outside a "church property"-building found on the block in order to loiter with intent for a potential target to prey upon as an assailant in conducting the 2nd-stage of the agenda I'm attempting to fulfill to complete all steps necessary in the process of self-enlightenment which I've set forth as a goal to achieve here in Minneapolis. The victim of choice is a specific female I've had the opportunity to notice in the area before at such an hour late on odd Saturday nights on the occasions in which I've chosen to venture to this particular location in order to scout out the neighborhood for potential targets who just so happen to be frequent visitors to that locale in the "after hours"-era of the perdiem-cycle of expiring time, once the neighboring streets appear to be vacant of any incoming pedestrians or motorists.

I did manage to commit the 2nd "sexcrime"-assault incident in attempting to complete the agenda which I'm pursuing in order to fulfill all requirements in the process of self-enlightenment which I've set forth for myself to *ultimately* finalize. I, of course, view the act of violating the Korean-American woman on this particular occasion as *necessary* in my attempt to pursue the agenda which I've set forth for myself to finalize in the "Perspective on the Process of Self-Enlightenment", viewing the incident as the necessary 2nd-stage in the process itself which I'm attempting to fulfill, yet another example of crime in which I select to violate the most ancient of "penal code"-regulations which humans sought to establish to safeguard the stability of a humane and decent society for the purpose of benefitting such a society's citizens with respect to their well-being and peace of mind, those being specific values which the citizenry trusts they're entitled to possess as "civilized" creatures co-habitating with each other in a human community. On completing the incident itself, I trust I'll receive what amounts to a particularly high degree of enlightenment (i.e., "cosmic knowledge"), which I'll benefit from upon the completion of the entire process of the "Perspective", allowing me to, thereby, bestow such wisdom on others seeking enlightenment in the world as well.

At the site of the violation itself, I had with me on the occasion occurring one week ago, as of SUN., Dec. 07, 2003, that is, of course, the assortment of "nocturnal"–warfare instruments which I keep handy for use once attempting to conduct a "sexcrime"-assault against a suitable female target in the pursuit of the agenda on "Self-Enlightenment" which I, here, in Minneapolis, have chosen to fervently attempt to complete for myself. I had with me, when assaulting the Korean-American female but a week ago, the boxcutting-blade, the 100-gram canister of "pepperspray", the anti-respiratory inhalant formula polluting the recipient's air-channeling passages with microscopic granules of toxic-level powder which the human lungs are incapable of adequately absorbing and expelling, and the stainless steel wrist-locking rings beneficial for use at the time of the "sexcrime"-incident in question.

At the site of the violation itself, I did commit an act of forced oral-stimulation of the male sex organ (i.e., the penis, that is) and, once again, an incident of sodomy (i.e., "rear-cavity" penetration, that would be) against the Korean crime-victim, while, yet again, the woman in question was bound with both arms behind her back with use of the stainless-steel wristlocking instruments available to me for use at the time in immobilizing the human target on hand.

Prior to initializing the "sexcrime"-assault against the particular female at the time of the incident in question, I, just before approaching the victim on the occasion, chose to utter, for the benefit of those on hand in the listening audience, the following words, as if to announce a declaration of victory in the quest I'm on to locate a suitable victim to serve me as a target in my attempt to complete a necessary stage in the agenda which I'm attempting to fulfill in order to finalize the process of enlightenment ... *"And, lo, the footman came and, thus, he chose to place the <u>second</u> sacrificial female on the altar as a gift to 'Wisdom', a tribute from the warlord emergent in him, a soul irrevocably sworn to abide by an oath of loyalty to Enlightenment itself!"*

I did, yet again, choose to utter unto the Korean-American female a line of <u>last</u> <u>words</u>, so to speak, to serve as a farewell prior to the final parting, as we, of course, went our separate ways upon completion of the assault itself. (... Ha! Ha! Ha! Ha! Ha!) Just prior to the moment of exiting the scene of the particular "sexcrime"-incident, occurring, once more, one week ago (SUN., Dec. 07, 2003), I, in fact, did inform the victim, while I saw her suffering in a state of respiratory-restriction due to the inhalant-formula I chose to fumigate her with, contaminating the air-channeling passages with the microscopic particles of lung irritant, that she, in fact, was not to inform local "law enforcement"-authorities (or anyone else, for that matter) about the incident of violation just transpiring against her at the unremorseful hands made use of in apprehending and abusing the Asiatic-American crime-victim (i.e., the "Asianamerican") in question on that particular occasion, old friends and constant companions whom I select to conveniently keep at close range.

Tasting Droplets of the Unforgettable Rain

By
Adrien L. Montgomery

<u>Cycle</u> <u>010</u>:

"After the 'Hat Trick', the Performer Tips His Visor in Acknowledging an Appreciative Audience Standing in Applause in Recognition of the Protagonist's Ability to Entertain Them."

<u>UTA</u> <u>Directive</u> <u>X</u>:

"Attention! Attention! ... The 'Raibus[AI]'-System Will Remain Idle Momentarily Until Transit-Workers Can Remove An Obstacle Found On The Tracks Ahead Of Us. Repeat, The 'Railbus[AI]'-System Will Remain Idle Momentarily Until Transit-Workers Can Remove An Obstacle Found On The Tracks Ahead Of Us."

("<u>UTA</u>": <u>U</u>rban <u>T</u>ransit <u>A</u>uthority)

The following announcement is spoken "on air" by the "after hours"-host of a broadcasting segment appearing on a ("['Nineteen-Eighties']-era/['Pop']-music")-radio station popular on the FM-band in the local region's radio market, who presents records ready for instant airplay at the station for a listenership selecting to tune in to the specific frequency found along the selection dial to hear the variety of hosts present to them a menu of Rock-music familiar to those remembering the "Popmusic"-era of the 1980's (i.e., the ['Arena']-Rock, ['Glam']-Metal, ['Hard']-Rock, ['Pop']-Rock, and, in even some cases, ['Alternative']-Rock), which became favorites for radio fans tuning in to "FM"-radio back in the "Eighties".

"Welcome, 'Rock & Rollers', to the Midnight-shift of the 'Rock Me House', tonight. I'm your grateful and engaging host, of course, 'Backstage' Carter Bachman. Why? ... Because, whenever a 'Hot Rock'-band visits the 'Twin Cities'-region to perform in concert for fans inhabiting the settlements found along the northern span of the Mississippi, that's exactly where I'll be on the night of the big gig ... '<u>backstage</u>', of course! And **you** can be there <u>with</u> me, if you're the lucky winner of one of our 'Meet-the-Band Quiz Contests'! ... This next track is going out to 'Ariq', who prefers to call himself the 'Lunarmaniac', who's just quietly keeping himself at home tonight in 'Laurel Park', listening to the late-night listener's favorite DJ, **me**, of course, on the 'Rock Me House'.... Now we'll all hear 'The Third Time Around' by Dragonflame, one of the great 'Eighties' bands, if I do say so myself. You have a decent night, Ariq, and, perhaps, it's better—for anyone

--()--
134
--()--

involved—that you <u>do</u> decide to keep yourself at home tonight.... Ha! Ha! Ha! Ha! You're listening to 'Backstage' Carter Bachman at KRMH 'Rock Me House' 103.5-FM in the 'Twin Cities'—Minneapolis and Saint Paul."

(-|<u>Calendar</u> <u>Date</u>: <u>SUN</u>., <u>Dec</u>. <u>21</u>, <u>2003</u>|-)

Here, I would prefer to indicate to persons in the reading audience that what is about to transpire in the lines of text which you will soon have the opportunity to review at your convenience, of course, will amount to what is basically a *summarization* of an incident which occurred earlier in the "narrative"-drama which currently unfolds in front of your *oh-so-attentive* eyes, old friends and familiar cohorts close by, which I do choose, here, to re-examine in this particular instance in order to ensure the audience on hand is aware of the exact reason as to why I did select to commit a specific "sexcrime"-assault against the particular victim in question in this case. I did choose, again, to commit an incident of aggression towards a female resident inhabiting a neighborhood within the vicinity of the "Central Commerce District" (one week ago, as of SUN., Dec. 14, 2003, that would be) to complete the 3rd-stage necessary in the agenda which I'm attempting to fulfill in order to finalize the steps appearing in the process of self-enlightenment, a program of stages which I set forth for myself to complete earlier on in the narrative in order to secure for myself what I trust, in the end, will be a higher degree of wisdom (i.e., "cosmic knowledge" in the world), which I'll then be able to bestow upon others who approach me in order to also seek enlightenment for themselves as well.

01)<u>Note</u>:
    a)<u>Assignment#</u>: 003
    b)<u>Date</u> <u>of</u> <u>Assignment's</u> <u>Occurrence</u>:
      --.SUN., December 14, 2003:
    c)<u>Specific</u> <u>Task</u> <u>to</u> <u>Fulfill</u>:
      --.The single instance of a felony-level "sexcrime"-assault against a female target whom the assailant (i.e., Ariq) determines can serve him as a suitable victim in the particular case in question
    d)<u>Summary</u> <u>of</u> <u>actions</u> <u>transpiring</u> <u>in</u> <u>the</u> <u>attempt</u> <u>to</u> <u>complete</u> <u>the</u> <u>specific</u> <u>assignment</u> <u>on</u> <u>record</u>:

I, Ariq, did choose to commit a <u>third</u> "sexcrime"-assault at a "church"-location near the "Uptown"-District of the Urbanzone which I just so happen to currently inhabit, at the "Fellowship of Our Lord's Frist Apostles", that is. I did begin the night's expedition while sitting aboard a "MetroTransit"-busroute and had, while on the mass-transit vehicle, the opportunity to strike up a conversation with a passenger happening to sit right next to me aboard the citywide shuttle-service. I chose to disboard the vehicle at a

--()--
135
--()--

stop in the "Uptown"-region and made myself wait for a particular female to casually walk past me. The female in question was, in fact, a Native-American woman who, at the time, was attempting to walk to a busroute-station three blocks up the street from where I stood in order to observe her. The assault did actually occur on Wyndale Ave., at a spot a fair distance down the street from a "convenience"-outlet, which I entered a while earlier in order to purchase a microwavable "barbeque-beef" sandwich and a 32-oz. cup of "Sprite™" Lemon-Lime soda. While outside the minimart-outlet, I consumed the sandwich I had in hand and the soda I acquired at a cola-dispensing fountain found at the rear of the convenience-store itself.

After eating, I began to march myself south on Wyndale Ave. until I did notice a young woman who was just stepping out of a parked vehicle positioned on the East-side of the asphalt auto-traffic route. I waited, while unnoticed by her, while the woman stepped away from her car and began to head south, in my direction on Wyndale Ave. Once I realized the woman had crossed a particular street ("Oak Grove Circle", that would be), I realized she'd, then, be forced to march past the "Protestant Church"-setting which stands on the corner of Wyndale Ave. and Carinolia Road, at which point I'd have the necessary opportunity to steer her, at knife-point, of course, into a stairwell that descends to a lower landing on the basement-level of a building behind the "church"-house itself, securing the privacy I'll require in order to initialize the specific assault I sought to begin on the exact occasion in question.

I did commit the 3rd "sexcrime"-assault incident against the unsuspecting female in question in attempting to complete the agenda which I'm pursuing in order to fulfill the requirements in the process of self-enlightenment which I've set forth for myself to ultimately finalize, here, in the state of Minnesota.

I, Ariq, of course, viewed the act of violating the Native-American woman on this particular occasion as a necessary stage in my attempt to pursue the agenda which I've set forth for myself to finalize in the "Philosophical Perspective on the Process of 'Self-Enlightenment' ", viewing the incident itself as the necessary 3rd-stage in the process which I'm attempting to fulfill, yet another violation against the most ancient of laws which humans sought to establish in order to safeguard the stability of a humane and decent society for the benefit of such a society's citizens with respect to their well-being and peace of mind, those being specific values which the citizenry trusts they're entitled to possess as "civilized" creatures co-habitating with each other in a human community. On completing the incident itself, I trust I'll receive what amounts to a particularly high degree of enlightenment (i.e., "cosmic knowledge"), which I'll benefit from upon the ultimate completion of the **entire** schedule itself, allowing me to, thereby, bestow such wisdom on others choosing to approach me in order to seek enlightenment in the world as well.

At the site of the violation itself (once again, 1 week ago, as of SUN., Dec. 14, 2003), I had with me, of course, the assortment of "nocturnal"-warfare instruments which I keep handy for use once attempting to conduct an assault against a female in the pursuit of the agenda on "Self-Enlightenment" which I, here, in Minneapolis, have chosen to undeniably a-dopt for myself to *ultimately* fulfill. I had with me the boxcutting-blade, the 100-gram aluminum canister of "pepperspray", the anti-respiratory inhalant formula to let me saturate a recipient's air-channeling system with microscopic granules of toxic-level powder which the human lungs are incapable of adequately absorbing and expelling, and the stainless steel wrist-locking rings for beneficial use at the time of the incident in question in order to assist in the act of immobilizing an assault-victim.

At the site of the violation, I did, yet again, commit an act of forced oral-stimulation of the male sex organ (i.e., penis), and, once again, an incident of sodomy (i.e., "rear-cavity" penetration) against the Native-American crime-victim, while, yet again, the woman in question was bound with arms in a pinching hold behind her back with use of the stainless-steel wristlocking instruments which I keep handy on such occasions.

Prior to initializing the "sexcrime"-assault against the particular female at the time of the incident in question, I, just prior to approaching the victim on the occasion, chose to utter, for the benefit of those on hand in the listening audience, the following words, as if to announce a declaration of victory in the particular quest I began in order to locate a suitable victim to serve me as a target in my attempt to complete a necessary stage in the agenda which I'm attempting to fulfill in order to finalize the process of self-enlightenment ... *"And, lo, the footman came and, thus, he chose to place the <u>third</u> sacrificial female on the altar as a gift to 'Wisdom', a tribute from the warlord emergent in him, a soul irrevocably sworn to abide by an oath of loyalty to Enlightenment itself!"*

I did select, upon parting ways, yet again, with the victim in question (i.e., the Native-American woman, a member of either the "Choctaw Nation"-tribal group or the "Chickasaw Nation"-tribal group here in the "Northern Plains"-section of the Midwestern US, I'm assuming), to speak to her a line of, once again, <u>last words</u> for the benefit of listeners in the audience on hand at the time. At the close of the "sexcrime"-assault incident, just prior to the moment at which I chose to exit the scene of the violation itself, i.e., the "Protestant Faith"-property location on Wyndale Avenue and Carinolia Road, I did inform the victim, while I saw her still suf-fering in the familiar state of respiratory-restriction due to the inhalant-formula I chose to fumigate her with, she, of course, was not to inform lo-cal "law enforcement"-authorities (or anyone else, for that matter) about the "sexcrime"-incident just transpiring against her at the pair of menacing hands which I, with a spasm of unrelenting rudeness, chose to place upon her in order to initialize and complete the incident of unlawful sexual aggression occurring against her on the grounds of the prayer house built for those subscribing to the ancient Christian scriptures which attendees on hand at the prayer house's weekly sermon believe in strictly abiding by.

Tasting Droplets of the Unforgettable Rain

By
Adrien L. Montgomery
Cycle 011:
"On the Occasional Night, the Predatory Soul Seeks to Appease its Appetite in Venturing Forth Towards a Familiar Hunting Ground, to Again Find Prey to Easily Feed Upon."

UTA Directive XI:
"Attention! Attention! … The 'Railbus[AI]'-Vehicle Will Be Boarded At This Station By The 'Metrotransit'-Police. Be Ready To Present Valid Tickets And Transit-Fare Passes To The Officers Upon Request. Repeat, The 'Railbus[AI]'-Vehicle Will Be Boarded At This Station By The 'Metrotransit'-Police. Be Ready To Present Valid Tickets And Transit-Fare Passes To The Officers Upon Request."
("UTA": Urban Transit Authority)

What follows in the ensuing segment is an announcement spoken by the anchorman of an evening news-broadcast at the ABC-TV Network's local affiliate-station in the "Twin Cities"-region (i.e., "WTWN-TV" News Channel 07), who hosts the news program occurring subsequent to the nationwide broadcast network's newscasting program seen at 5:30 p.m., C.S.T., who seeks to inform the populace inhabiting the region constituting the local television market in offering reports on noteworthy incidents occurring in the "Twin Cities"-region over the previous 24-hour term, since the beginning of the previous evening's on-air edition of the newscasting bureau's nightly episode.

"Good evening, I'm Jason Monroe, the host of WTWN-TV's evening newscast on ABC-TV's News Channel 07, 'Twin Cities Tonight', for SUN., Dec. 28, 2003. The top report our segment-producers have chosen to lead tonight's newscast is, of course, on the continuing case involving the series of 'sexual assault'-crimes against young females residing in the 'Minneapolis Greater Metropolitan Area'. The most up-to-date police reports released to the media by the Minneapolis Police Department indicate investigators in the agency's 'Sex Crimes'-Division are still active-ly searching for any available leads at all in the high-priority level local case that could help agents on staff at the citywide public safety office determine the identity and possible whereabouts of the assailant guilty of perpetrating the incidents of assault against women in the 'Central Commerce District' of Minneapolis. Investigators have produced an 'E-mail'-transmission which they believe is from the perpetrator himself informing any agents on staff in the 'Sex Crimes'-Division to avoid looking for him at any 'Boxcar Pizza[STF]'-outlet, due to the fact he stopped patronizing the well-known food-vending chain after the City Health Department suspended their license to sell alcohol…. Well, I guess that would mean the 'Boxcar Pizza[STF]'-outlets around the 'Minneapolis Metropolitan'-region are safe venues for the area's young women to visit at night, folks."

(-|Calendar Date: SUN., Dec. 28, 2003|-)

I do, here, old friends, select to indicate to the members of the reading audience on hand that, in all certainty, what transpires in the subsequent statement of mine will amount to what is merely a *summarization* of an incident which actually transpired earlier in the "narrative"-drama unfolding in front of your very eyes, in an instance occurring one week ago, to be precise (as of SUN., Dec. 21, 2003, that would be), which I choose, here, to re-examine in this particular instance, for the reader's benefit, in order to ensure the audience in attendance is aware of the exact reason as to why I chose to commit the "sexcrime"-assault against the victim in question, i.e., the young "Omani" female, that would be. I did so, I trust you would be ready to accept by this particular moment in the "narrative"-presentation on exhibit before the audience in attendance, in order to, yet again, attempt to complete the 4th-stage necessary in the specific agenda which I'm attempting to fulfill in order to finalize the steps in the "Process of Self-Enlightenment", a program of stages which I set forth for myself to complete, of course, at an earlier point in the narrative in order to secure for myself what I trust, in the end, will be a higher degree of "Cosmic Knowledge" in the world, which I'll then be able to bestow upon others who approach me to seek a higher degree of enlightenment as well.

01)Note:
    a)Assignment#: 004
    b)Date of Assignment's Occurrence:
      --.SUN., December 21, 2003:
    c)Specific Task to Fulfill:
      --.The single instance of a felony-level "sexcrime"-assault against a female target whom the assailant (i.e., Ariq) determines can serve him as a suitable victim in the particular case in question
    d)Summary of actions transpiring in the attempt to complete the specific assignment on record:

--()--
139
--()--

Adrien L. Montgomery
Tasting Droplets of the Unforgettable Rain
Official Imprint: "Dynamographx"

I did commit a <u>fourth</u> incident of sexual violation against a particular female on hand in order to continue to pursue the agenda I've chosen to adopt for myself, here, in the state of Minnesota, in fulfilling the "Perspective on 'Self-Enlightenment' " which I've set forth for myself to *ultimately* finalize with the aim of becoming an individual who possesses a higher degree of "enlightenment" (i.e., "spiritual wisdom", "cosmic knowledge", etc.) in the world which I can, *ultimately*, upon completion of the task which I've imposed on myself, bestow upon other members of humanity who also aim to seek a higher level of wisdom for themselves as well. In this particular instance, to conduct the crime of sexual assault, I did select for myself an "Omani" woman (a young Arab female) whom I witnessed walking from a car on Lakefront Avenue in the "Uptown"-District, heading west, presumably to the "Hennenburgh Transit Exchange Depot" found at the intersection of Lakefront Avenue and Hennenburgh Boulevard.

I, at once, upon realizing the opportunity at hand, chose to follow the woman in question quietly until I saw her stall herself at the intersection of Lakefront Avenue and So. Gamington Road, realizing, on the moment, I had, immediately, the obvious, ready-made option of steering the woman to a spot behind the high wood-crafted perimeter wall serving as a boundary between the "Protestant Church"-property on the corner of So. Gamington Road and Lakefront Avenue and the lot of vacant residential acreage just north of the "Church"-grounds—a conveniently isolating location which would offer to us a spot I would deem as adequate in its ability to provide us with a sufficient level of privacy which I, of course, would determine to be necessary in order to conduct the act of assault I must commit myself to conducting in order to complete the next stage in the agenda which I'm attempting to fulfill to finalize the "Perspective on 'Self-Enlightenment' ", a program of stages which I desire to see myself complete for the purpose of obtaining a higher degree of wisdom, enlightenment, or cosmic knowledge, etc., in the world at large, which we all happen to happily (or, perhaps, unhappily) inhabit. The name of the "church"-building itself is the "Eternal Redeemer's Church of the Northern Plains", a "Protestant Faith"-property serving as a service-site for the congregation desiring to assemble in its sanctuary each Sunday to receive the pastor's weekly sermon advising the church-goers on the path each one on hand must adopt in order to walk a road in the world the Lord would find acceptable for the righteous child to choose for himself in life.

Prior to approaching the particular victim in question on the occasion itself occurring in this instance a week ago, I had the opportunity to make note of an exhibition of "bumper"-stickers positioned on the rear-trunk of the woman's motor-vehicle, which she parked on the northside of Lakefront Avenue prior to going west on foot beside the urban autotraffic route. The bumper-stickers in question did, I'll note, just so happen to display imagery earmarking the vehicle's owner as a migrant hailing from the country of Oman, a monarchial state found in the southeastern corner of the Arabian peninsula, whose coastal boundaries run alongside the Gulf of Oman and the Arabian Sea. Here is, on the rear-trunk of the woman's parked motor-vehicle, which she left on the northside of Lakefront Avenue, on the fateful evening in question, one week ago, one sticker featuring an Omani national flag, a sticker with an image of the moon in the "crescent"-phase of the Earth-satellite in its monthlong era of transformation, alongside a five-pointed star, of course, the image being a symbol indicating allegiance to or origin in the Arab world, another sticker presenting a message featuring the "Arabic"-script of written-language across it, and a sticker with the silhouette of an architectural exhibit presenting the minarets, domes, and top-ornaments (i.e., spires) for use in earmarking the temple with the classical design of an Islamic mosque.

I did commit the 4th "sexcrime"-assault incident in attempting to complete the agenda which I'm pursuing in order to fulfill the requirements in the "Process of 'Self-Enlightenment' " which I've set forth for myself to finalize while residing here in Minnesota.

I, Ariq, of course, view the act of violating the Omani woman on this particular occasion as necessary in the attempt I'm adopting in order to pursue the agenda I've set forth for myself to finalize in the "Perspective on the Process of 'Self-Enlightenment' ", viewing the incident as the *necessary* 4th-stage in the program which I'm attempting to fulfill, yet another violation against the most ancient of laws which humans sought to establish in order to safeguard the stability of a humane and decent society for the benefit of such a society's citizens with respect to their well-being and peace of mind, those being specific values which the citizenry trusts they're entitled to possess as "civilized" creatures co-habitating with each other in a human community. On completing the incident itself, I do trust I'll receive what amounts to a particularly high degree of enlightenment (i.e., spiritual wisdom or "cosmic knowledge"), which I'll benefit from upon the completion of the **entire** process itself, allowing me, then, to, thereby, bestow such wisdom on others who seek such enlightenment for themselves as well in the world.

At the site of the violation itself, I had with me, of course, the assortment of "nocturnal"–warfare instruments which I keep handy for use in attempting to conduct an assault against a female in the pursuit of the agenda on enlightenment which I, here, in Minneapolis, have chosen to fervently attempt for myself. I had with me the boxcutting-blade, the 100-gram aluminum canister of "pepperspray", the anti-respiratory inhalant formula polluting the recipient's air-channeling passages with microscopic granules of toxic-level powder which the human lungs are incapable of adequately absorbing and expelling, and the stainless steel wrist-locking rings for beneficial use at the time of the incident in question in order to place any particular victim in the obligatory compliance-hold to pinch both arms behind the woman's back with a securing bond, for both my safety and, of course, her own as well. (… Ha! Ha! Ha! Ha!)

For dinner, which I had, approximately, 3 hours before venturing forth onto the streets of the city's "Central Commerce Zone" in order to initialize the "sexcrime"-assault incident against any unsuspecting female whom I found myself happening across on the unfortunate occasion in question in order to make yet another leap ahead in the agenda I've chosen to pursue in finalizing the steps necessary in the "Perspective on 'Self-Enlightenment' ", I chose to serve to myself what would amount to the ordinary "Saturday Night"-menu one would find (and quite possibly enjoy, as well) if choosing to visit me at home on the specific weekend evening. I had three beer-battered fish-fillets (oven-cooked, <u>not</u> microwave-warmed), Alaskan pollock serving as the item's aquatic dish (or, marine meat) on offer, of course. I had a few forkfuls of horseradish which I chose to use as a dipping sauce for the bites of fish I consumed while enjoying the "Dinnertime"-menu. I also had, on the kitchen counter, for my eating convenience, a basket of potato chips with onion dip and a couple of split-top dinner rolls with vegetable oil spread as a layering agent for the sourdough bread. I also had 2 12-oz. bottles of "Starscreamer^{UE}"-brand "Premium Black Lager" beer which I chose to pour into a "single liter"-size plastic drinking mug with ice cubes to chill the domestic-brand of lager from a tray in the freezer-section of the ("['In House']-refrigeration")-unit.

At the site of the "sexcrime"-incident itself, I did commit an act of forced oral-stimulation of the male sex organ (i.e., penis), and, once again, an incident of sodomy (i.e., "rear-cavity" penetration) against the Omani crime-victim, while, yet again, the woman in question was, in fact, bound with both arms behind her back with use of the stainless-steel wristlocking instruments I had on hand at the time of the criminal act itself for use in immobilizing a human in a solid, subduing hold.

Prior to initializing the "sexcrime"-assault against the particular female at the time of the incident in question, I, just prior to approaching the victim on the specific occasion, did utter, for the benefit of those on hand in the listening audience, the following words, as if to announce a declaration of victory in my quest to locate a suitable victim to serve me as a target in the attempt I'm pursuing to complete a necessary stage in the agenda which I'm choosing to fulfill in order to finalize the process of self-enlightenment … *"And, lo, the footman came and, thus, he chose to place the <u>fourth</u> sacrificial female on the altar as a gift to 'Wisdom', a tribute from the warlord emergent in him, a soul irrevocably sworn to abide by an oath of loyalty to Enlightenment itself!"*

In this particular instance of sexual assault on my part as a predator operating with a menacing intent in the city's "Central Commerce District", due to the date in question, positioning the incident itself inside of close proximity to the occurrence of Christmas Day on December's monthlong calendar, I said, in parting ways with the Omani woman after completing the occurrence of a "sexcrime"-assault against the female on site, the following words in order to announce what I trust exhibits an example of the spirit of the season in indicating my desire to see her enjoy a memorable Christmastime Holiday, that would be, after leaving her in a state of emotional stress, psychological trauma, physical injury, societal exile, and womanly shame, due to the recently emergent status she's had no other choice but to assume as a "sexcrime"-assault victim: "Merry Christmas and Have a Happy New Year! ... Or, *should* I say, 'Merry <u>Shitmas</u> and Have a <u>Crappy</u> New Year!' ... Ha! Ha! Ha! Ha! ... See you in 2004, my *ever-so-convenient* companion.... Ha! Ha! Ha! Ha! ... Goodbye, *oh-so-near* one!"

Beyond the moment of good Christmastime cheer which I chose to bring forth on the moment in question, I did speak what would amount to a series of *last words*, chosen expressly for the victim on site, that would be—just prior to the moment on which I chose to finally part ways with the Omani woman, after the close of the "sexcrime"-assault itself, of course.

I did, in fact, inform the victim, while I saw her suffering in the familiar state of respiratory-restriction due to the inhalant-formula of granular liquid-spray which I chose to fumigate her with, not to inform local "law enforcement"-authorities (or anyone else, for that matter) about the incident of violation just transpiring against her at the pair of remorseless hands I, the predator, chose to put to use in ruthlessly mistreating the Omani female on that occasion outside the confines of the "Protestant Church"-property found on the corner of Lakefront Avenue and So. Gamington Road.

Tasting Droplets of the Unforgettable Rain

By
Adrien L. Montgomery
<u>Cycle</u> <u>012</u>:
"While Enjoying the Season of Peace and Goodwill Towards Men, One Overriding Word of Advice Ensuring the Balance of the Individual Holiday-Observer Survives the Course of the Calendar of Celebrations Amounts to an Adage Which Cannot Be Dismissed by Those Seeking to Embrace the Festive Era with Others, Which Would, of Course, Read as Follows: 'Tis Better To Give Than To Receive!"

<u>UTA</u> <u>Directive</u> <u>XII</u>:
"Attention! Attention! ... Guests Aboard The ... 'CitiTraxx^{STF}' Railsystem-(X)

--()--
143
--()--

Adrien L. Montgomery

Tasting Droplets of the Unforgettable Rain

Official Imprint: "Dynamographx"

Vehicle Must Refrain From Speaking To Others Or Playing Music On Hand-Held Devices At Disruptively High Volumes. Repeat, Guests Aboard The 'CitiTraxx^{STF}' Railsystem-Vehicle Must Refrain From Speaking To Others Or Playing Music On Hand-Held Devices At Disruptively High Volumes."
("UTA": **U**rban **T**ransit **A**uthority)

What follows is an announcement made by the anchorman hosting the evening newscast of the local network-affiliate station in the "Twin Cities"-broadcasting market, for the CBS-TV Network's regional news partner, "WCTS-TV" News Channel 09 ("Action News Nine"), who's presenting public news updates to the "local area"-viewership to keep the "community"-inhabitants up-to-date regarding the police information found thus far relating to the ongoing case of the "sexcrime"-assailant, still determined to be at large in the "Central Commerce District" of the "Minneapolis Metropolitan Area" as of the date of the newscast segment itself. The anchor announces the latest report which local investigators in the "Sexual Predators"-Division have forwarded to the Press to keep the community on alert until the officers on staff at the city's Public Safety Agency can apprehend the party guilty of perpetrating such atrocious actions against local female residents.

"Welcome to 'Action News Nine' with Kenneth Crawlings for the date of SUN., Jan. 04, 2004. The lead report we begin with this evening, of course, covers the case involving the series of sexual assaults perpetrated by a local assailant whom the police have identified, thus far, as the 'Shadowslasher'. The most recent update on file indicates a professor of criminology at the University of Minnesota specializing in sexual predators, currently working hand-in-hand with investigators on the ongoing criminal case, has offered an additional nickname 'police agency'-employees can immediately put to use in referring to the assailant which the authorities are searching for at the moment. Professor Samuel Wellerman believes police and media agencies alike should, henceforth, refer to the predator guilty of conducting the series of assaults in the Minneapolis 'Central Commerce District' by the name of ... *'Suzannah Buttercup'?!* Says Professor Wellerman to the members of the local press today: 'Angering the predator is the best way to guarantee he starts making mistakes in his assaults against the women he preys on. Once that happens, investigators can easily gain leads which will assist the agency in finally apprehending him! ... Using <u>this</u> name in local media reports as an identifier for the perpetrator in these particular instances of crime should definitely infuriate such an individual as he, I'd have to say'."

(-|Calendar Date: <u>SUN</u>., <u>Jan</u>. <u>04</u>, <u>2004</u>|-)

--()--
144
--()--

I'm indicating, here, with this statement, to the members of the reading audience that what transpires in the following segment is basically a *summarization* of an incident which occurred earlier in the "narrative"-drama, which I'm choosing with this opportunity to re-examine in this particular instance in order to ensure the audience is aware of the exact reason as to why I chose to conduct the particular incident of indecent activity which I did agree to conduct on a recent occasion. The incident in question was necessary in order, of course, to complete the 5th-stage in the agenda which I'm attempting to fulfill in order to finalize the steps in the "Philosophical Perspective on the Process of 'Self-Enlightenment' ", a program of stages which I set forth for myself to complete earlier in the "narrative"-drama in order to secure for myself what I trust, in the end, will be a higher degree of wisdom (i.e., "cosmic knowledge") in the world, which I'll then be able to bestow upon others who approach me to also seek enlightenment for themselves as well.

01)<u>Note</u>:
    a)<u>Assignment#</u>: 005
    b)<u>Date of Assignment's Occurrence</u>:
      --.SUN., December 28, 2003:
    c)<u>Specific Task to Fulfill</u>:
      --.An incident of self-violation at the hands of another perpetrator to complete what I view as the <u>final</u> stage in the agenda which I'm attempting to pursue in order to fulfill the "Perspective on 'Self-Enlightenment' " which I desire to complete in order to obtain a higher level of wisdom (i.e., "cosmic knowledge") in the world at large, which I will, then, choose to bestow upon others seeking measures of spiritual wisdom from me in the world as well.
    d)<u>Summary of actions transpiring in the attempt to complete the specific assignment on record</u>:

I agreed to subject myself to an incident of sodomy at the hands of another <u>man</u>, which, in this specific incident, would be a Somali immigrant, i.e., a member of the Somali community residing in our city's "Central Commerce District" in high numbers since initially arriving in Minnesota as a "refugee"-community in 1995, that is. The man's name is "Ibrahim Hossein" and he claims he originally hails from Mogadishu, both the administrative center in and largest city of Somalia, a country found in the central-eastern sector of the African continent with an eastern shoreline running alongside the northwestern edge of an ever-idling Indian Ocean. The incident was meant on my part to fulfill all requirements set forth by me necessary to finalize the process of self-enlightenment in order to achieve the highest allotment of enlightenment which would guarantee the most beneficial reward yet—which I can secure for myself upon once completing the process of self-enrichment which I'm pursuing in the world.

<u>On the Incident of "Rear-Orifice" Penetration</u>:
I did choose to submit to an incident of sodomy (i.e., "rear-cavity" penetration) at the hands of a Somali immigrant man in an apartment on Rocolo Ave. and N. 4th Street (the "Fourth & Roc", that is), a complex to be found just one block north of the "Light Rail"-station which is situated on Rocolo Arcade and N. 5th Street.

The incident of rear-orifice penetration at the hands of the Somali immigrant man at the housing complex on N. 4th Street and Rocolo Arcade occurred on the night of SUN., Dec. 28, 2003. I did commit the <u>final</u> "sexcrime"-assault incident in attempting to complete the agenda which I'm pursuing in order to fulfill all requirements in the process of self-enlightenment which I've set forth for myself to finalize in pursuing "spiritual wisdom", the incident itself being an instance of <u>self</u>-violation at the hands of another perpetrator, who, in this instance, would, of course, be the Somali immigrant man in the apartment-unit on N. 4th Street and N. Rocolo Ave. (i.e., the "Fourth & Roc", again).

I, of course, viewed the act of self-violation at the hands of the Somali immigrant man on this particular occasion as *necessary* in my attempt to pursue the agenda which I've set forth for myself to finalize in the "Perspective on the Process of Self-Enlightenment", viewing the incident as the necessary (and <u>final</u>) stage in the specific process which I'm attempting to fulfill, yet another violation against the most ancient of laws which humans sought to establish to safeguard the stability of a humane and decent society for the benefit of such a society's citizens with respect to their well-being and peace of mind, those being specific values which the citizenry trusts they're entitled to possess as "civilized" creatures cohabitating with each other in a <u>human</u> community.

On completing the incident itself, I trust, I'll receive what amounts to a particularly high degree of enlightenment (i.e., "cosmic knowledge"), which I'll benefit from upon the completion of the process itself, allowing me to, thereby, bestow such wisdom on others seeking enlightenment as well in the world. In this particular instance, I trust, due to the fact the incident in question amounts to what is the <u>final</u>, or culminating, stage of the "Perspective on 'Self-Enlightenment' "—I do trust—upon the incident's completion, I will receive an *inordinately* high-level of enlightenment (or, "cosmic knowledge") bestowed upon me due to my choice to violate what would be, once again, ancient human laws established ages ago in order to safeguard the stability of a decent, humane society for the purpose of ensuring the well-being and peace of mind of citizens residing together in what they can declare to be a *civilized* community of human beings, i.e., a society of *evolved* creatures, <u>rather</u> than merely a gathering of *primitive* types.

With this particular incident, of course, I trust I've *finally* managed to complete all *necessary* stages on record to fulfill the requirements set forth in the "Perspective on Self-Enlightenment" which I established for myself to finalize at the beginning of the drama, the process by which one could attempt to pursue a higher degree of wisdom for himself in the world by completing an agenda in which he agrees to, once more, violate the most ancient of laws which humans sought to establish to safeguard the stability of a humane and decent society for the benefit of such a society's citizens with respect to their well-being and peace of mind, those being specific values which the citizenry trusts they're entitled to possess as "civilized" creatures co-habitating with each other in a human community, in order to receive various degrees of "cosmic knowledge" bestowed on such an individual with *each* separate act which he chooses to commit against such a codebook of behavioral precepts or strictures with the *ultimate* objective being to pursue a higher level of "spiritual wisdom".

At the location of the violation itself, I did have with me at the time, in all certainty, the familiar menu of "nocturnal"–warfare instruments which I keep handy for use once attempting to conduct an assault against a "female" in the pursuit of the agenda on enlightenment which I, here, in Minneapolis, have chosen to fervently attempt for myself. I had with me the boxcutting-blade, the 100-gram aluminum canister of "pepperspray", the anti-respiratory inhalant formula polluting the recipient's air-channeling passages with microscopic granules of a toxic-level powder which the human lungs are incapable of adequately absorbing and expelling, and the stainless steel wrist-locking rings—items for beneficial use at the time of the incident in question in order to immobilize an unwilling victim.

At the site of the violation, I was, on the night itself, subjected to an incident of rear-orifice penetration by the Somali immigrant, who placed me in the set of stainless steel wristlocking-rings to bind both my arms behind my back, in emulation of the compliance-hold which I, of course, subjected my female victims to earlier in the agenda which I chose to pursue for myself in Minnesota. I was then, in the apartment in the building on N. 4th Street and N. Rocolo Avenue (the "Fourth & Roc", that would be), forced to perform an incident of oral stimulation of the male sexual organ, once again, while still bound with the set of wristlocking-rings serving to bind my arms behind my back, to secure them in a pinching hold during the particular sexual act itself. I performed the incident of oral arousal of the male sexual organ while on my knees in front of the Somali man, the African immigrant, who stood naked before me, i.e., the "victim", that would be, in this particular instance. In the apartment complex on N. 4th Street and N. Rocolo Ave. (i.e., the "Fourth & Roc"), I was also subjected to a dosage of the pepperspray formula, the anti-respiratory inhalant-mixture of granules forming a toxic-level lung irritant entering the victim's air-channeling passages in the form of an aerosol solution comprising the anti-personnel grains of indigestible powder. I had to inhale the liquid-built aerosol-form respiratory-restrictor myself for the very first time that is, old friends and constant companions on hand…. Yuck!!

Prior to initializing the particular "sexcrime"-assault at the hands of the Somali immigrant man, a subscriber to the scriptural lessons found in old scrolls of the Islamic faith, I, just prior to entering the lobby-level of the apartment-complex (just north of the "CitiTraxx[STF]"-railsystem station), did choose to utter, for the benefit of those on hand in the listening audience, on the occasion, the following words, as if to announce a declaration of victory in my quest to locate a suitable *perpetrator* to serve as an "assailant" (in this case) in the attempt I chose to make in order to complete a necessary stage in the agenda I'm attempting to fulfill in order to finalize the process of self-enlightenment … *"And, lo, the footman came and, thus, he chose to place the <u>fifth</u> sacrificial human—himself—on the altar as a gift to 'Wisdom', a tribute from the warlord emergent in him, a soul irrevocably sworn to abide by an oath of loyalty to Enlightenment itself!"*

I did choose to have a "Dinnertime"-menu earlier in the evening prior to the decision on my part to venture forth onto the streets of the "Central Commerce District" on that specific date in question to travel to the apartment of the immigrant Somali man with the aim of attempting to complete the <u>final</u> stage in the agenda which I'm attempting to fulfill in the state of Minnesota in order to complete <u>all</u> requirements necessary to finalize the "Process of Self-Enlightenment" in order to receive a higher degree of wisdom (i.e., "Cosmic Knowledge") in the world. Prior to the incident of "rear-cavity" penetration at the hands of the Somali immigrant man, I chose to eat at a well-known "spaghetti house"-venue found just north of the "Central Commerce District", near the southern bank of the Mississippi River. The venue itself is known as "Pots, Pans, and Lotsa Pasta[UE]", an outlet appearing as one station in a nationwide chain of "spaghetti"-vending houses, with this restaurant in particular to be found on the corner of So. Washington Avenue and Oriole Avenue in the "South River"-District of the "North Metro"-Area.

As a child I remember going, on occasion, to the "Pots, Pans, and Lotsa Pasta[UE]" restaurant in Santa Lucia, California, which was in the "Oldtown"-District of the city. The venue itself stood beside a set of railroad tracks guiding extensive freight-engines carrying what would be industrial cargo to "rail transport"-depots found along the tracks further north of the bayside community which I had to reside in during that particular period. I remember the waiters working in the outlet's guest-seating room, using tubular rubber balloons in order to fashion animal-figures amounting to(X) instantly-made inflatable dolls for any children on hand to take home with them at the end of the evening. On one visit which my family and I paid to the location, a man sitting at the booth just beside ours asked one of the waiters for one of the tubular plastic balloons and shaped the balloon itself into an animal-figure before telling the waiter to hand it over to me in the next booth. ("Say, 'Thank You'!"—the parents did ask of me on receiving the gift from the dining guest in the next booth over.)

Yet, at the particular outlet I ate in prior to venturing to the Somali man's apartment (i.e., the "Fourth & Roc", of course) to <u>finally</u> fulfill all *necessary* requirements found in the "Perspective on Self-Enlightenment", the "Pots, Pans, and Lotsa Pasta[UE]" restaurant found on So. Washington Avenue and Oriole Avenue, that is, I didn't happen to notice any waiters using lengthy tubular plastic balloons to construct animal-figures by re-fashioning the balloons into dolls after inflating them. I.e., the kids attending the particular "spaghetti"-house venue didn't receive from the serving staff (or from guests) on hand the air-built animal-figures to take home with them at the end of their visit on that actual night. (((Sigh))).

Though I did manage to speak to the Somali immigrant in what would amount, I s'pose, to a set of *last words* occurring during the course of the incident of rear-orifice penetration which transpired in the apartment-complex on N. 4th Street and N. Rocolo Avenue (i.e., once again in a building known as the "Fourth & Roc"), uttering, despite the impediment to stable respiration caused by the aerosol-form granular inhalant-mixture, what would be words indicating to the immigrant man I, the "victim" in this specific case, do desire that he not inform any local "law enforcement"-agents (or anyone else, for that matter) about the incident occurring on the premises of the "tenancy"-complex (i.e., the "Fourth & Roc") in the "North Metro"-Area on that particular night in question, i.e., SUN., Dec. 28, 2003, that is…. Ha! Ha! Ha! Ha!

Tasting Droplets of the Unforgettable Rain

By
Adrien L. Montgomery
<u>Cycle 013</u>:
"When Traveling at Night, Choose a Chauffeur-Driven Vehicle to Permit Yourself as Occupant to Safely Voyage to the Nesting Station You're Hoping to Head to."

<u>UTA Directive XIII</u>:
"Attention! Attention! … The 'Cititraxx[STF]' Railsystem-Vehicle Will Be Delayed Momentarily At The Next Station While The Incoming Conductor Boards The Commuter Train In Order To Begin The Next Shift. Repeat, The

'Cititraxx[STF]' Railsystem-Vehicle Will Be Delayed Momentarily At The Next Station While The Incoming Conductor Boards The Commuter Train In Order To Begin The Next Shift."
("<u>UTA</u>": <u>U</u>rban <u>T</u>ransit <u>A</u>uthority)

The ensuing item is a news-update spoken by the anchorman of the "weekend"-edition of a nightly national newscast at the NBC-TV Network's local affiliate station in the "Twin Cities"-broadcasting market, i.e., "WMSP-TV" ("Evening News 03"), in a segment appearing "on air" on the affiliate-channel's Sunday evening local news program, to inform residents of the "Twin Cities"-region regarding reports on events producers at the affiliate-newsroom determine to be necessary to present to inhabitants of the "Minneapolis Greater Metropolitan Area" who choose to tune in to the news service's "Weekend Edition"-episode to update themselves on local events.

"Good Evening, ladies and gentlemen of Minneapolis and Saint Paul, I'm Philip Martleman, lead announcer of the NBC-TV Network's local news bureau, WMSP-TV 'News Channel 03', the flagship-station in the 'Twin Cities'-region for up-to-date events and affairs occurring in the southeastern-sector of the 'Land of 10,000 Lakes'. The lead segment on tonight's edition of 'Evening News 03' is, once again, concerning the continuing investigation by staffers at the Minneapolis Metropolitan Police Agency into the series of 'sexual assault'-crimes occurring at 'church'-properties in the city's 'Central Commerce District' over the past month. The lead criminal-profiler on hand at the 'Sex Crimes'-Division of the MPD has indicated that investigators have been questioning a man whom police determine to be their top suspect in the ongoing investigation of the case of 'rape'-crimes. The individual in question, one 'Lamar Lucas Montaine', who's currently employed as the barkeeper at the 'Gym Room', a gay nightclub found on N. Washington Ave. and N. Lumber St. in the 'Brick Wall'-District, indicates he's willing to apologize to the female victims he recently assaulted if squad-patrolmen at the 'MPD' agree to cancel their practice of conducting strip-searches of the male guests at the 'Gym Room' on Saturday nights. Says Lamar Lucas Montaine: 'Can't the police come to the party without *crashing* it?' "

(-|<u>Calendar</u> <u>Date</u>: <u>SUN</u>., <u>Jan</u>. <u>04</u>, <u>2004</u>|-)
What I'm indicating to you, old friends, with the scenario I, hereby, do present in the ensuing statement concerning the task I had to fulfill in traveling to a supermarket found in the local region on the date's specific occasion (i.e., "Lubrinski's Marketplace[AI]"), in order to acquire a list of "groceries"-items necessary in order to assemble ingredients for the preparation of "Breakfast"-, "Lunch"-, and "Dinner"-time menus which I'll be agreeably subsisting on over the span of the ensuing weeklong term as an

<table>
<tr><td>--()--</td></tr>
<tr><td>150</td></tr>
<tr><td>--()--</td></tr>
</table>

inhabitant currently selecting to reside in a residential complex found in the "Laurel Park"-District of the "Metro"-zone which I, at present, find myself existing in as the occupant, remember, of Apt. "#002", a unit on the basement-level of "The 'Falconeer' Building".

I did choose to travel on the evening transpiring to a local supermarket in order to acquire a list of groceries for myself to consume over the ensuing weeklong term at my convenience, as I determine the preparation of an adequate menu to be necessary from time to time, of course. Once outside the food market, at night, while standing in front of the entryway to the "groceries"-outlet (i.e., "Lubrinski's Marketplace[Al]"), I am awaiting the arrival of a taxi-cab which I called for via use of the ("['cellular']-service")-unit I carry with me on outdoor excursions from the cribbing-unit which I keep, in order to secure a safe-voyage home for myself after tonight's food-gathering task occurring at the market. Once inside the cab (a vanwagon with an immigrant driver from East Africa—probably Kenya), the "cabbie" sets the car radio's tuning pin to the Minneapolis affiliate-station of the Minnesota Public Radio Network, a statewide "public radio"-service broadcasting to residents of Minnesota a program of news, information, events, music, talk, entertainment, weather, traffic, etc., in order to keep its service-area's listenership as up-to-date as would be possible with notices meant to alert residents of the state as to any current events the radio-network's programming executives deem to be high-priority reports which the audience within the statewide network's broadcasting range should be aware of if choosing to tune in to the radio newscasting company for local community bulletins.

On the air, suddenly—to my surprise—there is a local police report, a "Community Alert Bulletin" relating to the series of "sexcrime"-incidents which I've just managed to complete as perpetrator in the agenda which I'm attempting to fulfill with respect to the requirements which I set forth for myself early in the "narrative"-drama regarding the "Perspective on 'Self-Enlightenment' " which I deem as necessary in order to achieve a higher level of enlightenment (or "cosmic knowledge") in the world at large, which I will, then, select to bestow upon others who seek from me enlightenment in the world as well.

The broadcast of the local police agency's "Community Alert Bulletin" reports to us on the police department's attempt to obtain any information leading local "law enforcement"-agents to successfully determine the identity and locate the whereabouts of the perpetrator guilty of committing the series of assaults against females residing in the "Central Commerce District" of Minneapolis.

Due to the transmission over the air of the police agency's "Community Alert Bulletin", the cab-driver (i.e., the Kenyan immigrant man) decides to initialize an extensive comment on the case involving the assailant still "at large" in the surrounding region which the man serves as a transportation-assistant seeking to aid residents with a convenient-level of vehicular travel from one spot in the area which he serves as a taxi-driver to another spot on the area's street map which the passenger in question, riding in the taxi's rear-seat, desires to venture to during the particular assignment bestowed upon the road-transport service's vehicle-captain, that is.

The cabbie, here, indicates to me he hopes the local police investigators soon apprehend the individual guilty of perpetrating the series of "sexcrime"-assaults against women occurring at "church"-locations in the "Central Commerce District" of the Urbanzone, due to the concerns over the case openly expressed to him by passengers whom he ferries around the town during the "after hours"-shift of road-service, particularly women. The cabbie, here, indicates to me that he's heard from several female passengers over the past month who blatantly comment to him in speaking of the fears they possess of walking around the streets alone at night, many of whom, nowadays, prefer to travel by taxi-cab, rather than attempt to walk home by foot, or by use of the "MetroTransit"-busroute system, fearing the assailant could be lurking near the vicinity of a bus-station just waiting for a female to stand alone at the route-stop in attempting to safely await the arrival of a busline for her to then board. The driver indicates the "MetroTransit"-buses reduce the frequency of their passenger-service after midnight, hence, creating the opportunity for a lengthy wait at a busroute-station if a woman is standing there alone, permitting any would-be assailant ample time to view her as a possible victim and steer her away from the bus stop and quickly maneuver her into an isolated, unviewable location at which point he could initialize a "sexcrime"-assault against her if the predator just happens to so choose.

The cab-driver (i.e., the Kenyan immigrant man), here, indicates he's had several women ask him to drive them to their cars over the past month, once the series of "sexcrime"-incidents began in the "Downtown"-District, in order to ensure they're not setting themselves up to be victimized by attempting to travel on foot to a parked car alone at night. The cabbie indicates his concern for female residents in the "Central Commerce District" who are forced to travel home from work alone after dark, considering the emergent danger presenting itself to such residents due to the presence of a sexual-predator who's seeking to prey upon isolated females caught out on the streets of the local urban-area alone after dark in merely attempting to walk themselves home from work or to a nearby parked vehicle.

However I, on realizing the specific "sexcrime"-assault which I did choose to commit against the Omani female victim as of SUN., Dec. 21, 2003, would amount, in fact, to the <u>final</u> incident to appear in the series of violations I have chosen to commit in order to attempt to fulfill the agenda

--()--
152
--()--

which I'm pursuing to finalize all *necessary* stages appearing in the process of self-enlightenment as required steps to complete on my part, which would be, indeed, the <u>final</u> incident of assault against women necessary on my part to commit in attempting to fulfill all essential aspects appearing on record in the "Perspective on the Process of 'Self-Enlightenment' " which I chose to set forth with the aim of attempting to complete while residing in Minneapolis, do, here, indicate to the driver I'm sure the females residing in the local region will soon no longer need to fear the presence of a perpetrator lurking menacingly about the area seeking to prey upon female residents caught alone on the streets at night while attempting to head home on the specific occasion at hand, that would be.

I, here, decide to tell the driver I'm *almost* positive the assailant in question will soon subside in the recent behavioral pattern set forth on his part of assaulting females on the streets after hours as a brutal serial rapist, due to the fact the community at large is aware of the ongoing case of assaults and the local "law enforcement"-agents are indeed likely to receive the whole-hearted support and eager assistance extended to the agency by community members in attempting to locate the assailant determined by investigators to still be "at large", if the perpetrator himself selects to remain in the region and continues to pursue the pattern of anti-societal crimes against local citizens after nightfall, that is. I tell the cab-driver, if the perpetrator has any level of alertness permitting him to recognize the environment which he happens to be currently facing, he will "**cease** <u>and</u> **desist**" from conducting any further attempts to continue the pattern of felony-level "sexcrime"-assaults which he's chosen to conduct in the region, for fear the police detectives, in such an event, will ultimately receive the opportunity to apprehend the assailant in question … once and for all.

I, here, realize, as well, the cabbie in question has no knowledge as to the fact the man who currently sits in the rear seat of the traveling vanwagon at the time of the specific occasion at hand (i.e., me, that is) *is*, <u>in</u> <u>fact</u>, the perpetrator of the series of "sexcrime"-assaults in the ongoing case of nocturnal urban criminal conduct occurring in the "Metropolitan"-Area which the "Sex Crimes"-Division staffers are currently attempting to successfully resolve by determining the ID of the assailant in question in order to, thereby, possibly locate the predator's whereabouts, which will perhaps lead to an immediate arrest of the party guilty of committing the <u>atrocious</u> actions against women in the "Downtown"-region during the shift of nocturnal hours.

I trust I did communicate to the cab-driver (i.e., the Kenyan immigrant man) what would indeed amount to a set of *last words*, or, a final farewell, so to speak, on parting ways with the African taxi-driver upon reaching the corner of Courier Street and Reddington Avenue, where, I'll here note, "The

'Falconeer' Building" stands, the housing-complex in which I do at present maintain lease-holding status as a tenant occupying a basement-level unit in the building (Apt. "#002"). I told the driver of the taxi-cab to have a "Happy New Year" and to not let himself be bothered with complaints made by female passengers whom he picks up reminding him of the danger they face after hours in choosing to walk home by themselves. I told him to merely do his job as the man ferrying people about the Urbanzone over the course of the "after hours"-shift and to let the police investigators following the case involving the predator guilty of committing "sexcrime"-assaults against women in the "Central Commerce District" to, honorably, do theirs, in accordance with the obligation which society has chosen to bestow upon them as "law enforcement"-agents entrusted with properly defending the public safety of all local citizens. (... Ha! Ha! Ha! Ha! Ha!)

Tasting Droplets of the Unforgettable Rain

By
Adrien L. Montgomery
Cycle <u>014</u>:
"If Safeguarding Nocturnal Behavior is a Priority of the Utmost Concern, One Rule Must Always Be Acknowledged by Such an Individual as a Vital Guideline Which Reads as Follows: 'Don't Talk to Strangers!' "

<u>UTA</u> <u>Directive</u> <u>XIV</u>:
"Attention! Attention! ... Passengers On Board The 'CitiTraxx[STF]' Railsystem-Vehicle Must Not Interfere With The Conductor Operating The Commuter Train While The Transporter Is Still In Motion! Repeat, Passengers On Board The 'CitiTraxx[STF]' Railsystem-Vehicle Must Not Interfere With The Conductor Operating The Commuter Train While The Transporter Is Still In Motion!"
("<u>UTA</u>": <u>U</u>rban <u>T</u>ransit <u>A</u>uthority)

There is a digital-screen billboard that stands atop the roof of a building appearing at the intersection of Hennenburgh Boulevard (a prime route for use by automoto-traffic running north and south) and Seventh Street (a frequent route for vehicular and pedestrian traffic running east and west)—with the building itself amounting to a large indoor retailing venue referred to as "Blockwalk Metrosquare 'A' "—which presents advertisements on its large electronic displaying board just one block west of the "First Avenue & 7th Street Entry"-venue found at the intersection of N. 1st Avenue and N. 7th Street in the city's "Downtown"-region.

On the large outdoor digital displaying board, the following announcement can be read by any pedestrians and motorists opting to travel through the

<table>
<tr><td>--()--</td></tr>
<tr><td>154</td></tr>
<tr><td>--()--</td></tr>
</table>

intersection at any hour of the day or night, as the specific sign itself appears once every 2 minutes while in rotation as one of several advertisements in a cycle which continually emerge on screen across the digital displaying board:

> *If you lived in Arizona, you'd enjoy a mild, wintertime climate.*
> *If you lived in Florida, you'd enjoy their sunswept coastline.*
> *If you lived in Wyoming, you'd enjoy breathtaking outdoor terrain.*
> *If you lived in Hawaii, you'd enjoy a relaxing beachfront lifestyle.*
> *If you lived … Huh??! …*

Well, I suppose what we're saying is, Minnesotans, remaining in this state, must be here for <u>some</u> reason, don't you think? … And we <u>know</u> what it is! … "Torini & Son Coffeeroom[UE]"! … Enjoy your life in the "Northstar State" (if you <u>have</u> to) by trying a variety of our amazing, fresh-roasted coffee-recipes today! (By the way, folks, we're in those other states, too! … Ha! Ha! Ha!)

(-|<u>Calendar</u> <u>Date</u>: <u>SUN</u>., <u>Jan</u>. <u>11</u>, <u>2004</u>|-)

I must here make note to you, once again, dear friends and followers alike, in a precursory statement to appear at the start of this particular segment of the "narrative"-drama, I trust, in accordance with the "Perspective on the Process of 'Self-Enlightenment' "—which I'm attempting to fulfill in Minneapolis by completing the necessary steps required of me in the program of stages constituting the process which I've set forth for myself to complete to then finalize the agenda in order to ultimately attain a higher degree of wisdom in the world, I did manage to conduct all of the *necessary* aspects appearing in the program of duties set forth in the perspective itself upon permitting myself to be subjected to an incident of sodomy (i.e., "rear-cavity" penetration, that is) at the hands of the Somali immigrant man (i.e., "Ibrahim Hossein", remember) in the apartment on N. Fourth Street and No. Rocolo Ave. (i.e., the "Fourth & Roc"), on Sun., Dec. 28, 2003. Due to the fact, I have indeed *finally* managed to fulfill the agenda which I set forth for myself to achieve earlier on, as I outlined such a program to you at the beginning, I do trust there remains, beyond today, **no** additional steps necessary appearing as aspects of the perspective left for me to fulfill to finalize the agenda itself. Hence, I trust I've managed to complete, by this date in question (SUN., Jan. 11, 2004), all <u>necessary</u> stages originally amounting to factors of the agenda itself necessary in order to, in the end, achieve a higher level of enlightenment (or, "cosmic knowledge"), in a *cumulative* measure, that would be, in the world, which I will then impart to others who approach me in order to seek such wisdom for themselves.

I'm at this moment aboard a public busroute leading commuters to the

--()--
155
--()--

"Northtown Transit Exchange Depot"-station which is found just outside the "Northtown Trading Emporium", an expansive retailing complex (i.e., "shopping mall") in the "Northtown"-region of the "Minneapolis Greater Metropolitan Area". I boarded the specific "MetroTransit"-busroute (the "10NT") at the "Leighmont Drive Transit Exchange Depot"-station at So. 10th Street and No. 3rd Avenue in the "Central Commerce District" with the aim of sleeping on board the running mass-transit vehicle while the "public commuter"-vehicle made the hourlong trek from the "Convention Center"-area in the city's "Central Commerce District" to the "Northtown Transit Exchange Depot"-station, the particular busroute's final stop in Northtown, Minnesota.

The attempt on my part to enjoy a nap aboard the running public-transporter occurs on Jan. 11, 2004, i.e., on a frost-ridden night found in the annual calendar's "Wintertime"-era, hence, permitting me to sleep aboard the busroute-vehicle while outside the snow harmlessly drifts to the earth, generously cloaking the region's outdoor acreage with a fresh layering of ice granules released from heavy beds of "precipitation"-material traversing the unlit ceiling which menacingly looms overhead, signaling its intent to subject the land beneath to a frigid discharge of frost in the "after hours"-term in question.

I did manage to fall asleep on the way up to the "Northtown Trading Emporium" at the "Northtown Transit Exchange Depot"-station only to be awakened at the busroute-stop by an African-American female driver, who told me I had to immediately disboard the bus to enable her to enjoy her "lunchbreak" aboard the bus at the public-transporter's "end of the line"-station (with her "lunchbreak" occurring after midnight, that would be[?]).

Yet, I cannot manage to find time to return to a peaceful, winter night's sleep aboard the busroute-vehicle which I'm using at this point to return to the "Leighmont Drive Transit Exchange Depot"-station at the corner of S. 10th Street and N. 3rd Ave. due to the fact that at the "Excelsior Ave."-bus stop, an access road which permits motorists to enter and exit the guest parking ground of the "Northtown Trading Emporium" at various driveways, an African-American man boarded the transit-shuttle and assumed a spot opposite mine on the bus's back row of seats, the bench at the rear of the bus which stretches from the vehicle's rear left wheel to its rear right wheel, offering to guests aboard the rolling "MetroTransit"-vehicle a wall-to-wall bench for use as seating space if necessary for passengers aboard to make use of during the late-afternoon "Rush Hour" commute they have to make while returning home after the workday.

The man on board began speaking loudly to a listener while using the "cellular service"-line unit he carries with him while assuming passenger space for himself at the back wall of the "commuter transit"-vehicle that's heading south towards its final station next to the Minneapolis Convention

Center within the southern sectors of the "Central Commerce District". The man appears to be conversing on the topic of an "R&B"-recording artist who became well-known to music fans in the early 1990's, releasing "song"-titles amounting to "single"-record discs receiving high-priority airplay on "R&B"-music channels appearing along the FM-band's tuning dial on radios back in the final decade of the 20th-Century that would be, thus, serving to disrupt any attempt on my part to begin a 2nd spell of "in traffic"-slumber on the ride back to the "Convention Center"-area of the "Downtown"-region.

I, unfortunately, had no choice, hence, but to encounter the black man, probably 24 years in age, while sitting aboard the "10LD"-busroute from the "Northtown Transit Exchange Depot"-station in the northeastern corner of the parking ground serving guests who arrive at the "Northtown"-retailing complex by car to the "Leighmont Drive Transit Exchange Depot"-station at the corner of S. 10th Street and N. 3rd Ave. in the "Central Commerce District" of the city.

While the man sits aboard the bench found at the back wall of the transit service-vehicle itself, the passenger space running atop one of the rear axles of the public-transporter, he turns towards me and continues to speak loudly while holding the "wireless service"-line unit in hand, not indicating as to whether or not he's attempting to address me (the co-passenger sharing space with him aboard the bus's rear bench) or the listener at the other end of the "telephone unit"-service line which he uses.

Yet, I, and the other passenger choosing to select seats for ourselves aboard the bench at the back of the mass-transit vehicle, do, unfortunately, engage each other in a rather lengthy, yet, uninspiring, I'd say, here, conversation which the other passenger initializes, as if he'd rather speak on a face-to-face basis to a person sitting close by than with a listener at the other end of the cellphone's communication-line, in order to, perhaps, avoid needing to shout to ensure the other person can hear him, choosing to interrupt the discussion ongoing with the listener at the telephone wire's other end in mid-syllable to begin addressing me, the "transit vehicle"-guest also sitting, along with him, on the bus's rear bench.

He, once again, begins to speak with me on the topic of a well-known "R&B"-act he favors as one being a devout fan, whose most notable "song"-titles appear in the playlist of ("['digital']-audiofile")-music tracks which the man has made available for instant playback in the menu of records appearing in the "dataplayer"-mechanism for use on the "cellular"-unit which he carries on him in hand at the time. The "R&B" act of note being a "vocal harmony"-act known as "Boy Voice Four", a band of four (or "quartet" of) African-American vocalists starting their career as a 4-part primarily "a cappella"-group in the early 1990's when the four men in the act were still actually teenagers, hence, the band's official group title, "Boy Voice Four".

The guest sitting at the opposite end of the bench which the both of us are using at the back wall of the "mass transit"-shuttle continues, here, to address me in conversation: "The 'Boy Voice Four' lead man is in jail again for cocaine possession? ... Damn! Heard he juss got outta 'Rehab', too. Next album's gunnah be delayed as well! ... <u>Shoot!</u>"

I merely nod, as if to indicate I understand exactly what the passenger's attempting to state to me at this point: "Too bad. They were a great group. I mean, I suppose I haven't heard anything from them lately. But, I remember a couple of their songs, though."

The black man nods, as if now recognizing a man of mutual interests, someone who shares his devotion to the group of "R&B"-singers: " 'Turnin' 'Round, Again' has gotta be my favorite.... 'Damsel-in-Distress' or 'Damsel in 'Dis Dress' (whatever it is[?]) is another one I *really* like."

I, realizing any attempt on my part to re-initialize a round of roadtime surrender to the spell of slumber is futile beyond this point, merely encourage him to focus on the music he's hearing on the cellphone's built-in playback-device: "I heard one of them died in a car accident a year ago. ... Probably not true, is it? Must have been another online anti-fan hoax."

Shakin' his head, almost furiously, at this point, in denying the scenario I enunciated regarding the fraudulent case publicizing the death of one of the man's musical heroes: "That was 'Maurice Cornell'. He was in an accident but wasn't hurt himself. 'Drunk Driving'! That was all. Apparently, he had to perform 'community service' for a weekend. That's it! He didn't die. He didn't kill anybody. Those were—what are they called?—**rumors**! ... Yeah, that's it! ... Only <u>rumors</u>!"

I merely watch the man as he appears to carefully select the next "song"-title from the menu of "audiofile"-selections appearing in the directory of music-tracks comprising the primary playlist available to him for instant access on the cellular telephone-unit: "I'm really a 'Blues' fan. Or, actually, more of a 'Blues'-Rock fan myself. And, I s'pose, a 'Folk'-Rock listener, too. I'm not really a fan of 'R&B' or 'Hip-Hop'."

Once again, here, the man shakes his head—almost furiously— decidedly condemning whatever it is I may have implied with respect to his particular musical tastes, seeing he appears to be a devout fan of the "R&B"-category of "Pop"-music: " 'Hip-Hop'?! ... That's just a bunch of gangstas shooting at each other with 9-millimeter pistols! Wish one of them would use an 'AK-47' to finish more of them off! (Ha! Ha!) Had a cousin who was shot by one of those gangstas after a 'Hip Hop'-concert back in '99. I hate **all** of those muthafuckin' so-called 'Hip-Hop' *artists*!"

Hoping, here, the man's actual route-stop is approaching to allow me to avoid hearing additional commentary from the "R&B"-fan on what it is a "musical"-style must express in the attitude it publicly presents in actual performance in order to qualify as a preferable artform in his eyes: "I guess I should try to listen to a little more 'R&B' in the future. If you say some of it's good! I might take a peek at their next album … 'Boy Voice Four'. I heard they did win a 'Grammy Award' several years ago."

The man begins to nod eagerly, indicating a certain level of satisfaction in noting the act he undeniably favors was chosen to receive such a public honor acknowledging them as deserving of the industry's recognition: " 'Best R&B Performance for the Year of 1997'! … The song?? It was 'Sheddin' Tears on Black Asphalt'! I got *that* one, too! It's one of my favorites. I listen to it … probably, every Friday night, while I'm drinking a case of the malt liquor—'Stormbreed 360^{UE}'! That's my brand!"

I merely watch as another passenger steps aboard the "MetroTransit"-shuttle at the busroute-stop at Central Ave. and E. Riverbank Street and finds a space for himself among seats in the forward section of the passenger-cabin aboard the "commuter"-vehicle: "Ever hear of them comin' to town? … Playin' at the 'Focuspoint^{AI} Arena' or at the 'Metropolitan Performance Hall'?"

The man appears to merely select yet another "song"-title to re-play for his listening convenience from the listing of music-tracks appearing in the menu of "audiofile"-options in the "R&B"-<u>only</u> playlist on the "cellular service"-device he holds in hand at the moment: "No, but I'm gunnah go on the Internet soon to find out when they're gunnah be comin' to town. Maybe I can get tickets, if I can afford it. I guess I can just watch one of their concerts at the ('U-Tube')-site, anyway."

Here, the man prepares himself to leave the interior comfort of the "public transit"-vehicle by rising gradually to his feet and stepping towards the exitway next to the busroute's "rear entry"-panels to ready himself to off-board the transporter once the vehicle arrives at the upcoming stop, at "N. Rocolo Ave. and 7th Street". The final words which the man chose to speak unto me as he walked from the rear bench stretching from wheel to wheel at the back wall of the transit-shuttle, again, re-confirmed to me the fraudulent reports appearing across the Internet regarding the lead vocalist fronting the group "Boy Voice Four" claiming the "R&B" maestro had died in a car accident a year ago were, once again, merely "rumors" initialized on the Web in what amounted to, again, an online anti-fan hoax presumably begun by a hater of the "R&B"-category of "Pop"-music.

I must make note, here, of the fact, at the rear section of the bus, just above the vehicle's rear axle of wheels, at the wall behind the final set of seats in the passenger-seating section, forming a bench of seats for guest convenience at the bus's back row, there is a large vent of air-channeling slots permitting the onboard heating-system to propel hot air into the bus's passenger cabin, offering to the onboard commuting busroute-users the convenience and comfort of a warm-air atmosphere while traveling aboard the "MetroTransit"-system's busroute.

I, here, witness the man offboard the "commuter transit"-vehicle, at the stop occurring at N. Rocolo Ave. and 7th Street, noting I am, as well, set to disboard the public transporter myself at the "Leighmont Drive Transit Exchange Depot"-station on the corner of S. 10th Street and N. 3rd Ave., just two blocks north of the "Convention Center" in the central-west sector of the "Central Commerce District".

In observance of the trivial exchange occurring between the young African-American passenger and myself aboard the "public transit"-vehicle a moment ago, I, here, must acknowledge the realization occurring on my part that the transit-passenger in question, seated opposite me on the bench at the back wall of the "commuter"-shuttle, is not aware of the fact I, Ariq Shoretempel, am the perpetrator guilty of committing the series of "sexcrime"-assaults occurring in recent weeks in the "after hours"-shift at various "church"-locations found in the "Central Commerce District" of the city. He failed to realize I'm the perpetrator still "at large" in the ongoing criminal case under investigation by detectives at the "Sex Crimes"-Division of the Minneapolis Metropolitan Police Force. (… Ha! Ha! Ha! Ha!)

The man merely wanted to discuss "song"-titles released in the 1990's by what is apparently an "R&B"-music act which he highly favors as an appreciator of the recording act's catalogue of "single"-record releases— "Boy Voice Four", a "vocal harmony"-group performing music primarily in the "a cappella"-style—as he merely chose to listen to different records of the band in the menu of ("['single']-play")-recordings he keeps in a songlist-file on the "cellular service"-device which he carries with him aboard the city's "public transit"-vehicles on occasions such as the one occurring tonight, at my expense, unfortunately, that would be. (((Sigh))).

Tasting Droplets of the Unforgettable Rain

By
Adrien L. Montgomery
Cycle <u>015</u>:

"If, as We're Told, the 'Postman *Always* Rings <u>Twice</u>', Then What I'd Offer to Any as a Word of Caution for Those Reluctant to Receive Any Visitors Deciding to Pay Unwelcome House-Calls Would Merely Be as Follows: 'Don't Answer Him the Second Time, Either!' "

UTA <u>Directive</u> <u>XV</u>:

"Attention! Attention! … Passengers Standing On The Loading Deck Awaiting An Inbound 'CitiTraxx[STF]' Railsystem-Vehicle Must Stand Behind The Yellow Safe-Boundary Zone. Repeat, Passengers Standing On The Loading Deck Awaiting An Inbound 'CitiTraxx[STF]' Railsystem-Vehicle Must Stand Behind The Yellow Safe-Boundary Zone!"

("<u>UTA</u>": <u>U</u>rban <u>T</u>ransit <u>A</u>uthority)

--()--
160
--()--

There is a digital-screen billboard that stands atop the roof of a building appearing on the southwestern corner of the intersection of So. 7th Street (an avenue in the business-park running from east to west) and Millington Street (a readily-accessible road for vehicular and pedestrian traffic running from north to south)—with the specific building of note being what appears to be nothing more than an abandoned commercial structure originally built to host "central"-offices (i.e., "headquarters") for various businesses operating as "tenants" inside its spacious "Downtown"-area suites, which is referred to as "Millington Street Plaza"—or, an announcing board which presents various advertisements and public advisories on its large electronic exhibition screen found just one block south and one block west of the "Hennepin County Medical Center" (or the "Hennepin Healthcare Corporation Complex") found on the northeastern corner of the intersection of So. 8th Street and Parkland Ave in the city's "Central Commerce District".

On the large outdoor digital exhibition screen the following announcement can be read by any pedestrians and vehicular-types passing through the intersection at any moment, daytime or nighttime, as the specific poster itself flashes on screen once after a short program of notices appears while in rotation as one of many commercial notices and public-advisories in a series which continually appears on screen across the digital exhibition board:

"Whether it's on the ride to work in the morning or on the ride back home in the evening, what you'd want is a good helping of aroma-rich coffee and a tasty bite of an oven-fresh muffin. We're here to help you enjoy <u>both</u>, whether you're heading out to the job or heading back to the house. Our job here is easy … it's to serve people something flavorful and ready-to-eat while they're on their way!"

We'll have the cup of "special recipe"-coffee immediately on the counter and an example of our bakeshop-skill instantly in your hand if you choose to stop by and walk into one of our eager-to-please kitchen-shops. (… By the way, even *if* you <u>don't</u> have a job right now, visiting an outlet of ours is a good excuse to get out of the house, at any rate…. Remember, we're "Bromili & Sons Café & Bakery^{UE}", the happy place found just around the corner!

(-|Calendar <u>Date</u>: <u>SUN</u>., Jan. <u>18, 2004</u>|-)

I'm standing on the lower floor of a " 'Safari House^{UE}' Bookshop"-venue in Bloomington, Minnesota, a city found merely 10 miles south of the Minneapolis "Central Commercial District", in the southeastern quadrant of

Adrien L. Montgomery
Tasting Droplets of the Unforgettable Rain
Official Imprint: "Dynamographx"

the state. I'm merely standing next to the spacious display of periodicals (newspaper- and magazine-editions) available for convenient use by any patrons on hand inside of the bookselling-outlet itself, a displaying stand of various publications from around the world in, of course, the periodical's most recently-published issue, which runs the length of one wall in the center of the bookvending-store's lower level (i.e., the first of two). I'm currently browsing, with a level of partial interest, a particular political affairs publication (i.e., *Global Forum*), a weekly publication presenting its readership with articles and updates regarding the state of international affairs emerging around the world on a week-to-week basis, to inform any readers anxious to learn of what the current class of world leaders is to prescribe as statesmen in order to ensure a scenario of diplomatic harmony prevails in the round of negotiations which the various political figures conduct with each other in ongoing conferences held for various reasons in capitals around the planet which each one of us calls home.

I, voluntarily, choose to return the issue of *Global Forum* to its specific place on the displaying rack of publications the venue presents to onsite patrons for convenient use while paying visit or for purchase as an item for use at the patron's leisure, rather than merely choosing to place the issue itself on a chair near the displaying racks for recent editions of popular weekly publications, due to the role of the venue's "re-shelver", a 19-year-old girl, a Caucasian who, for the most part, appears to be a "Punk"-style adolescent, whose job is to return to the shelves appearing around the venue's salesfloor the venue's merchandise, i.e., books, magazines, newspapers, toys, CD's, DVD's, children's games, etc., etc., which people move out of place while paying visit to the outlet itself and choose to leave on store premises upon deciding not to purchase the item in question at that particular time. Her job is merely to walk the store's floorspace and pick up a sales-item which a customer sought to drop from hand while on site after choosing not to buy it, forgetting to return it to its specific position in the array of the shop's table of merchandise, leaving the venue's "re-shelving"-girl, i.e., the "Punk"-style youth, to place the product back in its original position on the shelves of the extensive retailing outlet.

I'm walking from the magazine-stand I stood next to while browsing through the most recent issue of *Global Forum*, the "international affairs"-publication, and head across the venue's spacious sales-floor towards the entryway at the front of the building, next to the clerk's station at the checkout-counter. Upon approaching the doors at the front of the bookshop, I, almost tragically, happen to behold before me a sight which all but incites the spirit in me to seek for itself the nearest burial plot in order to securely keep itself safe from any threatening presence seeking to initialize its immediate (and terrible) undoing at the time. Before me, approaching at a leisurely step, is none *other* than the **Latina** female whom

I chose to assault (i.e., *violate* in a "sexcrime"-incident) in the early morning hours of SUN., Nov. 30, 2003 while on the grounds of the "True Minneapolite Church of Christ's Cross", a "Protestant Faith"-property found on the southeastern corner of the intersection of Hennenburgh Boulevard and Eleventh Street in the "Uptown"-District of the Urbanzone!!

She doesn't yet see me, however, due to the fact that while she is directly approaching, her stare appears to be focusing on something situated to her left at the northern wall of the large bookselling-venue, apparently directing her attention away from what's in front of her, serving as an immediate (and, I would have to here most thankfully add, *necessary*) distraction, steering her attention towards whatever she finds noteworthy on shelves or display racks at the venue's northern perimeter.

I immediately freeze myself in the path I'm choosing to make towards the venue's exit, instantly turning to my left in order to avoid any possibility of the Latina woman deciding to return her eyes to what's directly in front of her as she crosses the expansive floorspace of the bookselling-venue, which would provide her, possibly, with the opportunity to set eyes safely upon me, the assailant selecting to remorselessly violate her on that particular morning a month-and-a-half ago on the grounds of the "Protestant Faith"-center in what would obviously amount to a "felony"-level "sex crime"-assault incident which investigators on staff in the "Sex Crimes"-Division of the "Minneapolis Metropolitan Police Force" are currently examining as but one in a series of assaults which I managed to commit against females upon arriving in the state of Minnesota in late October of 2003.

I merely position myself as if I were a customer who just so happens to find interest in the table of books appearing just next to me on the venue's salesfloor, which is a display offering to patrons on hand a collection of notable literary works which "Everybody Can Enjoy", as the onsite-staffers claim upon the notice appearing as a sign situated on a wooden rail behind the stand itself which safely sets apart from the table-display the escalator-system elevating customers to the venue's upper-floor, its 2nd-level of merchandise-items on hand for patrons to possibly purchase during a leisurely visit to the bookselling-venue.

I decide to immediately pick up one of the works of "Classic Literature" appearing as noteworthy titles in their easily-seen position upon the table-exhibit appearing on the outlet's lower floor. Once I determine the danger on hand to no longer pose an immediate threat to me, assuming the Latina woman has casually walked past me in order to approach whatever item it was appearing at the wall on the venue's northern perimeter serving to distract her attention in that particular direction once she entered the venue itself as I, of course, almost tragically, chose to head for its exit on the occasion, I instantly turn towards the location's front entryway, seeing that the carpet-space stretching in front of me is in the clear, with no sight of the Latina woman in the immediate area of the bookshop and begin walking from the venue itself with a purposeful, yet not panic-ridden, pace, there being no reason to alert staffers on site to my exit, which might indicate to them I, a visitor choosing to rush from the store, may have chosen to pocket an item while on hand, and am leaving the premises without opting to pay for it at the sales-clerk's station at the front of the outlet.

I safely manage to exit the venue itself in a "stripmall"-location in the city of Bloomington, Minnesota and quickly situate myself inside a large grove of trees (standing leaflessly while suffering through the annual stage of barrenness, of course, in this era of the calendar, i.e., "Wintertime", that is) appearing at one end of a green belt (i.e., lawn path) sitting on the edge of the parking ground available for motorists to use as available space for the vehicle while the driver himself visits any one of the retailing venues operating along the perimeter of the extensive vehicle-convenience lot.

Upon safely securing myself from view behind the grove of trees at the edge of the asphalt parking ground, the first question coming to mind in view of the incident occurring inside the " 'Safari House^{UE}' Bookshop" concerns whether the Latina female actually resides in Bloomington, Minnesota or not, with an additional issue being to determine whether or not she might merely work in the area and reside elsewhere. Or, would she be, perhaps, just visiting a friend or relative who lives in the area on what would be an ordinarily routine Sunday afternoon??

Seeing the look appearing on her face as she, unknowingly, approached me while I stood, helplessly, not unlike the residents of a seaside settlement awaiting the apocalyptic arrival of a tidal wave rearing up in the ocean's suddenly menacing surface to approach their village while aiming, it would appear, to destroy any form of life found therein on that occasion, I can, here, easily determine the tone of her face to indicate she is, indeed, a woman who's recently suffered a shocking incident in her life. Her face appears to indicate the reaction a person would automatically adopt in the aftermath of a tragic occurrence which one would never expect to encounter herself at any point in life, with examples of such an occurrence being the unforeseeable death of a child, a notable accident resulting in a permanent injury to the person, the unexpected death of a spouse, the immediate end of a career, which serves as an event having lifelong implications, an example of such being the death, demise or disappearance of a family-run business that's been operated by members of the particular family for decades or, even, for generations.

On viewing the exact facial tone of the particular woman herself, I'd have, here, no other choice than to suggest … she would no longer be a Christian, due to the fact she was ruthlessly subjected to a "sexcrime"-assault incident on the grounds of a "Protestant Faith"-property while in the midst of performing an official role in which she serves members of the assembly who would choose to gather at the venue on the following morning to receive a message on the Lord's agenda for fellowship-members to abide by on a daily and weekly basis. Yet, "God" himself, the one the prayer hall honors in name, chose not to protect her from the particular assailant visiting the venue in order to violate an unsuspecting woman on its premises that night in November (i.e., me, remember). Hence, she believes God abandoned her and because of this failure on part of the Lord, she would certainly no longer be a Christian herself in heart. If she still has the job as a secretary at the church, she's only applying herself to keep the income which the position offers to her, not because she believes in working on behalf of the Good Lord in order to present His message to the <u>believers</u> found in the community in which she resides.

Despite the fact the Latina female, the one I just so happened to, again, almost tragically, encounter in the bookshop-venue which I just left behind me, did appear to have the look of one feeling both abandoned and betrayed by God above, I, here, must note, I still feel **no** sympathy towards her, the victim on the occasion in question, in light of the assault I chose to commit against her in order to violate her on the particular morning in question, a criminal incident, perhaps, serving to end the woman's belief in a benevolent and protecting God existing in Heaven to generously watch over the human inhabitants living on earth.

I must here choose to remind members of the audience on hand the sole motivation in my view for perpetrating the "sexcrime"-assault against the Latina female on the grounds of the "Protestant"-church property was, yet again, in order to complete all *necessary* steps appearing in the "Perspective on the Process of 'Self-Enlightenment' " which I've chosen to set forth for myself to fulfill as an agenda in the state—Minnesota—in order to attain a higher degree of wisdom (or, "cosmic knowledge"), by first completing all <u>required</u> aspects appearing in the program of stages comprising the perspective, which will then permit me to receive a *cumulative* level of wisdom once the entire agenda of tasks is fulfilled on my part, which I will then be able to impart to others who approach me in order to receive such enlightenment in the world for themselves as well.

However, I do realize that someone (whoever it might be) is apparently attempting to indicate to me the women whom I chose to violate at various venues around the "Central Commercial District" upon arriving as a resident in the state of Minnesota over 2-and-a-half months ago are still at large about me in the region. Perhaps the women themselves, at any time, could choose to conduct private surveillance upon me in order to collect details on me, the perpetrator, which one of the females could then forward to the agents investigating the "assault"-crimes on staff at the "Minneapolis Metropolitan Police Force". Or, even worse, a victim I chose to violate in the recent past might at one point follow me in order to determine the exact location of the particular residential address which I currently keep as a lease-holding tenant on the premises of "The 'Falconeer' Building", who could, then, forward the specific address to police investigators at the agency who would pay an unwelcome visit to the basement-level apartment unit which I occupy as a tenant-in-residence on site at the complex.

Due to the apocalyptic encounter I just underwent inside the confines of the bookvending-shop while here in Bloomington, I do, hereby, instantly determine I must make arrangements to immediately <u>vacate</u> the state of Minnesota as soon as is possible in order to avoid what could be another unforeseeable (and potentially tragic) encounter with any one of the women which I chose to victimize in the vicinity of the region's "Central Commercial District" on various nights since arriving in the state in late October of 2003. I, at once, also determine I'll require use of a pair of dark sunglasses, henceforth, in public in order to avoid any possible detection by one of the victims I might just so happen to encounter while innocently walking about town to conduct any errands I have to complete on the particular day in question.

Upon reviewing the face I so unfortunately happened to encounter while paying visit to the " 'Safari House[UE]' Bookshop" under the artificial source of "in house"-illumination available on the premises, I do, here, again, determine the Latina woman to be approximately 23 years in age, a physical trait which I first determined while encountering her on the site of the "Protestant Faith"-property over the course of the monumental incident transpiring at the close of November in the "Uptown"-District of the city's "Urbanzone".

What I, here, have no other choice but to say to any in the listening audience on hand in the moment is a statement which I first announced to you upon initially encountering the Latina female on the grounds of the "Protestant Church"-property in the early morning hours of Sun., Nov. 30, 2003, just prior to initializing the "sexcrime"-assault which I chose to commit against the female in order to begin achieving all *necessary* steps found in the "Perspective on 'Self-Enlightenment' " in order to fulfill the program of stages necessary to complete with the aim of receiving a *cumulative* level of wisdom (i.e., "cosmic knowledge"), which I will then be able to bestow upon others seeking such wisdom for themselves, in words echoing an announcement I made to others on hand in the recent past … which is to say … *"And, lo, the footman came and, thus, he chose to place the <u>first</u> sacrificial female on the altar as a gift to 'Wisdom', a tribute from the warlord emergent in him, a soul irrevocably sworn to abide by an oath of loyalty to Enlightenment itself!"*

Tasting Droplets of the

--()--
166
--()--

Unforgettable Rain

By
Adrien L. Montgomery

<u>Cycle 016</u>:

"And, at the Moment of the Child's Birth, There Came to the Location Three Wise Men, Choosing to Pay Tribute to the New-Born, Christened to Be One Receiving the High Favor of the Lord God, a Male Infant Born Beneath the Light of God's Unreluctant Approval."

<u>UTA Directive XVI</u>:

"Attention! Attention! … Passengers, Please Be Prepared To Present 'Farecard'-Passes And 'MetroTransit'-Tickets To Officers Of The 'Transit'-Security Force Stepping Aboard The 'CitiTraxx[STF]' Railsystem-Vehicle. Repeat, Passengers, Please Be Prepared To Present 'Farecard'-Passes And 'MetroTransit'-Tickets To Officers Of The 'Transit'-Security Force Stepping Aboard The 'CitiTraxx[STF]' Railsystem-Vehicle."

("<u>UTA</u>": <u>U</u>rban <u>T</u>ransit <u>A</u>uthority)

There is a digital-screen billboard that stands atop the roof of a building appearing on the northwestern corner of the intersection of N. 11th Street (an autoroute for frequent use by street-motorists running from east to west) and N. 1st Ave. (a user-friendly urban road for both vehicular and pedestrian traffic running from north to south)—with the building itself amounting to nothing less than the "Central Depot" for passengers boarding and offboarding the "Interstate Bus"-service vehicles which park inside the extensive garage in use as a loading zone for passengers and cargo which the "stagecoach"-transporter is to carry onto the depot found at the customer's ultimate destination at the end of the transportation service's lengthy route of travel. The screen itself being a notification board which presents a selection of advertisements and "community"-advisories on its expansive electronic exhibition monitor found just 5 blocks south of the streetside walkway leading game-ready fans to the entry gates of "Target Field"-baseball park, on N. 1st Ave. and N. 6th Street, which is the home playing field of the "Minnesota Twins", a professional baseball club in the "American League"-association of Major League Baseball, hosting opposing teams who visit Minnesota during the course of the league's schedule of contests to occur in its annual season of official competition.

On the expansive outdoor digital notification screen the following announcement can be reviewed by any pedestrians and motorists happening to travel through the intersection of N. 11th Street and N. 1st Ave. at any moment of the day or night, as the specific sign itself flashes on screen every so often while appearing in a short lineup of advertisements while in

(XOX)

--()--
167
--()--

a cycle as one of many notices and "community"-advisories which continually appear on screen across the outdoor digital exhibition-board:

"After hours, step into a place where people come to enjoy an atmosphere permitting them to relax after a long shift on the job, while sampling tastes of the several beverages available to patrons we welcome to our barroom and restaurant to recover after a difficult day at work. We'll set you up with a cold serving of any 'commercial'-brand or 'craft brewery'-brand beer order and an oven-fresh slice of any of our 'original recipe'-pizzas. Come in and enjoy yourself while watching your favorite local team perform on any one of our 'ultra high'-definition widescreen TV-monitors."

"We'll pour ounces of fresh beer straight from the tap and expertly bake a hand-made flavor-rich pizza for you to enjoy while visiting the comfortable dining house we keep open every night…. Let the workday disappear in just a few moments like the cloud of foam evaporating from the top of a fresh glass of beer…. Remember, we're 'Old Railroad Barroom Pizza[AI]', the place people enter to unwind after work!"

(-|Calendar Date: SUN., Jan. 25, 2004|-)

I'm standing beside a large empty building wall found at the southern end of an extensive parking ground that's situated just across the street from the " 'CitiTraxx[STF]' Railsystem"-station on the corner of N. 1st Ave. and N. 5th Street. Aboard the loading deck on the southern side of the commuter-service station, there's a large crowd of people awaiting the inbound rail-transporter to stop and permit those traveling further along the rail-tracks to step aboard a railsystem-compartment to access the transit-system's shuttling service for passengers desiring immediate station-to-station mobility.

Unfortunately, however, in needing to report to any observers close by who still just happen to be on hand by this point in the "narrative"-drama unfolding against the locational backdrop of the "Twin Cities"-region in the state of Minnesota, on this specific occasion, I have an unsettling event to report to you, oh *ever-so-constant* companions and cohorts. There is an incident occurring in which I am apprehended (i.e., put "in custody") by three agents of the "Minneapolis Metropolitan Police Force" as I choose to stand beside the prominent complex found at the southern end of a spacious, vacant parking land standing in between Hennenburgh Boulevard and N. 1st Ave., across the street from the " 'CitiTraxx[STF]' Railsystem"-station on N. 5th Street and N. 1st Ave., which would be in the "Brick Wall"-District, at the north end of the city's "Central Commercial District", actually.

The police agents on hand (the three officers) *actually* accuse me of defacing the wall found at the eastern end of a parking lot around 20 yards from N. 1ˢᵗ Ave., across the street from the "Butler Plaza"-building by spray-painting the face of the wall with simplistic samplings of "street"-graffiti. The policemen also accuse me of "disturbing the peace" by shouting profanities loudly at the crowd of people waiting atop the loading deck at the " 'CitiTraxx^STF' Railsystem"-station on N. 5ᵗʰ Street, as they await the arrival of the next inbound commuter-service train to carry the passengers to stations further along the eastbound road of tracks. The police decide, on the occasion, to enter my name (i.e., "Ariq Zarkahn Shoretempel") and the "DMV"-license number I have into the police agency's statewide screening-database in order to retrieve an ID-profile on me, the "suspect" currently in police custody, which could indicate a criminal record for the cops on site to conveniently review.

Just prior to the incident involving agents of the local "Minneapolis Metropolitan Police Department" momentarily apprehending me as a suspect in an instance of defacing private property, I chose, beforehand, to pay visit to a "multiplex"-auditorium in the "Central Commercial District" in order to view a screening-session inside one of the exhibition-rooms on site. I managed to enjoy, at the time, a screening of a recent "Christmastime"-release, a film the distributor's office decided to release onto screens across the US prior to the "Christmas Holiday"-season occurring over the 2-week term of observance (or vacationtime), beginning FRI., Dec. 19, 2003 up until SUN., Jan. 04, 2004, the final date in the early "Wintertime Holiday"-season permitted to any laborers expecting the standard "Christmas"-break allowing them to enjoy "Holiday"-time with family members during the annual "Season of Giving".

The title of the motion-picture which I screened at the "multiplex"-venue was "A Voice Unseen at the Top of the Stairs", an "R"-rated "Horror" movie I chose to watch in place of the other "Holiday"-releases which the venue presented to patrons upon theater-screens inside the house's film projection-rooms. I viewed the particular motion-picture in a screening-session at the "Blockwalk Metrosquare 'A' "-building, a large retailing complex, which stands in between N. 7ᵗʰ Street found at the building's south perimeter, N. 6ᵗʰ Street found at the building's north perimeter, Hennenburgh Boulevard on the building's eastern perimeter, and N. 1ˢᵗ Ave on the building's western perimeter.

As I'm being detained in a set of handcuffs (i.e., the police wristlocking rings in use by "law enforcement"-agents to immobilize the arms of a suspect in custody with a compliance-hold, instruments, as you would know, which I'm quite familiar with myself … ha! ha! ha!) by the side of one of the squadcars, an African-American man who appears to be about twenty years old in age suddenly begins to shout loudly in a particular spot of the spacious, vacant parking ground next to the wall found at the southern end of the asphalt lot, across the street from the " 'CitiTraxx^STF' Railsystem"-

station's boarding deck on N. 5th Street. The lead police officer on hand, an African-American patrolman, indicates the shouting man would possibly be the *actual* suspect the police are on site to respond to and immediately tells the other two officers to return to me, the original "suspect", the "DMV"-license and to liberate me from the pair of wristlocking-constraints I'm in. The lead officer, the "African-American" police squadmember, quickly walks over to the suspect, the *other* young black man, shouting profanities loudly near the wall at the southern end of the spacious, vacant parking ground across the street from the "'CitiTraxx^STF' Railsystem"-station on N. 5th Street, and begins to question him, the offending party in the area, the one apparently guilty of "disturbing the peace" by verbally harassing the people waiting atop the loading platform at the " 'CitiTraxx™' Railsystem"-station on N. 5th Street for the next inbound train to arrive to permit them to board prior to continuing eastwards down the set of rails.

The other two officers return to me the "DMV"-license which I was required to hand over to the agents upon request once they approached me as I innocently stood at the large, empty wall found at the eastern end of the parking-ground on N. 1st Ave. and release me from the set of wristcuffing-rings I'm currently bound by. I, admittedly, did happen to assume, at the moment, I, of course, feared the three agents on hand from the "Minneapolis Metropolitan Police Force" decided to apprehend me for the purposes of questioning me as a "prime"-suspect in the recent spate of "sexcrime"-assaults occurring around the "Central Commerce District" against females at "church"-locations after midnight, in moments transpiring just after the week's sacred "Seventh Day", the "Day of Service", had begun, since I arrived in the state of Minnesota in late October. At the moment, I, of course, was thinking, as the three street officers approached me after stepping out of "SUV"-patrol vehicles which they parked on the asphalt parking-ground across the street from the "Butler Plaza"-complex on N. 1st Ave., I'd never be heard from again and would, tragically, be consigned by a Minnesota "4th-District Court" judge to serve out a twenty-year sentence in a state "Maximum Security"-penitentiary after receiving a conviction (i.e., "guilty"-verdict) on charges of "felony"-level sexual assault, kidnapping, assault with a deadly weapon (i.e., the "boxcutting"-blade, remember), battery (use of the pepperspray-canister—the aerosol-form anti-respiratory inhalant mixture serving as the soluble lung irritant), etc. What the cops are saying to me at the moment is that a motorist driving south across the parking ground next to N. 1st Ave. spotted me next to the wall at the eastern end of the asphalt acreage built for vehicular convenience and assumed I was in the act of defacing the large blank wall with emblems of "street"-graffiti. The agents at the scene explain to me the wall itself is on a developer's private lot of property and the owner has had it repainted in several rounds due to local streetgang-members deciding to deface the large canvas of empty wall-space with "street"-tags to ID themselves as affiliates to a particular gang who stake claim to the neighborhood as its designated "turf"-ground. While members of a <u>rival</u> gang in the area will happen by and spray-paint the wall with "street"-tag markings in order to ID themselves as affiliates to an *opposing* gang in the area who *also* hold claim on the parking lot as "turf"-space belonging to their particular camp. One of the cops tells me I can't loiter on the parking-ground because the developer who owns the property doesn't want anyone defacing the wall with emblems of "street"-graffiti again and again. After receiving my "DMV"-license from the officers who entered the license's serial code to review an ID-profile on me on the police's statewide screening-database, I begin to head home on N. 1ˢᵗ Ave. to "The 'Falconeer' Building" found on Courier Street and Reddington Ave. in the "Laurel Park"-District of the city.

I, however, note, here, the three policemen who just so happened to make the momentary arrest on the empty, extensive parking-ground found on the southeastern corner of N. 1ˢᵗ Ave. and N. 5ᵗʰ Street, just across the street from the " 'CitiTraxx™' Railsystem"-station permitting passengers to wait upon the loading deck for the upcoming commuter-service train ready to offer them use of the citywide "Transit"-system to travel to stations appearing further east along the set of tracks all but blatantly appear to represent what I see as the three "wings of humanity", that is ... with one officer being a Chinese (or, an Asian man), representing the Orient, i.e., the Eastern wing of humanity and one officer being an African-American (or, a black man), representing Africa, i.e., the Southern wing of humanity and one officer being a Caucasian (or, a white man), representing Europe, i.e., the Western wing of humanity. I, here, must note the grouping of the three officers standing before me adequately stands in representation of the three arms (or "wings") of the human community on Earth, i.e., the Eastern, the Southern, and the Western! ... Ha! Ha! Ha!

Tasting Droplets of the Unforgettable Rain

By
Adrien L. Montgomery
<u>Cycle 017</u>:
"In a House of Jokers, the Wise Man Makes His Exit as Unnoticeable as Can Be, to Ensure His Hosts Do <u>Not</u> Instantly Extend an Invitation to Him to Return."

<u>UTA Directive XVII</u>:
"Attention! Attention! ... Passengers On Board The 'CitiTraxxˢᵀᶠ' Railsystem-Vehicle Are Not Permitted To Ignite Cigarettes While In Transit Aboard The

--()--
171
--()--

Commuter-Service. Please Extinguish All Cigarettes Prior To Boarding The Transporter. Repeat, Passengers On Board The 'CitiTraxx^{STF}' Railsystem-Vehicle Are Not Permitted To Ignite Cigarettes While In Transit Aboard The Commuter-Service. Please Extinguish All Cigarettes Prior To Boarding The Transporter."

("<u>UTA</u>": <u>U</u>rban <u>T</u>ransit <u>A</u>uthority)

What follows is an announcement read over the air by the afternoon "DJ" (Ronnie "Ringleader" MacRamses) at a "Classic Rock"-station broadcasting to residents inhabiting the "Greater Minneapolis Metro"-region (e.g., KQUE "The Quake" 101.5 FM), an FM "Rock" station found just beyond the "century"-mark, that is, in the local radio-market's tuning dial, known for offering to its listenership a playlist consisting of "Hard-Rock"-tracks and "Heavy Metal"-tracks originating from artists whose career-spotlight began (and, in many cases, died) in earlier decades (e.g.'s, the '70's, '80's, or '90's), only to leave in the path left behind them a number of widely known songs serving as anthems paying tribute to the particular bygone-era of "Rock" which listeners can always enjoy remembering upon hearing the particular tunes once again:

"... Meet 'Ariq Shoretempel', a new recording artist right out of our own neck of the woods, here, folks, in Minneapolis, Minnesota, who's just managed to achieve a long-held dream in life for himself ... the release of his first music 'CD'-project! ... The young Minnesotan is now attempting to raise his stock to the level of 'recording artist' with the release of a new 'Rock'-LP. Critics have noted the album appears to utilize a highly innova-tive approach with respect to the music's arrangement, relying upon single-instrument orchestration for most of the tracks on hand. The artist himself, Ariq, appears to merely be slapping a board by apparently standing next to the kitchen countertop inside of his house to generate the correct melodic tone he desires the album to include, as some critics have surmised. Observers prefer to note, as well, the artist's ingenious use of sound effects which appear throughout the album's tracklist. Listeners can frequently hear, if listening closely, odd sounds of peculiar origin, it would almost appear. For instance, the ringing of a doorbell, the ringing of an old landline telephone-unit, the barking of a dog in the distance, or, even, the ignition of car engine nearby, as if the performer chose to record the tracks inside, once again, someone's house, rather than make use of the technological assets available to musicians today in the confines of a state-of-the-art sound-recording studio. Critics believe the inclusion of such unique sound-f/x indicates an attempt on the performer's part to make comment on the tedious nature of household life encountered by many of us in today's world. The album also makes use of lengthy periods of silence

--()--
172
--()--

which merely serve to interrupt the musical passages on the 'LP'-disc, as if to comment on the near impossibility of human-to-human communication due to the ('["Internet"]-driven')-era which people, of course, find unavoidable, in today's world. The album's lyrical content appears to offer to its eager listeners what would amount to nothing more than a selection of random names and sequences of non-consecutive numbers. Ariq claims for the album's lyrical dimension, he often sought inspiration as a song-writer by reviewing a recent edition of the 'Yellow Pages' specifically compiled with the aim of noting business-listings for any residents of the 'Twin Cities'-region. Which, he claims, is why he chose to title the new 'CD'-project 'Place Ad Here'. The artist's use of local business 'contact'-listings found in the 'Yellow Pages' to compose messages in the music's lyrical content for radio-listeners to hear is an approach which won the artist praise from the 'environmentalist'-community for the naked comment it makes on the need for conservation in today's world. As the artist points out the blatant wastefulness of denuding forest-rich tracts of land merely to produce paper to make copies of a telephone book for area inhabitants, in light of the ability someone would have nowadays to easily look up the number he's searching for on a cellphone with access to the Web. The artist's lead vocal track is praised for appearing to be no less than a surprising tribute to the philosophy of 'Minimalism', as the performer merely appears to rely upon an approach similar to what you'd hear in an example of one choosing to present an instance of basic oratory or choosing to present speech in simplistic public address, rather than what you'd hear from a singer who's actually attempting to produce recognizable notes appearing in a musical scale.... Well, Ladies and Gentle-men of the 'Twin Cities'-region, now that you've heard the early reviews on the 'CD'-project, I'll let you decide for yourselves. **Here** it is, the first single-release from Ariq Shoretempel's new album, 'Place Ad Here', a song which appears for the most part to be a 'Blues'-Rock anthem, I would assume, called 'See Me at the Church, If You Dare'! ... Feel free to call us up, here, at KQUE 'The Quake' 101.5 FM and tell us if you like it!"

(-|Calendar <u>Date</u>: <u>SAT</u>., <u>J</u>an. <u>31</u>, <u>2004</u>|-)

(If the clown arrives without his costume, the makeup that masks him with an ever-smiling face will itself sufficiently indicate that a fool has chosen to enter among the company you keep.) ... I'm sitting in a "Realm of Jesters[ISS]" sandwich outlet that can, by any, be easily found on the corner of N. 1st Avenue and N. 3rd Street in the northern-central sector of Minneapolis's pedestrian-ready "Urbanzone", in a " 'sportsbar'-on-the-corner" community inside the "Brick Wall"-District, a neighborhood known for offering to residents of the "Downtown"-region of the metropolis an available array of eating choices and an assortment of end-of-the-evening

--()--
173
--()--

barhopping options which the weekending revelers can choose to enter in order to enjoy whatever conveniences and ready-to-order kitchen-recipes are on offer to patrons to purchase on the occasion after settling into a booth, table, sofa, chair or barstool inside the neighborhood's instantly re-enriching "after hours"-establishment—<u>reliably</u>, a customer-friendly house eager to receive the "after sunset"-sample of foot-traveling, cash-spending guests agreeing to automatically absorb the specific venue's all too tempting interior environment which expertly caters to arriving customers ready to resign themselves to the cradling comforts available on hand. It's just after 3:00 p.m., C.S.T., as of SAT., Jan. 31, 2004, on a day of frigid air-temperature in the specific area of territory which I just so happen to inhabit in this particular era of time, indicating the region's typical "Wintertime" climatic agenda, which serves to earmark the state as a "Northern Plains"-location, has, indeed, managed to arrive with its usual measure of inhospitable chilliness, of course, discomforting anyone found residing within the boundaries of the northern habitat's currently snow-rich environment.

The "Realm of Jesters[ISS]"-outlet is found on the corner of N. 1st Avenue and N. 3rd Street, on the northeastern corner of the particular intersection of the two Downtown motor-traffic routes drivers do utilize by daily routine. Inside the venue I occupy at the moment, there appears to be no less than <u>11</u>(!) state-of-the-art, widescreen TV-monitors, each being, of course, a "smart" LED-monitor with 4K-graphics and an Ultra High-Def resolution-level screen. At the front end of the venue itself there are 3 pinball machines for guests to use at their convenience, to play a round of pinball on one of the table-level systems standing along the "N. 1st Ave."-side of the building which the eating outlet sits in.

First, there's an "Untouchables"-pinball machine, an electronic game-room model featuring decorative imagery originating in the motion-picture production of the same title (i.e., "The Untouchables") released by "Paramount Pictures Corporation" in the Spring of 1987, focusing on the team of federal "law enforcement"-agents assigned to track the underworld enterprises of one "Al Capone", the "Chicagoland"-region Mafia-boss plaguing the Midwestern cosmopolis in the '20's and '30's with various criminal profit-making ventures. Next, there appears to be a "Battlestar Galactica"-pinball machine, using imagery originating in TV-advertisements and promotional-bulletins appearing in daily or weekly consumer-publications (newspaper and magazine) to announce the broadcast of the Sci-Fi series "Battlestar Galactica", which originally aired on ABC-TV in the late 1970's, i.e., from 1978 – 1979, the dates of the TV program's original era of broadcast. And, next, there appears to be a "Public Enemy"-pinball machine, a gaming-table using imagery featuring the "Hip-Hop" act known as "Public Enemy", East Coast "Rap"-community artists emerging in the late

1980's by publicly circulating "song"-titles notable for notifying the larger music universe of issues the African-American inhabitants of New York City encounter in life as a social block still struggling for equal standing within the broader set of residents co-existing inside the "Big Apple" (i.e., N.Y.C.).

There are several guest-seating booths found just near the "streetside"-window facing southwards (the outlet's perimeter along the "N. 3rd St."-side of the venue) and barrel-built tables and barstools found along the "streetside"-window facing westwards (the outlet's perimeter along the "N. 1st Ave."-side of the eating venue). Above the specific facility itself, there appears to be a separate nightclub (its name, "Nest of Serpents"), which features a dance floor, a live "DJ"-station, and several large chandeliers suspended from the outlet's ceiling offering an elegant level of interior illumination to patrons in attendance who might only hope to observe the guests selecting to let themselves physically participate in a group response to the music the DJ chooses to offer to the room's crowd of engaging evening guests. The nightclub-venue (i.e., "Nest of Serpents") is accessible through use of the "Airwalk"-system, an indoor bridge which permits pedestrians to utilize an elevated, enclosed footpath which stretches across N. 3rd St., above the street-level beneath it, the footbridge itself being level with the 2nd-story, that is, of the building which both the "Realm of Jesters[ISS]"-outlet and the "Nest of Vipers"-nightclub are housed in. There's an outdoor speaker-system along the "N. 1st Ave."-side of the venue, currently running music to any walking past the venue itself along the northwards foot-traffic route, which releases an example of "Heavy Metal"-music for the benefit of anyone approaching the venue on its west-ernside. Yet, I cannot, here, seem to identify the actual song itself by title or name of artist, though, I must, here, confess to being a genuine, long-term fan of the music category—"Metal"—that would be, my old friends.

There are two restrooms ("Male" and "Female") at the eastern end of the restaurant, on the "N. 3rd Street"-side of the outlet. The widescreen TV monitors positioned around the venue for the benefit of patrons to observe while standing or sitting in any particular spot upon the outlet's interior floorspace appear to be broadcasting to those on hand programming from 24-hour cable sports-networks (e.g.'s, "Golf Channel", "Tennis Network", "NBA Network", "MLB Network", "NASCAR Network", etc.) or programming from 24-hour cable news-networks (e.g.'s, CNN, Fox News, MSNBC, CNBC, etc.). There is a barroom "bouncer" on hand in the venue on Saturday nights to ensure there is no guest in attendance harassing or exhibiting hostile behavior towards the other patrons or house employees due to a state of intoxication occurring on the visitor's part at the time. To my knowledge, there appears to be a sales-counter near the eastern end of the venue, behind which one can easily detect the tap-levers ready for use in dispensing fresh, refrigerated ounces of lager-style beer, with each serving settling noisily into its glass with a foaming head of faint, carbon-rich fluid.

Of course, the establishment receives the benefit of an indoor climate-regulation system to maintain an acceptable temperature-level for patrons on site, in view of the frigid-level of Autumntime air outside the venue those entering the establishment at night are attempting to secure temporary relief from. In the outlet's spacious dining room, the ceiling features several exposed infrastructural beams overhead and exposed plumbing lines which apparently service the business-venue upstairs, i.e., the dance club ("Nest of Serpents"). There are several rotating ceiling fans suspended from the venue's overhead beams to assist in circulating the room's warm air about the operation's square-feet of available floorspace, a section of which any patron might select to assume for himself while eating or drinking inside the outlet found conveniently by the guest on hand in the "Brick Wall"-District of the town.

The menu includes sandwiches, coffee, wedge-fries, onion rings, coleslaw, brownies, sodas (with free-refills from soda-dispensing fountains near the venue's sales counter at the front of the large dining hall). There's a self-service soda-dispensing station, featuring a bank of release-ports in the outlet for guests to utilize if desiring a re-fill of cola in the plastic cup which the patron obtains from the sales-counter after ordering items on the menu-board appearing behind the clerk's counter.

I'm currently eating a Turkey sandwich with side-orders of coleslaw, wedge-fries and onion rings, with a soda from one of the dispensers on hand in the shop available to customers to receive free refills, selecting to consume on site a generous level of ounces of "Mountain Dew™"-brand "Mango Heat^R"-flavor tropical soda from one of the soda-dispensing fountains near the outlet's front-entryway. Some of the large widescreen TV-monitors found inside the fastfood-vending outlet appear to be showcasing programming off any one of the various cable-channels known for presenting a menu of music-video productions to the viewership choosing to tune in to the particular "specialty"-network ("M^{TV}", "VH1", or "BET").

In order to travel on foot to the "Realm of Jesters^{ISS}"-outlet from the corner of Reddington Avenue and Courier Street, the intersection at which "The 'Falconeer' Building" (the housing complex in which I currently reside as a lease-holding tenant) stands, I had to travel north on Reddington Ave. 6 blocks to the corner of Reddington Ave. and 8th St. On 8th St., I had to travel just one block east to the next corner, 8th St. and Hennenburgh Avenue, that would be. On Hennenburgh Ave., I had to travel 5 blocks north to the corner of Hennenburgh Ave. and 3rd St. On 3rd St., I had to travel just one block east to the corner of N. 3rd Street and N. 1st Avenue to arrive at the venue in question, "Realm of Jesters^{ISS}". The foodvending-outlet itself is found on the northeastern corner of the intersection of N. 1st Ave. and N. 3rd St.

I, here, do encounter, yet another guest on hand inside the eating venue itself, an elderly Caucasian woman, who chooses, here, to seat herself in a booth which is just in front of the one I currently occupy as a dining guest on the "N. 3rd Street"-side of the restaurant, right alongside the south-facing "streetside"-windows allowing any guests to monitor, if they so choose, the street traffic running outside the venue on N. 3rd St., the motor traffic or foot-travelers walking the concrete path beside the fastfood-station readily found inside the "Brick Wall"-District of the "Central Commerce District".

Initially, the woman appeared to be conversing with a particular man while first entering the venue as a patron just a few moments earlier, perhaps her husband or an elderly friend, selecting to accompany her to the particular site which she's choosing to pay visit to today in order to enjoy a menu of items available on the outlet's "lunchtime"-course of offerings. Yet, after exchanging a few comments with the woman, the man immediately chose to excuse himself and left the outlet's premises, leaving the woman to remain on site alone, it would appear. After receiving the order which she chose to place with the clerk at the front sales-counter, she chose a booth towards the eastern end of the venue, the one that just so happens to be in front of the one which I'm sitting in at the moment. Hence, the elderly woman is facing me at this point from the bench beside the table in the booth she currently occupies. The support-backs of the benches the booths offer to guests as seating space only rise to "shoulder"-height, as one sits upon the bench's level board, hence, one sitting in the booth the elderly female occupies can see one sitting in the next booth over, without obstruction, unfortunately for me, I do, here, prefer to add.

<u>Elderly Woman</u>:
(Here, she unshoulders the purse of personal items she carries with her as she settles herself onto the bench in the booth, placing the purse beside her on the furnishing piece she rests on.) "When you get older, it's harder to come to a decision in life. I had trouble at the counter determining whether I wanted the 'Grilled Chicken'-sandwich or the 'Meatball & Provolone'-sandwich which their menu displayed…. I'm 68 years old."

<u>Ariq</u>:
(Here, I refuse to admit to my own particular age, at first, as if the stranger is expecting me to agree to such an on-the-spot confession to her in a public place of customer convenience and comfort…. Sitting in the booth, alone, while continuing to munch on the remains of an onion ring which I've chosen to dip into a large paper cup of re-flavoring tomato paste, I choose to engage the elderly Caucasian woman.) "I'm twenty-six years old. I'm actually a software-developer currently residing in the 'Laurel Park'-neighborhood, next to the 'Convention Center'. I moved to Minnesota from

the San Francisco Bay Area over a month-and-a-half ago, in late October."

Elderly Woman:
(The customer chooses to set out on the table in front of her a napkin, she first unfolds, a plastic straw, she first unwraps, and plastic utensils from the racks available near the front sales-counter: a fork, a knife, and a spoon.) "That was my partner, the man I came in with, just a moment ago. He told me to return home before dark to make sure I'm off the streets before nightfall, fearing I might fall victim to the **predator** still at large in our area. What's the name the local news-channels use to describe him … the 'Shadowslasher'? … I used to attend one of the churches where the 'predator' chose to victimize a young woman. On Sunday, the 21st of December, I believe it was. At the 'First Metropolitan Church of the Resurrection'. I attended that church for a while in the past."

Ariq:
(I, here, immediately make note of the particular date and location to which the woman chooses to, here, reference in communicating with me…. The 'First Metropolitan Church of the Resurrection'. On SUN., Dec. 21, 2003. Yes, of course. That was one instance of a felony-level "sexcrime"-assault in which I chose to prey upon the 'Native American' woman, a victim, who, for better or worse, was obviously inebriated at the moment I chose to initialize the "sexcrime"-assault against her. I, here, note as well, this is merely the third incident in which someone in my midst has made mention of the case involving the serial rapist still at large in the 'Central Commerce District' without realizing I, Ariq, am the perpetrator of such offenses in question. Here, I consider immediately excusing myself from the venue, yet, I, rather, choose to remain, in order to finish eating the food and sipping the drink which I ordered on site, which I trust will serve me as a late lunchtime-meal on a Saturday afternoon.) "Oh? … The ongoing case we hear of in the newscasts by the local network-affiliates? … The so-called 'Shadowslasher'-crimes? This bothers a woman like you as well? … I s'pose I'm bothered by this case, too. If it seems to be upsetting to women in the region, such as yourself, I s'pose we all should hope the police manage to *some*how put an end to these crimes, for the sake of the community's peace of mind. So you can feel free to dine out at night without fearing an assailant might choose to *inexcusably* prey upon you."

Elderly Woman:
(Here, the woman bites into the "Meatball & Provolone"-sandwich she ordered off the menu-board behind the sales-clerk's counter at the front of the venue. She next sips at the plastic cup of soda kept on the table beside the tray holding the items she's selecting to eat while in the establishment

currently offering a customer-friendly indoor climate to guests on hand due to the "interior" heating-system in place.) "Tomorrow, I have to finish shoveling the snow off of the driveway <u>and</u> off of the walkway leading to the front door of the house…. I'm actually halfway done."

<u>Ariq</u>:
(Here, I would note, the woman in front of me is probably not going to attend an area church tomorrow to hear its minister deliver unto adherents of the faith in attendance a Sunday sermon. Instead, she'll be shoveling snow near the safe confines of her home residence. This could, perhaps, be due to the "sexcrime"-assaults I'm guilty of perpetrating in recent months, here, in Minnesota. I s'pose, at this point, women in the "Central Commerce District", particularly those most susceptible to victimization, such as the elderly, assume, at this moment in time, it's bad luck to venture to a local church on Sundays nowadays, at least until local "law enforcement"-agents manage to apprehend the perpetrator guilty of committing the assaults occurring thus far against women at local church-locations.) "There'll be another storm arriving in the 'Twin Cities'-region soon, probably in a week. You might have to obtain a motorized snow-removal system, rather than relying upon use of a hand-held shovel. There's simply less work for you to do. This storm is set to be just about as big as the last one, apparently. It'll hit the region with a formidable chill, a deep frost. The snow-level could apparently break all pre-existing records, I hear."

<u>Elderly</u> <u>Woman</u>:
(At this point, the woman merely begins to stare at me, with large, blank eyes, and starts to nod, as if acknowledging agreement on her part with something she recognizes and instantly chooses to accept. She appears, in nodding once again, to indicate approval of what it is she apparently beholds at the particular moment…. But, am I the one she recognizes she must accept or is it the "Meatball and Provolone"-sandwich she recognizes she must accept?? … She continues to munch on her late-afternoon meal at this moment inside the fastfood-outlet found within the urban boundaries of the "Brick Wall"-District.) "The last storm that hit the region was a terrible example of winter weather at its worst, I'd say. Which is why I still have to shovel snow from the driveway and front-walkway tomorrow, to clear the property of snowfall which prohibits me from being able to properly make use of the driveway and front-walkway. I hope the next storm isn't as bad…. I'm just *hoping* it isn't."

<u>Ariq</u>:
(I, here, assume the woman will be contacting her partner, the elderly man who chose to accompany her into the outlet's premises, by cellphone, later

Adrien L. Montgomery
Tasting Droplets of the Unforgettable Rain
Official Imprint: "Dynamographx"

on, and he'll return to pick her up, escorting her to the car and driving her home, to ensure she doesn't fall prey to any aspiring assailant lurking about the area, in an alley just waiting for a suitable target to appear in front of him to permit him to aim for the objective he seeks to see himself achieve on the particular night's itinerary.) "How's the 'Meatball & Provolone'? ... This time around did'ja make the right choice? ... The 'Turkey' I ordered is OK, I suppose. These onion rings are a bit tasty. Did'ja try one of their 'Craft Beers'? ... 'Wheelboat Brewers House[AI]'? ... 'Riverton Beermakers[AI]'? ... Oh, I see you ordered a plastic cup for the soda fountains? ... 'Cherry'-flavor cola, correct?"

<u>Elderly Woman</u>:
(The woman, here, uses the plastic fork she obtained at the utensils-bin in a station near the sales-clerk's counter at the front entrance of the outlet in order to lift a helping of the coleslaw from its paper serving carton to her eager mouth, apparently, ready to accept the strings of sauce-rich cabbage, as her appetite in the outlet indicates.) "Tell me something, young man.... Can you think of anything at this point that would <u>always</u> make you smile?"

<u>Ariq</u>:
(The woman's abrupt decision to offer unto me such a question catches me by surprise at the moment. Alarmed, to an extent, by the elderly woman's apparent intrusiveness, I at first refuse to respond to such a question, here, fearing I'll admit to finding pleasure in something which could, perhaps, confirm the woman's suspicions that the man sitting in the booth in front of hers is, in fact, the predator whom local agents of "law enforcement" are in the midst of attempting to apprehend for the benefit of those in the community—such as herself—desiring once again to enjoy the peace of mind everyone in an orderly society has the right to live with as a citizen in good standing. I begin to question the woman's motives in choosing, here, to communicate with me as she does.... Is she a retired policewoman?) "Actually, what makes me 'smile'—or, what makes me happy, I guess—is the ability to step into a venue such as the one which we currently find ourselves in today. The opportunity to walk into a place such as the one I happen to be enjoying as patron at this point, on a frosty day—such as the one transpiring at the moment—in order to momentarily escape what awaits us outside, is something I'd obviously believe deserves applause on my part."

<u>Elderly Woman</u>:
(The woman here, once again, merely bites into the "Meatball & Provolone"-sandwich in a "Potato"-bread hamburger bun, and, cautiously, munches on

the contents of the menu-item while a helping of the lunchtime-meal is still in her mouth.) "Actually, what makes <u>me</u> smile is seeing that a decent, upstanding young man … such as yourself, is able to behold a summoning light on the horizon to his east. I believe what you'll see is a bright future unfolding in front of you. For—behind you—on the horizon to your west, there appears a high-tide of darkness which you now have the opportunity to escape if you so choose to excuse yourself from the wave of death which steadily approaches you, silencing your path with the shadow it casts upon you, enshrouding you with a veil of doom, sewn together from your own sins, as if it were a tapestry of retribution to be placed over you as a blanket would cover a corpse in its grave."

<u>Ariq</u>:

(I, here, immediately make a note to myself to head home by first heading towards the parking lot outside the Post Office on 12th Street and N. Hawthorne Ave., in order to enter the driveway behind the "Townhouse Lofts"-building, an apartment complex on 11th Street and Hennenburgh Boulevard, in order to evade the elderly woman, if, for any reason, she chooses to follow me once I leave the "Realm of Jesters[ISS]"-outlet today.) "Y'know, I believe I do see what could possibly be a bright future ahead of me. Because I believe I'll soon be moving out of the state of Minnesota altogether in the near future. I must admit, I've seen more than my share of darkness since arriving in this state in October. *Of course*, it's because of the harsh climatic backdrop occurring over the past three months, which I personally find a bit too difficult to endure myself, regardless of what others inhabiting the region may feel about the lengthy term of 'Frost' be-sieging the community on an annual basis."

<u>Elderly Woman</u>:

(The woman, again, sips at the large paper cup she holds containing ounces of the "Black Patch[AI]"-brand "Root Beer"-soda which she chose at the station of soda-dispensing fountains found near the front-entryway of the foodvending-outlet. She, next, bites into the large almond-frosted brownie [a brownie sprinkled with finely-chopped almond-nuts] before, again, sipping from ounces in the paper cup of "Root Beer"-soda.) "I trust, young man, you, indeed, <u>are</u> on a path which will lead you to a horizon of morning sunlight, to the east that is, and you're ready to leave behind you the nocturnal storm which you've left in your recent past, even if that means you do, however, have to leave the state of Minnesota for good.... The darkness left in your wake must stay behind you, to the west that is, and can <u>never</u> emerge once more at any point in your future."

I, on hearing the woman's encouraging opinion indicating she desires I

--()--
181
--()--

follow through on the idea I raised about vacating the state to venture towards a community I'll encounter after distancing myself from the scene currently surrounding me, decide to consume the remaining portions of the "Turkey"-sandwich which I ordered at the outlet's sales-counter, as well as all that's left of the side-order of onion rings in the paper boat sitting on the plastic tray resting on the maple-built dining table found inside the booth which I solitarily do occupy at the moment.

I, here, assume the woman in the booth in front of the one I'm currently occupying is an "evangelist", whose real objective is to attempt to convert me to Christianity, aiming to ask me if I'm willing to accept "Christ" as my personal "Lord and Savior", thereby, becoming "Born Again" in the eyes of the Almighty, i.e., being, then, one who is safe from God's ultimate measure of justice towards the wicked.

I, here, decide to determine the elderly woman currently munching on a mouthful of the almond-frosted brownie she's holding in her right hand while continuing to consume the "lunchtime"-meal she entered the "foodvending"-outlet in order to eat in, at the time, opting to escape the presence of a cloud-ridden Saturday afternoon which awaits us both once venturing outside again, in fact, to be basically a harmless presence, and one who poses no threat to me at the moment. I.e., I no longer fear that she's an "undercover"-agent of the local police bureau's "Sex Crimes"-Division investigating the series of "felony"-level sexual assaults occurring over the past couple of months who, on assignment, chose to follow me into the venue to question me in a casual manner with respect to the alarming behavioral pattern emerging on my part in the recent past since arriving in the state. I quickly consume what remains of the "Turkey"-sandwich left on the wax-paper wrapper spread open on the plastic tray and consume the remaining ounces of the soda (the "Mountain Dew™"-brand "Mango Heat^R"-flavor tropical cola) in the plastic cup which the "sales counter"-clerk gave to me at the time I chose to place the order.

I prepare myself to finally exit the outlet and tell the elderly woman who consumes the lunchtime-menu made to fulfill the order she placed upon entering the venue to ensure she has a safe trip back home on this evening and I warn her not to over-exert herself in attempting to complete the "household"-chores which she has in store for herself to complete tomorrow, i.e., shoveling snow from the driveway <u>and</u> front-walkway at her address to clear the property of the "Wintertime" build-up of ice-granules left by the last storm which paid a very unwelcome visit, that is, to the local region we both happen to inhabit, a week earlier. (... Ha! Ha! Ha!)

Before exiting the venue, I dispose of the items of trash remaining on the plastic tray I carried from the table and I place the tray atop one of the trash-holding cabinets. I refill the paper soda cup I picked up at the sales counter when originally placing the order with ounces of "Mountain Dew™"-

brand "Mango Heat[R]"-flavor tropical soda at the station of cola-dispensing fountains near the venue's font-entryway and exit the outlet's user-friendly interior to venture into the frosty atmosphere offered by the streets of the surrounding area found in the "Brick Wall"-District of the city.

At this moment, upon finding myself once again outside the eating location itself, I must, I suppose, use the opportunity at hand to issue unto the reading audience following me thus far, a <u>final</u> farewell, expressing gratitude to one and all for accompanying me on the voyage towards a higher level of "Self-Enlightenment" by fulfilling all *necessary* stages of the "Perspective on Self-Enlightenment" which (both) you and I had the courage and confidence to embark upon together.... Hence, as if you are but a shadow to the figure I present to the moonlit asphalt roads which I'll walk during the odd nocturnal outing which I, of course, will ensure I keep on occasion, do (O devout disciples selecting to offer to me companionship) continue to assemble at "close range" and do continue to observe (on an intimate level of contact) the preceding series of lessons I've chosen to present, that you, as well, might discover the <u>genuine</u> value in what *exactly* it is which I'm attempting to illustrate to any and all for the purpose of permitting *some*one (i.e., the especially rare individual, that is) to adopt a path in the world at large which *could* possibly guide him to a heretofore unseen degree of wisdom (i.e., "cosmic knowledge") and, ultimately, to a previously unknown level of "Self-Enlightenment"! ... But, it is "Goodbye", I do, here, say ... a farewell to last only for but a brief moment until, O ever-present assembly of eager apostles, I choose to call upon you again! ... This, once more, is <u>Ariq</u> <u>Zarkahn</u> <u>Shoretempel</u> (i.e., the " 'After Hours' Assailant in the Metrozone of the 'Northern Plains' ") bidding the audience of loyal listeners on hand an honest "Goodbye"! ... And "<u>Goodnight</u>"! (... Ha! Ha! Ha! Ha! Ha!)

Upon issuing to you, friends and close associates alike, a final farewell for the purpose of acknowledging my long-standing audience, I, at once, here, make note of a sudden "cloudburst" occurring in the sky overhead, a rupture in the layering cloud-line menacingly appearing in the skies currently hovering over the local coordinates of land which manages, here, to release a tremendous downpour of liquid precipitation which inundates the ground of the "Brick Wall"-District with inches of water in what only appears to be a mere instance of time.

I quickly walk from the venue itself (the "Realm of Jesters[ISS]"-sandwich outlet), on the corner of N. 1st Ave. and N. 3rd Street by walking south 6 blocks to the northwestern corner of N. Hawthorne Avenue and N. 9th Street only to ("Lo and Behold! ...") *ultimately*—once the walk itself conveniently expires—find myself arriving at a "Protestant Church"-location found within the "Central Commerce District", the specific "fellowship"-venue being the "Assembly of the Lord's Sacred Crucifixion". I begin the afternoon's urban trek in the midst of the shattering arrival of rain by venturing south on N. 1st Ave., to head home to the "Falconeer"-building upon exiting the foodvending-outlet (i.e., "Realm of Jesters[ISS]"-outlet) on the particular Saturday at the end of January 2004. I walk past a clothing-outlet selling lingerie, nightwear apparel for women, and other items of apparently high sexual value for any parties interested in enlivening the "bedroom"-experience with assets one might deem as helpful (or even *necessary*) for a couple to make use of during their occasion of overnight intimacy. (... Ha! Ha! Ha!) I walk past the "Pegasus Bar & Grill" on the corner of N. 1st Ave. and 4th Street and continue to walk along N. 1st Avenue until encountering the "Sister Cities Brewery" on the corner of N. 1st Ave. and 5th Street, found right across the street from the " 'CitiTraxx[STF]'-Railsystem" station on Hennenburgh Boulevard and 5th Street.

I cross N. 1st Avenue at 5th Street and continue to head south towards the "Laurel Park"-region. I come to the intersection of N. 1st Ave. and 7th Street, the location of the "First Ave. and 7th-Street Entry"-nightclub venue. For a moment, I consider to pause at the "Events"-calendar posted on the wall outside the venue in order to review the upcoming acts on schedule to visit the well-known nightclub ("First Ave.") in the upcoming month, yet, I instead, continue ahead onto the next intersection.

On the corner of N. 9th Street and N. Hawthorne Avenue, there's an empty parking lot behind another nightclub (i.e., "The Hotel Babylon"), which is down the block from the "Halbarton House & Rooms" found on the corner of N. 1st Avenue and N. 8th Street. (The "Halbarton House & Rooms" is just one block south of the "First Avenue and 7th-St. Entry"-buildings, a nightclub-venue found on the corner of N. 1st Ave. and N. 7th St. in the "Central Commerce District".) Across the street from the empty parking lot on the northwestern-corner of N. 9th Street and N. Hawthorne Avenue is the site of the "Protestant Church"-location, called the "Assembly of the Lord's Sacred Crucifixion", found on the southwestern corner of the intersection of N. 9th Street and N. Hawthorne Avenue in the "Downtown"-zone.

I currently find myself standing on the black asphalt ground of the empty parking lot on the northwestern-corner of N. 9th Street and N. Hawthorne Ave., behind "The Hotel Babylon", while still holding the paper cup of "Mountain Dew[TM]"-brand "Mango Heat[R]"-flavor tropical cola in my right hand, as the rainwater crashes to the earth after freely dropping from the moisture-storage spaces in the cargo train of clouds appearing overhead as an ongoing storm passes through the "Minneapolis Greater Metro"-region, yet not before indicating to inhabitants found residing in the acres underneath the cloud-line as to what would accurately be the exact amount of water which it keeps in its transporting-tanks ready to level the land beneath with a torrential outburst of aerial precipitation.

I walk from the empty asphalt ground found behind the nightclub venue (i.e., "The Hotel Babylon"), itself on the corner of Hennenburgh Boulevard and N. 9th Street, and quickly cross N. 9th Street, an autotraffic-route which is accumulating a floor of rainwater due to the storm-waves of rain the menacing armada of clouds releases from overhead, with the street itself receiving a flooding amount of fresh water which immerses its surface beneath the kiloliters of the arriving storm-water. Once at the southwestern corner of the intersection, next to the "Protestant Faith"-location, I immediately notice the aluminum guide-channel leading rainwater from a roof-level gutter found on the edge of the building's roof, to, then, release the amount of precipitation which the roof-gutter collects onto the sidewalk running along N. 9th Street beside the urban "Church"-venue.

Permit me, old folks and friends alike, to, here, make record of the rain "runoff"-guide re-channeling water from the roof-gutter at the edge of the building's rooftop and to decide to fill the paper cup I have with ounces of the arriving rain-water rapidly running through the aluminum "runoff"-channel on the exterior wall of the church's streetside-property. I discard the remaining ounces of the "Mountain Dew™"-brand "Mango Heat^R"-flavor tropical soda-formula from the paper cola cup by throwing the fluid which the cup still includes into an elevated soil-pillow of plants set inside a large soil basin beside the exterior, street-level wall of the "Protestant"-church property and I then place the empty cup beneath the end of the rain "runoff"-guide re-channeling water from the gutter along the edge of the building's rooftop through the aluminum route to release the excess rain onto the sidewalk beside the church property itself. I watch the rain-water exiting the re-channeling guide rapidly collect itself in quickly-accumulating ounces (as if it were escaping the mouth of a running kitch-en-faucet), in order to fill the large paper cup with its "Wintertime"-stormwater, coming, of course, from the cloud-discharge of heavy precipitation found in the darkening sky overhead.

Lifting the large paper cup, full of the rain-water running through the re-channeling guide from the roof-gutter at the building's highest level, I begin to drink from the ounces of frigid rainwater caught in the cup I hold in hand beside the "Downtown"-property promoting the faith and fellowship prescribed to adherents in the "Protestant Church"-doctrines.

Upon allowing myself to consume ounces of the fresh storm liquid, I *immediately* realize what the rainwater inundating the earth from the overhead layering of clouds bloated with moisture-storage banks which currently threaten to overwhelm the "Greater Minneapolis Metro"-region with an almost apocalyptic flood of unending rainfall from the could-ridden sky is, hereby, offering to me on this specific Sunday—absolution! The rain-water falling from the sky threatening the inhabitants of the "Twin Cities"-region (i.e., water coming to earth from the sacred vessels found in the sunlit corridors of Heaven itself, in use, apparently, to ceremonially rehydrate the land beneath the cloud-train anxious to receive a generous level of fluid to quench its cries [inaudible to humans, that is] for the blessing of fresh rainfall in the Wintertime-season). The rainwater I consume while standing on the sidewalk outside the "Protestant"-church property found on the southwestern-corner of N. 9th Street and N. Hawthorne Ave. indicates, in the outdoor ounces I ingest from the paper cup I hold in hand, I am to be forgiven of the "sins" which I've left in the path running behind me since arriving in the state of Minnesota in October of 2003. (**Indentation**) These "sins", of course, being the actions I chose to commit upon deciding to adopt the agenda of fulfilling all *necessary* aspects of the "Perspective on 'Self-Enlightenment' ", a program of stages which I set forth for myself to fulfill in order to *ultimately* achieve a superior level of wisdom (or, "cosmic knowledge") which I could then impart to those who approach me in order to attain such wisdom for themselves in the world as well. (**Indentation**) The train of storm clouds continues to inundate the terrain beneath its "epic"-size moisture-storage tanks with a heretofore unseen amount of rainfall, in a storm leveling the land with a virtual inundation of water, basically indicating to me I am to be forgiven of the "sins" which I chose to commit earlier on in attempting to fulfill the agenda I set forth for myself to complete and will <u>not</u>, therefore, be subjected to a penalty upon the dispensing of justice from Heaven's virtually bottomless well of wrath, if I, hereby, do so choose to refrain from continuing to commit such atrocities against any females found currently residing in the "Minneapolis Greater Metropolitan Area" ... *forgiven*, that is, if I choose to avoid engaging in additional incidents of "felony"-level "sexcrime"-assault against female inhabitants of the region from today onwards in time. (**Indentation**) I, here, continue to drink eagerly from the ounces of fresh rainfall found in the large paper cup I still hold in hand as I stand beside the "Protestant Church"-venue (i.e., the "Assembly of the Lord's Sacred Crucifixion"), readily consuming the ounces of frosty rain-fluid in the paper cup I hold in hand which offers to me the water I managed to catch running through the aluminum "runoff"-guide re-channeling water from the building's roof-level gutter to the sidewalk beside the property of "Protestant"-fellowship, aware of the offer of <u>absolution</u> (i.e., immunity from justice) which Heaven extends to me at the moment, the rain storm signaling I, at this moment, assume a status in the eyes of the Almighty with which I am no longer due to receive any penalty appropriate in my case if considering the record of "sinful" actions (i.e., "atrocities") which I chose to commit against females in the state of Minnesota in attempting to fulfill the aspects of the "Perspective on 'Self-Enlightenment' " which I set forth for myself to complete in order to attain a higher level of wisdom (i.e., "spiritual knowledge") upon arriving in the state in late October of 2003.

    I do here, desire, to announce to all readers, the assembly of interested parties on hand being friends and close associates alike, I do indeed desire to immediately accept the offer of <u>absolution</u> (i.e., immunity from punishment) which Heaven presents unto me today, with the ounces of fresh rain-water found in the cup which I caught in the "runoff"-guide re-channeling water from the gutter at the building's rooftop level. The rainfall itself is—I note—a holy wave of storm-water sanctifying the one soul inhabiting terrain beneath its moisture-storage tanks alert enough to realize God offers to me an opportunity today to free myself from the penalty justifiably due to come unto me as punishment for the "sexcrime"-assaults which I chose to commit against females in the region in fulfilling the agenda I set forth for myself early on in order to achieve enlightenment on arriving in the state of Minnesota. I, Ariq, do, today, hereby, promise I will avoid continuing on a course of such socially unacceptable conduct in exchange for the gift of "absolution" which God, hereby, agrees to bestow on me, freeing me from the just penalty due for sins in the past, seeing that I, Ariq, do, hereby, choose to avoid repeating the antisocial path of behavior which I did leave in the trail behind me over the past 2-and-a-half months as a resident, here, in the state of Minnesota.

I do, once again, hereby, promise to refrain in the future from initializing another series of "sexcrime"-assaults against females residing in the region similar to the record of "felony"-level offenses which I just let myself commit in the recent weeks since arriving in Minnesota.

I freely consume the remaining ounces of rainwater left in the paper cup I received at the "Realm of Jesters[ISS]"-outlet on N. 1st Ave. and N. 3rd Street and instantly realize I am, in fact, no longer due to receive a just penalty appropriate in my case as determined by the hand of the Almighty if con-sidering the path of atrocities left in the road I chose to adopt for myself upon arriving in the state in order to fulfill the agenda I set forth at the beginning in attempting to fulfill all *necessary* aspects in the "Perspective on 'Self-Enlightenment' ". The penalty which God would seek to bestow on such an individual guilty of perpetrating the "sexcrime"-offenses I chose to commit against women in the state could, as the elderly woman at the foodvending-outlet chose to indicate to me as I sat in the booth just in front of hers while innocently eating the "lunchtime"-menu I chose to purchase at the outlet, amount to <u>death</u> itself! (((Sigh))).

I, at once, begin to walk east on N. 9th Street, towards Hennenburgh Boulevard, in order to maneuver myself towards the basement-level apartment I occupy as a lease-holding tenant in the "Falconeer"-complex on Reddington Avenue and Courier Street, while being fully aware of the offer of <u>absolution</u> (i.e., immunity from a penalty due for sins in one's past) which Heaven chooses to extend to me today with the ounces of rainfall found in the paper cup I was able to fill at the bottom of the aluminum "runoff"-guide beside the "Protestant Faith"-building, a genuine offering of forgiveness <u>and</u> deliverance (potentially, from <u>death</u>, as the elderly woman at the "Realm of Jesters[ISS]"-outlet chose to indicate to me earlier today), which I, of course, once again, chose to immediately accept from Heaven's outstretched hand of charity.

I note, here, as I reach the northwestern-corner of the intersection of Hennenburgh Boulevard and N. 9th Street, the rainfall arriving on earth from the armada of cargo-holding rain clouds traveling through the sky overhead ... with the airboats themselves almost appearing to be similar to large ocean-going vessels traversing an expanse of sea-space in heading to the next port which the convoy of ships is to sail to in its worldwide voyage—with the rain steadily flooding the "Downtown"-boulevard with inches of water released from the cloud-line above as a fluid-discharge soaking the soil beneath with a blessing of liquid quenching and silencing the earth's audible cries for instant precipitation. I now cross Hennenburgh Boulevard and carefully sip from the paper cup I hold in hand the final few ounces of rainfall which I caught from the water "runoff"-guide found alongside the exterior wall of the "Protestant Faith"-building, on the corner of N. 9th Street and N. Hawthorne Ave., permitting myself to taste and savor what would amount to the last ounces left of what I would, at the moment, determine to be nothing less than an Earth-storm offering to me, here, what must be an "<u>unforgettable</u> rain"!! [!!Issuing 'Emoticon' Alert!! (} ; >)]

Tasting Droplets of the Unforgettable Rain

By
Adrien L. Montgomery
<u>Cycle 018</u>:
"An Office in the Clouds Permits the Employee on Hand to View the World from a Lofty Plateau.... Yet, Without Question, the Task of Rising to That Level Is, However, a Chore Many Would Prefer Not to Endure."

<u>UTA Directive XVIII</u>:
"Attention! Attention! ... Passengers Aboard The 'CitiTraxx[STF]' Railsystem-Vehicle Must Not Attempt To Interfere With Or Prevent The Closing Of The Commuter-Service's 'Entry/Exit'-Doors. Repeat, Passengers Aboard The 'CitiTraxx[STF]' Railsystem-Vehicle Must Not Attempt To Interfere With Or Prevent The Closing Of The Commuter-Service's 'Entry/Exit'-Doors."
("<u>UTA</u>": <u>U</u>rban <u>T</u>ransit <u>A</u>uthority)

On the southeastern corner of the intersection of N. 4th Street and N. 1st Ave., in the "Brick Wall"-District of the city's central acreage of urban real estate, there's a "Jazz" nightclub, an "after hours"-venue offering to its patrons onsite-entertainment from various touring ensembles who perform

--()--
188
--()--

compositions known to belong to the "Jazz"-style category of music. The night-spot in question is the "Sioux Nation Jazz Room and Restaurant", a popular spot in the city's "Brick Wall"-District serving to its guests a menu of "bar & grill"-cuisine and a program of music, as performed by the "Jazz"-ensembles paying visit to the club *each* and <u>every</u> night of the week.

Here, the house's manager, Rickie "Quick Mouth" Mazalburgh, is intro-ducing to the audience-members in attendance the Jazz ensemble which is scheduled to perform on the venue's stage on the occasion, in order to entertain the patrons with selections of well-known Jazz compositions, which the band includes in its repertoire as a traveling Jazz orchestra:

<u>Rickie "Quick Mouth" Mazalburgh</u>:
"Tonight's act is a well-known Jazz quartet hailing from Starkville, Mississippi, who are currently making their way around the country on their first coast-to-coast tour, after having made quite a name for themselves in 'Jazz'- and 'Blues'-rooms around the South. People, <u>here</u> they are, 'State of Blouisiana', ready to perform for us classic and original compositions of 'Mississippi Delta' Blues. Let's welcome them to our stage tonight with a warm round of applause, ladies and gentlemen of the 'Sioux Nation'. (And we've heard folks in the southern states are already *begging* them to return.) At the 'Sioux Nation Jazz Room and Restaurant', <u>here</u> for two nights only, ladies and gentlemen, it's 'State of Blouisiana'! ..."

(-|<u>Calendar</u> <u>Date</u>: <u>MON</u>., <u>Feb</u>. <u>02</u>, <u>2004</u>|-)
I'm now sitting on a bench at the spacious countertop serving as a table at which I sit while I fulfill tasks during the day as a programmer employed by the tech-firm I currently work for, "Hyper Mind, Inc.", a company whose central office (i.e., headquarters) is found on the eastern side of Arquette Ave., in between 11th Street and 10th Street, in the city's "Central Commercial District", in what would constitute a "Business Plaza"-section of "corporate"-properties occupying three squares (or blocks of "Downtown"-acreage), extending from Arquette Ave. on the west to Louisville Ave. on the east. The "office" I occupy is on the 4th-story of a 4-floor corporate property, and the specific station I utilize to complete the various tasks which I'm required to perform and fulfill as a programmer employed by the tech-firm is situated in the northeastern corner of the 4th-floor level of the large corporate building-location.

The floor I'm on appears almost as a production-floor which you'd be likely to find on the premises of an assembly plant, with the floor itself being similar in immediate appearance to what you'd probably witness in a "warehouse"-facility in use for work in assembling machinery or industrial equipment. My particular work-space is actually a table, having a surface being around the height of a typical kitchen-countertop in the US (i.e., 42-

in. above the floor that would be), and, while at the table, I sit on a bench built for one person (i.e., a single-seater), which is on casters (or wheels), permitting me to move the bench along the edge of the lengthy table itself without needing to remove myself from the bench's seat in order to push it further along the furnishing's length.

On the spacious table-surface I work at (as one, that is, with there being no other employees or co-workers sitting alongside of me at the table I use in completing the variety of assignments which I must fulfill in a daily shift at the office), I'm allowed to listen to a portable radio-receiving system which I keep on the table's surface next to me during the work day, with the tuning pin usually set to the frequency indicator permitting the system to receive the signal of a well-known "Classic Rock"-station found in the local broadcasting market, "KHSE 'The House' 95.8 FM", a local broadcaster airing a daily menu of "Heavy Rock"-songs usually originating as single-record discs for radio-playback in the 1970's or 1980's. As far as I can tell, there is no other employee working in the floorspace near the northeastern corner of the 4th-story of the office-property who appears to find the open-speaker receiving-unit I use during the day to be a distraction of any kind at all. No one on the floor has ever chosen to pay visit to my particular table to make note of a song being broadcast by the radio-station at any particular time, indicating others in the office could be listening to the music along with me, explaining the volume which I set the receiver to could serve as a distraction for others working on the floor.

The floor's supervisor (or "foreman", that is), Christopher Mariar, has, on occasion, suggested I attempt to make use of a set of headphones ("Bluetooth[R]"-enabled) to listen to a playlist of "Classic Rock"-tunes appearing in a songlist compiled in a roster of "audiofile"-units in a database for (["sound"]-data)-playback in order to avoid use of a radio with open-output speakers which others might find to be disturbing while focusing on the tasks they're assigned to fulfill during the work-shift.

I told Christopher that wearing the "Bluetooth[R]"-enabled headphones all day would be too uncomfortable for me to do and I would, therefore, not be able to focus on fulfilling the tasks I'm required to complete each day, hence, I choose, rather, to make use of the radio-receiving unit which relies on open-speaker sound-production as a radio source while in the office.

One aspect of the job which I do appreciate is the fact I can clothe myself in what would ordinarily be viewed as *casual* attire when on the premises of the workplace during the daily shift, e.g., black jeans and long-sleeve T-shirts as opposed to dress slacks, button-front collar shirts and neck-ties, items of attire which I'd care not to outfit myself with each day of the workweek. As I indicated earlier, the 4th-floor of the corporate-property serving as the central offices for "Hyper Mind, Inc.", the tech-firm which currently keeps me on staff as one of its computer-programmers, operates in a manner similar to what one would see on the production-floor of a large assembly plant, whose onsite-employees are working to put together machinery or industrial equipment as a team of production-technicians. Hence, at the office on the 4th-floor of the company's headquarters found on Arquette Ave. in the "Business Plaza"-section of the city's "Central Commercial District", there's no reason for any of us on staff to bother at-tiring ourselves with formal office-clothing prior to arriving at the jobsite *each* and <u>every</u> day of the workweek to begin fulfilling the variety of assignments required of the staffers on site.

Currently, what I'm working on at this particular moment is the task of re-editing a program which I'm writing for use as a software-project the company's attempting to produce which will serve as a tool enabling its sales-staffers (a department occupying the building's 2nd-floor) to maintain an up-to-date level of communication with clients of the firm who've bene-fitted from the services we offer to those existing in the tech-market in the past. The sales-staffers will be able to automatically transmit ("['Email']-notification")-reminders to our recent clients indicating the service which the particular business or individual sought our assistance with in order to indicate to the company the benefits it will receive if choosing to utilize our services again. In the past, the customer service representatives (i.e., the "CSR" 's) on the building's 2nd-floor were not doing a reliable job of following up with former clients of ours every three months in order to offer to perform any service the client would require a software firm to perform on its behalf, and the sales team's management wanted the policy of re-connecting with former clients to occur in an automated-system, hence, requesting the programmers—the department occupying the building's 4th-floor—design a system enabling the sales department to transmit ("['E-mail']-notification")-reminders to former clients of ours indicating to them the services they required we perform for them in the past, along with notices indicating the rates we charge for such services currently, the job-approval rating the particular client awarded to us for the work we performed on their behalf, contact information on the current "CSR" assigned to the specific client, notes on the additional software-services we can currently offer to them, etc., etc.

The company's CEO, Timothy Laugong, a Chinese-American man (i.e., a "Chinamerican"-type) decided to have a local cabinet-making firm ("Against the Grain[AI]") build tables, benches, chairs, cabinets, shelving-units, bookcases, and countertops for the programmers to make use of as office-furnishings on the 4th-floor of the company's "Downtown"-corporate property situated in the "Business Plaza"-sector of the city's expansive "Central Commercial District". Hence, the floor's foreman "Christopher Mariar" chose to position a work-station for me on the floor's northeastern corner, merely comprising a spacious "dinnertable"-size work-desk and a

--()--
191
--()--

one-seat bench on wheels for the occupant to utilize during the workday. I must, here, admit the workspace I make use of is in a rather remote or isolated sector of the floorspace available to us on the building's 4th-floor, indicating Christopher desired to see me occupy what would be a <u>solitary</u> work-station each day, perhaps, not just to permit me the space I require in order to dutifully complete the assignments I'm required to fulfill but also to ensure no other employee working on the building's top floor would necessarily need to put up with me on a daily basis.... Ha! Ha! Ha! Christopher obviously sees me as a co-worker whom others in the office would prefer not to deal with during the workday.... Well, considering the nocturnal operations I'm guilty of conducting at "Protestant Faith"-properties around the region of the "Central Commercial District" of the city since arriving in the state of Minnesota in late October in order to complete all *necessary* stages in the "Perspective on 'Self-Enlightenment' " I set forth earlier on with the aim of acquiring a higher degree of wisdom (i.e., "Cosmic Knowledge"), which I will, then, impart to any who approach me to acquire such wisdom for themselves, could you really blame any of them, old friends and *ever-so-close* companions at hand? ... Ha! Ha! Ha!

I've already chosen to notify the company's CEO, Timothy Laugong, the Chinamerican executive, of my recent decision to relocate myself to the city of Taos, New Mexico in order to vacate the state of Minnesota as quickly as is possible in order to avoid being seen by any of the females whom I chose to victimize at local "church"-properties in the recent instances of "felony"-level "sexcrime"-assault, who could, then, perhaps, collect necessary information on me, the likely assailant, and then make report on me as a "suspect" in the series of "assault"-cases to the investigators in the "Sex Crimes"-Division at the "Minneapolis Metropolitan Police Force". The foreman in charge of the 4th-floor of the building, Christopher Mariar, is scheduled, I hear, to pay visit to the work-station which I occupy in order to discuss my decision to quit the company without submitting to the executive-staff the <u>required</u> 3-month notice indicating the employee's decision to terminate any contractual obligations required of him as a member of the corporation's "official" work-force.

Just as I'm about to adjust the volume-level of the open-output speaker-system on the radio-receiving unit found on the tabletop just to the left of the "workstation"-computer I'm using in order to re-edit the programming components of the software-project I'm completing on behalf of the company's sales department found on the building's 2nd-story, I note Christopher Mariar, the supervisor (or "foreman") of the company's programming operation on the 4th-floor, is walking over to the side of the table I'm currently utilizing as a work-station available for use in fulfilling assignments required of me *each* and <u>every</u> day at the office.

Christopher, a Caucasian male, who is 41 years in age, stands here at a position across the table-top from where I currently sit upon the one-seat bench I use while working at the spacious, yet solitary, desk-station: "Well, I hear you're trying to leave us *immediately*. What's this … 'Tahoe'? Isn't that in California? … 'Lake Tahoe', it is. Who's telling you to *leave?"*

I merely adjust the volume-level of the radio-receiving unit's open-output speaker-system, in order to guarantee music the radio emits is not serving as a distraction to Christopher during the discussion: "No, it's 'Taos' in *New Mexico*. <u>Not</u> 'Lake Tahoe' in California. I'm quitting the job, terminating employment at 'Hyper Mind, Inc.', as of MON., Mar. 01, 2004. I've always wanted to live in New Mexico. In December, I just decided not to delay the transfer any longer."

Christopher looks at the radio-receiving unit indicating the speakers are running a music-station's signal while knowing quite well I will not lower the radio's volume-level any further, as the music program available to listeners of the station "KHSE 'The House' 95.8 FM" is a privilege I enjoy during the day which I'm not willing to deny myself at anytime while sitting at the table I'm assigned to in the northeastern corner of the 4th-floor's extensive office-space: "Is it a girlfriend? … That's it, huh? Your girlfriend now wants the two of you to move out to Lake Tahoe, I mean, to New Mexico, as quickly as possible, doesn't she? *Every* **time** an employee quits without submitting the <u>required</u> 3-month notice, it's always because *her* husband had to take a job in another state, or because *his* fiancé was sick and tired of living in the bone-chilling 'meat locker' of a state we Minnesotans like to call 'home'!"

I notice other employees on the floor watching Christopher as he stands alongside the work-table I occupy as an onsite-station during the completion of the daily duties which I'm required to fulfill on the job and realize people around the office must have heard he said he'd "lower the boom" on me for terminating contractual obligations at the tech-firm without issuing proper notification first: "It's a great place to live. There's the 'Taos Ski Valley' just northeast of the city and there's a championship-caliber 18-hole golf course in Taos County as well. At this point, I'd simply prefer to live out west. A lot of people do, but I'm actually going to **do** it. I'm just not going to delay it any further."

Christopher, obviously hesitant to erupt with a reminder that I'm violating the company's policy requiring all employees on the 4th-floor deciding to terminate employment with the tech-firm submit a 3-month notice of retirement which the executive-staffers can review and discuss with the employee in order to ensure a degree of necessary coordination occurs with respect to the task of hiring a programmer to assume the position which the first employee is choosing to vacate: "Haven't you been up to the 'North Woods'? … My sister and her husband have a cabin up there on 'Lake Moose Leg' in the northwestern part of the state. I'll assume you'd enjoy it <u>here</u>, *if* you simply discovered what was offered to us!"

I adjust the radio receiving-unit to indicate a favorite song of mine is currently emanating from the system's open-output speakers, as if to tell Christopher the song itself is more important to me than anything he has to say about remaining in Minnesota rather than following through with my decision to migrate to the state of New Mexico in April: "No! March 1st is going to be my last day on the job at 'Hyper Mind, Inc.' I'm moving to Taos on April 1st. There's no reversing this decision on my part. Nothing you say to me will matter beyond this point. Timothy's simply going to have to find a replacement to assume the position of 'Onsite Operations'-programmer. I'll finish the software-project I'm developing for the sales-staffers on the 2nd-floor before I quit on March 1st. You don't have to worry about that. Tell Timothy the new 'client connection'-platform will be ready before I vacate."

Christopher motions with his right hand that I'm to adjust the volume-level on the radio's open-output speakers in order to lower the sound which the radio currently emits at an easily audible level: "So long as the sales-staffers on the 2nd-floor can make use of the 'client reconnection'-software program, I don't believe Timothy will refuse to grant you the 'early retirement'-package employees usually receive from the company. You've only been with us for four months, but you've done a lot of good work for us, Ariq. I assume Timothy would want to keep you on board as a 'remote project'-specialist after you leave in March."

Lowering the radio's output-level by nothing more than a degree in order to marginally comply with Christopher's pleas to reduce the receiving-unit's sound-volume, I adjust the speaker's control knob: "I can work as a 'remote project'-specialist for 'Hyper Mind, Inc.' for a while after I set myself up in New Mexico. I'm not willing to take any projects with me. I'll notify you after I'm stationed in New Mexico if I'm still willing to work for 'Hyper Mind, Inc.' Obviously, it could take me a while to find a programming job in Taos, at any rate."

Christopher turns to observe the idle employees on staff loitering around the spacious extent of the 4th-story's production-floor, realizing the three or four co-workers watching him are expecting to see him "lower the boom" on me for choosing to terminate all contractual obligations I'm required to fulfill at the company <u>without</u> first submitting a 3-month notice indicating my intent to vacate the position to the executive-level staffers situated in corporate offices on the building's 1st-floor: "**Taos, New Mexico**?! ... You'll be *damned* lucky to find a good-paying programming job in that place, I bet you! You're *damn* right about <u>that</u>! I'll tell Timothy today it appears as though you'd be willing to stay on board for a while as a 'remote project'-specialist after you're re-stationed in New Mexico. He'll probably agree to keep you on board as long as you'd like. Instead of receiving the 'early retirement'-package, I guess you'll request a 'transfer'-

package to cover the basic requirements of getting yourself set up in your next location. I'll tell him later today."

I peck at the keyboard on the "workstation"-computer system resting atop the extensive table-space serving as the office desk I utilize in completing tasks which I'm to fulfill as an employee of the tech-firm during the workweek, indicating to Christopher my desire to return to the assignment at hand: "You can tell him to hold off on the 'early retirement'-package until I'm in New Mexico. I'll notify 'Hyper Mind, Inc.' once I'm there if I'm still willing to work for the company. The 'remote project'-specialist job would have to permit me a *full*-time (<u>not</u> *part*-time) salary, however. I'll be arriving in New Mexico on April 01 and I'll notify you of my decision with respect to the 'transfer'-package sometime later in April."

Christopher, here, merely nods, as if to indicate he'll abide by my instructions with respect to possibly extending any contractual obligations which the firm requests that I fulfill after I've managed to adequately relocate myself to New Mexico in April. He simply turns to acknowledge the radio receiving-unit resting on the spacious desktop I'm occupying as the sole occupant of the station set up in the northeastern corner of the 4th-floor's production space, and turns to observe the idle employees on hand standing around the extensive floorspace of the building's top level, realizing they were expecting canon-fire from him after he approached the work-space which I make use of in the floor's remote corner. He again turns to me, offering a faint, but sincere smile and turns around again, walking from the extensive "dinnertable"-size desk-space which I'm currently occupying as an employee on the corporate property's 4th-floor in order to fulfill the various assignments presented to me on a week-to-week basis at the tech-firm, "Hyper Mind, Inc."

For the record, Christopher Mariar, the supervisor (or "foreman") of the corporate office's 4th-floor (i.e., the company's programming department) is an openly <u>gay</u> man, i.e., a homosexual, that is, or, an "ass-meister", that would be. (… I've seen him at bars and restaurants around the "Central Commercial District" of the city on "dates" of his, that would be, on evenings in which he agrees to play escort to another male while the pairing select to dine together at a top-rated eating venue available to guests visiting any such location to be found in the "Downtown"-acreage of the Urbanzone.) Every time a <u>male</u> employee quits the company's programming department, Christopher ends up requesting that the person remain on board rather than see the employee terminate affiliation with "Hyper Mind, Inc." I suppose Christopher sees the employee as just another potential target of his which he had plans to *ultimately* get around to approaching sooner or later. For the executive team, the employee deciding to close out **all** contractual obligations which he's required by specifics of the initial agreement to fulfill represents the loss of a proficient programmer, yet, to Christopher, the employee's decision to quit represents the loss of what was once a promising opportunity which he'll have no chance to explore in the future.... Ha! Ha! Ha! Ha!

Tasting Droplets of the
Unforgettable Rain

By
Adrien L. Montgomery
Cycle <u>019</u>:
"When 'Little Red Riding Hood' Chooses to Pay Visit to the Grandmother's House, She Knows Not the Wolf Who Hides Himself Inside Has Already Eaten the Home's Helpless Occupant and Awaits the Approaching Arrival of a <u>Second</u> Course to Soon Be Served to Him!"

<u>UTA</u> <u>Directive</u> <u>XIX</u>:
"Attention! Attention! ... Passengers Aboard The 'CitiTraxx^{STF}' Railsystem-Vehicle Musn't Leave Any Personal Items Aboard The Commuter-Service Train's Guest Compartment. Please Gather All Personal Items Before Exiting At The Next Station. Repeat, Passengers Aboard The 'CitiTraxx^{STF}' Railsystem-Vehicle Musn't Leave Any Personal Items Aboard The Commuter-Service Train's Guest Compartment. Please Gather All Personal Items Before Exiting At The Next Station."
("<u>UTA</u>": <u>Urban</u> <u>Transit</u> <u>Authority</u>)

On the westernside of Rocolo Ave. No., i.e., on a span of the urban auto-traffic thoroughfare known locally as "Rocolo Arcade", indicating its use to area inhabitants as a pedestrian-ready retailing district, there is a well-known nightspot found on Rocolo Arcade in between 10th Street, the motor-traffic road just to the north of the venue and 11th Street, the motor-traffic road just to the south of the venue, referred to as the "Wheelboat Music Room and Restaurant", a night-spot offering to its clientele a menu of musical acts chosen to perform on the venue's performance platform on the particular night patrons select to pay visit to the music club in question to hear the artists scheduled to entertain the house audience on that specific occasion.

On this specific evening the restaurant's host and manager, Mason "Another Round" Murielle, stands before the crowd on hand inside the well-known night-club found on Rocolo Arcade in the city's "Central Commercial District", in order to present to guests of the venue the actual musical act chosen to entertain the patrons on hand on that particular occasion with valued selections from the group's catalogue of recordings which the band-members have already been able to release on "LP"-discs and digital "audiofile"-units available for purchase at datavending-pages online for any music fans. Mason "Another Round" Murielle, at the moment, prepares the audience to welcome to the stage the act which the crowd eagerly arrived to observe on the venue's well-lit performing floor for artists chosen to offer to the club's patrons examples of the musical tastes apparently setting them apart in the eyes of the anxious fans arriving on hand to enjoy the particular band.

<u>Mason</u> "<u>Another Round</u>" <u>Murielle</u>:
"Ladies and gentlemen in attendance tonight at the 'Wheelboat Music Room and Restaurant', it is my proud privilege to present to you a favorite of our audience here in the 'Twin Cities'-region of the Midwest, who, again, have agreed to travel to our state in order to perform before the fans always ready to receive the highly-favored musicians and welcome them once again to the city known for appreciating a higher caliber of musical artists such as those set to perform for you tonight. You've seen them on our humble but discriminating stage before, but here they <u>are</u>, yet again, ready to entertain those of us in the 'Twin Cities' with their unique and unparalleled variety of 'Folk'-Rock melodies.... It's a group we'll always welcome aboard the 'Wheelboat Music Room and Restaurant' for yet another trip down the rambling Mississippi River. Ladies and gentlemen of the 'Twin Cities', once again, it's 'A Room Without Walls'! Let's hear a good round of applause for these celebrated icons of independent 'Folk'-Rock!"

<u>(-|Calendar</u> <u>Date</u>: <u>MON</u>., <u>Feb</u>. <u>09</u>, <u>2004</u>|-)
I'm merely, at this point, which would appear to be approximately just 10 minutes before 7:00 p.m., C.S.T., as of MON., Feb. 09, 2004, sitting on a sofa—a three-cushion furnishing built for use on a house's "family"-room floor, I s'pose, one featuring leather upholstery and a low-rising supporting frame at its rear, with the sofa's back rising to the level of a person's shoulders if one sits atop any of its spacious, comforting seat-cushions. This, once again, dear friends and *ever-so-faithful* followers, would be at the apartment-unit which I currently occupy, on a solitary basis, that would be, as a lease-holding tenant inside "The 'Falconeer' Building", a housing-complex found on the corner of the intersection of Courier Street and Reddington Ave. in the "Laurel Park"-District of the Urbanzone, a residential establishment found a mere 2 city blocks west of the Minneapolis Convention Center.

I'm merely, at the moment, sitting upon the leather-built sofa on the floor of the apartment-unit watching a program appearing at the time on the surface of the widescreen TV-monitor i.e., a "Samsung™"-brand "LED"-screen which is mounted to the northern wall of the apartment's front room with use of applicable mounting-hardware which came with the "TV"-set itself. The front of the apartment is a room which I've furnished in order

--()--
197
--()--

to serve as basically a "family"-room setting, a bedroom, a work-space, and a dining area. I'm currently watching a game show ("Riddles 'R' Us") on KWST-TV Channel 13, a local-market "Fox Broadcasting Corporation"-affiliate in the "Twin Cities"-region for a viewership in the "over-the-air" television audience capable of tuning in to the locally-operated station in the "Minneapolis Metropolitan"-area.

I'm merely selecting at the moment, while sitting in front of the widescreen TV-monitor on the northern wall of the apartment-unit I inhabit, drinking cans from a case of "Schwarmann[UE]"-brand "National Reserve"-recipe "Red Lager"-style beer cans (from the "Essinghof-Prazburgh[AI]" Company in Wichita, Kansas), while watching the programming which the widescreen TV-monitor exhibits to me at the moment—the 12-oz. cans of "Red Lager"-style beer are, of course, kept on the 2nd rack (from the top) in the kitchen refrigerator's "fresh foods"-compartment to ensure the beverage features a frosty punch to it upon the moment of consumption on my part. I've actually chosen to pour a couple cans of the beer-formula into a large drinking mug in order to add to the serving of alcohol a few ice cubes from one of the plastic trays which I keep in the refrigerator's "freezer"-compartment to instantly add to any cold beverage an even stronger chill in order to spike the fluid's fresh taste with additional spirit.

What I'm really doing at the time as I lounge in front of the "Samsung[TM]"-brand widescreen "LED"-built TV-monitor is merely awaiting the arrival of "Suzie Wolvershire", the building manager of the "Falconeer", who ordinarily works out of the landlord's leasing-office on "Autumn Leaf Circle", whom I'm expecting to pay a visit to me tonight in order for her to examine a leak occurring at present in the apartment's bathroom. The leak is due to a loose control-knob which regulates the intake of water flowing into the radiator-unit in the bathroom from a feeding-pipe leading to the apartment's bathroom from the boiler-room which is found at the eastside end of the basement-level floor in the "Falconeer"-complex. What I've done, recently, in order to remedy the situation at hand which allows the leaking control-knob to flood the apartment's bathroom with a puddle of water by the end of each day, is to place a plastic paint-mixing tray underneath the radiator-unit's control-knob in order to catch any water dripping from the knob which would ultimately run across the bathroom's tile flooring material and settle onto the space beneath the bathtub, ultimately forming a large puddle in the bathroom by the end of each day on which the building's boiler is running.

Due to the fact the local weather forecasting reports indicate the low-temperature levels for the following week will decline to points below 0-degrees Fahrenheit, I'm certain the building's "maintenance"-attendant ("Jessie") will keep the building's boiler running continually over the next several days, guaranteeing the leak from the intake-pipe's control-knob will be constant, possibly releasing a sizable flood onto the floor of the apartment's bathroom.

As of MON., Feb. 02, 2004, I placed a notice in the dropbox behind the dropslot in Apt. "#001"—the manager's residence—which Suzie Wolvershire, the property manager, has never chosen to occupy herself to serve us as an onsite-manager of the property, preferring rather to work out of the landlord's office on "Autumn Leaf Circle" and pay occasional visit to the property during the weeknights at some time between 6:00 p.m. and 7:00 p.m., indicating to the landlord's office I intend to vacate "The 'Falconeer' Building" as a tenant as of THU., Apr. 01, 2004, in order to relocate myself, immediately thereafter, to the city of Taos, New Mexico.

At just after 7:00 p.m., C.S.T., at 7:02 p.m., to be precise, I do hear a knock at the apartment's front door, which I answer by merely calling to the visitor on hand while still sitting atop the left-side cushion of the leather-built sofa found against the southern wall of the apartment-unit on the basement-level of the "Falconeer"-complex. The guest identifies herself as "Suzie Wolvershire", the building's manager, visiting directly from the landlord's leasing-office on "Autumn Leaf Circle". I at once lift myself off the sofa-furnishing's spacious, comforting end-cushion and walk over to the apartment-unit's front door to answer it and permit the manager to enter the unit in order to inspect the leak occurring beneath the radiator-unit in the apartment's bathroom. I let her into the unit and immediately lead her into the bathroom, to allow her to inspect the leak occurring from the intake-pipe's control knob which produces an amount of water accumulating on the tile floor which amounts to a large puddle which I have to mop up at the end of every day. (... Ughhh!!)

Inside the apartment-unit's bathroom, I make note of the steam-radiator unit's control-knob which is found against the southern wall of the bathroom, telling her I noticed water accumulating on the floor of the bathroom in a puddle forming underneath the bathtub in early January and, hence, have been living with the particular room "maintenance"-issue for over a month by today's date, attempting myself to resolve the issue with respect to the accumulation of water due to the leaking control-knob by mopping up the puddle forming beneath the tub every night and by placing a plastic paint-mixing tray on the floor beneath the control-knob to catch any water leaking from the radiator-unit's water intake-pipe.

Suzie observes the leaking intake-pipe and nods her head in order to indicate she'll make note of the "maintenance"-issue to personnel on staff in the landlord's office tomorrow: "I guess I'll call 'Jessie' and tell him you have an emergency 'maintenance'-issue to deal with. He'll probably come by tomorrow morning. I'll tell him to stop by your apartment as early as possible. That would be just after 8:00 a.m., I believe."

I point out the level of water-accumulation appearing in a puddle on the

--()--
199
--()--

floor of the bathroom at the time: "I've had to mop-up <u>every</u> night since early <u>January</u>! Tell him he *has* to be <u>here</u> tomorrow morning. This isn't something he can delay until Friday afternoon. If he does that, he might forget and I'll have to suffer with this over the weekend!"

Suzie, here, shakes her head to indicate she, as well, believes what I have on the premises of my particular unit qualifies as an "emergency"-job for the building's "maintenance"-agent, Jessie, to respond to: "I'll tell him it's an emergency. *I'm* the <u>manager</u> of the building. I'm the one at the leasing-office who coordinates 'maintenance'-jobs for all the members of the 'maintenance'-crew which services the buildings which 'Dorellen Properties, Inc.' has in its 'real estate'-portfolio at the moment. *If* I tell him your job is a <u>priority</u>, he'll be <u>here</u> tomorrow morning!"

I point out the sizable puddle of water appearing on the tile flooring material of the apartment-unit's bathroom to ensure she sees the severity of the situation I'm having to endure due to the leaking control-knob: "See all this water?! I gotta clean this up tonight with a mop. I drain the mop onto the floor of the bathtub to get rid of the water leaking from the steam-radiator. I don't want to keep doing that!"

Suzie, again, shakes her head to indicate she agrees with the assessment I'm offering indicating the problem at hand transpiring on the floor of the apartment-unit's bathroom is <u>indeed</u> an "emergency"-job for the building's "maintenance"-agent, "Jessie", to immediately handle due to the leaking intake-pipe which is producing a problematic amount of water *each* and <u>every</u> day in the bathroom: "He'll be here! I reassure you. Once I tell him you have an 'emergency'-level leak that's creating a large puddle, a minor flood, on the floor of your bathroom, he'll visit your place '<u>first-thing</u>' tomorrow morning!"

I nod, to signal I'm satisfied with the fact the building manager, "Suzie", at the moment apparently accepts the "maintenance"-issue transpiring in the apartment-unit's bathroom as an "emergency"-level job, indicating she will inform "Jessie" the repair of the radiator-unit's intake-pipe in my apartment should be the priority occurring at the top of his list of "Jobs to Do" tomorrow morning: "I should have said something earlier, but I didn't think anything would get done due to the fact I noticed the leak right after the end of the 'Holiday'-season and, therefore, assumed the 'maintenance'-man was still on his 'Christmas'-vacation."

Suzie takes a second look at the intake-pipe's leaking control-knob and crouches on the floor of the bathroom in order to inspect the puddle appearing beneath the bathtub, before standing again to indicate she's seen what she's needed to see to then file a "maintenance"-report with Jessie, the building's "maintenance"-agent, on the "emergency"-level leak occurring in Ariq Shoretempel's apartment-unit in Apt. "#002" at "The 'Falconeer' Building": "Well … I suppose you will be leaving the 'Falconeer'-

complex on April 01, a couple months from now, huh, Ariq?"

I nod, surprised she's chosen to raise the decision made on my part to immediately terminate the 12-month leasing-agreement I've kept on file in the landlord's office on "Autumn Leaf Circle" since late October of 2003: "Yeah, I guess I've disqualified myself from the security-deposit 'P.J.' required I transfer to 'Dorellen Properties, Inc.' upon agreeing to lease the unit in October. I'm not going to ask him to return the security-deposit I have on record with the office when I vacate the building in April."

Suzie begins to exit the bathroom unit, indicating her intention to leave the apartment-unit after adequately inspecting the intake-pipe's leak and the water puddle appearing on the bathroom floor, with both problems obviously presenting to her an "emergency"-level "maintenance"-issue which she'll report to Jessie, the building's "maintenance"-agent, tomorrow morning: "Do you need the deposit back in order to move to Tijuana? ... That's in Mexico, right? Most tenants indicate they need the security-deposit returned to them on immediately vacating their units in order to rent out the next apartment they find for themselves."

I follow Suzie into the kitchen as she waits on the floor of the apartment-unit's oven-room, asking me to respond to the issue of the security-deposit currently kept on file under my name with the "leasing"-office on "Autumn Leaf Circle": "No! ... I'm not moving to Tijuana, Mexico—I'm moving to Taos, New Mexico! It's a ski resort in the 'Rocky Mountain Range'. I was there to enjoy the skiing a couple times when I was a kid. The city of Taos isn't that far from the 'Taos Ski Valley', the region's actual ski area."

Suzie, here, turns around, after hearing me specify as to where exactly I'll be heading upon terminating my status as a lease-holding tenant residing on site in the "Falconeer"-complex, yet, suddenly appears to freeze herself as she faces the far end of the kitchen countertop which extends from the kitchen's entrance, next to the front door of the building-unit, to the southern wall of the room. All but tragically, I'd, here, have no other choice than to state to any and all still standing by in the audience of listeners remaining on hand at this particular moment in the "narrative"-drama unfolding before all witnesses in attendance, on the kitchen countertop, at the southern wall of the room, what we both, Suzie and I, at the moment, unfortunately choose to set eyes upon would be nothing less than the instruments amounting to the assortment of items I kept with me for use as a "nocturnal"-warfare kit of assets which I made of use when choosing to violate females at the "Protestant Faith"-locations found around the "Central Commercial District" in the early morning hours of the particular organization's "Day of Service" (i.e., Sunday), since arriving in the state of Minnesota in late October in order to fulfill all necessary aspects of the "Perspective on 'Self-Enlightenment'" which I set forth for myself to conclude early on in order to finalize a program of stages permitting me to receive a *cumulative* level of enlightenment (i.e., "Cosmic Knowledge") upon the agenda's completion, which I could then impart to others who approach me seeking such wisdom for themselves in the world we inhabit.

On the kitchen countertop, against the southern wall of the unit, we both see what appears to be a kit of items including the 100-gram canister of pepperspray, the anti-respiratory inhalant consisting of an aerosol-form particulate-mixture enabling me to fumigate the victim's breathing-channels with a lung-irritant inducing a constricted process of respiration on the part of the female on hand, the set of stainless steel wristlocking-rings for use in conjoining the victim's wrists in a pinching hold behind her back in order to deny her the ability to resist the act of "rear-cavity" penetration which I sought to inflict upon any of the women during the "sexcrime"-assault, and the "FineCrafters[AI]"-brand boxcutting knife with its 25-millimeter "stainless steel"-blade for use in quieting any assault-victim who may select to notify any others in the region surrounding the site of the "sexcrime"-assault by screeching audibly to alert anyone nearby as to the predicament of endangerment she, at the moment, appears to be enduring at my unmerciful hands. (… Ha! Ha! Ha!)

In a panic, I realize I have to explain the presence of the incriminating items before Suzie Wolvershire leaves the apartment with the image of such a threatening assortment of tools still fresh in her memory: "Those items belong to a cousin of mine--'Raymond Blautaine'. He's a patrolman working at the 'Minneapolis Public Safety Administration'-office on N. 5th Street and Oregon Ave. He left those items here on Friday night after the end of his shift. He stopped by because he said he might be able to fix the leak in the bathroom which I showed to you. He said he'd have to stop by a hardware-emporium first and pick up a new control-knob. I told him to forget about it and that I'd simply have the building 'maintenance'-man stop by and fix it this week. I called him up last night and he said he'd swing by tomorrow and pick up the items belonging to him."

Suzie merely begins to gradually head towards the apartment-unit's front door, while nodding her head, indicating she accepts the explanation I offer in order to excuse the presence of the incriminating assortment of items (i.e., the kit of "nocturnal"-warfare instruments) which I have resting, unfortunately, in open-view, on the apartment-unit's kitchen-countertop: "Oh, yes! … I'll tell 'Jessie', tomorrow, to stop by your apartment and repair the leaking intake-pipe in your bathroom, so you won't have to worry about it anymore, 'Ariq'."

Suzie appears, at this moment, to instantly accept the excuse which I offered for the presence of the alarming items appearing on the kitchen-countertop, indicating she'll allow herself to instantly delete any memory of the instruments which she saw in the apartment's kitchen the moment she exits the front door of the unit, ensuring any memory of the incriminating assortment of items found on hand isn't able to lurk problematically at the back of her mind, until *ultimately* the image of the "nocturnal"-warfare kit itself pressures her into raising the issue (the odd presence of such unusual instruments) with a third party, i.e., possibly investigators at the "Minneapolis Metropolitan Police Force", currently conducting an ongoing examination into the series of "sexcrime"-cases occurring in the "Central Commercial District" since November at "Protestant Church"-locations found in spaces around the expansive "Urbanzone" I inhabit.

Suzie informs me again she'll make sure "Jessie" arrives early tomorrow morning (i.e., "first-thing") in order to remedy the "emergency"-level "maintenance"-issue currently transpiring in the apartment-unit's bathroom and thanks me for allowing her into the apartment to inspect the ongoing problem itself, i.e., the leaking control-knob of the intake-pipe on the bathroom's steam-radiator appliance. Once she vacates the unit and I gently close the apartment's front door behind her after her casual, unburdensome exit, I quickly recover the assortment of "nocturnal"-warfare instruments from atop the apartment's kitchen-countertop and decide to place them out of view, on the floor of the room's clothing closet, right next to a portable "AM/FM" stereo cassette-recorder system, against one wall of the large wardrobe-chamber, to ensure the items themselves no longer offer any evidence of the occupant's recent nocturnal activities if I'm visited again by any employees of "Dorellen Properties, Inc.", who might choose to enter the unit as guests for any reason whatsoever in the near future, before I, that is, manage to vacate the building altogether and migrate to the convenient sanctuary of Taos, New Mexico on THU., Apr. 01, 2004, that is. *(Oh, boy! …)*

Tasting Droplets of the Unforgettable Rain

By
Adrien L. Montgomery
Cycle <u>020</u>:
"The Starring Performer Offers a Sincere Farewell to All Choosing to Attend the Exhibition of Drama Which He Chose to Offer to Everyone Deciding to Become a Member of the Loyal Audience Which He Always Found Close at Hand."

<u>UTA</u> Directive <u>XX</u>:
"Attention! Attention! … All Rail-Transit Guests, Your 'CitiTraxx[STF]' 'Railsystem'-Vehicle Has Arrived At The Commuter-Service Route's Final Station. All Passengers Are, Hereby, Required To Offboard The Mass-Transit Multi-Cabin Transporter. Repeat, All Rail-Transit Guests, Your 'CitiTraxx[STF]' 'Railsystem'-Vehicle Has Arrived At The Commuter-Service(X)

Route's Final Station. All Passengers Are, Hereby, Required To Offboard The Mass-Transit Multi-Cabin Transporter."
("UTA": **U**rban **T**ransit **A**uthority)

The following oral comment amounts to an actual statement found on an ("['audiofile']/['databyte']")-voice record of Ariq Shoretempel's responses in a digital recording made with use of a suite of sound-recording software-programs by a supervising physician during an approximately "up-to-date" neuro-analytical interviewing period with the patient in question (i.e., "Ariq Shoretempel") …

Supervising Physician:
Dr. Martha-Esther Belinmoor, M.D., Ph.D.
(Therapeutic/Clinical Psychiatrist)

Date of Diagnostic Examination: FRI., Mar. 19 of 2004

"I believe I'd view 'Taos' as a sanctuary offering to me a necessary suspension of the particular difficulties I've found myself encountering while residing in the state of Minnesota. The city itself—'Taos'—is located in the northern-central sector of New Mexico, amid the extent of the 'Sangre De Cristo' chain of summits, a 'subrange' forming the tail end, that is, of the 'Rockies'. I believe such a tranquil location, the region of northern New Mexico, will offer unto me the solitude and serenity which I require at this moment of my life in order to recover from the hotbed of destabilizing pressures which I've unfortunately found myself encountering while a resident of the state of Minnesota."

Patient Undergoing Examination: "Ariq Zarkahn Shoretempel"
Noteworthy Traits:
(--26 Years Old--)
(--African-American--)
(--Male--)
(--Software-Developer--)
(--Taos Resident--)
(--Outlaw Still "At Large"--)

(-|Calendar Date: TUE., Apr. 27, 2004|-)

I'm sitting in a private dining compartment inside the "Flag Fort Apache Dining Club" in the lodging village found at the foot of the central mountain at the "Taos Ski Valley" resort in Taos County, New Mexico, a "skiing mountain"-area found among the peaks of the "Sangre De Cristo" (i.e., "Blood of Christ") mountain chain in the northern-central sector of the state of New Mexico. The "Sangre De Cristo" subrange constitutes a rolling span

--()--
204
--()--

forming the peaks amounting to the southernmost extent of the Rocky Mountain Range of crests in the earth's crust running almost as a spinal-track northwards, across the western states of the US and into Canada.

The dining compartment or cabin I'm occupying at the moment serves as a private cabin or booth to permit a group of restaurant guests to assemble at table inside the private room in order to enjoy a lunchtime (or, dinnertime) menu offered on site by the eating venue's kitchen-staff while also retaining the ability and opportunity to converse among themselves on a private level without fearing diners at tables or booths nearby also on the outlet's dining floor could possibly overhear what a particular group seated for the establishment's dining service just so happens to be discussing at the moment, thereby, dissuading any patrons selecting to enter the outlet itself from freely conversing on the topic the table deems to be of particular importance at the time to the customers congregating around the furnishing built for dining convenience.

On the table before me rests the order I chose to select from the menu brought to me upon sitting on the bench found against a partition of the private compartment, with the compartment itself being built to accommodate four diners who could occupy the cabin for a private dinner-time meal—with the booth itself offering its guests a table, a built-in long bench against one wall, and, just opposite the bench, two wooden dining chairs, with the legs of each chair freely standing beneath the table, permitting guests maneuvering ability unlike those who've chosen to seat themselves upon the long bench built into the booth's partitioning wall.

I'm currently enjoying samples of the serving the onsite kitchen-staffers chose expressly for me as I indicated earlier to the waiter advising me on the menu's options upon placing an order for him to transfer to the employees working in the dining house's running oven-room. I'm currently eating from a serving which includes the house's "Alaskan King Crab Legs", "Scalloped Potatoes", "Tomato and Onion Salad", "Mushroom Pan Roast" (with a seasoning sample of Parmesan cheese as a topping sauce), "Garlic Bread", and a glass of "Espumante", a sparkling white wine originating in a vineyard-tract found inside the acreage encompassing southern Portugal.

The restaurant itself (i.e., the "Flag Fort Apache Dining Club") is a well-known "apres ski" (i.e., "evening-time") dining establishment which itself was owned back in the late 1980's (1988 and 1989—each year being an occasion in which I paid visit to the "Taos Ski Valley" as a child during the "Christmastime"-break from school occurring at the end of the calendar year) by a man (a "Jean-Paul") who was a member of France's Olympic Squad in the 1968 "Winter Games" hosted by the town of Grenoble, France (at the "Chamrousse" ski resort), who competed on the French team in the "Men's Slalom"-event, a contest occurring at the "Alpine"-skiing venue of competition during that particular Olympiad. The restaurant, of known era, served a menu of French cuisine due to the fact the kitchen was then run by a "French"-style chef, who was actually a Frenchman himself, hailing from a high-altitude village in the French Alps, that being an alpine settlement near "Mont-Blanc".

In addition to the particular private dining compartment which I currently occupy, there is a row of similar compartments along the northern perimeter of the establishment itself, with the perimeter wall consisting of large window-plates permitting guests choosing to seat themselves inside the private compartments to enjoy the menu while setting eyes upon the slopes of the Ski Valley's central mountain, a highly forested peak, offering to its guests several advanced-level ski runs which the vacationers can attempt to negotiate at their own pace and (if told beforehand) at their own discretion. (… Ha! Ha! Ha!) At the rear end of the venue there's a large, brick-built fireplace, a log-burning hearth, set off from the surrounding floorspace by a circular retaining wall which permits guests on hand the opportunity to seat themselves in large sofa-chairs found near the brick-built retaining wall of the fireplace while absorbing the warmth originating from the flames which gradually eat away at the bark-less logs of bare tree-wood arranged in the fire-pit's center to foster a large exhibition of burning which produces an almost fragrant cloud of fragile smoke that escapes into the aluminum routing-pipe found above the brick-built fire-pit which channels the fire's fumes through the restaurant's ceiling and into the mountain air outside the dining house.

There's a staircase behind the fireplace that leads to an upper-level of dining tables found on the 2nd-floor of the dining establishment. The 2nd-level offers to patrons an additional set of private dining compartments which the guests can enter in order to enjoy the opportunity to initiate a dinnertime discussion without needing to concern themselves with others nearby overhearing the comments they exchange while sharing the menu on hand at the dining floor's private table.

I'm currently residing in a condominium in the nearby city of Taos (or, the "Town of Taos", as the locals prefer to make note of in referring to their particular city), and have already chosen to notify Christopher Mariar (i.e., the supervisor [or, foreman] of the programming department found up on the 4th-floor of the complex serving as the corporate property of "Hyper Mind, Inc.", the tech-firm employing me as a software-designer while I inhabited the city of Minneapolis, Minnesota) that I'd be willing to accept the position of "remote project"-specialist which he offered to me during the discussion which transpired between us at the work-table I made use of as a programmer on the company's production-floor on the date of MON., Feb. 02, 2004, when he paid visit to the station I utilize in order to discuss my decision to terminate all contractual-obligations due to be fulfilled on my part at the company while not <u>first</u> submitting the <u>required</u>

3-month termination notice, which is standard in accordance with the firm's personnel-policies. I indicated to Christopher in an over-the-phone conversation I had with him a week ago, I'd accept the position so long as the job of "remote project"-specialist allowed me a <u>full</u>-time (*not* <u>part</u>-time) salary with the tech-firm.

As I indicated earlier, I had no choice other than to relocate to another part of the country, i.e., to a place outside of the "Twin Cities"-region in order to avoid detection (and possible apprehension) by any one of the **4** victims whom I chose to prey upon while attempting to fulfill the *necessary* stages required by the "Perspective on 'Self-Enlightenment' " which I set forth for myself to complete early on in the "narrative"-drama which unfolds for your very eyes, my loyal and *oh-so-close* companions at hand, which mandated I fulfill an agenda constituting a program of separate stages in order to receive, in the end, a *cumulative* level of self-enlightenment (or, "Cosmic Knowledge") which I could then impart to others seeking me out in order to acquire such wisdom for themselves to possess in the world.

I already informed the audience as to the unfortunate fact that I did inconveniently endure an encounter with the Latina woman as of SUN., Jan. 18, at the bookstore-venue in Bloomington, Minnesota, the first victim appearing in the roster of female victims I chose to violate while residing in the state of Minnesota in order to complete the self-imposed agenda of self-enlightenment I sought to achieve as one seeking a higher degree of wisdom in the world. Tragically, almost, I did happen to run into *each* of the remaining <u>three</u> women in places around the "Central Commercial District" of the city as well over the course of an era stretching from mid-February to mid-March, with the encounters themselves only serving to reinforce the view that I had no other option left to me as an individual than to relocate myself as soon as would be possible to a settlement which would be found outside the "Twin Cities"-region of Minnesota in order to avoid possible detection by any one of the four female victims which I chose to violate in completing all *necessary* stages of the agenda at hand.

I did run into the 2nd victim, i.e., the Korean woman, in a "Pirate's Beach Videosellers^{AI}"-outlet, as I paid visit to the retailer to browse titles available on the "Blu-ray™ Disc"-format to view at home. She did, I note, appear to exhibit an undeniable level of hostility in the openly troubled face I saw her exhibit to the world at large while selecting to secretly watch her while in the store myself as a patron. The indication of hostility appearing on the Korean-American female's face as she chose to review "DVD"-titles on offer inside the videoselling-shop suggests, I'd say, she's disregarded any opinion asserting the world she inhabitants exhibits a state of moral stability expressing the balance of positive versus negative energy at large across the face of the Universe, trusting rather the world she unfortunately inhabits, instead, exhibits a *disproportionately* high degree of immorality to it, rather than a level of equality existing between positive and negative forces. I did encounter the 3rd victim, i.e., the Native-American woman, while she sat on a bench late one-night outside the "YWCA^R" fitness club found on the corner of Arquette Avenue and N. 7th Street, who had in hand a large can of malt liquor or beer, which itself was dressed with a brown paper "liquor"-store bag which the outlets offer to customers to allow them to immediately consume the contents of the can or bottle they chose to purchase at the location while still out in public, on the streets, that is, within the vicinity of the liquor-vending outlet itself. I did come across the 4th victim, i.e., the Omani woman, while, once again, inside the "Pots, Pans, and Lotsa Pasta^(UE)"-venue which I frequent from time to time as a guest in order to enjoy what the restaurant's menu offers to its appreciative public, the crowd of onsite-patrons choosing to dine on the outlet's "house"-offerings. She was with a male partner … a boyfriend, perhaps? (… Or, a fiancé, possibly?) While observing her I noted he laughed gleefully after apparently making a comment he believed to be funny, yet, she merely responded with a noticeable and lingering contempt in her eyes as she silently stared at him…. Mmmmm??

In <u>each</u> of the encounters which I, here, do make note of, the women failed, of course, to recognize (or even notice) me as I observed each within immediate proximity of the subject due to the fact I, after encountering the Latina woman in the bookvending-shop in Bloomington, chose, as I earlier indicated, to always ensure I wore a pair of dark sunglasses whenever in public to ensure I wouldn't be recognizable to any of the female victims whom I chose to violate at "church"-locations around the "Central Commercial District" of the city in the early morning hours of the specific venue's "Day of Service", i.e., Sunday, of course. This being in order to avoid detection by the women who could, then, notify investigators in the "Sex Crimes"-Division at the "Minneapolis Metropolitan Police Force" currently examining evidence found in the ongoing case of "sexcrime"-assaults which I, of course, am guilty of perpetrating at "Protestant"-faith houses found around the "Central Commercial District" of the city.

For the record, old friends, I didn't come to encounter on any occasion in a particular spot around the "Central Commercial District" one "Ibrahim Hossein", the Somali immigrant man (from Mogadishu, that would be) whom I became "victim" to myself in an apartment-unit on N. 4th Street and N. Rocolo Ave. (i.e., the "Fourth & Roc"), though I could have easily paid visit to him again anytime I so desired due to the fact I already knew of the man's residential address. It's unlikely that Ibrahim Hossein, the participant whose assistance I chose to solicit in order to facilitate the act of <u>re</u>-playing the assaults themselves (in a reversal of roles, that would be), with me, the assailant, instead, serving as "victim", in the instance of intercourse which I shared with the Somali man on that night in December of 2003, determines me to be a "prime"-suspect in the series of "sexcrime"-assault incidents occurring at "Protestant Faith"-venues in the city's "Central Commercial District" in the months of November and December of 2003, upon my arrival in the state of Minnesota in order to complete the agenda on self-enlightenment which I sought to fulfill as a resident while inhabiting the Urbanzone found in the southeastern sector of the state.

Due to the stress I acquired due to the encounters occurring, one by one, that would be, with former victims of mine almost tragically presenting themselves to me in various incidents around the city's "Central Commercial District", I had no other choice than to travel to the Hennepin Healthcare Corporation's "Central Medical Complex" found on N. 7th Street and Parkland Ave. in order to pay visit to the "Adult Crisis Ward" in order to meet with the psychiatric-services specialist on hand to request I be prescribed a daily dosage of "Xanax"-capsules in order to alleviate the degree of stress which I was undergoing due to the presence of the females still at large in the region and the possible threat of encountering any one of them in a public spot, which, of course, would leave me vulnerable to possible detection by the particular female on hand.

I underwent an interview with Dr. Martha-Esther Belinmoor in the "psychiatric treatment"-wing of the Hennepin Healthcare Corporation's "Central Medical Complex" (i.e., the "Adult Crisis Ward") in order to request the physician on hand prescribe for me the necessary capsules of "Xanax" to aid in alleviating the stress which I found myself enduring due to constantly encountering the females whom I chose to victimize at "Protestant Church"-locations in the "Central Commercial District" in attempting to fulfill the self-chosen agenda on self-enlightenment I sought to complete in the state of Minnesota after arriving in October of 2003. After the diagnostic interview with the physician, I asked that she fulfill the prescription of "Xanax"-capsules at the healthcare complex's own onsite pharmacy located on an underground-level of the medical care institution for my convenience in, thereby, enabling me to immediately obtain the "Xanax"-prescription and leave the hospital's "psychiatric treatment"-wing (i.e., the "Adult Crisis Ward", that is) with a new prescription of the medication in hand as I headed home—back to "The 'Falconeer' Building" in Laurel Park.

As far as the "Philosophical Perspective on the Process of 'Self-Enlightenment' " which I proposed earlier on in the "narrative"-drama which you were allowed to watch unfold before your unbelieving eyes, I'm not certain as to whether or not I <u>will</u> receive a *cumulative* degree of spiritual wisdom (i.e., "Cosmic Knowledge") ultimately which I, of course, can then choose to impart to others who approach me in order to seek such wisdom for themselves to possess in the world we all unfortunately have to inhabit. I did, of course, in the end, complete <u>all</u> aspects in the agenda *necessary* for me to fulfill in order to complete the program of stages which the perspective comprised at the beginning of the struggle itself, yet, to date, after fulfilling <u>all</u> stages the process required of me over the months of November and December of 2003, culminating with the incident of intercourse (i.e., "rear-cavity" penetration) which I underwent with the help of the Somali immigrant man, one "Ibrahim Hossein", in an apartment-unit found in the building on N. 4th Street and N. Rocolo Arcade (i.e., the "Fourth & Roc"), I haven't received the *cumulative* level of self-enlightenment still due me, as an individual in the world who managed to complete an agenda promising to him a superior degree of "Spiritual Wisdom". Whether I, at one particular point, will *ultimately* become the recipient of a higher level of spiritual wisdom (i.e., "Cosmic Knowledge") or not, due to the completion of the "Perspective on 'Self-Enlightenment' " which I managed to close out in Minnesota during the time I spent in the state as an inhabitant still remains to be seen, I s'pose, my friends and ever-faithful followers.

The waiter at once chooses to approach the private dining compartment I conveniently enjoy as a guest of the dining establishment (i.e., "Flag Fort Apache Dining Club") found at the foot of the Taos Ski Valley's central mountain, which offers to its on-slope recreating clientele the opportunity to make use of advanced-level ski runs which the participants can hope to successfully navigate without inadvertently coming to incur injuries to themselves while attempting to make it safely to the foot of the steep skiing venue, and quickly knocks at the pair of sliding wood panels to announce his intention to enter the private dining compartment which I currently enjoy as the cabin's solitary occupant and sole diner (receiving, once again, a "table for one" ... ha! ha! ha!). The waiter enters the compartment with a circular wine tray in hand which carries on it a pitcher of fresh water and a second glass of the "Espumante"-variety Portuguese spirit, the sparkling white wine from a field in the southern wine-making region in the peninsular, western-European country. He immediately places a new empty drinking glass on the table in front of me and fills it with water from the pitcher he holds in hand—placing the 2nd glass of white wine on the table as well. He then lifts the first glass of wine from the table and raises its rim to a point being no more than an inch above the mouth of the 2nd glass, motioning with his hand as to whether or not he has my permission to pour the contents remaining in the first glass into the 2nd glass of fresh wine to permit me to enjoy what's left of the wine in the original serving along with the ounces in the 2nd serving of sparkling wine. I nod, indicating he can place what is left of the wine remaining in the first glass into the 2nd glass of the "Espumante"-mixture on the table.

For an instant, old friends and familiar followers on hand, I think of lifting the 2nd glass of sparkling white wine, the "Espumante"-variety spirit originating in terrain found in the busily harvested vineyard-regions of southern Portugal to my mouth to sip at its contents directly in front of the

--()--
CCX
--()--

waiter who's standing beside me in the private dinning compartment, a secluded booth for guests in the "Flag Fort Apache Dining Club", just to sample an ounce of the fresh wine before he leaves the private dining cabin to return the first glass, safely empty at this point, to the eating establishment's kitchen … but I don't. (((Sigh))).

(!START OF INTERMISSION!)

"Ladies and Gentlemen, we will pause momentarily in the presentation of tonight's proceedings for a brief "Intermission" which must, in view of what is necessary at this particular instance of time, transpire until we can continue with the exhibition of each remaining segment which our evening program includes for the audience-members still on hand to observe at their convenience …"

(!INTERMISSION!)

Upon a black multiplex screen, the following sign appears in large print as if as in warning to all witnessing the screen's current visible content:

(!INTERMISSION!)

(A notice appears upon the screen at the theater's front perimeter along with a vocal reading that accompanies the print material alerting the screening's guests of a pause that is to occur in the room's ongoing presentation.)

"Ladies and Gentlemen, there will be a brief pause in the proceedings at this particular time. We, of course, do apologize for any inconvenience that this interruption might present to our viewing audience. We will continue with our feature drama as soon as we find it technically possible to do so. Until then, we ask that you all enjoy this brief intermission …"

((While you, of course, are still "in audience" in the multiplex building's screening room, where those on hand are watching the menu of "teaser trailer"-ads appearing on the house's widescale nylon screen the following "Motion Picture"-preview begins running through the projectionist's lens …))

Screen Teaser-Trailer's "Voice Over"-Announcer:

"This summer, theaters around the world will be introduced to the one superhero who, alone, is ready to face a new millennium of crises. The one sent to New York City to save its citizens from the dangers of this, an ever-threatening era. We do, of course, now speak of one man and of one man only! … A man who never learned the meaning of the word '**fear**'…. A man who never learned the meaning of the word '**dread**'…. A man who never

--()--
CCXI
--()--

learned the meaning of the word '**cowardice**'.... A man whose disadvantages in childhood left him with a <u>very</u> limited vocabulary, to state the obvious. The city's 'public school'-system may have failed him.... But, he won't fail <u>you</u>!! We do, of course, speak of none other than ... **AFROMAN**!!!"

((On screen, a woman stops in the middle of an intersection's crosswalk and looks desperately into the skies hovering above her.))

<u>Woman</u> <u>in</u> <u>the</u> <u>Crosswalk</u>:
"AFROMAN!! AFROMAN!! ... Where *are* <u>you</u>?! We <u>need</u> *you*! Help us! ... Help us!"

"<u>Voice</u> <u>Over</u>"-<u>Announcer</u>:
"You've heard of Superman, the 'Man of Steel'. Now meet AFROMAN, the 'Man of Style'.... Faster than a '2004 Rimagan[AI] Imperium[UE] Class IX S.U.V.' exceeding the legal speed limit!! ... Able to leap ghetto rooftops without the use of PCP capsules!! ... More powerful than an 'Order to Appear' summons issued by 'Child Support'-services for derelict payment obligations!! AFROMAN's promise to be 'at the scene' in 30 minutes or less is a guarantee you'll get from him and him **alone**. (Or from 'Funnie Car[STF] Pizza', too, I reckon.)"

((On screen, a man standing on the balcony of a highrise apartment-unit reacts to a figure flying through the air above the bustling streets of Manhattan's "Uptown"-District.))

<u>Man</u> <u>on</u> <u>the</u> <u>Balcony</u>:
"**Look**! Up in the sky! ... Superman? ... Batman? **No**!! It's ... it's ... AFROMAN!! It's AFROMAN!!"

"<u>Voice</u> <u>Over</u>"-<u>Announcer</u>:
"If you're ever in trouble ... just dial '**9-1-1**'. If the police fail to respond ... <u>then</u> call AFROMAN!! If you're in danger, AFROMAN can save you. (... Possibly.) Whenever danger threatens the citizenry of the 'Big Apple', AFROMAN will be there. (... If you're patient.) ... A one-time statistic! A longtime participant in various county-, state-, and federal-level 'public aid'-benefits programs! <u>Now</u> ... hero to an entire city! (... Even if it's **not** 'New York'.) AFROMAN! ... If ever you need help, he's the <u>final</u> call you'll *need* to make. (... <u>Also</u>, he's the <u>last</u> man you'll *want* to ask.) ... If you have <u>no</u> hope... you have AFROMAN!!"

((On screen, the Chief of the New York City Police Agency stands in a con-

--()--
CCXII
--()--

ference room with other high-ranking officers while deciding the latest route to pursue in urban "public safety"-operations.))

<u>New</u> <u>York</u> <u>City's</u> <u>Chief</u> <u>of</u> <u>Police</u>:
"This city needs help! … Our circumstances have left us with only one option. And I think we all know what that option is, don't we, gentlemen? … Call AFROMAN!! We'll use the special AFROsignal^{UE}!!"

((A searchlight with a 69-inch diameter across its lamp projects the silhouette of a gigantic "Afro"-style hairdo against the clouds that hover over New York County's softly-lit nocturnal skyline.))

((On screen, AFROMAN is eating dinner out on the terrace of his top-floor "penthouse"-apartment in posh "Central Park West" and sees the "AFROsignal^{UE}" lighting up the clouds drifting almost unnoticeably overhead.))

AFROMAN:
"Damn! I had 'Cajun Style' Chicken Wings, too! … With 'Angelhair' Coleslaw, French Butter Croissants and 'Louisiana-Style^{UE}' Pasta Salad! And <u>these</u> … the Bourbon Street^{STF} Breadsticks and Nu O'leenz^{UE} 'Just Like Home' Fries with Dixietime^{ESU} 'Mesquite' Grill Sauce, as well! Damn! … I'll just tell the 'poh-leece' I've been taken hostage by 'al-Qaeda'…. Them poh-leece can't leave me be foh a single minute! … Damn!"

<u>"Voice</u> <u>Over"</u>-Announcer:
"Born in a shelter for teen mothers in the slums of New York's Harlem section in the early 1970's (<u>in</u> the 'Age of Jive' <u>and</u> the 'Era of Groove'), raised in the 'Marble Street Orphan's Home', educated by New York State's Board on Youth Offender Facilities and Programs (… at only a modest perannum price to New York's taxpaying residents, I might, here, conveniently add) … AFROMAN is <u>always</u> ready to rescue those persons he finds in impossible peril…. AFROMAN is <u>always</u> anxious to save any citizen in need of swift safeguarding…. AFROMAN is <u>always</u> eager to reclaim any resident of our region he believes to be unrecoverably at risk…. AFROMAN! The <u>ever</u>-loyal friend to every law-biding local."

((On screen, AFROMAN is soaring through the skies over the southeastern section of Manhattan Island in the city of New York, New York, i.e., the "Big Apple", using the antigravitational energy which the custom-built "AFROsuit^{UE}" allows him to generate at will. Yet, even at "full speed", he still witnesses a flock of crows float calmly past him, without appearing to exert

(XOX)

any overtly high degree of effort on their part in quickly outsailing the airborne urban champion of public safety.))

<u>AFROMAN</u>:
"Damn! They iz sumthin' wrong with 'dis here 'AFROsuit^{UE}'. Can't even keep up with the birds that be flyin' south for the winter. Wonder if they iz headin' for Savannah or Jacksonville? There shou'd be a special resort for vacation-seeking superheroes in Louisiana or Mississippi. 'Cuz I do need to get away from it all and recharge 'dis superhero's super SOUL on occasion!!"

<u>"Voice Over"-Announcer</u>:
"AFROMAN's here to help all community members unfortunately finding themselves as victims of the mindless criminal behavior upsetting urban life today. He'll come to aid all those in jeopardy! (… If he's not in jail himself for accidentally flooding a prime traffic-route again with his faulty fire-fighting equipment.) AFROMAN's here to seek nonviolent resolutions to all disputes occurring between neighbors and friends alike. He'll help resolve issues dividing New York's usually upbeat, easy-going populace. (… If he's not fighting with the New York Air Transit Control Commission over having to re-design the 'AFROsuit^{UE}' with a searchlight that allows him to be seen by airline pilots at night.) AFROMAN's here to help turn lives around by telling the wrongdoer to turn over a new leaf and to co-exist with the community at large as a person who respects other people and property. He'll advise others to begin life anew on the right side of the law. (… If he's not too busy chasing down the guy who tried to break into the 'AFROspeeder^{UE}' while carrying a running gasoline motorsaw in his hands.)"

((On screen, AFROMAN is heading towards the rooftop of a burning "tenement"-building in the northern-eastern residential region of Bronx County, in the city's uppermost end geographically. He's there to rescue from the rooftop a young boy and the helpless family pet, a male Burmese kitten. AFROMAN quickly spots the two survivors attempting to flee from the building blaze [an inferno most likely begun by a nearby fire-worshipping fool (… <u>gawd</u>!)] by waiting atop the "tenement"-house's roof for a rescue team to eventually arrive.))

<u>AFROMAN</u>:
"Damn! I better save that damn little kittie kat! Look at its face! … Damnit!! That face look juss like my Uncle Willie! Uhmm … that kittie look juss like muh uncle Willie from Cincinnati! The kittie's like a little four-legged version of old Uncle Willie from Cincinnati, Ohio!! I gotta save that little kittie and that little kid from that damn house-fire some 'mofo' juss started

--()--
CCXIV
--()--

for the Hell of it! Damn fire-lovin' muthuhfuckas! I'll juss pick 'em both up and set 'em down inside the basketball court over in the neighborhood's recreational greenblock.... Damn! Look at that little '**Uncle Willie**'!!"

<u>"Voice Over"</u>-<u>Announcer</u>:
"... <u>Born</u> to a father who quickly found himself pursuing a particular approach to life which he saw as infinitely more acceptable to him than merely agreeing to raise <u>five</u> (... uhmmm, or rather, <u>one</u>, that is) children with a 'social services'-recipient in a 'public housing'-operation alongside the southwestern embankment of the Harlem River.... <u>Raised</u> by a mother who had to suffer miserably due to the irresponsible organizers running the variety of '(<u>pro</u>-"sobriety")'-programs and '(<u>anti</u>-"dependency")'-courses which the 'Eastside Agency on Child Fortification and Safety' had her attending in order to qualify for continuing permonth welfare -benefits.... <u>Bred</u> on a **dream** ... to ensure both the security and peace of mind of New York City's amiable, infectiously-upbeat community of charitable citizens. ... 'AFROMAN'!! ... The <u>one</u> name all New Yorkers (cops and criminals alike, actually) never care to speak aloud. The <u>one</u> name everyone in New York would most quickly associate with '**DANGER**'! The <u>one</u> name everyone in New York would most quickly associate with '**CATASTROPHE**'! The <u>one</u> name everyone in New York would most quickly associate with '**DOOM**'! The <u>one</u> man solely responsible for more calls citywide to local area 'Emergency Response' dispatch-operators than even Osama bin Laden himself! ... 'AFROMAN'!! ... The <u>one</u> name all New Yorkers (cops and criminals alike, actually) fear to mention the most!"

((On screen, AFROMAN is standing atop the "United Nations Headquarters" building in the southern-eastern quadrant of Manhattan Island [New York County], just distant from the water's edge of the East River's narrowing shore-to-shore span. He's waving heartily to travelers aboard a triple-engine, extra-capacity Helius-Wexter^{STF} Corporation V5-Z09 jumboliner, with a twin-aisle flight cabin and cross-continental air-range that's slowly vacating the flight-space over Manhattan's "Midtown"-District. Our hero, AFROMAN, enthusiastically salutes the air passengers, bidding each a happy farewell and a safe voyage on their sky-level adventure to ground terminals in the distance that will bring a secure end to the air-route they're braving aboard the jumbosize commercial jetliner.))

<u>AFROMAN</u>:
"Well, I hope at least them people up there aren't hi-jacked by a group of Islamic terrorists.... Is there **no** decency left in this world today?? People can't even enjoy a safe vacation with their families on board a jet-plane without being afraid of an al-Qaeda cell waging an unofficial '<u>jihad</u>' against

--()--

CCXV

--()--

innocent transcontinental flightgoers. What's next?? ... <u>Moslem</u> extremists trying to blow up rollercoaster rides because turning people upside-down that close to Heaven violates a rule on the afterlife found in verses of the 'Islamic'-scriptures?? ..."

> '... To the mortal, there is but one invitation
> on offer to gain entry onto Heaven's soil,
> and if a man is to fail in earning admission
> on the first, to the Human world he shall return
> never again.'

"Well, I guess that's jus' the wild-ass world we're all livin' in righ'tcheer in the twenty-first century, isn't it? It just goes to prove the old rule of the fearless explorer ..."

> '... In a world that is, to you, <u>unknown</u>,
> you can't avoid facing dangers that are,
> to you, <u>unknowable</u>!'

((On screen, an adult couple standing on a sidewalk in New York's " 'Midtown' District"-region watches while AFROMAN initializes a flight directive from the rooftop of the "UN Headquarters"-complex that stands alongside the familiar East River's southwestern embankment. AFROMAN safely re-enters the airspace stretching over Manhattan's monumental skyline.))

<u>Woman</u> <u>on</u> <u>the</u> <u>Sidewalk</u>:
"Look! ... It's AFROMAN! He's ... he's **here**! The one man known to help the citizens of New York, if ever troubles arise. Thank you, AFROMAN! Thank you for helping the good people of Manhattan! Today he's at the 'UN'-building! Probably to help negotiate 'antiproliferation' talks between the US and Iran. For, we know the Iranian government is attempting to build 'ballistic' warheads and the US government bravely opposes such designs on the part of Tehran's regime. **See**!! He even cares about saving humanity from a nuclear catastrophe!! We should **all** be thankful AFROMAN is ready and willing to help the **whole** world survive in this stomach-wrenching era. We salute you AFROMAN! Thank you! Thank you, sir!"

<u>Man</u> <u>on</u> <u>the</u> <u>Sidewalk</u>:
"YES!! ... All I can say is 'AFROMAN' is my hero! I've loved him ever since I first moved to New York.... That would be about a year ago, I guess. Trust me, he's made this city what it is today! If it weren't for AFROMAN, we'd all have to rely upon the old '911' crisis-hotline. (Not too reassuring, I can tell

--()--
CCXVI
--()--

you.) But he responds more quickly, especially when it comes to attending to citizens in emergency situations residing in our habitat's welfare-ridden neighborhoods … like 'Harlem', of course."

((AFROMAN aims himself towards Central Park's southwestern corner, waving merrily to the citizens below who stand upon the ground-level concrete footpaths of New York County's " 'Midtown' District"-section. The people stop in amazement and watch the local folk-hero float effortlessly through the skyspace that stretches over the southern area of New York's Manhattan Island.))

<u>AFROMAN</u>:
"If fast assistance is what the event requires, I'll offer whatever I can, whenever I can, my good citizens! Remember … the <u>one</u> name you need to know if mortal danger ever seems inescapable … '**AFROMAN**'! … Yes! I'm ready to fight against any threat the decent, upstanding residents of New York can't combat themselves…. My name is all you good folks gotta know! … Just *remember* it when encountering *any* catastrophe!"

<u>"Voice Over"-Announcer</u>:
"Meet AFROMAN!! … It's always a bad 'hair day' for criminals when this superhero's superfro is pumped up. With a hairstyle rivaled in strength only by 'AstroTurf^{TM}', AFROMAN has a head for heroic deeds and the 'AFROpick^{UE}' to prove it, too. This summer, only in local theaters, watch AFROMAN catch these urban ne'er-do-well's while wearing the widescreen megafro that only a *true* urban hero could have…. AFROMAN! He's comin' at'cha with a lotta courage in his heart and with a large comb in his hair!"

(A notice, once again, appears against the screen at the front end of the showing house along with a vocal announcement which reads aloud the print material noting the end of the brief segment of "Half Time" entertainment which the house chose to offer to its audience.)

"Ladies and Gentlemen, we do thank you for exhibiting such patience during this minor break in tonight's 'feature'-screening. We, once again, do apologize for any disruption which this short interval in the evening's program may have had upon the audience's opportunity and ability to review the showing with pleasure. We do, hereby, resume tonight's primary event with your delight as our only central concern. Again, we do apologize for any inconvenience this brief 'INTERMISSION' might have brought to those patrons who are in attendance tonight."

Upon the black multiplex screen, a second sign appears in large print, once

--()--

CCXVII

--()--

again, in an announcement to all observing the screen's single page of text material:

(!**INTERMISSION**!)

The page of sign material disappears from the multiplex room's large nylon screen and the black vacant sheet appearing across the house's front wall begins to gradually brighten with the colorful cinematic imagery which fills up the frames of "feature"-level motion-film footage …

(!**INTERMISSION**!)

"Ladies and Gentlemen, we do, once again, select, here, to offer apologies to all those in attendance at tonight's film-screening for requiring patrons to endure the brief pause occurring in the evening's program of installments which we present for the benefit of our viewing audience. At this moment, we do, hereby, resume the presentation appearing in the menu of segments still on hand for guests of the house to review over the course of the remaining exhibitions still to occur before you on the occasion …"

(!**END OF INTERMISSION**!)

Scriptograph^{UE} One
The "Shadowslasher" Volumes
(Book I: "Tasting Droplets of the Unforgettable Rain")
A Novel By
Adrien L. Montgomery

("<u>Welcome</u>, <u>Ladies</u> <u>and</u> <u>Gentlemen</u>, <u>to</u> <u>the</u>
<u>Closing</u> <u>of</u> <u>the</u> <u>Series</u> <u>of</u> <u>Sectional-Units</u> …")

<u>A</u> <u>Particular</u> "<u>Dialogue</u>"-<u>Script</u> <u>Excerpt</u> <u>to</u> <u>Only</u> <u>So</u> <u>Noticeably</u> <u>Appear</u> <u>Just</u>
<u>After</u> <u>the</u> <u>Closing</u> <u>of</u> <u>the</u> <u>Series</u> <u>of</u> "<u>Sectional-Units</u>"

("<u>Dialogue</u>"-<u>Script</u> <u>Excerpt</u>)

"… I fear that a high number of people might never be heard from or seen again if they simply assume these radical theories from Minnesota aren't a tremendous problem for us to reckon with. I find there is no choice other than to seek a solution to utilize before this particular program of reasoning alters the basic character of the world which we've known up until this point in time and turns the future onto its ear…."

Robbie Carterson
a.k.a., "Johnnie DiCorisselli"
(In the Feature "Motion-Picture")

--()--
CCXVIII
--()--

Standing Still Beside the Final Horizon of Time
(1991)

"Oh, Wait! We're Almost Near the End! ..."
(Epilogue)

You watch rain that still falls from a series of storms that died over the planting lands several ages ago. The droplets themselves arrive with a prehistoric mist that softly collects itself against your flesh. The rainfall is, perhaps, just the ghost of a tempest that ran itself aground in an earlier, pre-medieval era. Yet, on this particular night, you open your mouth and, at once, you find you're tasting the water of a cloudburst that's falling noisily to the soil only after traversing both land and time to reach you.
Adrien L. Montgomery

Adrien's Here to Explain Everything ... And Make a Habit Out of It
[!!Emoticon Alert!! (} ; >)]

In the narrative project "Scriptograph^UE One [The 'Shadowslasher' Volumes (Book I: 'Tasting Droplets of the Unforgettable Rain')]", the protagonist, Ariq Zarkahn Shoretempel, believes that he will attain a "sum level" of enlightenment once he commits the *ultimate* act of evil, which, in his eyes, would amount to an act of self-violation, i.e., submitting to an incident of "sodomy" at the hands of another (i.e., "rear-cavity" penetration). The protagonist trusts that with <u>every</u> act of evil he commits (i.e., the variety of sexual assaults), he will gain a certain degree of "enlightenment" or level of spiritual wisdom. He initiates a series of "sexcrime"-acts under the belief that the actions themselves will guarantee he will achieve a level of *spiritual* knowledge which no other human being possesses. He's actually on a quest for wisdom, rather than on a rampage or a spree of violence. The protagonist, Ariq Zarkahn Shoretempel, is intending to develop into a "God"-like individual, i.e., a creature with a—heretofore unseen—level of *spiritual* knowledge, possessing a level of enlightenment which no other human being in the world would possess.

In truth, Ariq's "Philosophical Perspective" (as he so deems it) isn't truly as malevolent as it first might seem (to him, at any rate, that is). He believes in violating society's laws (i.e., committing acts of rape or crimes of sexual assault), yet, he trusts he's actually acquiring degrees of wisdom (with each particular act) which will serve to enlighten him, to make him "God"-like or *super*natural regarding his personal level of "spiritual" knowledge, that is. If, in fact, he can become superior to all other humans concerning the level of enlightenment he attains, he can, *ultimately*, use this degree of knowledge or wisdom to enlighten and illuminate others. I.e., once "Ariq" attains the highest level of knowledge he possibly can acquire, he will be
(XOX)

--()--
CCXIX
--()--

only like "God" himself, and will, at that point, be able to bestow this specific level of wisdom and knowledge upon other people as well.

Hence, "Ariq" is actually attempting to put himself in a position in which he can benefit others by granting to them the wisdom and knowledge which he trusts he's acquiring through the campaign against humans and against social law which he conducts throughout the course of the text's narrative, in committing the noteworthy series of "sexcrime"-assaults which the reader pays witness to over the course of the project's extent of narrative material. Even though "Ariq", at the onset, appears to be strictly interested in committing evil, self-oriented acts, he assumes he will be capable of using the specific degrees of knowledge which he gains through the particular criminal actions in order to benefit other humans seeking enlightenment as well. Therefore, what he's doing with regard to the sexual assaults isn't as truly as "evil" a behavioral pattern as it first might seem (in the protagonist's view, that would be). He knows of no other way in which to obtain the enlightenment which he, first, must obtain, and, then, be in possession of in order to ultimately help others in becoming *genuinely* knowledgeable as well. In short, "Ariq" is committing the variety of sexcrimes over the course of the project's dramatic material in order to, in the end, become to others what would *ultimately* be seen as a societal "benefactor" of sorts. I.e., he is putting himself on a path which humanity itself will <u>ultimately</u> find beneficial, and this is what the definition of "goodness" is, as "Ariq" views the matter—to do, that is, whatever you must do in order to, in the end, ensure you are a *benefit* to humanity.

<u>Note</u>:

((The subsequent information includes points on the narrative which are to occur in the sequel [or, part 2] of the fictional project known, heretofore, as "Scriptograph^{UE} One [The 'Shadowslasher' Volumes (Book I: 'Tasting Droplets of the Unforgettable Rain')]", hence, if you desire to safeguard yourself against any knowledge of events/incidents to occur in the second half of the dramatic tale, you should choose to forego reading the following material in such case.))

Of course, in the end, "Ariq" fails to attain *any* level or degree of enlightenment (or *spiritual* wisdom) through the commission of the various sexual assaults the reader watches him enact throughout the narrative's length (i.e., the series of "rape"-incidents/"sexcrime"-assaults). He, in the end, admits faults with the "Philosophical Perspective" which he chose to present early on to the readers and sought to benefit from (and "Ariq" makes note of the <u>ultimate</u> futility of the crimes themselves, that is, specifically with regard to the genuine lack of enlightenment or wisdom resulting from the series of antisocial actions which he chose to mindfully commit over the course of the dramatic presentation's material). Even the ultimate act of evil (in his estimation, that is), i.e., submitting to an incident of "sodomy" at the hands of another (i.e., "rear-cavity" penetration)—he notes—results in no real gain on his part concerning the level of spiritual knowledge or enlightenment which he believes he should possess. "Ariq", seeing the *purpose* of whatever life he's to live in this world is not to pursue "enlightenment" through the commission of "sexcrime"-assaults on various women, begins to suspect he might not have *any* purpose at all in the world. Upon debating with himself as to whether or not he'll *ultimately* discover the true purpose which the Cosmos may have had on reserve for him to fulfill at the moment of his birth, "Ariq" concludes the narrative with a probing statement on individual human psychology, a topic whose various aspects he chose to observe within himself and within others over the course of the personal odyssey which he underwent throughout the span of the narrative's series of dramatic incidents.

<u>Note</u>:

((Due to what appears in the "narrative"-presentation which this specific volume includes—i.e., "Scriptograph[UE] One [The 'Shadowslasher' Volumes (Book I: 'Tasting Droplets of the Unforgettable Rain')]"—the stages necessary to exhibit to readers in order to permit audience-members on hand to witness the dramatic-scenario unfold to assume a state of completion for readers to behold at the volume's end do occur in a satisfactory-level of development considering the current volume available to members of the reading public. Hence, beyond the current project at hand, the author, i.e., Adrien L. Montgomery, will not find it a requirement to release a 2nd volume [i.e., "Part II"] in order to present for the reader's benefit additional stages which he would deem as necessary in order to permit the dramatic-scenario at work in the protagonist's tale to unfold in order for the full narrative to assume a state of finality or completion for the reading audience to witness.))

Adrien L. Montgomery
(Author)

<u>"Betcha Figured I Wouldn't Remember, Didn'tchoo?"</u>

It is often assumed that the novelist is, perhaps, the last remaining artist who is capable of completing a "professional" task or assignment wholly on his own in actual design. Despite the overall validity of this particular viewpoint, I do trust this particular work is the result of a number of conscientious individuals, choosing to ensure, in spite of all difficulties, that the work of fiction which you've just had the opportunity to read appears in the most well-designed and reader-friendly version that it possibly could appear in. Hence, I would prefer to use this moment to say

--()--
CCXXI
--()--

Adrien L. Montgomery
Tasting Droplets of the Unforgettable Rain
Official Imprint: "Dynamographx"

"Thank You" to all those whose efforts contributed to the outcome of this particular publishing project, "Scriptograph[UE] One [The 'Shadowslasher' Volumes (Book I: 'Tasting Droplets of the Unforgettable Rain')]".

First, let me express a special gratitude to the publishing house of this specific work (that is, "Dynamographx[R, TM]", i.e., Adrien L. Montgomery's own production studio, of course). If not for certain decisions and priorities assumed on the company's part, this particular narrative-project would not be in your hands today in its present state, my dear friends. Secondly, I want to thank any and all "staff"-members of the specific house in question for their diligence in producing what I feel is a project which succeeds on *each* level that I originally did desire to see it succeed upon.

There, absolutely, in any campaign of this diameter, are individuals in particular whose own efforts would warrant special attention on the part of the author, which, of course, in this case, would be me ("Adrien L. Montgomery", that is). I'd want to use this particular moment to thank *every*one on hand at "Dynamographx[R, TM]" whose determination and focus made possible the volume of fiction which multitudes of fiction fans can enjoy and discuss as of today. To these particular individuals whose personal diligence and enthusiasm were vital in determining the very results of the publishing process which this project had to undergo at "Dynamographx[R, TM]", I do, hereby, desire to say the following words in, I believe, the sincerest of tones: "Thank you, my dear friends and partners, for guaranteeing the end results of our joint production effort are on the particular level which the narrative-project at hand exhibits—both in its general scope and in its specific aspects—to readers everywhere who are enjoying the work today!"

The people inside the organizational structure of "Dynamographx[R, TM]" whom I'd choose to elect for any such recognition would appear (in any official listing of names) in no particular order of stature or official rank within this particular house's chain of seniority regarding its creative and administrative personnel. Each of the individuals I'd prefer to thank at this particular moment would, in my particular estimation, warrant an equal measure of gratitude and appreciation on my part.

It is with the sincerest gratitude that I do choose to make note of my particular debt to all specific individuals who, through effort and motivation upon each person's part, made sure that this "novel" project, i.e., the work of fiction which you've now had the opportunity to read through and consider, my good friends, was sent to you in precisely the condition and quality in which it was. I'm certain that you, too, would desire to express your many thanks to the individuals whose tremendous efforts ensured I could bring this narrative project to you in the particular degree of value and on the specific level of integrity which you've found it to possess in its final state upon an initial reading of the "fiction"-project itself

on your part, dear readers.
Adrien L. Montgomery
(Author …)

Scriptograph^{UE} One
The "Shadowslasher" Volumes
(Book I: "Tasting Droplets of the Unforgettable Rain")
A Novel By
Adrien L. Montgomery

<u>Author</u> <u>Comments</u> <u>on</u> <u>the</u> <u>Book</u> <u>as</u> <u>a</u> "<u>Philosophical</u>" <u>Novel</u>
I, hereby, indicate to members of the reading audience, in a document to appear, here, at the close of the project, what the readers have just had the opportunity to review amounts to what is nothing less than a "philosophical" novel. I, hereby, indicate what a "narrative"-project must present to its audience, formally, to, thereby, qualify as being a "philosophical" novel as opposed to a "dramatic" novel or a "psychological" novel or a "character" novel, etc. I, hereby, outline for the audience the exact points comprising the "Philosophical Perspective on the Process of 'Self-Enlightenment' " which Ariq sets out to fulfill in order to achieve a higher degree of wisdom (i.e., "Cosmic Knowledge") in the world in which he resides, which he can, then, share with others who approach him to attain such wisdom as well for themselves as mortals existing on Earth.

Ariq trusts with <u>each</u> action he commits in violation of the most ancient laws in existence prescribed by humans ages ago to safeguard the stability of a humane and decent society in order to ensure the peace of mind and well-being of its citizens (values which the society members trust they're entitled to enjoy as individuals choosing to cohabitate with each other in a civilized human community), he will, then, receive a certain measure of "cosmic knowledge" imparted to him from the stars overlooking the inhabitants of earth from Heaven. And, once he commits what amounts to the severest action of violation against the most ancient of human laws (self-violation at the hands of a separate perpetrator), Ariq assumes he will, then, receive what amounts to the greatest measure of wisdom imparted to him from the stars illuminating Earth from a distance.

Upon completion of the entire process of enlightenment, once he manages to fulfill the agenda he set forth for himself to initialize at the start of the narrative, he will, then, receive a *cumulative* level of wisdom which will permit him to, then, become, a fully enlightened creature, i.e., one who is "God"-like with respect to the level of cosmic knowledge which he possesses and is able to share with others who seek such wisdom for themselves in the world. Ariq trusts upon achieving such a status with respect to the level of wisdom which he'll attain once he manages to fulfill the agenda he's set forth for himself to finalize concerning the perspective on self-enlightenment, he'll become a <u>good</u> person, i.e., one who serves as an asset, or benefactor, to the world at large, as opposed to one who merely exists as a parasite who feeds off the community he inhabits without returning anything of value to the society in which he resides.

He believes that in being an asset, i.e., benefactor, at the end of the process of enlightenment which he strives to achieve over the course of the narrative, he will attain the status of "good" person, i.e., one who helps others (in his case, in imparting knowledge to them), despite the fact he may have chosen to commit "evil" deeds (i.e., crimes or sins) in order to complete the program set forth in fulfilling the stages necessary to finalize the process of enlightenment, permitting him, ultimately, to secure a superior rank of individual wisdom. His view being that the commission of a crime (violation of a female) will, <u>ultimately</u>, lead to a degree of wisdom imparted from the stars illuminating the land from skies overhead is, in his outlook, a necessary struggle (or battle which he had to unfortunately wage) in order to *ultimately* gain the measure of wisdom which each act of violation (or "sexcrime"-incident) entitled him to receive.

Ariq's agenda in completing the "Process of 'Self-Enlightenment' " (despite the terrible atrocities which he commits against females in the region in which he resides) is to *ultimately* become what he sees as an asset or "benefactor" to the community to which he belongs and seeks to serve as a "patriarch" (which would, in fact, be the very community [i.e., Minneapolis] which he *initially* chose to tyrannize as a <u>predator</u> in violating women in order to complete the steps necessary in the "Perspective on 'Self-Enlightenment' " which he attempts to finalize as one seeking a higher degree of wisdom which he will be able, and willing, to impart to members of the community in which he resides who seek from him a higher level of wisdom in the world at large as well).

Adrien L. Montgomery
Author
--."Scriptograph^{UE} One (The 'Shadowslasher' Volumes [Book I: 'Tasting Droplets of the Unforgettable Rain'])"
Minneapolis, Minnesota (U.S.A.)
Date: FRI., Nov. 15, 2019

<u>The Traveler's Road Runs Its Course</u> (((("Sniffle"))))
<u>Hello, Again, Dear Reader</u>:

This, once again, is Adrien L. Montgomery, the author of the narrative project "Scriptograph^{UE} One [The 'Shadowslasher' Volumes (Book I: 'Tasting Droplets of the Unforgettable Rain')]". I desire to thank you once more, my friend, for choosing to select (and pre-occupy yourself with) the preceding

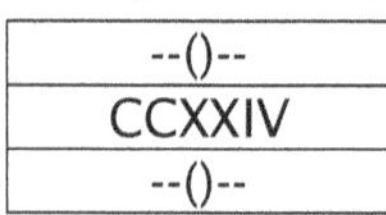

--()--
CCXXIV
--()--

work of fiction. I, the novelist, could not actually do the job I desire to do if, in fact, you yourself chose to avoid journeying through the specific project of fiction which I did manage (with the publishing of this book-project) to release to the reading public. There is, I'm sure you'll agree, my friend, truth to the famous statement "… It takes <u>two</u> to Tango".

I do trust that you found this particular text to be a rewarding reading experience. Perhaps, you should put it aside for a while and let the narrative's subject material gradually present itself to you, again, as you conveniently raise questions on the book's material content from time to time.

I do believe, with this particular book-project, I was able to create a work of "Literary"-fiction which the average **adult** reader could find, on one hand, *amusing*, and, on the other hand, *enriching*, on both an <u>intellectual</u> and a <u>spiritual</u> level. I did **not** desire, in composing the text, to merely do nothing more than present overtly "intellectual" opinions on man's nature, or on society, etc., etc. Nor did I simply desire to request that the reader tune in to Nature and encounter her stateliness on strictly a "metaphysical" or "spiritual" level. I **did** want to create a **novel** which would appeal to the reader on another level as well. I attempted to ensure this particular work of fiction is one which could satisfy the reader's desire for a "lively" and "entertaining" dramatic tale.

I must again state how satisfied I am with the particular edition of the novel which you now have in hand, dear reader. I couldn't be any happier with the <u>final</u> "draft" (or version) of the text which I released through the publishing house "Dynamographx[R,TM]". Nor could I be any more impressed, at this particular moment, with the high integrity of the narrative volume's various production elements. The decisions made during the publishing process itself were, obviously, made under careful review on the part of the "Dynamographx[R,TM]" team of "staff"-personnel. The production team which the publisher assigned to this book-project diligently sought to attend to <u>every</u> element of the final version of the narrative. The results of this attentiveness are, of course, in the assemblage of words and pages which you now hold in your hands, my dear friend.

I trust that you, the reader, found, in your review of the text, that there is much more to this work of literature than the incidents of extreme misogyny on exhibit at times. The offenses which the protagonist commits against females (using the utmost in maliciousness, I must, here, admit) are, of course, <u>not</u> the *primary* issue which the material content presents, yet, merely serve to initiate a discussion on the aspects of the human individual's psychological structuring, I can, here, assure you.

You, perhaps, are also seeing that inside this narrative work, you've found particular views on man's unchanging nature and views on the current state of society which you shall continue to offer questions on and, perhaps, choose to discuss with others, even if those companions of yours haven't already read this book themselves, "Scriptograph[UE] One (The 'Shadowslasher' Volumes [Book I: 'Tasting Droplets of the Unforgettable Rain'])".

I would want to assume that the exercise of reading this piece of literature was for you, the reader, as rewarding an experience as the exercise of writing this fictional text was for me, the writer. The craft of writing is, of course, a "team" event. The novelist must, of course, have in sight a particular reader for whom his works are composed and by whom those works are evaluated. (In short, to, once again, use a familiar quote, "… It takes <u>two</u> to Tango", my dear friend.) I can at this point only *assume* that your opinion of the novel is as high as I had imagined it would be while laboring on this work. (Though, if you manage to encounter me at a "['book'-signing]"-event or at a "['book'-reading]"-event, you can let me know *exactly* what it is the specific narrative-project seems to offer to you, in particular.)

I, again, should tell you that a <u>second</u> manuscript is currently in its formative stage and should become available to *any* and **all** interested readers at some point in the near future. If you did enjoy reading "Scriptograph[UE] One (The 'Shadowslasher' Volumes [Book I: 'Tasting Droplets of the Unforgettable Rain'])", I can promise that you will *probably* enjoy the next project to a similar extent, my friend.

I must, once again, to show my appreciation to **all** choosing to read through this particular piece of fiction, use the following words in the sincerest of voices: "Thank you, dear readers, for both your time and your patience in hearing me out". I do believe that you would, if it were possible, show me a similar gratitude for receiving the opportunity to read this particular book, a *novel*, that I've created for <u>adult</u> fiction fans to both entertain <u>and</u> enrich themselves with (intellectually *and* spiritually, that is).

We've come, I do regret, to the particular time at which I must issue a genuine and poignant farewell to **all** who've taken the opportunity to discover any messages which are solidly beneath the ink which appears on the book's sheets of paper. I do, hereby, bid you all, dear readers, a reluctant goodbye and trust you might sometime return to this book of mine (or to, perhaps, a subsequent narrative project) to re-experience the delight which you felt on first turning the pages of this particular narrative-text. Goodbye, my dear friends, and do not hesitate to call upon me again soon!

Adrien L. Montgomery
Author
--."Scriptograph[UE] One (The 'Shadowslasher' Volumes [Book I: 'Tasting
    Droplets of the Unforgettable Rain'])"
Minneapolis, Minnesota (U.S.A.)

Date: WED., Nov. 06, 2019

The Author's Final Words … (Or, "One Author Commentating …")

--.One author commentating … on the view that a novel (such an effort being nothing less than a panoramic work of narrative fiction) would, in fact, serve (in and of itself) a purpose concerning the particular value the text material presents to the eyes of an attentive reading community.

--.One author commentating … on the view that there is, I trust, an obligation on the reader's part to openly discuss and share the admirable points of a satisfying work of creative writing with other individuals who might also prefer to review such a work of narrative fiction themselves.

--.One author commentating … on the view that the reader must discuss with others any particular book actually proving of value with regard to the statement such a work offers to people on the table of psychosocial human behavioral traits existing in communities resident in major "Urbanzones" found inside the contemporary United States or elsewhere.

--.One author commentating … on the view that no one should dissuade himself from notifying others on the enlightenment you did personally receive in having had the opportunity to read an observant work of narrative fiction, particularly one that includes acute commentaries on the dominant sociobehavioral traits existing in major urban communities of current "time"-eras.

--.One author commentating … on the view that it is, in fact, the reader's purpose (upon reviewing a work of narrative fiction which one finds to be satisfying) to offer opinion on what, in fact, the work itself had to give to the reader with particular respect to any comment the author's text presents on the human behavioral characteristics occurring inside population centers in the USA's network of "Urbanzones".

--.One author commentating … on the view that the reader's obligation upon reviewing any particular work of narrative fiction which one believes to be highly illuminating concerning the statement which the book actually makes on the particular psychosocial issues prevalent today would be, in fact, to offer a personal comment on the work itself in response. ("What is your comment? …")

--.I do believe the volume which you have just had the opportunity to review, my companion, consists, through the entirety of its table of dramatic elements, of material which would be capable of generating a positive, fostering spirit in whoever it is who might read the work and choose to discuss its narrative contents with other book-readers. I do believe this particular narrative work is a composition which is capable of producing a "salving" effect upon the community of readers who choose to expose themselves to the statements the text itself presents on the psychosocial behavioral characteristics which happen with a high level of occurrence inside the major urban environments existing in the United States (and elsewhere) today. Would you prefer to add an opinion on any specific presentation there is of social traits dominant in the particular community in which you, O reader, find yourself currently residing? Do not hesitate to offer to others any statement which you believe would be a valid assessment of the prevailing characteristics one might witness inside the human community which you yourself appear to be an associate to in today's world, my dear friend …

Adrien L. Montgomery
(Author …)
(Minneapolis, Minnesota)

Scriptograph[UE] One
The "Shadowslasher" Volumes
(Book I: "Tasting Droplets of the Unforgettable Rain")
A Novel By
Adrien L. Montgomery
(XOX)

(… <u>Bonus</u> <u>Sequence</u> …)
<u>The</u> <u>Author</u> <u>Offers</u> <u>a</u> <u>Poem</u> <u>to</u> <u>the</u> <u>Patient</u> <u>Listeners</u>

I did desire, dear readers, to share with you, using this particular opportunity, a particular work of verse which I made time to complete alongside the fictional project "Scriptograph[UE] One (The 'Shadowslasher' Volumes [Book I: 'Tasting Droplets of the Unforgettable Rain'])". This particular work of poetical narrative, which I do believe is not awkwardly, to any extent whatsoever, part of this project's package of fictional material due to the fact that the work itself already appears, to an extent, in a particular re-working, inside a dramatical episode which the narrative-project already includes. The first verse of the following poetic composition appears initially in a section of the narrative text which you, my friends, have just been able to review (in "Cycle 06: 'Even in its Mask … the Wolf Can't Help But Drool' ")/"Scriptograph[UE] One (The 'Shadowslasher' Volumes [Book I: 'Tasting Droplets of the Unforgettable Rain'])". Inside the particular scenario in which the verse itself appears on page, an African-American character is singing aloud while heading south atop Reddington Avenue's western sidewalk. The African-American singer in question, here, is about 21 years in age. The songtrack which the man performs is an "Adult"-Rock single, a "Pop"-music anthem, of sorts, which the man performs in the "a cappella" (i.e., "voice only"-music) tradition, of course, being alone on the streets after daytime's busier hours. The single, according to Ariq's information on the music track's history, became a familiar radio tune in the late 1990's. Its original performers were, to note, according to Ariq, an

--()--
CCXXVIII
--()--

("['Acoustical']-Rock")-act out of Orlando, Florida. The title of the specific "single"-track itself is "Last Friday Night's Affair". According to Ariq, once again, the single became a constant music clip on commercial "Rock" and "Pop" stations across the US at the time (i.e., late 1990's). The African-American street-singer is reciting in song what amounts to the first stanza of the following poetical work. "Ariq", in the narrative episode, states the track is a "single"-release by the band "Ghettoblaster Farm" that appears on the group's CD *Seeing the Immortal Church Burning*. The single release became a chart hit on radio channels in the Summertime months of 1998 (June, July, August, and September), with the particular record receiving maximum priority-rotation on FM "Rock"-stations over the course of that particular solar-season. What follows is the exact excerpt detailing the words which the street-singer recites to the empty outdoor avenue in the particular scene of mention occurring in "Cycle 06: 'Even in its Mask … the Wolf Can't Help But Drool' ", a particular dramatic episode appearing in the preceding narrative project:

I've gotta far march out to the town's "Bar Park" tonight …
*I'll search 'til I find a room brimming with **both** a high song and spirit.*
I'm gunna march 'til the doors of the "Bar Park" cross into view!
*Tonight, I'll **know** the spot that's got the right heart—indeed, I'll hear it.*
The past workweek's just a faint, ghostly, mist-hidden dream …
*In just this one elapsing minute, I am, **at last**, alive again!*
The road I'm on tonight will lead me right to "Heaven's Stairs"!
I'll find the "The Brickstreet Cellar" and enter it through its door—
*Hear me sing in praise just **once**! In closing, what must I say? … "<u>Amen</u>"!*

The first verse of the song the man sings is, yet again, actually an alternate version (i.e., a variation on the original) of the first stanza appearing in the original poem "Omniverse[UE] I: 'Beerlover in the Barrelroom on Thirstender St.' ", a work which I did compose, once again, while laboring over the same period of time on the text of the novel-project "Scriptograph[UE] One (The 'Shadowslasher' Volumes [Book I: 'Tasting Droplets of the Unforgettable Rain'])". I do desire you, the reading audience, to review the following poetical writing project ("Omniverse[UE] I: 'Beerlover in the Barrelroom on Thirstender St.' ") and determine the value of the writing's artistry, dramatical scenario, sociological perspective, etc., etc. The poem is the only one in verse format which I believe, as of today, I'm capable of presenting to a reading audience in a complete and satisfactory state of compositional excellence. For readers of the fiction project, perhaps you might enjoy a poetical effort on just this one particular occasion to review critically. For traditional fans of the verse format, I do believe you will find that this particular work matches up with

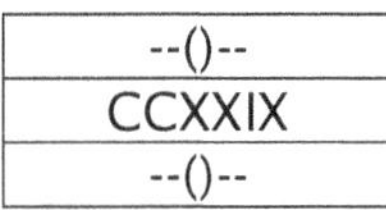

the criteria which you would normally use in evaluating the verse examples which you've come to happily review and enthusiastically treasure over the course of the lifelong fondness for poems and the poets creating them which you've been maintaining during the time which you've spent as a continuing reader of creative writings. Here, again, my loyal readers, is, in its complete state of composition, the original poetic work which I did finish while, simultaneously, laboring on the manuscript project "Scriptograph^UE One (The 'Shadowslasher' Volumes [Book I: 'Tasting Droplets of the Unforgettable Rain'])". It is my sincerest desire that you, faithful listeners, do review the following work and, again, find … in its artistry, dramatical scenario, and in the sociological perspective on the urbanistic backdrop which it offers to you … a distinct, detectable narrative offering—in addition to an actual "philosophical" viewpoint. Thank you, again, patient readers, for selecting to hear me out on this particular issue and, again, for utilizing this particular moment to read the following work of verse …

Omniverse^UE I:
"Beerlover in the Barrelroom on Thirstender Street"
A Poem By
Adrien L. Montgomery

(-|Date of Completion: FRI., Aug. 29, 2025|-)
I'm on the long march down to "Thirstender Street" tonight …
I'll search 'til I see a room running high in **both** its song and spirit.
I'm gunna march 'til the doors of "Thirstender Street" cross into view!
In time, I'll **know** the spot that's got the right heart—ahead, I'll hear it.
The past workweek's just a faint, ghostly, fog-ridden dream …
In just a brief, short-running minute, I am, **at last**, alive again!
The lone road I'm on tonight will lead me to the "Ever After" realm!
I'll find the "The Open Caske House" and enter it through its door—
Hear me sing in praise just **once**! What, in closing, might I say? … "Amen"!

Already, I'm at, t'night (Friday), the door to the song-house's front room!
I see guests at the tables on the walk by the beerhall's entrance stairs;
Soup or a salad it is, with a tall lagermug, cold and on tap, I assume.

Inside … I ask for fresh beer from the large pine barrel of black ale—
I'm hearing a "Blues" CD that the room's high ceiling speakers roll.…
I watch the "Folk/Rock"-act preparing on the club's corner stage …
The crowds en route outside enter bars to reinstate any common soul.
Turning to the "Extrascreen^ISS", I see it's running "JAZZ-TV^STF" …
Our house's "barfly" shoots rounds of pool on the bar's billiards table.

--()--
CCXXX
--()--

ALM
TDOTUR
2026

Adrien L. Montgomery
Tasting Droplets of the Unforgettable Rain
Original Year of Publication: 2026

But, I ask the bar's host to put a "Scotch-on-the-Rocks" in a beermug;
Here, the "Folk/Rock"-act ("Pagan Bride") offers us a barroom ballad.
Tonight, I guess, I'll start to sing it, too, if, later, I am still able....
("The End")

Omniverse[UE] I
"Beerlover in the Barrelroom on Thirstender Street"
A Poem By
Adrien L. Montgomery

(-|Author's "Portrait"-Photo In Year 2018|-)

Adrien L. Montgomery
(Author ...)

Scriptograph[UE] One
The "Shadowslasher" Volumes
(Book I: "Tasting Droplets of the Unforgettable Rain")
A Novel By
Adrien L. Montgomery

Author's Announcement Condemning the Mistreatment of Animals
I, do, hereby, desire to utilize the opportunity, here, on hand, to officially condemn the practice of "bullfighting", as the event, known the world-over, occurs, today, in its ongoing state of aspects, my friends. Bullfighting (as the term itself appears in usage, in referring to the particu-

(XOX)

--()--
CCXXXI
--()--

lar "sport" in question) permits the unnecessary mistreatment of a living creature, as the deliberate harm which the animal suffers transpires unto it for no other reason than to <u>entertain</u> a crowd of spectators observing the showcase of abuse from seats surrounding the arena (i.e., the "bullring" or *"plaza de toros"*).

While the bull itself poses no threat to any extent to the human community on hand to observe the deliberate cruelty which the contestants *("toreros"*, i.e., "bullfighters") inflict upon it, the spectating audience arrives at the event for the sole purpose of seeing the display of unjustifiable cruelty to an animal not guilty of inflicting any harm whatsoever to either the human observers watching the event in the spectating stands or to the team of "bullfighters" selecting to inflict undue suffering upon the creature for the sole purpose of entertainment (i.e., the *"picadores"*, the *"banderillos"*, the *"mozo de espadas"*, and the *"matador"*), the actions transpiring during a *"corrida de toros"* or *"encierro"* (in each case, "bullfight" or "running of the bulls") occur to do apparently nothing other than inflict undue and unjustifiable suffering, pain, humiliation, degradation, misery, and death upon the animal serving as object of the aggression on the part of the human competitors on hand.

I do, hereby, seek to utilize this particular statement appearing before the readers of this specific project of "narrative"-fiction to officially <u>condemn</u> the practice known as "bullfighting" as the "spectator"-event occurs around the world in countries wherein the deliberate mistreatment of "fighting" bulls (creatures especially bred, raised, and trained as contestants against the *"toreros"* in bullrings) occurs on a recurring basis.

What the practice of "bullfighting" itself amounts to is nothing less than the unnecessary abuse and mistreatment of an animal (innocent of committing any acts of harm against the community of human spectators in attendance at the events and innocent of posing any threat to human animal-handlers in charge of keeping the bull during its maturation as a "fighter") with the intent of permitting human observers on hand at the bullrings to witness such <u>crimes</u> occurring which amount to nothing other than the malicious mistreatment, humiliation, and, ultimately, murder of an animal not guilty of any acts of aggression against either the humans managing the creature prior to its induction into the bullring (usually the day of its death) or to the humans visiting the arena as spectators to witness acts of cruelty occurring to the animal as performed by the team of *"toreros"*, lead by the *"matador de toros"* (i.e., "killer of the bulls").

I do, hereby, encourage anyone selecting to read this particular statement announcing a protest against the continuation of unnecessarily exhibiting undue <u>torture</u> and suffering unto an <u>innocent</u> animal for the sole purpose of *entertaining* the crowd of observers on hand at the "bullfighting" events to join local "anti-bullfighting" programs found in the

--()--

CCXXXII

--()--

particular communities, cities, and countries in which you happen to reside in order to announce a public rejection of the practice known as "bullfighting"--that the "tradition" involving the unjustifiable and unnecessary abuse, mistreatment, torture, and murder of an animal innocent itself of any acts of aggression against members of the human community around it will come to an end as quickly as is possible in countries around the planet which still permit the terrible public "spectator"-event to occur. Thank you, again, dear readers, for hearing the announcement I do, hereby, make in protest of the cruel and unnecessary practice of "bullfighting" which I do offer unto <u>all</u> available readers with this specific comment that such a demonstration of unnecessary animal abuse should be, ultimately, discontinued as an exhibition for spectators to behold at events staged solely for the purpose of slaughtering a "fighting" bull to entertain the crowd on hand in what is nothing more than an <u>inhumane</u> and <u>reprehensible</u> public spectacle.

Adrien L. Montgomery
Author
--."Scriptograph^{UE} One (The 'Shadowslasher' Volumes [Book I: 'Tasting
   Droplets of the Unforgettable Rain'])"
Minneapolis, Minnesota (U.S.A.)
Date: FRI., Nov. 08, 2019

<u>(|The "Official Declaration of Authorship"-Certificate|)</u>
<u>Date of Official Declaration</u>: FRI., Nov. 08, 2019
<u>Holder of the Official Declaration</u>: Adrien L. Montgomery

<u>(I)</u>
<u>Purpose of "Declaration"-Certificate on Behalf of Author</u>
<u>"Adrien L. Montgomery"</u>:
I, Adrien L. Montgomery, author of the preceding literary property, hereby, recognized in title as "Scriptograph^{UE} One (The 'Shadowslasher' Volumes [Book I: 'Tasting Droplets of the Unforgettable Rain'])" do, hereby (in the oath appearing as the statement which this document presents), swear to being the actual originator and official author of all sectors, subsectors, documents, subdocuments, parts and materials appearing in the preceding work of literary (i.e., "creative"/"fictional"/"poetic"/"nonfictional"/"instruc-tional"/and "advisory") properties which this specific publication presents to any and all readers selecting to review to any extent the "in print"-communications found within the publication's content.

<u>(II)</u>
<u>Statement Testifying to the Credibility of the Preceding Oath</u>

--()--
CCXXXIII
--()--

<u>Attesting to the Genuine Identity of the Present Literary Property's
Original and Official Author</u>:

I, the undersigned, do, hereby, proclaim the preceding oath sworn on the part of the "author" (i.e., Adrien L. Montgomery) to be a legitimate admission on the author's part which serves to duly attest to the credibility with respect to the claims on part of the undersigned (i.e., Adrien) concerning the actual identity of the individual actually due <u>total</u> credit for originating, completing, and presenting the preceding literary property ("Scriptograph^{UE} One [The 'Shadowslasher' Volumes (Book I: 'Tasting Droplets of the Unforgettable Rain')]") to be an act of valid witnessing on the undersigned's part genuinely testifying as to the identity of the preceding work's original and official author (i.e., "Adrien L. Montgomery").

01)>Section "A":
    --.Official "Signature" of the Literary Property's "Author":

    )) ____ ((
    --.(On this Date of ... FRI., Nov. 08, 2019)

02)>Section "B":
    --.Official "Name-in-Print" of the Literary Property's "Author":

    )) ____ ((
    --.(On this Date of ... FRI., Nov. 08, 2019)

(The preceding "Signature" and "Name-in-Print" both indicate, for the signatory's benefit, the specific document on hand <u>officially</u> identifies one "Adrien L. Montgomery" as being the <u>sole</u> author of the actual literary property, hereby, recognized in title, for legal verification, as "Scriptograph^{UE} One [The 'Shadowslasher' Volumes (Book I: 'Tasting Droplets of the Unforgettable Rain')]".)

(<u>III</u>)

<u>Official Act of "Notarization" Legitimizing the Preceding Oath and
Signature as Genuine Records Admissible as Official Documents in a
Forum Existing Under the Jurisdictional Authority of All Relevant
Legal Codes</u>:

For the purposes of legitimizing the preceding "Declaration"-certificate on the author's own behalf (i.e., "Adrien L. Montgomery") in the advent of any proprietary dispute arising upon which the document on hand must appear as evidence on exhibit in a forum existing under the jurisdictional authority of state-, federal-, or international-level legal codebooks (i.e., known as "compacts", "conventions", "treaties", etc.) governing the rightful process by which the originator of any literary properties on record may make claim to an agency or agent authorized to determine the legitimacy with respect to any petitioner's claim to property rights regarding use of a particular literary property, I do, hereby, present to any agency or agent possessing such authority in determining the credibility of any petitioner's claims of ownership the following "Stamp", "Signature", and "Name-in-Print" of a duly authorized "Notary Public" possessing a commission in good standing:

01)>Section "A":
    --.Official "Stamp" of the "Notary Public":

    ))____((
    --.(On this Date of … FRI., Nov. 08, 2019)

02)>Section "B":
    --.Official "Signature" of the "Notary Public":

    ))____((
    --.(On this Date of … FRI., Nov. 08, 2019)

03)>Section "C":
    --.Official "Name-in-Print" of the "Notary Public":

    ))____((
    --.(On this Date of … FRI., Nov. 08, 2019)

The preceding "notarization"-process did occur on the premises of "The Bulletin Board[STF]"-outlet found at the following business-address:

"The Bulletin Board[STF]"
Suite #229
50 South 6th Street
("['Downtown'/@'Butcher Plaza']")
Minneapolis, MN 55402

Notes on the "Pinball"-Machine Titles Appearing in the Preceding "Narrative"-Project in "Cycle 17"

--()--
CCXXXV
--()--

<u>(The "Pinball"-Machine Titles in List Appear in Alphabetical Order in Acknowledgement of the Title's First Letter Itself)</u>
<u>(Note: 001)</u>
a)"Battlestar Galactica". TV drama-production broadcast in week-to-week installments. Produced by NBC Universal Media, L.L.C. Airing from Sept. 17, 1978 to Apr. 29, 1979. Broadcast by the ABC Television Corporation. Number of episodes in original series: 23. (Page# 192)
b)"Public Enemy". "Hip Hop"-style music-recording group. Era of Commercial Activity: 1985 (&continuing thereafter). (Membership: Drayton Jr., William Jonathan/Griffin, Richard/Lord, DJ/Ridenhour, Carlton Douglas /Rogers, Norman/Wynn, Khari James). (Page# 192)
c)"Untouchables, The". "Feature"-category "motion-picture" drama-production. Distributed by "Paramount Pictures Corporation". Official Public Release Date: WED., Jun. 03, 1987. Original Screening Time: 01 hrs., 59 mns. Original Exhibition Market: United States of America. (Page# 192)

<u>"On Screen"-notification to "Internet"-audiences spanning the measurable extent of the officially-known globe</u> …
You have been watching a presentation by "Dynamographx^R Paperworks™"

<u>"MADE IN U.S.A."</u>
By
Adrien L. Montgomery

!!Thank You!!

Berkeley, California
San Francisco, California
Minneapolis, Minnesota
Taos, New Mexico

<u>Information Page on the Narrative Project's "Production Services"-Facility (i.e., "Printing Site")</u>
<u>Note:</u>
All "printing/mass processing"-services necessary to produce paper-built copies of the preceding "narrative 'printerwritten' "-manuscript project-- known, heretofore, on record as "Scriptograph^{UE} One (The 'Shadowslasher' Volumes [Book I: 'Tasting Droplets of the Unforgettable Rain'])"--did transpire at the following production-venue in the state of Minnesota …

<u>Address of the "production services"-facility (i.e., the "printing site") on record as the narrative project's "printing/mass processing"-location:</u>
<u>(01)</u>

--()--
CCXXXVI
--()--

"Lightning Source[TM] L.L.C."
("['Print-on-Demand']-service")-facilities
Ingram Book Group L.L.C.
(<u>02</u>)
"Dynamographx[R] Paperworks[TM]"
("['Printshop']-service")-facility
Minneapolis, Minnesota

(Year of Project's Initial Round of Printing: 2026)

<u>Infosheet</u> <u>on</u> <u>the</u> <u>Photographer's</u> <u>ID</u>:
The three "Portrait"-photographs of the Author (i.e., "Adrien L. Montgomery") which appear on pages in the book-project "Tasting Droplets of the
Unforgettable Rain" for the convenience of the volume's readers (one [on
page-# "CCXXXI"], and one [on page-# "CCXXXVIII"], and one [on page-#
"CCXL?"/("N/A")]--the "Backside"-coversheet) are, hereby, attributed in
name to the actual photographer producing the three photographs on the
author's behalf for the specific project in question (i.e., "T.D.O.T.U.R."), i.e.,
Jonathan Conklin at the "Jonathan Conklin Photography"-studio in
Minneapolis, Minnesota in March of 2018.

<u>"Topside"</u>- & <u>"Backside"</u>-<u>Coversheet</u> <u>Design</u> <u>Credits</u>

-<u>i</u>-
The "Frontside"-coversheet design (i.e., page# "N/A")
By Adrien L. Montgomery

-<u>ii</u>-
The "Backside"-coversheet design (i.e., page# "N/A")
By Adrien L. Montgomery

-<u>iii</u>-
The "Frontside"-coversheet design with respect to the specific page's
composition of visible material, arrangement of all text-data elements,
actual coloring of all visible print-material, and other elements constituting
the particular page's resulting presentation of any and all text-data
material elements appearing within the scope of the page itself (e.g.'s,
"Font"-style, "Points"-level, lines of demarcation, margin-settings, etc.)
appears in place due to assembly by Adrien L. Montgomery.

-<u>iv</u>-
The "Backside"-coversheet design with respect to the specific page's
composition of visible material, arrangement of all text-data elements,(X)

| --()-- |
| CCXXXVII |
| --()-- |

actual coloring of all visible print-material, and other elements constituting the particular page's resulting presentation of any and all text-data material elements appearing within the scope of the page itself (e.g.'s, "Font"-style, "Points"-level, lines of demarcation, margin-settings, etc.) appears in place due to assembly by Adrien L. Montgomery.

Tasting Droplets of the Unforgettable Rain
A Novel By
Adrien L. Montgomery

(… A Presentation Of …)
(… **Dynamographx**[R] **Paperworks**[TM] …)
(… The Official Imprint …)
"… Listen to a Voice Always on the Vanguard"
"… Illustrating the Beauty of Dynamic Motion"

Adrien L. Montgomery
(Date of Photo: March of 2018)

Official Declaration of Authorship (O.D.A.) 2019
Adrien L. Montgomery
(https://www.youtube.com/channel/@adrienlmontgomery)

Author's <u>Official</u> <u>Wordcount</u>-<u>Report</u>:
This final notice I've chosen to present for the benefit of the reading audience, hereby, announces the "narrative"-project, heretofore, known as "Tasting Droplets of the Unforgettable Rain" (i.e., the preceding work of ["('Adult')-Literary"]-fiction), includes in its "print"-edition format, with respect to its sheets of text-data material (acknowledging all pages appearing in the project itself: the "Frontside"-coversheet, the "Backside"-coversheet, the "Spine", and the "Interiorsheets"-file), the following number

(XOX)

--()--
CCXXXVIII
--()--

of words in its total wordcount: 110,997 (exact countup)

A Notice on the Legal Use of Digital-Images Appearing on Volume's "Frontside"-Coversheet and "Backside"-Coversheet:

The author did receive an "Enhanced License" from the "Shutterstock" Internet-Database entitling Dynamographx^R (Imprint) with the privilege of using the digital-image appearing on the volume's "Frontside"-Coversheet (i.e., "Solar Radiance Illuminating Planet Earth") in an unlimited number of reprintings for use in public distribution of the novel, heretofore, known in title as "Tasting Droplets of the Unforgettable Rain" and entitling Dynamographx^R (Imprint) with the privilege of using the digital-image appearing on the volume's "Backside"-Coversheet (i.e., "Nuclear Cloud Igniting Atmosphere with Atomic Radiance") in an unlimited number of re-printings for use in public distribution of the novel, heretofore, known in title as "Tasting Droplets of the Unforgettable Rain".

Adrien L. Montgomery
(Author ...)
(Minneapolis, Minnesota)

Author's "Zero Error"-Approach to "Proofreading"-/"Typesetting"-Phase Put to Use in Developmental-Stages of Project's Production-Cycle:

Total number of errors appearing in the preceding series of pages appearing in the narrative-project's "POD"-edition copy (i.e., "paperback"-version) due to issues relating to failure to attend to incorrect spelling, failure to apply necessary grammatical rules, failure to reform faulty sentence-structuring, punctuation, margin-settings, paragraph-settings, or due to inappropriate use of any text-effects (e.g.'s, underlining, italicizing, boldfacing, use of superscript, use of subscript, etc.): **00.00(!)**